FAMOUS
LAST
WORDS

SARA HAMMEL

Published by SARA HAMMEL

For information, address sarahammelbooks@gmail.com.

www.sarahammelbooks.com

Cover design by Laurie Anne T. Ernst

1

Beverly Hills
#88, #89, #90, #91, #92

John Travolta: *Sweet and fun. Surprisingly accessible. A little dopey. Treated me like a person, not dog crap. Called me Lorraine.* **Flo Rida**: *Amiable and engaging. Smells amazing. Asked him what scent he was wearing, joked he wouldn't tell me, then didn't. Gave me fun quotes about his old pal Beyoncé—editors will be ecstatic.* **Katie Couric:** *Social butterfly. Tweets a lot. Had some wine, slapped my face.*

When I'm done with my notes on Katie, I shut my book, slip it in my handbag, and crane my neck to see who's coming down the red carpet next. A roar rips through the pack of photographers as Oprah arrives in a cloud of bronze taffeta. The reporter stationed next to me behind the velvet rope, a man-bun-wearing hipster called Lance, catches my eye.

"By the way, what happened with Katie Couric?" He asks as we wait for Oprah to make her way to us. "Are you, like, never going to wash that cheek again?"

Oh, I definitely will. This very night, in fact, because Katie's move was maybe a Level 5 insult out of the ten levels of celebrity misbehavior. But Lance, whose name I only recently learned because I've been calling him Hipster Reporter since the day I met him, won't stop staring at me, so I give in and defend Katie's honor. It wasn't 100 percent her fault she hit me.

"I told her, 'I know you might want to slap me for asking this, but we'd love an update on your love life considering what's been in the news lately,'" I say. "So she obliged."

Lance cocks his head as if he's confused, but any celebrity journalist worth his salt knows Katie can get prickly when asked about her personal life. She'd maintained that famous watermelon-wedge smile as her hand slid smoothly across my cheek in a faux-slap. Like many others trickling on to the red carpet from the VIP cocktail hour, she smelled slightly, pleasantly of fancy booze.

Hipster shrugs. "I guess you can't really blame her."

Sure I can, I think. I blame all the celebrities for their transgressions, whether colorful, sinister, or downright illegal. It's a weird time to be covering Hollywood. Tonight alone, every celeb I've met has been connected to some form of controversy, scandal, or accusation—and you never know if something worse is about to explode from beneath their carefully crafted images. In the months since I embarked on my quest to interview exactly 107 celebrities, I've met wonderful has-beens, half the Hollywood B-list, and a gloriously grubby selection of A-listers. Some behave like the best friend you always wanted, others like insufferable brats. Trying to figure out the truth about these people is exhausting. I've had some shocking glimpses behind the curtain on this journey, though, and I suspect I'm in for more before it is over.

Oprah is getting closer. She's now using Steven Spielberg like a shield, standing behind him and grasping his shoulders as reporters lob questions at her. Apparently, this particular brand of attention—chaotic, out-of-control, and diffuse—is not her favorite. I call out to her, and as Steven steps away to speak to a *Variety* reporter, she is left exposed. She walks over and glances down at the paper taped to the ground with *Augusta Noble, CelebLife magazine* handwritten on it. Oprah, who is grand and luminous, could say my name in her greeting; some celebs do. She chooses not to.

"Yes?" she inquires. She is my Number 91. I am so, so close.

"Vacations," I blurt. "Where will your next one be, and what will you be doing?"

She doesn't have to think about that for long.

"I went truffle hunting this year," Oprah replies after a moment, not quite answering the question. "Truffles and Italy—is there anything better?"

If a billionaire says it, it must be true. "Absolutely nothing," I agree.

I ask her the question I *really* want the answer to. "Tell me the truth—you can trust me," I assure her. "Do you actually eat pasta and bread and still lose weight?" I'm incredulous. I eat both and never shrink, no matter how many planks and reverse crunches I attempt.

"Of course," she says with signature Oprah passion. "I wouldn't give those up. Are you kidding me?"

"I wouldn't kid you," I reply. "But seriously," I persist, "you eat carbs even during times like these, when you have to fit into gorgeous clothes day after day?" Tonight's Sterling Star Awards Dinner is the last awards season event before the ones people truly care about: the Golden Globes and the Academy Awards.

As I hold my phone—which doubles as a recorder—near her mouth, a call comes in. My heart sinks and my stomach tightens when I see the contact flash across the screen in capital letters: *THERAPIST*. I keep a listening face on for Oprah as I cancel the call with one stealthy thumb.

"It's a long haul," our maybe-possible-future-president acknowledges. "You have to keep your balance—not starve yourself, not overdo it." I nod along with her. *Good advice, Oprah. Shame it's of no use to me right now. Can you tell me how to avoid a murder rap when I can't remember anything I did?*

"OK?" she inquires crisply. This is celeb-speak for, *Gotta go. Please stop asking me dumb questions.*

"Of course," I smile. "Thanks so much."

With that, she is gone. I stare at my phone as if the voicemail notification will disappear in a *poof* if I wish hard enough. It doesn't, and I'm left to field an attack of grief, panic, guilt, and doom that comes whenever I'm forced to think about New York. The guilt—that's the worst. It's still gnawing away at me like a million little cookie monsters on a pile of Oreos. The therapist has tried valiantly to help me curb it, uttering her favorite quote in nearly every session we had before I quit: "Guilt is a useless emotion. Set it aside, and *that's* when you will begin to heal." She was never impressed by *my* favorite quote: "Makes sense. Never going to happen."

What Caroline went through was my fault. And what happened to the others…well, I still can't remember exactly what went down, but the police seem to think I had something to do with it. The details of that day—the hours over which the horrific event occurred—remain cruelly abbreviated in my mind. I recall the vivid colors of my best friend Caroline lying in her bed covered in blood, but I can't remember how we got to that point, what role I played, or why I was the last one standing.

I put the phone to one ear and stick a finger in the other to block out the noise of shouting photographers and loudly fawning reporters. I pray the message is not a direct order to return to face the consequences of my "selective amnesia," as they call it. (What a ridiculous term—I'm not *selecting* any of this.) I wince and hit the "play" button.

"Hello, Augusta," the therapist is saying. "I'm trying you one last time. *Please* call me back when you get this. The police are asking me for a progress report, and I don't know what to tell them—if I have to say you're MIA, well, I'm afraid it won't be good for you. You know I'm in your corner…" She pauses, clears her throat, then adds, "Just get back to me and we can schedule a phone session. You're running out of time. *Please.*"

Click.

I close my eyes and let my arms fall to my sides. Of course she wants me back; she didn't want me to leave in the first place. She said I was running away, that I should stay in Manhattan and "do the work" to reboot my memory. But after weeks on her saggy velvet couch talking about my childhood and my feelings, I was only getting worse, biting my nails to the quick, sabotaging my job at *Newstime*, missing deadlines, and calling in sick to eat fudge-brownie ice cream and stare into space. In the end, it was the therapist's own obsession with the past that gave me the idea for the mission I'm on. She asked me two pointed questions: "When did you last feel safe, Augusta?" And, "Can you remember a time when you were truly happy?"

I could; it was easy. The worst and best times of my life dovetailed during the shit-show that was high school, when my existence was so profoundly miserable and I was such a shy, awkward misfit that I sometimes wondered if I'd even make it out from under the bedcovers to physically get to college. It turned out only one thing could save me; only one thing *did* save me. Celebrities—those beautiful, twinkly eyed, perfect specimens—came to my rescue. Suddenly, *voila*, everything in my life started to get better.

The photographers start shouting again, jolting me back into the moment. I take some breaths and start to calm down. I see Jack Black drawing near. I regain my composure as he stops in front of me and casts a glance down at the paper with my name on it. This man with his shaggy hair, a huge grin that takes up his whole face, and a suit that looks fetchingly uncomfortable, looks me in the eye. "How the hell are you, Augusta Noble?" he asks.

"Hi, Jack Black. I'm great. How are you?" I smile back at him, because his good cheer is contagious.

See? Celebrities always make it better.

2

Must. Call. Best. Friend. My hand is shaking with humiliation as I dial the payphone next to the principal's office. I'm tapping my foot, listening to the long, shrill rings, glancing around nervously as lunch comes to an end and the hallway starts to fill up. *Answer the damn phone, Caroline. We have a Code Red.* My cool urban friend should be home; Cambridge kids are allowed to leave campus for lunch and she almost always does, usually to smoke weed at her friend Lincoln's apartment because he has parents only in the most basic sense of the word.

I hear a click, then a voice. "Caroline," I say, "I did it. And it was—"

"You *did* it?" she shrieks. "No way! I can't— well, honestly, I thought you'd chicken out. So? Was I right? Was he psyched?"

I check to make sure no one's near enough to hear me. "It was the most mortifying experience of my life," I tell her. "He said, and I quote, 'Prom? With *you?*'"

"*No* he didn't," Caroline says. She's chewing something.

"*Yes* he did," I reply. "Then he kind of laughed, and I freaked out and couldn't think of anything else to say so I just stood there with my mouth open, and he finally said, 'Are you kidding? Wait—are you serious? I don't even know what's happening right now…' Then he walked away."

"Oh, fuck," Caroline groans, then swallows. "I'm so sorry, Auggie. Really. I had no idea. I mean, from what you said, he's not exactly fighting off the girls…"

"He's not," I confirm. I resist the urge to pick at a piece of hardened pink gum on the silver face of the phone. "Why is this so fucking hard, Caro?" I lean against the wall and close my eyes.

She sighs. "I don't know, Augusta, but screw him. You don't want to go with a tool like that anyway."

"But, really." I turn to the wall when I hear some kids coming down the hall. "It's not like I'm trying to go with the captain of the lacrosse team. Jono is full geek! I'm talking greasy skin, pants hiked up too high, personality of maybe a three out of ten."

Caroline laughs sympathetically, but I don't see anything funny about this. The big dance is Saturday. Even the dorkiest, shyest, most awkward kids have dates. Sally Mawchuk has the worst skin ever and she has a date, as does Chloe Barnes, who still wears braces and her hair looks like she sticks her finger in an electric socket every morning. What do they want from me? I mean, I'm not hideous. I even accidentally lost a load of much-maligned "baby fat" (as my mother called it long past infancy) after spending two summers at Camp Nature in Vermont, which Caroline and I dubbed Camp Naked because of all the co-ed skinny-dipping, and where Ben Affleck also went when he was young. (The scoop on Ben: My former babysitter shared a bunk with his ex-girlfriend Cheyenne, who was super nice and cool and apparently Ben didn't deserve her. He did pushups on the grass outside the boys' bunk to try to impress the girls, wore dreadful orange Hawaiian shirts, and walked around with a superiority complex because he was on public television in *Voyage of the Mimi*. Other than that, my babysitter said he was a nice enough guy…*back then.*)

I'm not going to cry. I'm not going to wither like a petunia in the desert. I won't give any of them the satisfaction. *Don't cry, don't cry, don't cry.*

"Look," Caroline says. "Prom is an overrated teenage ritual hellfire anyway. You should be glad you're not—"

"Hang on," I interrupt. I hear someone calling me from down the hall.

"Augusta! Augusta Noble. I've been looking for you."

Margy Gertz, executive editor of the *Samuel Adams High School Bugle*, marches up to me. "We need you, Augusta," she says. "We need you bad."

I catch a ride to the event with the newspaper's faculty adviser, Mr. Tanner.

"Now," he says as he maneuvers his rattling old Buick as close to the Bison Lodge as he can get, "today we display the utmost professionalism. Do as you're told, be polite, but get your questions in—don't be afraid."

I barely hear him. Of course I'm afraid. I'm about to meet *the* John F. Kennedy, Jr., who broke every girl's heart at Sam Adams High when he married a mantis-like creature called Carolyn, and who today is making a surprise pit stop in our sleepy suburb to shore up support for his uncle Ted Kennedy's senate campaign. Both Margy and Kenny (the assistant managing editor) have AP exams this afternoon, which leaves me to handle the biggest story the *Bugle* has ever covered.

"Security is tight, so make sure you have your press pass in hand at all times," Mr. Tanner advises as he drops me at the outskirts of an excited mob. I sigh, wonder why the hell I agreed to this, and weave my way to the door, flashing the pass as I go. They're going to eat me alive. The most scandalous thing I've covered so far is a bake sale where someone found beetles on the sugar cookies.

"You're over there," the check-in guy says when I get to the entrance. "In the press pen. No questions allowed—you are not to address Mr. Kennedy in any way."

The event space is the size of our school gym. I look where the guy directed me and see a pack of hot, frowning, grown-up reporters crowded together behind a rope, squirming like farmed fish. *Oh hell, no.* In an instant, I'm no longer Augusta, High School Loser. I'm Augusta, Girl Reporter, and I'm here to get a scoop.

"I forgot something," I tell the check-in guy, then turn and run out of there.

I have a hunch. I stroll through the crowd waiting to catch a glimpse of John. On the drive in, I'd noticed a shiny, fancy town car parked behind the building, and as I come around the corner now I see it's still there. I slip under the chain strung across the entrance and stand a few feet from the vehicle, doing my best to be inconspicuous. It occurs to me I might be arrested, and that it would be worth it. I don't give a shit about consequences. Getting arrested or yelled at or banned from the paper would be a delight compared to being dissed by the third-dorkiest boy in my school.

A half-hour later, a white-haired Bison unhooks the chain across the drive. There, walking quickly behind him, is John F. Kennedy, Jr. My body is coursing with adrenaline and I fear I'm going to hyperventilate like I did with Jono this morning, and clearly this is too much for me. JFK, Jr. has no formal security team, but the Bison escorting him have their steely eyes on me. John is immaculately turned out in a double-breasted navy suit and maroon tie. He raises his eyebrows expectantly and side-eyes his handler, a guy in khaki pants and a salmon shirt straining at the buttons. I brandish my notebook like a white flag.

"I'm Augusta Noble with the *Samuel Adams Regional High School Bugle*," I say quickly, crisply, like they do on the nightly news, and I'm shocked by the confidence in my own voice. "What do you want people to know about your uncle?" It had taken me all afternoon to settle on this question.

I'm shocked when John stops, turns, and speaks to me. So shocked, in fact, that I drop my pen and it hits the asphalt with a *click clack click*. John bends down and picks it up for me without missing a beat.

It's the eyes that get me: I'll never forget those eyes, a deep hazel that turns chocolate and then hazel and chocolate again in the sunlight. I have the full attention of our country's version of royalty shining on me. It is hot here.

"Vote for Ted Kennedy," the coolest man alive is saying. "Get out and make calls. Show up. Make a difference. As my uncle once said, 'The work goes on, the cause endures, the hope still lives, and the dream shall never die.'"

I'm scribbling as fast as I can in my reporter's note-book. I'm moved by what he's saying, but also thrown by his unpresidential way of speaking. I had never heard this about John-John, but it's sadly true: He lacks a certain *gravitas*. I feel terrible even thinking it, especially because

11

he's probably launching my career right now *and* he picked up my pen—which, by the way, I'm going to lock up and never touch again—but his delivery is California surfer meets frat boy. I get the feeling he'd rather be kayaking shirtless in the Hudson with Daryl Hannah, or maybe his wife, or maybe me.

"Hello?" he prompts, snapping me out of my thoughts. "Is there anything else?" I realize I've stopped writing and he's stopped talking. I glance down at my scribbled notes, which read something along the lines of *I wanna tall ppl to vote fur my wurkel.*

Salmon-shirt guy shakes his head sternly. "Young lady, please move aside. Mr. Kennedy is late for his next appearance."

But Mr. Kennedy's eyes are still fixed on me.

Ask him to prom. Come on, chicken, ask him. It could be a great campaign stunt: *Prodigal nephew takes pathetic dork to prom.*

"It's OK, I have a minute," John says to calm the Bison. "Now. What else can I tell the *Bugle*?"

I have to know. I have to ask. What's the worst he could do to me?

3

There are a number of creative tactics a serious American journalist can use to get her foot in the door to *CelebLife* magazine's London bureau. Mine entails eating British nachos (this is an oxymoron) and sipping a gloopy strawberry margarita while trying to impress the international bureau chief.

"Do you like celebrities?" Stanley Rader asks me, his man-hands wrapped around his pint glass like two overgrown starfish.

"Who doesn't?" I throw back to him.

"Do you *follow* celebrities? What do you read?"

I'd been asked that second question before, in almost every interview for a writing job, in fact, and the correct answer always includes at least two of the following: *The Times*, *The Economist*, *The New Yorker, The Washington Post* and *The Atlantic.*

I reply, "*CelebLife*, of course. *Star Scene, Supermarket Scoop*, *Teen Vogue*, and…well, sometimes I check out *The New Yorker.* Oh, and the *New York Post* goes without saying."

Stanley is a sturdy black man wearing a slightly too-tight button-down gingham shirt. He's stern in an authentic way, and he's busy intriguing me over apps and cocktails at a touristy yet strangely comforting Texas Embassy restaurant by the Charing Cross Tube stop. We're both American expats, and sometimes, however uncool it is, you want a taste of home.

"What I'm looking for in a reporter," he says, "is the sweet spot. Do you know why it's so hard to get hired at *CelebLife*?"

I shake my head. I do not know. But if it's anywhere near as hard as it was to get this meeting, I'm in trouble. Stanley squints at me, and I'm glad the place is low-lit because I am certain he is attempting to see through me.

"Because," he explains, "I need people with hard-news experience—one of my best women in Spain is an award-winning war correspondent—who know the difference between Dermot Mulroney and Dylan McDermott, can recite a few lyrics off Taylor Swift's latest album, and can charm Michael Douglas at a party into talking about his sex life with Catherine. You with me?"

I nod. I am.

"So," he says, rescuing a tortilla chip from its congealed cheese prison, "news experience alone does not impress me. Do you, or do you not, love celebrities?"

He crunches down on his chip.

"I've loved celebrities since I was a kid," I tell him. "Everyone I know reads *CelebLife*. I have had it in my—" *don't say bathroom, don't say bathroom*—"life for many years."

Stanley folds his arm on the table and leans in. "That's great," he says in a way that seems like he doesn't think it's great. "But to work here, you have to have an encyclopedic knowledge of celebrities and their histories. I can't hire someone and have her ask Angelina how Brad's doing."

"I understand," I nod seriously. "I can do it."

He narrows his eyes, takes a sip of beer, and regards me with some skepticism. The most enthusiasm he's shown all evening is when I explained I can legally work in the UK because I was born here when my parents were teaching at London School of Economics.

"I see you conducted a couple celeb interviews in high school, but your CV doesn't exactly reflect a life of celebrity fandom," Stanley says. "You went from interning for a Capitol Hill wire service to covering cops and crime for a newspaper, and finally to *Newstime* in New York, right? You've spent the past two years covering hard news and corporate scandals. Where does Katy Perry fit into that?"

He should check out a photograph of my childhood bedroom, where only a few slivers of dove-grey paint were visible between the celebrity posters.

"Since you ask," I say, "pick a celeb with a robust Instagram presence. Anyone you want."

Stanley doesn't hesitate. "OK, I'll play. Gigi Hadid."

"Gigi Hadid," I repeat. "Too easy. Just got back from the Maldives after a secret-not-secret cover shoot for *Sports Illustrated*. Posted as if in real time but she's already back in L.A., which I know because she was papped at LAX yesterday."

He appears roundly unimpressed. "Viola Davis," he says.

His attempt to throw me with an oldie will not work. "Inspirational quote of the day, paraphrased: 'Womanhood is you. Womanhood is everything that's inside of you.' Etc. etc."

The quote is from a while back, but I am positive Stanley will not know that. He will also not be aware of the tactic my mother, the estimable professor Jemima Noble, taught me to nail any job interview: Make up your own question beforehand, then offer up the answer when things get sticky. Before meeting Stanley, I studied social media for hours, discovered who has the biggest followings, then crosschecked those names with most the popular posts on *CelebLife*'s Web site over time.

Stanley regards me with an unreadable expression that includes the tiniest upturn of one side of his mouth. Either it's a half-smile, or he has gas from the beans we've just eaten. Without a word, he raises a finger and calls for the bill (in the UK, it's not a check; never a check). I pull out my empty wallet, but Stanley shakes his head and slides his credit card across the table.

I feel slightly ill. This was my one chance—this was *it*. Stanley only agreed to meet with me because my friend Rachel got *her* close pal who works in *CelebLife*'s New York headquarters to push my resume forward. I'd been emailing and calling editors for weeks before it finally dawned on me they were never going to respond. According to Rachel's friend, *CelebLife* gets a thousand resumes a week from starry eyed movie nerds and aspiring fashionistas, which was bad news for me because it meant there was nothing available in Los Angeles or New York. Then I thought, how many of these would-be reporters have British passports? Rachel saw my point and went to work snagging this meeting for me. But now, as Stanley and I leave the bustling restaurant, I'm afraid I blew my shot. Out on the street, on a clear night in this perpetually wet city, Stanley stops and faces me.

"One more question," he says, searching my eyes. "Why leave a full-time job at *Newstime* for a freelance gig? I want to stress again we have *no* staff positions available for the foreseeable future. I can't give you benefits, vacation, or full-time work. Why leave? Why now?"

Why now. He'll never know the real answer to that if I can help it. He won't know I quit my writing job at one of the top newsweeklies loudly, dramatically, and in front of everyone, or that I did it because of a cheese pizza, or that the worst thing that can happen to someone actually *happened* to me and my friend, and that it was my fault. He won't know that I lost my shit and can't handle any of it. And he certainly won't know I'm begging him to hire me because hobnobbing with the beautiful people can cure all your ills, and that I have more ills than I can count.

"It's something I've always wanted to do," I reply, shrugging. "I thought it was time to go for it."

Stanley's demeanor remains neutral, unreadable. I decide he was a Marine in another life.

"I'll be in touch," he says. I thank him for the meeting and he turns to walk toward the Tube, a slab of a man I estimate to be is in his late thirties who's maintained gobs of muscles from his youth, but let trips to the pub widen and expand around them, especially in the middle.

As I watch him go, I have an uneasy feeling I'll never hear from him again. I stand on the street and wait for him to disappear so I don't run into him on the train platform, then pull the custom-made reporter's notebook out of my handbag and fan through all the empty pages I'm determined to fill. The goal was 107 celebrities from the moment I devised the plan while sitting on the therapist's couch: It was the exact number of posters on my bedroom walls growing up. (Attempting to interview every *actual* poster person was too much of a stretch, especially because some, including River Phoenix and Jonathan Brandis, have sadly died.) I haven't told anyone about my quest; I know it would sound silly to some and delusional to others, but it makes perfect sense to me. After weeks of intensive therapy to try to deal with the trauma of that day, I still lacked a solid, tangible plan to get myself out of the hole I was in. I needed something more than a floating concept of healing, a vague idea of forgiveness, a promise of recovered memories that never showed themselves. The idea came to me when I was talking to the therapist about high school. As I rattled on, I was reminded of a quote from Albert Schweitzer my mother shared with me when I was young: "In everyone's life, at some time, our inner fire goes out. It is then burst into flame by an encounter with another human being. We should all be thankful for those people who rekindle the inner spirit."

I had to get out of New York. I had to get off that sofa. I had to *remember*. As the therapist talked about letting go of the past, I thought about getting away. What if I went out and met *all* the celebrities? What if, just like when I was a teenager, hanging with the stars could fix everything? What if celebrities could rekindle my spirit, nudge my memory, and take the pain away, even for a little while?

As I hold my notebook now, I flip to the back cover where Albert's quote is inscribed in loopy script across the still-shiny pink pleather. Stanley *has* to give me a chance—he must. If it doesn't work out for me at *CelebLife* in London, I have nowhere left to go. I figure the coast is clear by now, so I place the notebook back in my bag and start making my way to the Tube.

4

The cab whizzes away from the Clarence hotel, and I begin to relax as I watch the blue-grey River Liffey rolling by on my right. Water always has that effect on me.

I go over my notes for tonight's event and say a little prayer that Bono is in a good mood. Stanley did indeed call me with an assignment after making me wait four torturous days during which I decided he hated me, I probably had cilantro in my teeth during the whole dinner, and I'd never get another journalism job anywhere ever. This doesn't necessarily mean I nailed the interview: He made a point of telling me I got the gig only after the original reporter came down with strep throat, then warned me (half-jokingly, I hope) not to come back to London without quotes from A-list names.

"We're here, madam," the driver says, and I hand him some euros, including a nice tip, and step out. He pulls away and I stand in place outside the stadium, breathing, centering, preparing to nail my one chance to get in with the long-lived *CelebLife*, America's sweetheart of a brand that reaches something like seventy million gossip-hungry readers every week.

I'm early, so it's still quiet inside the huge VIP area, other than staff bustling about. It's a bit busier in a back corner my personal PR rep takes me to, where I immediately see Colin Farrell holding a clear fizzy drink (I'm thinking gin and tonic) in one hand and a cigarette in the other. His light brown eyes are wide in the face of a small but impassioned crowd surrounding him. His dark brown hair is worn shaggy and longish; day-old scruff leaves a shadow on his face.

"We're ready, Colin," a guy standing next to a cameraman says.

A petite woman with flawless skin—I recognize her as Colin's sister Claudine, who could give any A-lister a run for her money in the beauty stakes—takes his cigarette and the drink, juggling them with the two phones she's carrying. Three other women and two security guards watch as the actor gives an interview to the charity's house media team. Colin talks earnestly about the importance of "giving back," and about the inner strength displayed by children with physical and mental challenges. He tops it off with his love for events where he can interact with kids.

"I can see you're happy here," observes the producer, who's also Irish, "away from all the glitz. I've seen you out before, and you're normally press-shy, to say the least."

I don't know what the guy is talking about. This is glitz central, starting with Golden-Globe-winning Colin himself, who is gorgeous and dark in person, and emits pheromones that make me a bit wobbly. *Stop it.* Sure, it's Colin Farrell, but swooning on the job is unprofessional. Anyway, we're in a well-lit, roomy space decorated in soft ecru, high above a stadium where U2 and Bon Jovi will be giving a private performance in a couple of hours. Five bars scattered around the VIP party are serving Perrier-Jouët rose. Like I said—glitz.

"I'm enjoying it," Colin agrees in extreme Irish. "I'm chuffed." He speaks quickly, shyly. "This is better than the Oscars and all those things—it's for all the right reasons."

The cameraman looks up from his lens and nods. "That was great, Colin. Really great. Thanks, mate."

Colin nods. "Whatever you need."

I turn to my handler, a redheaded string bean called Shandy who does PR for the All Children Rock! charity, which is throwing this mega-bash.

"He seems genuine," I say under my breath.

Shandy nods and whispers behind a cupped hand, "He bought *every single* child a special outfit for tonight. Three hundred of the little buggers. Paid for everything himself."

I continue pushing back any lustful thoughts and glance up at Colin, whose sparkling drink in a cut-glass tumbler is back in his grasp. Even if—*if*—his Hollywood glory days are behind him, he's in his native Ireland so everyone wants a piece of him. I feel an adrenaline surge. It's my turn. I flip on my recorder and hold a pen as backup. I step toward him, but Shandy holds me back with one straight arm. She says to his sister Claudine, "Can he do a quick hit with *CelebLife* magazine?"

A frowny faced woman with slick frosted hair intervenes, shakes her head vehemently, gets between Colin and me. She nods to him and they speed-walk away from us. This doesn't work for me. I was flown here from London to get quotes from three particular stars, and I'm not leaving without them.

I pretend I don't notice the rejection and follow Colin's crew. Shandy cheers me on with a whisper and a light elbow in the ribs: "Go for it."

"Colin," I say, trying not to sound out of breath as we speed along. "I'm with *CelebLife* magazine. Why is this cause so important to you?"

I brace for a smack from Claudine or a shank in the gut from one of the unobtrusive guards. But, whaddaya know? Colin turns and replies, "It's for the kids. It's *so* important. I wouldn't miss it."

Sour-faced rep whirls on me without missing a step. "He doesn't have time. Colin, let's go. We have to get to rehearsal." Colin keeps moving.

I'm still in their wake. "Does being a dad make this charity even closer to your heart?"

The actor stops, forcing his entourage to skid to a jumbled halt, then turns to face me. My own heart is in my throat. The frowning lady is trying to pull him away.

"In spite of everything, it changed me," Colin tells me. The woman lets go of him, resigned. "Watching them grow up is the best, man. I just try not to mess them up too much."

I may be new at *CelebLife*, but I know this is gold, Jerry. *Gold*. *CelebLife* will print anything with the following words in the headline: *baby, marriage, divorce, dad,* and most of all, *hot dad,* because those are ultra-clicky. I am disproportionately grateful for the crumbs Colin's thrown me, but, to be fair, the stakes are high for me. *Thank you, Number 5.*

Colin stays rooted, searching my eyes. "Will that work?" His voice is soft. My knees would buckle if I let them, due to the Irish accent and the intense, big brown eyes. But I don't, because lusting after interview subjects is creepy.

"That works great," I say, and he nods, turns, and leaves.

This is how celebrities live. You hear about it, but you don't really *get* it until you gain entry to their rarefied, lubricated world. The charity concert is being held at an indoor stadium, and I'm sunk into a white love seat in the massive glassed-in area high above the stage, sipping Champagne and picking at a plate cobbled together from a buffet of acres of king crab legs, a seafood tower, mini-sandwiches, a pasta station, and every kind of salad. Shandy left me here with these parting words: *If you see a celebrity*, she'd said before taking off to do her PR thing, *go for it*.

I keep an eye out for the other big names I'm after. The good news is, *CelebLife* has the exclusive on this behind-the-scenes VIP affair, which means I don't have the added stress of worrying about evading and beating the competition. I open my journal and make some notes on Colin. We're off to a roaring start, and I've decided that from now on, all of my celebrity quarry will receive rankings. Colin gets a 9.0 out of 10 for giving me a story, for being kind, and for being a former A-lister with current B+ potential. I write underneath, *Life lesson: Never take no for an answer the first time. It can be the difference between failing it and nailing it.*

I set down my plate, check my teeth for errant parsley, apply some lip-gloss, and mosey over to the bar in search of Champagne and celebrities. *Bingo*. Owen Wilson has come in with a posse of young beauties with impossible hair straight out of a Garnier Fructis commercial. I finish my Champagne, wait for him to pass by, and trail him and the ladies to the bar.

I'm not sure whether to interrupt them or not. Stanley's other mandate, *Whatever you do, don't piss off the celebrities,* is clashing with the *Don't come back without quotes* threat. I decide to order two Champagnes and offer Owen one, but as I pass him he stops suddenly and I bump into him.

"So sorry," I say, horrified.

"It's all good," he smiles.

I decide he's genuinely forgiven me. "Hey, Owen, I'm Augusta Noble with *CelebLife*. Do you have a moment to chat?"

"Sure. How's it going?" His voice is soft, lilting, and slightly nasal. The girls look bored and head to the bar, leaving me alone with Owen. Wearing a smooth, tailored suit and sky-blue shirt and sporting a bit of golden scruff on his face, he reminds me of a slower-talking version of his character in *Wedding Crashers* (and *The Internship*, and *Hall Pass*, and *Marley & Me…*).

"Nice party, right?" I turn on my recorder.

He heartily agrees.

"How do you like Dublin?"

His eyes widen and he starts to get excited, as if he *really, really* loves this town. He grabs my arm with excitement, gripping *hard*. I see that famous nose close-up, and it is spectacular—flattened and prominent, crooked and perfect, and undeniably penis-shaped. His shaggy, wavy hair is a sunny shade of butterscotch. He proclaims that he has *never* been to such an adorable city. "It's so mellow and the people are so friendly," he expounds. "I just love it—don't you?"

"Absolutely," I agree, as he lets go of my arm. It's a bit hot where his hand was, but it was a friendly grab, so I'm fine with it. "What brings you here?" I ask. "You must be a huge fan of the charity."

"Sure," he drawls in a way that makes me think he's not entirely familiar with what they do. "You know…the organizers called me, and I'd heard Dublin was a cool city, so here I am. It's a great cause, right?"

That's about all I have time for because the beauties are back and want their celebrity returned to them; they close in and I thank him for his time. He smiles at me. "Have fun," he says.

Back on my sofa, I glance around every few seconds but spy only commoners. I flip open my notebook, and I think about the bored models. I write, *This is what it's like to be a celebrity: people fly you places and treat you like a king just because you're you, and beauty follows. Score: 8.2.*

It is only after I scrawl my last line that a cold panic grips me: Thank God I never got that drink for him. From what I've read, it's quite possible Owen is sober, or trying to be, and it had completely slipped my mind. Offering him a drink could've been catastrophic for both of us. I take another walk and grab a Champagne for myself, and after a few moments I begin to feel the first semblance of calm since I arrived in Dublin. Maybe moving from New York to London in one swift yank wasn't so insane after all.

Shandy finds me on my sofa. She stands over me and eyes my half-empty glass. Three badges around her neck weigh her down, along with a cellphone and a Secret-Service-type earpiece.

"*What*?" She shrieks to whoever is in her ear. She gestures wildly for me to get *up, up, up.* "Gotta go," she says to whomever. "Come," she says to me.

She turns and we move in long, quick strides. We break into a run. An entourage emerges from an elevator up ahead and moves swiftly, as a pack. Their vibe says, *We are racing to the ER to save lives. Make way!* We fall in behind the group, and I see Mr. Jon Bon Jovi cossetted by two layers of handlers. This is not how it was supposed to go down. Jon and I should be alone in an all-white suite with Diptyque candles and yoga music piping in as I pepper him with fascinating questions.

"OK, go," Shandy urges, nudging me in the back. But Jonnie-Boy is walking away, and also talking to someone else.

"*Now! This is your chance,*" she hisses. "Go!"

This cannot be happening. I'm supposed to interview a major star's back while running in heels, full on buttered rolls and bubbly? Everyone's in earshot. His entourage. Security. Charity staffers. It feels like we're going fifteen miles an hour. The exit door, mocking me in all its angry bright neon, is yards ahead and I have four questions Stanley wants me to ask. I can't go back with *one* piddling answer, let alone zero. I'm livin' on a prayer as I make the snap decision to fire off a question about the event. I know full well that if it's all I can get from Jon, it will be useless because quotes about "giving back" do not make a story.

"How important is this charity to you?" I ask, my voice coming out far louder than intended. Jon returns a rote, one-sentence answer in a flat voice, turning his head a few degrees in my direction so he will appear to be making an effort.

Still moving, I grit my teeth and throw him one of the "fun" questions—an easy one, if not slightly inane. I try to jazz it up with a perky voice. "If you had to wear the same T-shirt every day, what would it say?"

This time, he swivels far enough that his eyes meet mine. He has bags under his eyes and his overall skin tone is craggier than in photos. The way his upper lip curves and the shape of his nose give him a feline quality. "It would say, 'I Love Dublin,'" he says.

He's talking to someone else now. I have seconds before he reaches the exit.

Reporting 101: Always get specifics. Details make the story. "Fascinating!" I shout. "What is it about the city that you love so much?"

He slows, turns. "And WHAT does this have to do with what we're talking about? Right. *Nothing*," he snarls. "That's enough. We're done here."

That's enough is said in the way you might tell a crazy person to stop throwing rocks at you. The door flies open and he is gone. I am flabbergasted. Is this the same guy who does photo ops for his favorite causes, grinning and hugging the less fortunate people who gaze upon him with wide-eyed worship? I am reeling from a public rebuke for such a benign query—in the name of charity, no less. It is *how* Jon spoke to me, more than what he said, that stung. Normally in the course of doing my reportorial duty, I am prepared for who's going to be combative: a CEO asked why his stock is down or a police chief confronted about rising crime in his city will be on the offense, and I'm always ready for it. The rest of the time, I expect people in the grown-up work world to be professional and polite— yes, even celebrities.

Shandy and I come to a stop as Jon disappears. She widens her eyes and bares her teeth at me in a manic attempt at a smile. "Did you get what you needed? Two down, right?" She's touching her earpiece again.

"Let me ask you a question," I say slowly. She nods. "Did Jon, Bono, and Colin agree to do interviews?"

"Well," she chirps, "they didn't *not* agree to do interviews. And," she adds tantalizingly, "remember this is all exclusive. You're the only reporter we let into the party."

Great. I can see it now: *EXCLUSIVE! Augusta Noble Dissed by Aging Rocker in Excruciating Blaze of Non-Glory.*

"Why don't you head back to the buffet? I hear the lobster salad is to die for," she suggests.

"Will do. Call me if you see Bono," I reply, then head to my favorite sofa and pull out the notebook. My chest tightens. I feel panicky, dizzy. *Breathe.* Since that horrific day, the panic attacks come out of nowhere, from the quietest corners. It is like stepping into a one-way street, watching out for cars coming from one direction, then getting slammed by a drunk driver speeding the other way. Owen touching me should've set me off more than Bon Jovi running away, but no. I feel air in my lungs and recognize this attack isn't a big one; it's a rogue wave, not a tsunami.

I sip my drink. The therapist calls alcohol "the ultimate fake friend"—something about hangovers, increased anxiety, and messing with brain function—but so far my old pal Champagne has proved to be a reliable ally.

Breathe. Focus. Celebrities are wonderful and beautiful and, ultimately, an escape from the excruciating agony of being alive. Living in their orbit can cure you if you let it. I tap my pen on the cover of my notebook. Rating Jon won't be hard; coming up with some fresh, descriptive adjectives to describe my new feelings toward him might take a while, though.

Obnoxious. That's one, I decide as I scan the still-chilled-out party for more action. It's all very civilized; I think I see onyx-haired Dylan McDermott sipping a clear drink up at the bar. I smile to myself thinking about Stanley's interview question—I'm certain I'm looking at *Dylan*, not Dermot. Where are all the naughty celebrity party antics we always hear so much about? I take a break from thinking about Bon Jovi and hop up off my seat to do some recon behind the scenes.

5

Massachusetts, 1999

JFK, Jr. awaits my question. I grip my pen until my knuckles hurt.

"Will you ever run for president?" I blurt. I ditched the prom question at the last second—I'm bold sometimes, but not delusional.

John half-smiles, meets my eyes, and almost knocks me down with the charisma shooting out of his body in invisible charisma rays. He leans down and I get a good sniff of him; his scent is a mixture of soap and man.

"I very well might," John says softly into my ear. "But I have a lot of things to do first. Talk to me in ten years."

He straightens up as the Bison guarding him says, "That's enough, young lady. Scoot on back inside, please."

Everything freezes around me. The world has stopped. *This* is it—the moment I know what I'm going to do with my life. I'm going to be a journalist. It hadn't occurred to me before; I only joined the paper after the guidance counselor threatened to sign me up for the glee club if I didn't pick my own extracurricular activity. I love to write and apparently, when it comes to work, I'm able to talk to people without stuttering or sweating. It's as if the pen and the notebook are my superhero powers and the reporter is a character I'm playing. *She* does the talking, and she's awesome at this.

I cap my pen, high on adrenaline and a shot of hope that life might not be entirely shitty forever. I'm finished trying to impress high school boys. John F. Kennedy, Jr., liked me. He *saw* me. I smile, give a little squeal and a hop, and head back inside to call my mom for a ride.

On Saturday night, I stay on the phone with Caroline talking through the finer points of *The Lost Boys* again, and she sticks to her theory that the half-vampire transformation represents Michael risking his soul to try and fit in. I've known Caroline since we were six, when our families moved in across the street from each other two days apart during the hottest August in recorded history. I wish we'd never left Cambridge—a funky little city in Greater Boston where old-fashioned cheesefests like prom are regularly boycotted by the cynical urban kids—but my parents decided a bigger house in the "safe" suburbs would provide a better childhood for my brother and me.

It's not *sad* I'm skipping prom, it's "the *coolest*," Caroline swears.

We eat popcorn together from four towns away, and for a while it doesn't feel like I'm missing out on anything, especially when I start to get maudlin and Caroline points out, "Oh, get over yourself. Anyone can go to prom. How many people get to interview John F. Kennedy, Jr.?"

She has a point. I was a minor celebrity at school for about two days, and the big Boston papers picked up my "claims" about John's presidential plans, though they didn't name me.

"Screw them, anyway," Caroline adds. "Lincoln's having a party next Saturday night. Borrow your parents' minivan and get yourself into the city. We'll show you suburban softies how it's done."

I'm not sure she realizes her friends don't think much more of me than my own classmates, but it never seems to matter. Caroline doesn't give a shit what other people think. When she's by your side, you're always one of the cool kids.

"Different but always together," I say when it's time to go.

"Best friends forever," she replies, just like always.

I lie back in bed after we hang up and stare at the brand-new JFK Jr. poster on the ceiling above me. He's replaced Leo DiCaprio from *Titanic*. I've had an ongoing battle with my mother—a women's history professor who minored in psychology and keeps a signed copy of Gloria Steinem's *Outrageous Acts and Everyday Rebellions* displayed on its own shelf in our living room—dating back to my first poster, which was Mark-Paul Gosselaar from *Saved by the Bell*. Mom doesn't mind Alanis Morissette or Alicia Keys, but Mark-Paul, Ralph Macchio (I've seen *The Karate Kid* at least seventy-nine times), Brad Pitt (long-haired *Legends of the Fall* Brad, natch), Joshua Jackson, Puff Daddy, even the more cerebral Ethan Hawke, all make her curl her toes. As a compromise, she tried to make me sprinkle in a bunch of what she calls "world changers." I resisted with such ferocity that she ended up settling for one. Being an incurable wise-ass, instead of the Betty Friedans or Stephen Hawkings I knew she wanted, I chose a poster of the guy who invented the pencil. His name is Conrad Gessner. You can also buy mugs with his face on them.

I check the time: one a.m. The prom parties should be over soon, I think, though I don't really know because I've never been. I lie in bed, stare at the faces surrounding me, and think, *What if I met them all? Every one?* I don't need high school losers when I have John, Leo, Brad, and the gang.

Someday, maybe.

6

#8, #9, #10

I venture out the same door Bon Jovi disappeared through earlier. It leads to a maze of hallways with scuffed white linoleum flooring lined with a series of closed doors. I walk slowly, stopping at each door to try to hear celebrity related noise. I pass an elevator bank that presumably leads down to the stadium stage, and after another twenty feet or so, I come upon a door with a plastic yellow star taped to it that happens to be cracked open. I hear sniffing inside, like someone has a bad cold. *Do I dare go in?* I finger the pass around my neck, which I earlier flipped over so instead of a blaring "Media" label, it shows the All Children Rock! logo. I push the door open.

When I step inside the small room, I am taken aback. Sticking out six feet from my face is the butt of a man in snug jeans; he is bent over the corner of a table weighed down with drinks and appetizers on which two white lines of powder are laid out unironically between a can of Diet Coke and a bowl of chips. I hear the snorting sound as he rises and does the requisite huffing for the finale: "*Ahhhhhhh.*"

Shit. I shouldn't be here. I'm about to turn on my heel when the man swivels around.

I'm so shocked I actually *gasp*. The snorter is that A-list Action Star—the all-American boy-turned-man, only a few years older than I, adorable, likeable, pretty, and…so, so famous. His lifetime box-office total is rocketing toward a billion and he's not yet thirty-five. He wasn't on the list Stanley gave me, so I'm not sure what to do.

The actor's eyes flick to the plastic pass around my neck. He puts on a movie-star smile.

I do a quick sweep of the room and note a back way out. We're the only ones here.

"Want some?" He asks me, extending a rolled-up hundred-dollar bill.

I'm so dead.

I reach out instinctively because I don't want to upset him. *Don't piss off the celebrities* is ringing in my ear—but so is, *What are you doing? You can't do coke with this A-List Action Star. That's a hard no.*

I'm frozen in place as the money hangs in the air. It's not the coke that's freaking me out—it's the when, where, and with whom. It's five-o'clock in the evening at a children's charity event, and this guy is a poster boy for clean-cut.

Just as I'm about to squeak out, *No, thanks, I had some earlier*, the back door bursts open and a squat man in a tailored suit and an oddly square, close-shorn haircut enters. He's staring down at his phone as he barks, "Hey, man, really—we've got to get down to rehearsal. Let's *go.*"

The actor turns to answer the guy—and I race out the door. In my wake, I hear the squat man shout, "Who the fuck was that?"

I'm frantically searching for an escape route in this endless hallway. The man is yelling, "You stay here—I'll go get her! We need to know who the hell caught you putting that shit up your nose."

I'm running in heels now; I slow down to try the next door I come to. It's locked. I run a few feet to the next one, and as I turn the handle violently, I throw all my body weight on the door—and it opens. I fall in, stumbling into something wet and squishy with my right foot. I then get a slimy, smelly mass of tentacles in my face. I stifle a scream and pull the door shut behind me, shaking off the floppy strings as I do. I shift, turn on my phone's flashlight, and see I've crashed into a cleaning closet, stepped in a pile of wet rags, and been slapped in the face by an old mop. I catch my breath, shut my light off, and put my ear close to the door. I can hear the man stomping down the hall, talking to someone, probably on the phone because I only hear his voice: "Yes, *yes*. He says there's no way she caught it on video. Yes, she had a *pass*, Mark. If this gets out—yes, I know she can't prove anything, but even the suggestion— yes. Let me know if you see her."

I hear him walk by very, very slowly, and when his footsteps grow quieter, I start counting to a hundred. I make it to twenty before I abandon the countdown, because I hear a sudden ruckus that sounds a lot like a rock-and-roll entourage. Someone calls out, "Bono, you're up for sound check in five!"

As I step gingerly into the hallway, I almost run into The Edge. He walks by me, beanie cap pulled down tight, small eyes focused straight ahead. I opt not to bother him. The entourage is still rushing through the hallway. I turn on my recorder and wait for Bono, who passes by thirty seconds behind The Edge. I jump into the scrum.

"How did you choose the music to fit tonight's cause?" I shout as I do my second running interview of the day. Bono turns his head while powerwalking to the elevator bank. His famous glasses, the lenses a bright vermillion, obscure his eyes. "We chose the most beautiful music," he shouts as the elevator doors open.

It is enough—or will be, once I watch the show and fill in the specifics. More important, now I can tell people I've interviewed Bono. I head back to the party to try to pick up any straggling stars before the concert starts, but first I pull my straight blonde hair back into a low ponytail and cover my short-sleeved deep maroon dress (H&M, three seasons ago) with a black sweater I've had tied around my waist. That'll alter a couple of the descriptors of the woman A-List Action Star's people are looking for.

I head into the party and run into Dylan McDermott gazing down at the sound check below. He's so dashing in black tie I decide he could be the next James Bond. (Producers, are you listening?) He's happy to chat when I approach him and even asks if he can get me a drink. I request club soda, then check my list of questions while he's at the bar. When he returns, I toss out one of the least-dumb ones, which is still a question a third-grader might ask a baboon.

"Do you have a life motto or slogan?" I ask, hoping I'm not visibly wincing. "If so, what is it and why?"

Who the hell walks around with a life motto or slogan? I wouldn't have an answer for such a witless enquiry. Dylan smiles at me, nods, and in true gentlemanly fashion takes the question, and me, seriously.

"It would have to be, 'I love C & C," he replies. "For Coco and Charlotte."

I sip fizzy water and hold my recorder as subtly as I can as he speaks about his daughters, about how his love for them is as wide as the Grand Canyon. I feel my ovaries twitch, and I could talk to him for ages, which means it's time to let him go.

"Enjoy the concert," he tells me, and I thank him for his time before heading out to find my seat in the VIP box, where I make some notes before the show begins. It occurs to me as I debate whether to give Dylan an 8.5 or an 8.8 (sadly, he loses points for not being A-list) that I am overly grateful for being treated with respect by a celebrity who knows he's talking to our millions of readers. I tap my pen some more, then write out three words: *Celebrity Stockholm Syndrome*. That applies to me; it is the label I have just invented for celebrity reporters who have to put up with jerks, then swoon at the tiniest crumb of kindness. I make a mental note to avoid it in the future.

I put my notebook away to enjoy the show, but walk out when Bon Jovi comes on—I never liked his music much anyway. Back inside, I run a Yammer search for the A-List Action Star's management team. I didn't think it would be this easy, but Square Head pops up instantly. Turns out the guy who was chasing me is one Ivan Deaver, power publicist to the stars, A-List Action Star's personal pit bull and the architect of his phony all-American, corn-fed image. An article listing him as the seventh most powerful person in Hollywood notes he earned his nickname, "Deaver the Deceiver," by lying constantly to the media about his clients. *Great*. I can only pray I don't run into him before the night is through. I make a quick note about the action star in my book, and decide a guy offering me drugs counts toward my total. I step back out to the stadium in time to see the action star introducing U2's closing set. The crowd goes wild as he chokes up talking about "the inspirational kids" and about how he was dyslexic in school. I guess the cocaine did its job, because he puts on a great act. After that, when U2 plays "Sunday Bloody Sunday," I get emotional because it's so powerful, and because it feels like the only real, true thing that's happened tonight.

In the taxi on the way back to the Clarence, I'm too exhausted to feel anything—either excitement or failure—though I manage to make time to overthink things. Either I suck at this celebrity journalism thing, or a lot of celebrities are assholes. I'm willing to entertain the idea that both things are somewhat true, but that doesn't make me feel any better. *Good god.* A drug den at a benefit for kids. Dissed by an aging rocker. What am I doing here?

I'm living on borrowed time in my parents' Wimbledon flat, which they bought when I was just a fetus. I can stay only until the decrepit bathroom and creaky floors are renovated, at which point they'll resume renting the place to actual paying tenants. I think about quitting. Already, at Number 10, part of me wants out. Already, this quest isn't what I thought it would be. How can I possibly subject myself to *ninety-seven more* of these people?

But no, a voice says. *There must be more good ones than bad. Finish this. Nothing will get better if you give up.* I make a note in the book under my final interview of the night: *No matter how many times you fall, get up again. Fall down seven times, get up eight.*

7

I pull open the heavy door and step into the Farnsboro Skating Rink, recoiling at the blast of smelly, chilled air hitting me in the face. It's like being in a refrigerator full of teenage boys' sneakers. I pad across the foam floor and remind myself to act interested in this so-called "celebrity" charity hockey game, which, in this part of the world, usually means a vicious blood match between the Bison Lodge and the local Knitting Club.

I'm two weeks away from heading off to college, and it's been a tough summer. I was on my uncle's dinghy when I heard about John Kennedy's plane going down. A fisherman steered close to us and yelled across the water in a Gloucesterman's accent rough as a rusted razorblade, *You heard? It's bad.* When he told us, I gagged, leaned over the side of the boat, and prepared to throw up (I didn't). I tried to see beneath the ripples and thought, *It's so cold down there. John-John can't be at the bottom of this same ocean.* Selfishly, losing him meant losing hope; his death was an abrupt end to my dream of a future where I was normal, even thriving. I always thought we'd meet again and I'd be able to thank him, maybe even work with him.

I still feel guilty for leveraging our interview to secure a two-week summer internship with the *Suburban Boston Times Daily* before I leave for Virginia. I'm getting paid in gas money and tuna sandwiches from the newsroom vending machine. To make matters worse, there was an end-of-summer party for graduating seniors last night, which I heard about accidentally while shopping for tampons at the drugstore. Amanda, my alleged best friend at Sam Adams who doesn't always include me in things, wouldn't call me back, so I had to find out where the party was by driving around town in my parents' minivan. I got a hit at the home of one Billy Ronson, lacrosse captain. His front lawn was spilling over with excited seniors about to be freshmen again. I parked one house away under a tree with my lights off and watched my classmates giggling and dancing and drinking from red cups, and I desperately wanted a red cup in my hand, too. I felt sick about missing another teenage rite of passage, but I couldn't go in on my own; I wasn't brave enough.

I was left trying to solve the unanswerable problem: *What is wrong with me?*

I shake thoughts of last night's party out of my head as a sandy-haired man in a blue hockey uniform rushes up to me as I approach the ice.

"Can I help you?"

"I'm here for the event—Augusta Noble with *The Boston Suburban Daily Times*?"

"Oh," he says, giving me a once-over. "Right. You look young, sorry. You're the first one here—you came at a good time. I'm Robert, press officer for the charity."

I stand at the edge of the rink as athletic males whizz along the ice and mill about at the edges with fetchingly sweaty tendrils of hair pasted to their faces.

"You're going to want Matthew Perry," the guy's saying as surveys the ice.

"Matthew Perry? Ha," I chuckle. "Same name as the guy on *Friends*." Same as the guy on the wall behind my bed, along with the rest of the cast.

Robert turns to me with an odd look on his face. "Right. The guy from *Friends*. You'll also want to talk to Jason Priestley, I assume."

"Yeah," I chuckle. *You bet I would.* Jason Priestley is also on my wall.

Come to think of it, none of the guys on the ice look like members of the Landesboro Bison Lodge. I whip out my compact and check my face. The concealer is doing a fine job of hiding the puffiness leftover from last night's crying jag; it seems the ice pack and zucchini slices actually worked. (We were out of cucumbers, so in desperation I lay in bed with squash discs on my eyelids.) I put away the mirror, take another look around, and there, halfway across the ice, is Chandler Bing. I mean, Matthew Perry. I'm instantly nervous bordering on freaking out.

Robert has been signaling the guys, and Matt, bulked out with protective pads, catches my eye and races in our direction, gripping his hockey stick in both hands. I flinch as he barrels at me, but at the last second, he *whooshes* to a sexy ice-stop, expertly twisting to the side and kicking up a cloud of crystals.

"This is Augusta Noble from the *Boston Suburbs Daily* newspaper," Robert says incorrectly.

"Hey," Matt says.

"Hey," I say.

My interview with one of the biggest TV stars in America is off to a cracking start. I picture the ghosts of Martha Gellhorn and Nellie Bly shaking their heads.

Robert steps away and I work hard to focus. I manage to ask about the charity Matthew is here to raise money for.

"It's an amazing feeling," he replies, smiling shyly, not a cocky Chandler vibe to be felt. "It's an honor. I grew up in Ottawa, skating on the canal through the city, so this is where I feel my best."

And suddenly, thank God, here she is again: Augusta, girl reporter.

"So, you're good?" I name the only Canadian hockey player I know. "Like, Wayne Gretzky good?"

He cocks his head. "Not Wayne Gretzky good," he confesses. "But since he's retired, I think there's a spot open. I might try out. What do you think?"

It's the *way* he says it that gets me. I giggle and he waits for my answer. *What do I think?* I think nothing. My brain currently is as sharp as the oatmeal my dad manages to burn every morning.

"I…think you're smoking," I babble. *Someone save me.* "I mean…I think you're *cool*. Hot. I mean great. At hockey. And acting."

Matthew smiles sympathetically, which is a step up from condescending, but still stings.

"Why don't you give it a try?" He holds out a hand.

"I've got sandals on," I point out.

"Not a problem. It's got a good bit of snow on the surface. I'll keep you upright. Come on."

He's got a dimpled, adorable smile on as he pulls off a bulky glove, so I take his hand. Thankfully, I don't show surprise when I see he's missing half his middle finger; I never knew he was digitally challenged. He holds my hand tight, and as soon as my sandal touches ice, it seems I'm OK and, stupidly, I let go of his hand. I take one step and

I'm falling, waving my arms like a windmill to right myself, and Matt can't help because he's in front of me and he's on skates, and as I'm toppling backwards to my certain death, I feel arms catch me, envelop me, and set me upright.

Whoever it is holds me up until I'm safely off the ice. Matt skates over and takes my hand, concerned. "You OK? Sorry…I thought I had you…"

I turn to see who the Hercules of the hour is and find a tall, lanky guy with shaggy, sandy-blond hair. "Thanks," I say, and the guy nods, glancing down at my inappropriate footwear.

"Try not to cross any frozen lakes in those things," he says.

"I'm going to the beach later," I lie. He has great eyelashes, dark and long, framing emerald-green eyes.

"I'd like to see that," he says, and I almost fall over again because his eyes are connecting with mine like we're the only people here. He's not much older than I am; somewhere between nineteen and twenty-five, I'd say. My hero cocks his chin as a goodbye, then skates off to join another group across the rink.

I figure Matt owes me after my brush with death. I ask casually, "So, Matthew…are you seeing anyone since Julia Roberts? Our readers would love to know."

He appears taken aback, and I'm guessing the fact that I'm barely more than a high school kid combined with the fact that he almost caused my premature demise is the reason he doesn't skate off in a huff.

"Not seriously," he claims. "Julia's a hard act to follow." And there is my headline. *Thank you, Chandler.*

Robert races over to us. He's got a colleague in tow, a young woman with a clipboard who's blinking rapidly, along with the guy who caught me. He needs a haircut. He's staring at me.

"This is Tristan Catlin," the blinking PR woman tells me. She consults her clipboard. "The *Globe* didn't want him…Associated Press, that's a *no*…let's see…*The Worcester Telegram* said nope, too. I'm assuming you don't want to talk to him either…"

Now *I'm* blinking too fast. *Ouch.* Tristan is looking down at the ice; he kicks at some of the snow Matt peeled off earlier with his grand entrance.

I say loudly, "I'd love to interview Tristan. Our readers are always excited to know about up-and-coming stars."

She shrugs, nods, and reads in a monotone from a press release: "'In the pilot for situation comedy *He's On Fire,* newcomer Tristan Catlin plays the foil for main character Buster McGraw (Ashton Kutcher), a Texas oil heir who loses everything to a wildfire.'"

She looks up at me. "Sounds fun, right?"

They're all staring at me, including Matthew. I have nothing to ask this guy. I'm unnerved by the look he has in his eyes—if I didn't know better, I'd say he kind of likes me.

Matthew swivels when he hears his name, then waves to us and skates off. I'm left alone with Tristan, who smiles and says, "Ask me anything."

I'm wavering under his intense gaze, but I manage to scrabble together a question. "What's harder: Ice skating or acting?"

He throws his head back and laughs. "You know what?" he says, growing serious, "It's acting—by far. People think it's easy, that you just need a pretty face, but it's a tough thing to do well. I can only hope I'm lucky enough to make it in this business."

I nod and noticed he's moved a few inches closer to me. As I'm thinking about something else to ask him, Robert walks up to us.

"Miss Noble…Augusta. We need you. Jason has three minutes before his *Globe* interview."

"I'm sorry," I say to Tristan.

"My loss," he says. He waves at me and skates off alone, and I feel a pang, because I know what it's like to be leftovers.

I follow Robert to the other side of the rink. When we get to Jason, who stands in front of me like a blue knight in shoulder pads with his hockey-stick sword, I'm the other me again, confident and a little cocky. Jason is shorter than Matt and Tristan, but prettier and equally athletic.

"I didn't know you were a hockey fan," I say.

"It feels great to be on skates again," he says, smiling. He gestures at the hunky Canadian hockey players whizzing around behind him. "And for such a great cause."

I have a ton more questions, but blinking lady is back. "Jason," she says, "we need you *now—Boston Herald*'s doing a big feature on the game."

"Hey," Jason says to me. "Sorry about this. Great to meet you."

I read recently in *Star Scene* that some guest stars have claimed the *90210* leads won't let people look them in the eye, let alone talk to them. I found no evidence of this kind of superiority complex with Jason. He looked me in the eye longer than any boy I've gone to school with for the last seven years.

On my way out, I see Tristan skating alone. He's racing, gliding, and taking corners gracefully, moving like an athlete. He's quite sexy from afar, but I forget about him as soon as I start the car because I've got an exclusive Matthew Perry story to write up.

8

The day I arrive back in London, exhausted from staying up all night in the Clarence bar filing a story about Colin Farrell's parenting tips, Stanley shoots me an email inviting me to *CelebLife*'s London HQ "to talk about Dublin." I find their offices in an old converted mansion off the Strand. I'm expecting to be cowed by a sleek, glamorous space humming with size-zero editors wearing five-inch Jimmy Choos, rushing out for coffee with Benedict Cumberbatch. I step off the elevator into a creaky, open-plan office with four desks shoved together in a hundred-square-foot space. There's a whiff of decaying newsprint in the air. The décor is Ye Olde English: stained wood, intricate wainscoting and high ceilings. Phones are buried under stacks of newspapers, their tangled cords peeking out beneath the tabloids and broadsheets. It feels a lot like my old newsroom back in Massachusetts (apart from the antique fixtures) and I feel instantly, oddly, at home. A bespectacled young man sitting at one of the desks glances up.

"Hello," he says in a British accent.

"Hi," I say in American. "I'm Augusta Noble, here to see Stanley."

"Robbie." He nods hello and points down a hallway off to my left, his right.

I make my way down, noting staffers staring at computer screens in three offices along the way. I stop at the last one, a corner office with a modest wooden desk and a giant monitor. Stanley is typing ferociously, his meaty fingers bouncing over the keyboard like sausages on a hot grill.

He glances up and says as if it's a huge surprise to see me, "Oh, Augusta! Hello. Come in."

I sit in one of his guest chairs. He keeps typing, and after a minute or two I shift in my seat, stressed and uncomfortable, in part because I've worn my one good suit and after a few weeks of hanging at the Fox & Grapes drinking pints of cider and black, the pants seems to have shrunk.

Stanley slams one final key with a flourish and crosses his arms on the desk in front of his keyboard.

"Bon Jovi," he says, "didn't like you."

I clear my throat. "Did he say that?"

"No," he laughs. "Your file did."

He reads from his monitor. "'Jon stormed away without so much as a look back, and I can only hope he's nicer to the needy children than he was to *CelebLife*'s reporter.' Don't take it personally. He was the same way with one of our New York correspondents a while back, when she did a sit-down with him. Trust me: They're not all like that."

I'm nodding like it's no big deal, but a rock star snapping at me on what should be a delightful and fluffy assignment is a new one for me. Time to get used to it, I guess.

Stanley adds, "Always remember it's just a job. Get what you need and get out of there." He smiles. "Maybe he was having a bad day."

I did consider the Bad Day Defense, but I'm not buying it. We all have bad days; my life has been one long terrible day since the nightmare at Caroline's, and yet I manage to remain professional and polite.

"Look," Stanley says, leaning forward, laying his palms on his desktop. "It's more common than not for the big stars to be narcissists, divas, or both. They can be great with their peers and bosses—basically the powerful people who can do things for them. They can also be kind to the homeless, sick children, and rescue dogs, because it makes them feel like saints. The thing is," he says, "a lot of them have trouble with the middle."

"You and I being 'the middle' in this scenario," I confirm.

"Precisely. You can't make this fun for our readers if you don't have a little fun yourself, Augusta. Try not to take it so seriously."

Interesting, considering he was serious as a heart surgeon when he was grilling me over nachos at our first meeting. I nod again. I'm getting nervous; I'm not sure I've wowed him. I go for broke and figure I'd better tell him everything. "There's one more thing I didn't tell you about Dublin," I say carefully.

He raises his eyebrows. "Oh?"

"It's about a very famous action star." *Don't do it.* "I was looking for the bathroom, and…"

I proceed to tell Stanley every detail about our cocaine confrontation, except the part about how I was in fact looking for a scandal, *not* a toilet, when I took a stroll through the stadium.

"Wow," he says at the end, shaking his head. "Just…wow."

"I know, right?"

He leans forward and grabs his mouse. "This," he says, "is the part where I ask why you didn't tell me right away."

I can feel myself starting to turn red. Editors insist you inform them about everything, which reporters rarely do, so when they find out you've betrayed them, there's usually trouble.

"I thought I was doing the right thing," I reply sheepishly. "This Deaver guy was beside himself and I was afraid no one would believe me. Then I calmed down a bit, and realized I should've told you. It was my first day with *CelebLife*, and I thought it might cause trouble if I said anything."

"Fair enough," he nods, then turns to his monitor and starts typing. "But don't make a habit of it—tell me everything you find, and I'll decide what's worth covering, OK?" I nod, and he continues, still typing. "I'm going to tell you something, but you have to keep it between us."

"Of course." I'm on the edge of my seat.

Still punching the keys, Stanley says, "We've been tipped off over the past year about this guy's drug use. We could never nail it down, and neither could the scandal sheets or gossip Web sites. There's all this attention on opioids right now, but we're hearing he favors coke, heroin, and occasionally, a hit of meth."

"Holy shit," I say. "He looks so healthy…"

"I know, I know. It's sad—he clearly needs help." He looks from his keyboard. "OK. I've let the editors in New York know about your big scoop. Your instincts were right, by the way—we wouldn't write about what you saw, but it's an important piece of background reporting for any big future story."

"You mean, if this action star does something crazy, checks into rehab, or both," I say, "you'll have my story as confirmation."

"Correct. Tell you what, Augusta. Why don't you stay for the day? I'll put you to work and you can see how things are done. If you still want to work here, I'm happy to give you a shot."

"I'd love that," I say. "Thank you!"

He reveals my hourly rate which, when I make some quick calculations, adds up to twice my salary at *Newstime*. He adds, "You'll invoice, what, thirty-two hours or so for this past trip…?"

More calculations. That's at least one month's rent toward my own flat after my parents kick me out of theirs. I suppress a smile; this is a huge relief.

Stanley dismisses me by gesturing to the door. "Robbie will set you up," he says.

As I head down the hall, he shouts after me, "Hey—don't get used to traveling. You're new—this Dublin thing was a fluke, you understand?"

I smile to myself and keep walking. I find Robbie munching on potato chips.

"Crisps?" he asks, holding out the silvery bag. I check the label: They're Sunday Ham-flavored.

"No, thanks," I say.

He sets the bag down. "You staying?"

"Yep."

He sets me up at the desk diagonal to his, with my back facing the entrance. I take a good look at him. He's too young for me, but I can imagine the girls dig him: He's about six feet tall, well-built though on the thin side, with glasses semi-obscuring what appears to be a cute face—kind of like if Clark Kent and Ryan Reynolds had a kid.

Robbie dumps a colorful pile of British newspapers in front of me. "Go through these, please," he says. "Note anything that looks interesting."

With those vague instructions, I leaf through them all. I'm lost in a *Daily Snitch* story about Justin Bieber supposedly texting the Queen to try to get into her knickers when a turquoise-haired intern strolls in with a bunch of cappuccinos.

"Hi, I'm Poppy. Been staking out Kensington Palace," she tells me. "Didn't know you existed, though, so no coffee for you, sorry."

"Augusta. That's OK," I respond, but she's already moved on.

Stanley calls Robbie to announce that the bureau meeting is starting. Everyone's invited, including me, beauty/fashion/news writer Gillian Adlington, royals reporter Barton McPhee, Robbie, even blue-haired Poppy. In forty minutes, I learn that half of what's published in *CelebLife* magazine does not match what the staff believes to be true. Officially, they'd never pit Meghan Markle against Kate Middleton; in fact, the magazine calls them "great friends." However, apart from Barton—who never has a negative word to say about any royals—the others believe Kate Middleton is ultra-lazy and phones in her not-so-frequent charity visits, and that Meaghan is going to eclipse her in every way. I learn that *CelebLife* is all about territory: London mustn't tread on L.A.'s turf, and they, in turn, better stay out of Miami's way. And don't get them started on New York, which has been caught calling Gwyneth's people even though she's now L.A.-based. So far, it appears that at *CelebLife*, for every hour you spend in the presence of an actual celebrity, there is a full week of talking about them, reading about them, calling their friends, and other downright cringe-worthy crap to endure.

When I get back to Wimbledon at the end of the day, I let myself into my parents' flat and feel a wave of emptiness. I trudge up the stairs and land in a gloomy living room, flip on the lights, and move to the kitchen to find the half-bottle of white Burgundy that's just past my two-days-open limit. I pour the rest of it into a glass and drink it standing against the counter. I go to bed early, making a silent wish that my next assignment will come the next day.

The call doesn't come, so I am left alone with an endless span of time. The gap between Stanley saying he'll call and Stanley actually calling seems to stretch out to infinity. In the meantime, while I have friends-of-friends I'm supposed to call for a social life—a new mom whose American husband is a big-time investment banker, a married woman who lives an hour away, a fellow single woman who hasn't returned the emails I sent when I got here—I can't bring myself to make the effort. In the next few days I walk London alone, sipping espresso at Costa, visiting Green Park, Buckingham Palace, and Kensington Palace. I stick closer to home for pints of Strongbow and black and goat-cheese salads at Fox & Grapes on Wimbledon Common. Just when I'm starting to freak out that Stanley was telling me what I wanted to hear so I'd leave his office and never come back, the call comes. It's Robbie this time.

"I have another big one for you," he says. "You know, I've never known a stringer to be thrown in at the deep end like this before. Stanley must like you."

I am profoundly relieved. Stanley's approval, after all, is tied directly to my ability to support myself. The specter of slinking back to Jemima and August's retirement townhouse in Cambridge, where Friday nights are Bible readings for academic analysis and bashing Freud in between glasses of sickly white Zinfandel and cups of Lemon Zinger, looms like a medieval punishment for my hubris in ditching everything I had in New York.

"Anyway," Robbie continues, chewing something that sounds suspiciously like his beloved pig crisps, "Barton's in Monaco for a ball and the rest of us are too bloody tired to work a twelve-hour day on a Sunday, even if it means Champagne and Prince Harry. So…you available?"

9

It's the night after my Matthew Perry interview and I'm blasting Alanis Morissette when my mother creeps into my room, something she routinely does while blaming my "loud" music for masking her alleged knocking.

She's smiling. Usually, she stops by when she wants me to clean something, is worried about me, or has bad news.

"I haven't seen you so happy since your JFK interview," she observes, tucking a curl behind one ear. "Is it Matthew?"

I nod. "And the job," I say, then fill her in on how Jim the surly features editor with a heart of gold loved my exclusive about Julia Roberts, and is putting my story on the *Suburban Boston Times Daily* front page for the next day (bottom left corner, but still).

She squeals—something the serious professor is not prone to do—and hugs me. Sometimes I wonder if she really gave birth to me. Her appearance is the first suspect piece of evidence: she was born with thick, wavy hair with glints of auburn while I got a thin curtain of stringy blonde; she's a slender pear and I'm a full-on apple, which is the worst fruit you can be. Pears are OK, bananas better still. After the kids in fifth grade dubbed me Miss Piggy, I decided that I was actually a pineapple: sweet inside, but with the thickest, roughest, prickliest skin. Just try and get to me. You can't; I won't let you.

"Your first professional byline before you're even in college," Jemima says. "Make sure you tell dad when he gets back."

I shrug. August Noble (yes, my parents did this), a professor of physics who makes a hobby of philosophy, is traveling again, giving talks on his latest paper about this neuron or that proton. When he is around, he keeps his talking to a minimum. And anyway, I'm good for once. It's now been proved to me that celebrities make everything OK. They've raised me up when the rest of the world stomped on me. They see me when no one else does. They're beautiful in a way the Samuel Adams High School student body only wishes it was. They are the cool kids of real life, and let's face it, high school's over.

"I have something for you," Jemima says. I'd been wondering about the cream-colored box she's carrying.

"Never stop asking questions," mom says, offering it to me with both hands outstretched. "Stay brave."

I don't know what to say. I never thought of myself as brave, but courage is an attribute my mother worships above almost any other. I open the box and find the reporter's notebook to end all reporter's notebooks. It the requisite spiral binding across the top, and the shiny light pink cover is monogrammed in sweeping gold calligraphy: *A.X.N.*

"Don't worry," Jemima says as I rub my fingers over the smooth cover, then across the embossed initials for Augusta Xanthe Noble. "It's pleather. I had it made for you after your JFK interview."

I bring it to my nose and indeed it is faux leather, a requirement for me as I've been repulsed by killing, eating, and wearing dead animals since I visited a working farm as a kindergartner. I try to be that person they say could never hurt a fly. I even hate killing ants, and as terrifying as spiders are, I don't believe I have the right to take their lives. Yep—even my own parents say I have issues.

Mom sits on the edge of my bed as I flip open the book and finger the crisp, fresh pages. "Write about John and Matthew and your experience at the newspaper—all of it," she says. "From the first moment you saw John right up until now. These are only your first pages. You have a career ahead of you as a journalist—if that's what you want. And you know…" She trails off, then clears her throat. "Journaling is a great way to process loss."

"I'm doing better," I assure her. There's been a lot of crying in this house since John died. "It's so hard to understand how a person could be alive and vibrant one second, and then *poof*…he's gone. It's like…it's like he *got* me when no one at school ever did."

She smiles and nods. "You're going to love college, Augusta," my mom says. "People will see you for who you are now. It's where we can reinvent ourselves—or re-introduce the person we've always been. It's a fresh start."

She puts her fist under her chin. She's therapizing me, something she's done since I was little because she is a frustrated analyst at heart and will never admit it. Out of nowhere, she hits me with a big question.

"How many would it take, Augusta?" she asks. "How many people wanting to be your friend, telling you you're beautiful, wanting to be around you—how many would make you happy?"

I think for a moment, then sweep my eyes around the room. When I was stuck at home on prom night, I took inventory and counted exactly 107 posters on these walls.

Some are admittedly glorified magazine pages torn from the middle of *Tiger Beat*, but that allows me to squeeze more in.

"How about 107?" I reply, making a sweeping gesture around the room. "That sounds about right. Yes. I'd like 107 friends."

"Is quantity really what matters?" She asks.

"Did you ever go to high school?"

She lets out a part sigh, part laugh. "Fair enough."

She's quiet for a moment, then says, "None of that will make it better, you know." She lays her right palm on her chest. "The answer is in here. That's the only way you're ever going to be truly happy. The rest is just posters."

That's what they all say. Little does she know that fantasies are what keep me going. They're about beautiful celebrities, yes, but also about L.A., where it's always sunny and life is Malibu and mountains and margaritas by the sea. Leo DiCaprio, infinity pools, convertibles, blue skies, Sunset Boulevard. Who wouldn't be happy with all that?

My mother rises, walks to the door, then stops. "Check inside the back cover," she says, pointing to the book still in my hands. "You found your fire. Now you need to keep the flame alive." She nods to me, then closes the door behind her.

I flip to the back of the book and find an inscription embossed in gold: *In everyone's life, at some time, our inner fire goes out. It is then burst into flame by an encounter with another human being. We should all be thankful for those people who rekindle the inner spirit. —Albert Schweitzer*

I read it over and over until I have it memorized, then turn Alanis back on and decide it's probably about time to call Caroline.

10

#11, #12, #13

At six feet two inches of solid, flab-free charm, Prince Harry doesn't disappoint in the flesh. He oozes authenticity and underarm sweat as he interacts with fans before his big polo match: The man in a wheelchair gets a hearty laugh and a warm handshake; a shy, lonesome woman gets an upper-arm squeeze and an *almost*-flirty hello; the young military man who shouts, *Oy oy! Sir!* gets a shout, a joyful laugh, and a bear hug, *Oy, squaddie.*

I'm jotting down every nip of detail as I follow Harry, who rose to the rank of captain in the British army, while keeping my feelings entirely professional. (OK, *somewhat* professional. For those who aren't ginger fans, the boy has a presence, a musk, a *way* about him that transcends type.) *The handsome prince, his jodhpurs clinging to his strong build, made even the most jaded VIPs swoon Sunday as he prepared to take on rival polo hunk/BFF Nacho Figueras.* I've learned there is no superlative too gooey, no prose too fawning, for *CelebLife* magazine. I'm secretly glad Meghan Markle isn't coming today. This way, I get Harry all to myself.

The back of my neck starts to sweat so I run my fingers through my hair to air it out, then check my compact and blot my cheeks and forehead. I'm not seeing any big stars apart from Harry. Windsor Great Park is like a pasture within a forest, huge and green and full of leggy, upper-crust women, rich men, and C-, D-, and F-list actors. Harry pays most attention to those with the no-frills tickets trapped in the general admission pen. Eventually, Harry waves goodbye to his fans as he's whisked away by handlers.

The event's rep, a young blonde with a clipboard and an east London accent, sidles up to me. "Time for lunch," she says quietly, handing me a small envelope and a vermillion wristband. "Be discreet, OK? Only four of you are invited in."

I find my table under a VIP tent decorated with a sea of white roses, peonies, and sweet peas, circling until I land on my name, handwritten in careful calligraphy: *Amanda Noble*. Close enough. I'm the first one here so I stand awkwardly over my chair looking out for Harry, who's allegedly stopping by before the match. It doesn't take long to spot him within a crowd of linen suits and strapless summer dresses swelling around one table. My own tablemates appear one by one, and I smile and nod as we all take our seats. Harry is surprisingly accessible, his protection detail clearly trained in discretion.

"I have a good view," a deep voice next to me says in a posh British accent. "But you know he's off the market, right?"

I turn to see a striking man whose light-brown eyes are focused on me with some amusement.

"I am aware," I reply. "Anyway, he's not my type. I'd wither away behind those palace walls with that stuffy family."

"Noted," he says. "Don't hurt your neck—he'll be surrounded the entire time. And he won't eat. He's got a match shortly."

The man is smiling in the languid way inherently confident people do. He's tall, wide-shouldered, tanned (evident from a pale mark under his watch), and boasts a healthy head of wavy chestnut hair.

"I'll try to be more subtle," I say. "But keeping an eye on him is part of my job, so…"

I take a look around the table. To my left is a bald guy who looks about my age. He catches my eye. "You're a journalist?" he asks, buttering his roll.

"Yes," I confirm.

"Any scoops on Harry today, then?"

"I couldn't tell you even if there were," I reply dryly. I reach over the centerpiece of roses and grab a white roll.

He chuckles, then holds out his hand. "…Or you'd have to kill me, I get it. Brian Malcolm with *The Daily Snitch*. Not too many Americans here. Who are you with?"

"Augusta Noble," I say, shaking his hand. "With *CelebLife*. It's an American mag—"

"I know it, of course. What's your readership these days?"

I lift my Champagne, twirl the stem in my fingers. "Something like seventy million if you count the Web site, I think." I take a long sip, then have another look in Harry's direction, but he remains all but hidden behind a wall of rich white people.

"About twenty times ours, then." Brian shakes his head, picks up his Champagne, and downs half of it in one.

The tall guy on my right extends his hand. "Alexander Matten," he says. "Pleased to meet you." He has a firm shake.

"Augusta Noble. You're a reporter, too?" I ask, checking him out. He's got a playful grin and a dimple in one cheek.

"I am, indeed."

A server stands over us with two bottles of wine. "Red or white, madam?"

I ask for white and he pours me a glass of Chenin blanc as another waiter drops a beet salad in front of me.

"What gave me away?" Alexander asks, then requests a glass of red wine from the hovering server.

"You were getting in my business," I say. "Classic reporter move."

He throws his head back and rewards me with a deep laugh. We all start picking at our salads.

"Do you cover the royals?" I ask when I'm done chewing a piece of arugula.

"I cover everything," he replies, stabbing at a baby yellow beet.

"He's a smug bugger, isn't he?" Brian chimes in. "He's not kidding—he travels the world for the best stories. Typical *International Post:* Oxbridge brains and American arrogance." He winks at me. "No offense."

"Offense taken." I sip more bubbly. I always thought the "Champagne lifestyle" of the rich and famous was a metaphor, but it seems I was painfully naïve.

"I like her," Brian from *The Daily Snitch* drawls.

Alexander keeps chewing.

Halfway through the main course, during which I'm picking at the select vegetables that haven't touched the beef on my plate, Alexander leans over. "There," he whispers in my ear. I get butterflies out of nowhere, and I'm not sure who caused them.

Harry is walking by our table on his way out, and as we all shout *good luck*, the freckled prince shoots me a direct look I feel in the pit of my stomach. Alexander sees this and makes a face, like, *Yes. That happened.*

I start coughing, take a sip of water, and croak, "Be right back," as if I'm running to the bathroom. I'm not, of course. If you want to know what a famous person is really like, you have to be his assistant. The next best thing is to catch sight of him with commoners, while out of the view of cameras and the public.

Is Harry really as charismatic, kind, and humble as he seems? We'll see. I follow his entourage at a distance until they're near the main building, where I presume Harry will finish preparing for the match. They're not letting anyone with a camera near him, but a soft, befuddled, blonde American pretending to be lost gets in with the scrum as he slips down a narrow walkway. The event people are fawning: *Do you want water? Are you OK? Do you need anything? Is that dust on your shoe? I've got a handkerchief.* Harry is calm and friendly. *No, no; don't worry. Please. I'm fine. I'm having a lovely time. I'll get some water in a bit.* One of the handlers gets too close and nips Harry's heel. *I'm so sorry Your Highness. Oh, dear*—but Harry is unbothered.

Oh, dear is right, because I'm caught—a big guy seems to realize I'm not officially with this gang. When I see him heading my way, I turn on my heel and beeline it back to my table. I'm just in time for profiteroles and coffee, and I smile to myself as I recall my JFK Jr. days. Sneaking around can be dangerously fun.

During the match, my new reporter friends and I sip more Champagne under cover of bright umbrellas and glance occasionally at the dashing men on their steeds. I circulate through the crowd, chatting about polo and the gorgeous weather and asking everyone I encounter about Harry—

just as Stanley told me to. I'm thrilled when I get an anecdote about how Harry is, and I quote, "incredible in bed—like, *amazing*. Unlike certain other royals I will not mention." When I ask the very drunk English twenty-something how she knows this, she wags her finger at me and slurs, "Nice try, American gossip *mazageen* girl. *Not* tellin'.'"

At halftime, when it's time to stomp the divots, I mosey out onto the grass and tap my toe on some flopping lumps of turf, trying to remember how Julia Roberts did it in *Pretty Woman*.

"Come on. Put some effort into it," Alexander says as he comes up next to me. He finds a divot and grinds into it with one shiny loafer, and I decide to one-up him. I place the ball of my sandal on a lump and push hard.

The glob of grass shoves in easily, creating a bigger hole so my foot caves in and dirt covers my toes. "Happy now?" I pretend snap, shaking my foot, then trying in vain to brush the dirt off.

"You'll be OK," Alexander says, pulling a handkerchief from his pocket and kneeling to wipe my sandal. I feel the warm cloth brushing off the dust until my pink toes are almost clean. He stands, puts the handkerchief back in his pocket.

He stays close and in the bright sun I realize how good-looking he is, and how tall—easily six-foot-two. For some reason, he is smiling at me. I should mention, I'm kind of hot in England, and I don't know why. American boys tend to think I'm too "curvy," not cute enough, and definitely too outspoken. British boys find me intriguing and sometimes even…*adorable*. It's weird.

"Polo looks dangerous," I say to keep him standing there. "I just hope the poor horses aren't mistreated."

"Ah," he says. "An animal lover. That's why you didn't eat your lunch."

Interesting…he noticed.

He assures me, "I think you'll find these particular horses sleep in air-conditioned stalls and eat the finest organic carrots."

He nods to the empty glass in my hand. "Shall we get you a refill? I know a secret bar in the back of the tent that never has a line."

"Thanks," I smile. "But I'm working. I've had enough for now."

I watch him walk away just as everyone's ushered off the field in preparation for the second half to begin. I wander back to the tent alone, the straps of my wedge sandals digging into the backs of my ankles. I've turned Alexander off. I say the words to myself again, the ones I've tried to stop repeating: *You're awkward, off-putting…there he goes. See?*

Dancing with princesses is no big deal when you've had approximately two or five drinks. The two sisters bop rhythmically on the raised wooden floor, working their shoulders and doing some foot-shuffling worthy of a high-school dance. Beatrice and Eugenie Mountbatten-Windsor have matching freckled noses and auburn hair just like in their photos, but they're prettier in the flesh. They show no signs of suspecting that I snuck into this VVIP after party, a basic but exclusive affair under a white tent with easily penetrable walls.

It is not lost on me that the two royal twenty-somethings are free-range partiers tonight, with no obvious guards or security. The match is over, the hoi polloi have gone, but the after party has some life left in it. Flailing along with the sisters is my last hurrah before my car arrives. It's killing me not to talk to them, but Stanley forbade it, explaining it's a huge no-no for reporters to address royalty unless the meeting has been previously arranged—and that's ultra-rare. I'm still looking for Harry just for observation, but buzz in the tent is he headed back to London.

Evening is coming and the air smells of dirt and cut grass and men's sweat and horses. I'm focusing on my new best princess friends, and as one of my favorite oldies comes on—"This Is What You Came For"—I try out some more energetic moves. My wedges are great on grass but wrong for drunken dancing. My heel slips on a wet spot and I go down hard, slamming my hip and elbow on the wood. In that moment, when I'm certain I'm a two-step away from getting trampled, the princesses hover above me. Their quick exchange of eye contact conveys concern. Rihanna is still singing and I am thinking, *This is NOT what I came for.* Beatrice mouths, *Are you OK?* I hold up my hand like I'm fine, then I roll to my side and scramble to get to my feet with a modicum of grace, but it's slippery, and it takes me a few tries.

I'm fine! I shout, giving the ladies a thumbs-up, but of course I'm not; I'm horrified. It's time to go. I give the princesses a wave and they nod in response. I head outside to find the town car I ordered, glancing around for Alexander, whom I haven't seen since the polo tent. As soon as the door of the car closes behind me and it's quiet, my VIP status disappears and I feel a stab of loneliness. I take out the notebook. I hold my pen over the next blank page and reevaluate the rules I set for myself when I embarked on this quest, which included the following: (1) Every celebrity I speak to counts toward the total; (2) Don't stop until 107. Now that I've reached Number 13, I decide any meaningful encounter should qualify. I didn't have to *speak* to Prince Harry. He looked straight at me and that is enough. If the encounter moves me, it counts.

I start scribbling about falling on the dance floor, and add at the end, *P.S.: Some princesses have hips. Not all women have to be as thin as Kate Middleton—they are beautiful as they are. I am beautiful as I am.* I pause and think about crossing out that last line; I still do not believe it, no matter how often I repeat it. I leave it as it is.

I'm not sure I'll ever tell anyone about my goal. Caroline was one who always shook her head at my secret love of the stars. "Your parents are professors of everything a celebrity is not. How did you become so obsessed?" she once asked. I didn't tell her the sad truth: the celebrities were my friends. While I was locked in my room reading all the *Little House on the Prairie* books and *Are You There God? It's Me, Margaret* five times, the posters were there with me. When I cried after school because there was no one to sit with at lunch, I knew they'd be there when I got home, smiling out at me from the walls. Jason Patric from *Lost Boys*, Neve Campbell and the entire cast of *Party of Five*, Johnny Depp and Winona Ryder, Tom Cruise and Iceman Val Kilmer. I can almost hear what Caroline would say if I told her.

What are you trying to achieve with this plan of yours?

I have to find my fire again. The flame that makes me brave enough to remember.

It's silly. You know that, right? Celebrities are phonies with money and festering narcissistic wounds that will never heal.

They make me feel better.

It's not real.

I'm so glad you're here. I thought you'd never speak to me again.

I'm not. You're imagining it. MURDERER.

"Madam? We're here." The driver jolts me awake in Wimbledon.

I blink the sleep out of my eyes, trudge up the stairs, and write up a story about the dashing, polo-playing prince. I email it to the fifteen editors back in the U.S. Stanley told me to, fall into bed just before three, and sink into a hard, dreamless sleep.

11

I meet Caroline for our official goodbye on the patio at Au Bon Pain in Harvard Square. She's going to college in upstate New York with her semi-foster brother Lincoln and her supermodel friend Ginger. I'm going to Virginia by myself.

"I'm worried," I tell her, slurping iced mocha, "that you'll change. Ginger knows some hard-core people. Those model types eat tissues for lunch, you know. Cocaine flows like wine."

Caroline smiles. "You'll always be Number One," she says. She's finished her espresso and is sipping green tea. She has a far greater tolerance for caffeine than I do. "Ginger is *barely* Number Two, anyway. You know how hard it is to like someone who doesn't get out of bed for less than ten-thousand bucks a day?"

I don't believe her, but it's sweet she tried. "I wish my parents had never made us leave Cambridge," I grumble. "I would've turned out so much cooler."

"Fuck the suburbs," she agrees. "But you know, there are still plenty of assholes in the city. Everyone at my school competes to see who can be the most alternative. I swear Lincoln's got no skin left—he's tattooed everything but the soles of his feet."

She grasps her tea with two hands. "To tell you the truth," she says, "I'm relieved to get out of here. I'm ready to meet some new people. High school boys bore me."

I squint at her. "But you're, like, the hottest chick in your school. You have nowhere to go but down on the popularity scale."

She laughs. "I'm not sure that's true," she says unconvincingly. "Either way, I'm ready for a fresh start in New York."

I slurp the rest of my coffee and shake the ice. Evening is coming and I feel a wave of melancholy as I watch a fire-eater wowing a crowd and a man doing backflips on the bricks not far from us. Eleven years ago, Caroline and I shared a toy on her porch a few streets away from here while our parents set up our new homes, hers with handmade tapestries and socialist propaganda, mine with Spanish tiles and a new couch from Jordan's Furniture. The first time she came over, she stood in the kitchen shaking her head. "Paper towels," she said. "Do you know how wasteful that is?" She was wearing a No Nukes T-shirt. We were seven.

"I want a blueberry muffin," I say.

"No time," Caroline shakes her head. "Let's take a walk."

We pass by the Store 24 where I bought my very first soda when my parents gave me money to pick up bread, then the CVS where Caroline was caught shoplifting a lipstick freshman year. She told them she'd taken the tube of Magenta Dream to use in an art project, and offered to make the manager's kid a bracelet, so they let her go. Being adorable, with a nose like Stephanie Seymour's, lips like Claudia Schiffer's, and cheekbones like Christy Turlington's didn't hurt her cause. If she were taller, she'd be the model, not Ginger.

"Lincoln's having a goodbye party for everyone tonight," Caroline says as we weave through the zombie-like tourists. "Why don't you come?"

"I'm still tired from our school's end-of-summer thing back in Landesboro," I tell her. "It was a rager. But…I guess I can make it. I feel like I know all your friends anyway."

Two lies in one statement. Sometimes I can't tell Caroline how bad it is.

I leave Lincoln's party early. I say it's so I can finish packing, but it's because no one's talking to me. Caroline follows me out to the courtyard of his building and hugs me.

"You're going to have a blast in college," she says into my ear. "They'll see what I've seen all along. Don't *you* go changing too much." She pulls away and I see her eyes welling up. My tears are already spilling. "You'll probably join a sorority and date some frat boy named Brett," she says, choking up.

"And you'll become the first female president of the Dead Heads Society of New York and everyone who comes near you will pass out from Patchouli fumes," I reply.

We laugh through our tears. She takes my hand.

"Different but always together," I say, squeezing hard.

"Best friends forever," she says.

I release first, then wave goodbye. I see Lincoln in the doorway behind us, a broad, tall boy with a man's body. "Caro!" he yells. "We need you for strip Yahtzee. You're on my team."

"Bye, Big Linc," I wave. He waves back, but his eyes are on Caroline.

She blows me a kiss, turns and runs back inside, her cut-off jean shorts riding up her slim, tanned legs. I cry all the way home, but it's not totally out of sadness—a part of me is excited and optimistic about what's to come.

12

Stanley summons me to the office the Tuesday after the polo event.

"Hi Robbie," I wave as I walk in at the appointed hour of noon. "Stanley in his office?"

"He is," Robbie nods, making a face. "Good luck."

I head down the hall and stand in Stanley's doorway until he looks up, unsmiling. I take that as an invitation to come in and sit in his guest chair.

"I liked your Prince Harry story," he says by way of a greeting.

"Thanks," I say. My first official CelebLife.com byline has all the details about Harry's day, insider observations, and quotes from royal hangers-on.

"The thing is, there are no celebrity interviews in your file. You gotta interview the *celebs*."

"But there weren't any—"

He reads from his monitor. "The *Mail* had some good stuff. What about Annabelle Wallis?"

"She didn't want to talk on the carpet…"

"So you get her at the party."

"I thought I wasn't supposed to harass the celebrities?"

He sighs. "She's not Julia Roberts. It's fine to pursue someone like her." He glares at something on his screen. "What if Harry squeezed Annabelle's butt and told her she was pretty, and she was ready to talk all about it to you? *That's* news."

"Do we think Harry would do such a thing?"

He turns his glare on me.

I'm fired. Fuck, I'm fired. I'm learning the major downside of freelancing: you're only as good as your last assignment, and you can be let go on a whim.

Stanley flicks his fingers toward the door. "Robbie will set you up." He picks up his phone receiver.

"What?"

"Set you up. For the day. Thanks."

I rise from my chair and have a momentary desire to quit. I don't need this push-pull crap.

As I head out the door, Stanley adds without looking up, "I could use you all week."

Then again, I'll probably stay. One week's pay at *CelebLife* is a month's rent in a modest flat, so I stroll down the hall to find my old friend Robbie.

He sets me up at a station across from Poppy, and the two of us fall into a chatty rhythm of tracking down celebrities on social media—Twitter has Tom Hiddleston at lunch with a mystery woman, and an Instagram post indicates Kim Kardashian is at the Dorchester, so we have to find out what they ate, who they're with, why they're in London.

Throughout the week, I watch how celebrity magazine staffers live. I learn they're always on their phones, they're on call twenty-four/seven in case there's a Brangelina-level divorce, and there's no such thing as overtime pay. I, on the other hand, get paid for every minute I'm even thinking about an assignment for this magazine. And, since this is England, who needs company health insurance? Things I find out in the daily meetings: Don't pitch Woody Harrelson for a story, ever, because one of the top editors, a shrill woman called Uvula Garsh, can't stand him for undisclosed reasons. I learn that *CelebLife* often knows who's pregnant but—allegedly out of decency—won't tell unless the celebrity herself reveals it, even if she's waddling around with a gigantic bump, swollen ankles, and a freshly bought breast pump in hand. I learn about a couple of closeted actors and an aging former A-lister who recently miscarried. Her younger husband is going to leave her soon. I learn a world-famous star who has never been able to escape the gay rumors in spite of having had a wife and kids is actually straight. "Straight," Gillian explained, "but asexual." *Mind blown.*

I'm searching social media for mentions of Harry Styles one evening when the staff starts traipsing by my desk one after the other and gathering at the elevator bank. I'm wondering what I'm being left out of this time when Robbie says crisply, "Hurry it up, lazy bones."

"Hurry for…what?"

"Monthly madness."

I stay seated.

"*Drinks*," he says, enunciating as if I am a simpleton. "So we don't go bonkers working at this place."

He had me at "drinks." I shut down my computer, suddenly craving a pint and a reason to stop overthinking everything. I fall in with the group as they stroll down the Strand, turn at a quiet corner, and file into the Hog & Leaf. It's a dark pub that smells of old beer and still carries the aura of stale cigarettes from when they were legal. Stanley pays for all the drinks, as well as some unhealthy apps including frites and Belgian mayo. I watch the bureau interact and tease one another and talk about things other than work, bad bosses, money, status and their phones.

Stanley is in fine form, treating me like one of the gang. When Barton says in front of everyone that the bureau is better off with me in it, I think I might've found my place. These can be my people. This can be my where I stop for a while. No one knows my past or sees my baggage, and it's freeing.

13

#14, #15

Things go quiet after my week working in *CelebLife's* office. I use the time to speed-walk the hill from my flat to Wimbledon Common repeatedly until I am able to run it. I've been spending less time at the pub and more time walking, headphones in, watching people, trying to get out of my own head.

I am surveying my tiny closet after a particularly rigorous workout, followed by a hot shower, when I find myself talking to my clothes: "Are there any clean black outfits in here? Really? Where's that stretchy top…"

My phone rings; I throw myself onto the bed and answer on the second ring. "Hi, Stanley."

"I got something for you," he says. "I was going to send Robbie, but I could use someone with more on-the-ground experience. This one's going to be intense."

"I can do intense," I assure him. "What is it I'll be doing?"

"You're off to Switzerland to chase royals. Find out where the hell Harry and Meghan are. We know Wills and Kate are skiing in Klosters, but no one can pin down where the other two are. If they're in Klosters as a foursome, it's up to you to find them."

"Sounds good," I say, and he mumbles his thanks and hangs up.

When I arrive in Klosters, the weather is bitter and the sky is gray. Job Number One, after checking into my chalet-style lodge, is to find the royals. Problem is, there are something like eighty-five ski runs. They could be on any one of them—or could already be in front of a fire drinking hot cocoa.

I dump my bags and hike over to the only run that has a raging après ski bar at the bottom. The circular bar offers 360-degree views through temporary walls made of plastic sheeting. My chances of running into the royal dears are slim, but they've been photographed here in the past, so it's a bet I'm willing to make. I order a Swiss rum-and-soda situation and as I wait for the drink to materialize, I check out a brown-haired, broad-shouldered man in a snazzy red ski jacket—the only other solo person here. This place is the definition of *après ski*, a semi-outdoor bar that allows people to glide off the lift, whip off their skis, and have a drink in hand in seconds. Everyone is loud, ruddy faced, wild-haired, and high on endorphins. I sit with a view of the lift and sip my drink. My eyes flit back to the guy. There are too many puffy jackets between us to get a decent view, but then, as a gesticulating woman between us shifts, I see his face. He sees mine. My heart soars, then sticks in my throat.

It is Alexander from polo. More frightening than that, instead of the blank look I expect (either that or a flicker of recognition followed by a sigh of, *Oh shit, I have to make conversation with that chick from Windsor who I stupidly flirted with when I was drunk on Champagne*), I get the face lighting up and the sparkling eyes, and, most heart-leapingly, the lifting of the beer signaling he's leaving his seat. He's coming over.

I'm feeling strangely confident. Winter gear suits me. My big yet sleek velveteen black coat slims, lengthens, and covers up every sin. Rosy cheeks and big smile top off the look. He walks over to me and I look up at him from my stool.

"Hi," I say, smiling like a high school girl. "What are you doing here?"

"Same thing as you, I expect," he says in that refined public school accent.

There is no stool for him. He is pressed close to me by the crowd, so I have an excellent view of his ski tan, the just-slightly-crooked nose, the brownish-hazel eyes. A loud Australian hops off a stool and Alex drags it closer and hops on, facing me; our knees are forced to touch.

"I thought you covered a bit of everything," I say. "Seems to me you're all about the royals."

"Slow news week. I figured a trip to the Swiss Alps would be a worthy diversion."

He sips his beer, turns serious. "The job's changing," he shrugs. "It doesn't offer quite the free rein it used to. The unspoken rule now is cover whatever you want—as long as it gets clicks. There didn't used to be that caveat."

He looks past me at the mountain, and I turn to follow his gaze.

"Have you seen them today?" I ask.

He nods. "I skied behind William and Kate. They're both better than I am." He smiles. "I'll catch them on the slopes tomorrow, too, I hope. You going up?"

"Of course." *On foot*, I don't add. I don't dangle by a hook on a tiny wire over alpine crevasses, nor do I career down mountains on waxed wooden sticks. I'm afraid of heights and broken limbs, which makes *après* ski my sport of choice.

I employ my most casual, *Whatever, it's no big deal, but…* face. "Have you seen Harry and Meghan?" I ask. "I hear they're around, too."

"They're not here," he says with such confidence I'm a bit confused.

"Are we sure they're not holed up in a chalet somewhere?"

"Definitely not." Alexander is typing something on his phone. "We'd know."

Excellent. I shoot Stanley a text: *Source says H&M definitely NOT in town. Will try to get paps to confirm. More later.*

I get an instant note in return: *OK. Make sure you keep tabs on W&K.*

Alexander and I chat about what Will and Kate have been up to, where they might go tonight, how stunning Switzerland is, until our drinks are gone. He asks me what I'm having and I keep it simple: "White wine—whatever they have." We catch up over one more drink and then it turns out I've chosen my station well.

"Look," Alexander says. "They're here."

I glance out the window and see three photographers rise up out of nowhere. Alexander and I run out of the bar and stake out separate positions. I have a close-up view as the royal couple alights from the lift; I sip my wine casually and try not to look like a stalker fangirl. William and Kate swish smoothly, expertly toward us.

William jokes and laughs with a burly royal protection officer, but he soon swaps his cheery demeanor for an expression of concentration as he waddles over to lay his skis in the rack between the lift and the bar a few feet from me. His wife continues grinning incessantly at nothing. The prince—who is tall and lean and possesses prominent teeth in a light shade of mustard—says something to a friend. Kate flashes her dimples, never letting her face fall. I don't know how she keeps it up like that. I smile in solidarity, just to see what it feels like to grin from ear-to-ear eternally. It feels awkward, painful and false.

I see up close that she is notably thin, even with her gear on. She has mirrored ski goggles perched on her head and brown, twisty sausage curls tumbling along her shoulders. A fitted white ski jacket contrasts strikingly with her dark locks. The pair heads to a waiting van, and his highness ducks in first, without throwing his wife so much as a glance. She follows behind him, dimples still dazzling the photographers. Once the van doors slam shut, I imagine that grin settling into resting bitch face from its exposure to us filthy commoners.

This is great color, and I want to get this on paper, *stat*. Alexander, who will need to file immediately too, touches my shoulder.

"We're all doing dinner later. Meet at my hotel bar at eight?"

I don't know who we "all" are, but I'm in, of course. Alexander is clearly connected, so I'm confident that wherever he goes, the royals will be. I watch him walk out of the bar, serious and brilliant at his job, which makes him even more attractive.

I race to my hotel, throw together a file of everything I know so far, then head back out to cram in some "back-reporting"—following in royal footprints, slouching into bars and restaurants, acting casual and saying in Germanglish, *Hey, yeah, so, um… seen any princes lately? Maybe a Duchess or two?* You'd be surprised how many yesses I get. I get news of the *après-ski* four-dollar slippery nipple shots the young aristocrats knocked back the night before, and the rowdy evening that followed on the outdoor deck, away from prying eyes. When I ask if the couple seems close, I get no reports of affection or even friendly proximity. It seems they tend to socialize separately, at opposite ends of the room or table.

I'm giddy about the reporting I send to Stanley and Barton. I celebrate for exactly one minute, then commence worrying about finding Will and Kate cavorting around Klosters by night. I shower, blow-dry my hair into submission, and attempt a smoky eye. I throw on a black pencil skirt and stretchy black top, and paint on some peachy lip-gloss and head out to Alexander's hotel.

The chalet-style accommodation he's staying in has a gorgeous, intimate restaurant in its basement. I descend the winding stone stairs into a cozy room with a rustic bar glowing with soft lights. He is there, drinking alone. Alexander smiles at me and I break into a wide grin; I can't help myself. He pulls out a stool, and I slide on.

"What'll it be for the American? White wine, perhaps?"

"Fendant," I tell him—my official new Swiss favorite. I had it on the plane ride over: it's got the tiniest bit of fizz and a hint of sweetness.

Meanwhile, Alexander has remembered what I drink. Like we're on a second date.

"How did you do today?" he asks. It's what reporters ask each other on assignment. *What did you get? More than I did? Less? A scoop I need to warn my editors about?*

"Pretty good," I tell him. "There were some caramel vodka shots consumed, from what I hear."

"Oh? That doesn't sound very royal."

"Agreed," I smile. "But I've got it on good authority they were tossing them back like it was freshman year of college."

"Well, then," he says. "In honor of your investigative coup, I think we need to do some caramel shots." Before I can protest, he signals the waiter and orders two.

The barman sets them in front of us, and Alexander holds his up. I follow suit. "To Prince William, his slightly dull bride, and the fact that the world's fascination with them has brought us to these utterly delightful surroundings."

"Hear, hear," I grin as we clink shot glasses. We both drink and slam our glasses on the bar.

After that, we make flirty small talk and I can tell he is attracted to the foreign thing: exotic accents, cultural differences, newness. As blond as he is dark, as brashly American as he is posh British, I seem to fascinate him, and the feeling is mutual. In the middle of all this, his phone rings. He makes an apologetic face, holds up a finger, then answers.

"I can't now," he tells the person. "When I get home. Yes—*mm hmm*. I'll fix the gutters when I get back. I told you…*yes*." I hear the ring of a woman's voice on the other end. "I can't do anything from here. Try not to worry. You know Branford can always take care of it…yes…I know…I'll call you tomorrow. OK. *Yes*. Me too." He sighs, presses cancel, smiles tightly and apologetically at me again.

My stomach drops. I swallow, gulp, try not to freak out. That sounded extremely domestic. I shoot a glance at

Alexander's left hand. No wedding ring and no indent or tan line, either. Then again, Prince William himself doesn't wear a band. The bartender delivers our next round and I grab my wine and sip, keeping the glass at my mouth to hide my frown and my disappointment. This has happened to me all my life: I think a guy is into me, but he's flirting out of boredom, or finds me interesting simply because I'm the only one there to talk to, or is utterly unavailable. I'm always reading *meaning* into everything. I should know better.

I'm quiet for a moment, and so is Alexander, who apparently doesn't feel the need to offer an explanation. Even before our drinks are finished I say, "Shall we get going?"

My focus is back on work. I'm determined to find those royals, with or without Alexander, who may or may not be married or living with some British skankaroo with dirty gutters.

14

I manage to act like everything is normal over a boiling cauldron of fondue that would make a germaphobe shudder. We dip our forks in the same pot over and over— *we* meaning Alexander, a few photographers, and another reporter, Mia somebody from the *Daily Review* whom Alexander seems to know well and is oddly cool to me.

When all that's left in the pot is a raw garlic clove and hardened remnants of Gruyere, we move on to the royals' favorite party palace, the only disco in Klosters. Casa Antica is a rustic "nightclub" typical of small Swiss towns. No velvet ropes, no VIP lounge area, no clipboard-wielding gatekeeper. It's got basic stools, some little round tables, exposed beams, an incongruous disco ball, and a selection of creatively vile shooters for late-night binge drinking.

As we walk in we stumble on the Holy Grail wrapped in glossy locks (her) and a booming voice (him), along with Kate's commoner sister and her famous butt. The rest of our crew acts like this is just another night out, but I'm beside myself to be this close. We sit at the bar while the royals guffaw and make merry in a back room a few feet away. Alexander hands me a cocktail, and as he chats with Mia, I watch history unfold. The prince is holding court in a corner, his distinctive voice rising above the din, while the wife sits across the room, drifting back occasionally to check in with him. I picture her asking him what he needs, what he wants. It reminds me of a servant-master relationship; not the sexy kind, the know-your-place kind.

A pretty blonde, one of the only females in the group, laughs too hard at something Wills says and…did I just see Waity Katie shoot her a death glare? There have been reports of Kate's jealousy of other females who got too near Wills during the years she pined for the engagement ring. There is never a kiss exchanged between them, nor do I see Princey-poo tend to his bride in any way. No one bothers them or even seems to notice royals are in residence. In the game of What are They Really Like, William is what you'd expect, but Kate is different. Her shy, awkward smiles at events, her soft stumbling through one-minute speeches she still has to read from notes? There's nothing of that here. She carries herself like one who spent her life seeking the tiara—and got it.

None in our group goes near them, but I head to the loo right about the time Kate's coming out. As I pass her, there is no polite nod or *excuse me* or *hello*. It's not crowded; it's just me and her and a notably subtle royal protection officer who lets me get closer than I ever dreamed I could. The fact that she is just a few years older than I am but looks forty-five is a stark warning against smoking. The Duchess *not* smiling, and she looks like a different person. She's wearing thick, coal-black eyeliner. For those who report her as five-foot-ten, stop—she's five-seven at most. She veers toward her royal pack as I keep moving toward the bathroom.

When I make it back to the bar, it's Alexander's turn to go. I slide onto the stool next to Mia. "Do you know Alexander well?" I ask, while deciding what to drink next.

Mia, whose light brown hair is thin like mine and reminds me it's time I got a trim, looks past me at William, who's guffawing about something.

"I bump into him quite a bit on assignments," she replies. "I cover royals exclusively and he often gets nudged in that direction because of his position."

"His position?"

She glances sideways at me.

"I thought he covered world affairs," I push. "That no one could tell him what to write about. That's the whole mystique of the Round the World gig, isn't it?"

"Not so much anymore," she shrugs, echoing what Alexander told me. "Times are changing."

The change; it's everywhere in journalism. I feel it in the air, when I'm in the office, when I see rampant mistakes and shoddy reporting every day even on so-called respectable news sites. The money is draining away, and with it the quality of content, and the jobs.

"So…you all travel a lot, huh? Does Alexander ever bring his girlfriend on assignment?" I look away, squeeze my eyes shut. *Calm down. Too obvious.* "I mean…do any of you bring your significant others?"

"Good Lord, no." Mia shakes her head. "Too many hours, too much pressure. The partners never understand why you can't plan a delightful sit-down dinner with them 'after work.'" She chuckles sardonically. "There is no 'after work' when you're hunting exclusives."

I don't see how I can ask anything more without giving myself away. Mia finishes her neat vodka and adds, "And anyway, there's no girlfriend to bring, far as I know. Alexander is as single as any of us."

I clear my throat. *Casual, casual.* "Oh? Earlier he was taking a call from…I thought…"

"Alexander? Oh…" Mia shakes her head. "That was probably his mum. She got the historic family mansion in Belgravia in the divorce and is always bothering him about something."

I'm finding it difficult to act uninterested. "Historic?" I inquire.

"He's Matten-*Thorpe*," Mia tells me, like I'm an idiot. "As in Viscount Alexander Matten-Thorpe? He drops Thorpe for work. Never wants special treatment—or to be perceived as such."

"So his father is…"

"An Earl. You wouldn't know it, right? His family practically disowned him for going into journalism, especially when he started covering the royal family, who are, of course, distant relatives." She finishes her vodka, then adds, "Except his mother, I mean. She's American and always wanted him to forge his own way. Shame she won't let her staff take care of her, though, instead of relying on Alexander so much."

My face must show my relief, because she asks, "Why? Are you interested in him or something?" She takes a closer look at me, then swivels her neck to see Alexander making his way back from the bathroom. His royal blue button-down shirt brings out his ski tan, and he has that dimple; he's a standout who makes the prince look ancient and bland. It makes sense now when I see William throw Alexander a subtle nod, a tilt of the chin, like, *Hello, third cousin once removed.*

"No," I say to Mia coolly. "It's just I'm new around here, trying to get the lay of the land."

She shrugs as if she doesn't care—or doesn't believe me—and downs the rest of her vodka.

Alexander smiles at us, sits next to me. "You ladies doing OK? Drinks for anyone?"

I'm nursing a warm cranberry vodka and could use a refresher. "Champagne," I say.

About twelve-thirty, the royals order a round of six Jägermeister shots. And that is all we are going to see. Because we're caught.

A royal minder comes out of nowhere and part-sidles, part storms up to my three associates. I'm sitting at the edge of the group pretending I don't know them. "That's enough," he says. "You go or William goes."

He doesn't have to spell out that if *William's* crew has to leave, the palace will be furious, which will in turn infuriate our bosses. We can't have that. I act natural, stare straight ahead at the wall. Sip my drink robotically. Alas, I too am screwed. Mia throws me under the bus, happily and with no shame. She slides off her stool and says loudly to the royal minder, "SHE'S A REPORTER, TOO." How very unsportsmanlike. When the journalist you're with is not a direct competitor, there is no need to screw her over. I would have been happy to share any late-night details in the morning.

When we're congregated outside in the snow, Alexander says quietly in my ear, "Nightcap?"

I look up at him. "Absolutely," I say. I am lightheaded.

He says goodbye to the others, and the photographer says he has to finish up some work. Mia glances at me sideways, loathe to let me go off alone lest I sniff out some exclusive news. But she's not invited, so she crunches off into the night with the photographer, who gallantly offered to see her home.

Alexander and I wander into the first bar we see and settle into a small booth. We joke about Americans versus Brits because it involves never-ending hilarity (we both hate Marmite! It's aluMINIUM, not alumiNUM!). We sit close. His photographer joins us after a couple more drinks, and we all get a bit drunk, and before we know it, it's closing time. We three step outside into the crisp Swiss air, which is a kind of clean that's hard to find anywhere anymore, and pad along on the snow under stars set against a licorice sky. Alexander reaches out and takes my hand; I clutch it, then let it go. It's big, warm, and soft. His hotel is first; mine is far past it, up a steep hill. They insist I come back for another nightcap. We are buzzed, we are exhausted, and we all have a big day tomorrow.

When we make it inside the hotel, the photographer immediately bids us goodnight. Without a word, Alexander takes my hand and leads me to his room. I am so hypnotized I don't have the brainpower to overthink what's happening next or worry about my body's imperfections. This man likes me. I lust him. He sits on the edge of the bed, pulls me down next to him. He gives me *that* look. My lungs are devoid of oxygen. He leans in and touches my lips with his. It is perfect; it is like we were meant to be here, right now, doing this. He smells of German beer. He is slow, exploratory, soft, and heart-stoppingly skilled. His hands start moving; I slowly, gently pull my lips away.

"I…um…I'm supposed to be here for work," I tell him. "I feel a little strange mixing my job and…" I say it. "Pleasure." I don't want to ruin this before it starts. One-night-stands with people I don't give a shit about are one thing, but this guy…if I let my guard down and then he never calls, it will hurt too much. That, and I remain riddled with guilt about what happened to Caroline, so happiness and well-being are not on the menu for me right now. Also, I'm wearing gigantic tummy crushing underpants.

He looks confused, disappointed, and exhausted all at once, but he gives me one more soft kiss, then collapses back on the bed. "I understand," he says, and I think he actually might. "Stay," he adds, scooting further to one side. "Don't go."

I lie down and almost immediately fall asleep in my clothes, wondering if I'm a wimpy idiot who just missed a chance I might not have again. I console myself that tomorrow is another day.

After four hours' sleep I sneak out of Alexander's room and race up the road to my chalet. I bang out a colorful review of the previous night's antics, and Stanley writes back almost instantly: *Nice file. Check in as soon as you get something today.*

Nice??! It appears the richer and more exclusive my reporting is, the more Stanley expects. After a quick face wash, tooth cleaning, and change of clothes, I walk the town and talk to more people, and discover that Will, Kate and company will be having a private dinner catered in tonight. This means all us newshounds are free for at least for part of the evening.

I run into one of the photographers from last night sitting at a table at an outdoor cafe. "You heard the royals are eating in tonight?" I confirm.

He nods, and I inquire, "Any plans for us all to meet up for dinner?"

He shakes his head, plays with his lens. "I'll be outside the chalet trying to catch them coming out after the meal. Alexander's gone, you know. Another assignment in Italy or some bollocks."

He smiles tightly, answers a call, and walks away. My heart is heavy. It didn't occur to me until right now that we never even exchanged numbers. I thought there would be more time.

15

"The name of the band is All of It?"

"Yes. All of It."

Caroline rolls her eyes. "Besides being thoroughly unimaginative, it's pretty arrogant."

I try to get up from the beanbag, a difficult endeavor because it's tragically been leaking beans for a while.

"Turn on your computer," I tell her. I clamber to my feet and type in a search for All of It's last performance.

She squints at the screen. "Ponytail Man there, trying to block the lead singer so he gets all the attention?"

"That's the one. He's hot," I tell her. "Best kisser ever."

He is. He was almost every first for me, though he doesn't know that, and it's sophomore year of college and I still haven't allowed him to go all the way even though there are twenty girls at every show trying to get into his cargo shorts. I've accepted the fact that I'm still behind other girls my age, but the good news is, inexperience is easily mistaken for a blazing case of Hard to Get. Band Guy has never met resistance like mine, and it's partly why we've lasted a whole three months.

"You were right," I tell Caroline. "College is amazing. I made senior writer on the paper this year, and I'm doing investigations into the money they spend on men's sports vs. women's, and I kind of have a boyfriend, and I have good girlfriends, too—no one like you, of course. But still. Real ones I can trust."

Everything changed the day I set foot on campus. People treated me like I was normal, included me, told me their stories, and asked me about mine. Many of my tales were lies, including the one about my ex-boyfriend Jordan who sadly went to UCLA on a baseball scholarship so the distance was too great to maintain our epic love story.

I add, "I haven't closed the deal with the band guy yet…I'm not sure it's ever going to be exclusive with us, but still…"

"There's no closing the deal with a band guy," Caroline says. "There's only doing the deed and getting the hell out of there. There's always another girl lined up."

"Not him," I shake my head. "He's picky."

"Picky, my ass."

"It's good to see you again," I reply with a measure of snark.

It *is* good to see her, even if for one night after the drive from hell with a college friend who's visiting her boyfriend and offered to drop me at Caroline's upstate New York school. I check out the décor of their dorm room. Caroline's imprint is a heavy, beloved jade elephant her late uncle left her when we were twelve. I also notice what's missing: her art. She started Caroline's Crafts junior year of high school to earn pocket money, and she's incredible at it: she can make stunning necklaces out of second-hand copper wire and earrings out of an old penny, some beads, and a couple of paperclips. Her room at home drips with bits of metal, gems, jade and wire she's hoarded; here, her studio is relegated to one box shoved in a corner.

"You ready?" Caroline asks, putting in some hoop earrings she made senior year.

I spruce up my makeup and we set off for a party at Lincoln's off-campus house. As we fight our way through the living room to get outside where the beer is, Caroline sees someone she knows who has some questions about their geography homework, so I keep moving and run into Lincoln at the keg. It's the first time I've seen him since his pre-college party, and he's wearing the same clothes he was then: a black Red Hot Chili Peppers T-shirt and baggy army pants.

He selects a red cup and fills it for me. "How's college treating you?" he asks. He doesn't smile; he's making forced, polite conversation.

"It's great," I reply. "You?"

"It's OK." He hands me my beer. "I'm only here for Caroline, you know?"

No, I didn't know. "What do you mean?" I ask, taking a sip, the foam covering my lip so I have to lick it off.

"I'm not meant for higher education. I hate school—always have. But someone has to look out for her."

"But Lincoln," I half laugh, "you got a full scholarship. You're smarter than all of these people."

He shrugs, stares at the beer gun. "I'm good at school," he says. "Doesn't mean I should be at one."

Caroline comes out and Lincoln notices her. From then on, he doesn't take his eyes off my friend, though we are still, ostensibly, chatting. "You know," I say casually, "Caroline can take care of herself. You don't have to worry so much."

"Of course I do," he says. "It's my job."

Not knowing how to respond to that, I bid him adieu and join Caroline under a tree where she's talking to some emo girls. They smile tightly at me and take off, and I quote, *to do some drugs.* "What's going on with you and Linc?" I ask Caroline when we're alone.

"I'm not sure," she shrugs. "I love him like family—and I'm way too comfortable with him. But I can't seem to meet a guy who *thrills* me, you know?"

I never got those two. Lincoln lived with her family on and off over the years, usually when his mom was on a weeklong bender. I know they called themselves a couple at one point, but I was never sure exactly what that meant for them.

"I get it," I tell Caroline, but I really don't, because plenty of guys "thrill" me these days. Right now, in fact, a brooding one with thick black hair is giving me the low-lidded sultry eye from across the room. He's bordering on beautiful, with delicate features and wide brown eyes.

"How hot is *he*?" I elbow Caroline and nod subtly toward him. "He's been giving me the eye for the past half-hour."

"That's Dash. He's a man-whore," Caroline replies. "He gives everyone the eye."

"Ouch," I say, making a face at her.

"I didn't mean it like that! I just want you to know you can do better."

"Who here is *better*, exactly? He's hot, I'm technically single, why shouldn't I go for it?"

She examines me for a moment. "You're right. Go. Sow your wild oats."

I can see she's torn: happy to see me having a good time but worried I'm being an idiot. It's past time for me to be an idiot. It's my turn.

Caroline is in a foul mood when she picks me up at Dash's house the next morning to drive me to the bus station.

"You know," she says as we wait at a red light. "Guys will still like you even if you don't put out right away. The right guys will, anyway…"

"What?" I feel bile rising in my throat. Everything tastes and smells like rotten beer. "It's *college*, Caroline. When did you turn into such a prude?"

"I just want you to be safe and smart. Is that so wrong?"

"Slut-shaming," I shoot back, "is not a good look. Not that I have to justify myself to you, but I didn't sleep with him. We fooled around a little. That's all."

"I'm not slut-shaming you," she hits back. "I want you to know you're a gorgeous, smart woman. You don't have to get drunk and go home with random guys."

I don't know what convent Caroline just came out of, but I hope college isn't going to ruin us. Something feels different. We were pulled apart when she stayed in Cambridge and I moved out to the suburbs, but we kept coming back together like two ends of a stretched rubber band. College, sex, growing up, New York; we're diverging in ways I fear could create an impassable chasm.

"Different but always together," I say when she stops on the curb outside the bus station.

She doesn't miss a beat. "Best friends forever."

We sit quietly for a moment, and I involuntarily belch.

"Gross," she says.

"I just wanted to have some fun."

"I know." She drapes a slight, pale arm around my wide shoulders. "I just don't want anything to happen to you."

"You don't always have to protect me." *I'm not the shy loser I once was.*

"But I always will. Deal with it."

16

#16, #17, #18, #19, #20, #21

The afternoon bartender at Fox & Grapes knows me now. He's gay, which is great because I'm celibate and we can flirt shamelessly without confusion or consequence. He seems quite posh (apart from the working in a pub thing), with public-school-boy-neat hair and an upper-class accent.

"I guess I'll have one more," I inform him. He pulls me a pint of Strongbow and squirts in some glorified Ribena. "Hey, Edward. Random question…how big a deal is it in this country to be an earl or whatever?"

"An earl or *whatever*?" He sets a frosty pint in front of me.

It's quiet in the pub, because of course it's quiet at three-thirty. When you're only somewhat employed and get all your exercising and emailing over with by three and it's already getting dark because it's England, there is nothing else to do but go to the pub.

"Yeah. An earl. Or a…viscount."

"Well," Edward says, picking up a glass and polishing it with a suspiciously grey rag, "it's a *very* big deal to them. Most of them are landed, of course, and have a spot in the House of Lords. You thinking of anyone in particular?"

I shake my head. He finishes the glass and selects another. "Well, a lot of them find themselves land rich and cash poor—upkeep of those castles cost a bloody fortune. So, they're not always as wealthy as you think, but they are our aristocracy, so I guess—well, I guess it is a big deal."

A senior citizen walks in with his chocolate Labrador and sits at the bar. Edward goes over to confer with him, nods, then starts pulling a pint of Guinness.

"What about Viscount whatshisname…Alexander Matten something?" I ask.

"Ah," Edward says as he waits for the head to dissipate on the Guinness. "The heir apparent. Matten-Thorpe. All you have to do is Yammer him, girl. He's only one of England's most eligible bachelors. And wouldn't you know it—he's bloody *straight*."

He sets the pint in front of the man, then turns back to me.

"You know," he says slyly, "he's famous for not having a type. He's dated a law student in between socialites—I think there was even a gigantic volleyball player in there somewhere. I think he likes Americans, too." He raises one eyebrow.

I shrug. "I was just curious. We know some of the same people."

Of course I've already Yammered Alexander extensively and obsessively, but journalists are tough to cyberstalk because our bylines come up in search results before anything else. Edward's revelation is bad news for me. The more eligible Alexander is, the less chance of our flirtation going anywhere. He's probably on assignment in the Amazon right now, *not* trying to find WiFi so he can *not* research me. I did find one *Tatler* piece about his breakup with a socialite who everyone thought would be the one, and no one knows why it ended, and everyone keeps trying to set him up with Penelope von Smythington-Somebody and Isabella Gloucestershire-Pinkerton-Whatever.

My phone rattles on the bar next to me and I sit up straight. It's Stanley, who never calls just to shoot the breeze. "Hi," I say, hopping off my stool and stepping out to the narrow country lane.

"Hey," Stanley says. "Can you travel tomorrow?"

"You know," I reply mock-innocently, "I seem to remember somebody telling me I shouldn't expect any travel…"

"Shut it and book your flight." I can hear his semi-smile over the phone. "We're slammed right now, especially with Gillian on holiday. You want me to say it? *We need you.*"

"Well. If you put it that way." I can't help it. I like the guy. He's nothing like my boss at *Newstime*, a fey, milquetoast man with colorless lips and no passion for our business.

"Call the travel department and get a flight to Lisbon tonight or tomorrow—one or two nights, up to you. Just make sure you're there in time for the party. Red carpet starts at five tomorrow. I'll email you everything."

He fills me in on a few more details, then signs off. I step back into the pub, drain my pint, and give the bartender a wave. "See you next time, Eddie. Gotta work."

He waves back and smiles, and I think that when it comes time to get my own place, I might stick with Wimbledon. I'm starting to like it here.

It's my first time in Lisbon. I'm sure it's nice, but all I'm seeing are some palm trees and a flash of the Atlantic in the distance as I finish my last red-carpet interview and prepare to hit the after party. One-time *Desperate Housewives* star

Teri Hatcher was the definition of *meh*, grudgingly answering one question about "giving back," so she has to get a low score (4.0). I'm holding out hope for higher-wattage interviews at the party.

I sashay up to the guys in tuxedos with the magic clipboards guarding the entrance. I am rooting around in my purse for my ticket when a woman runs up to me.

"*There* you are. I'm sorry I'm late. So sorry." The stranger is a confident Brit with a clipped accent, maybe five-foot-four, sunburned nose, bleach-blonde pixie cut.

I'm rooting around in my handbag for my ticket while the gigantic bouncer watches me suspiciously. I raise my eyes and see my new friend standing on tiptoes to look at his clipboard.

"Got it." I produce my ticket. He waves me in, but holds a hand up at my new "friend."

"Don't need a ticket," she tells him. "I'm with Jean Alesi." She gestures toward the clipboard. "See?"

He runs a finger along the names, and stops quickly, then nods. "OK. Have a good night."

She strides in behind me and we both stop at the bar. "I'm Mallory with *The London Herald,*" she says. "I do their nightlife column. We don't get invited to a lot of stuff outside England."

"Augusta," I say. "With *CelebLife*. Nice to meet you."

Mallory orders a vodka tonic and, as it turns out they don't do cranberry here, I get a vodka and pineapple. I watch the guy make it. It is about ninety percent vodka.

"Who are you after today?" Mallory asks.

"Same as you, I'm sure."

"I hope they show up," she says, glancing around the room, which is nowhere near full yet because we are unfashionably early. "See ya in a bit. I'm off to do a circle."

I find a velvet ottoman in a dark corner and start making some notes from the red carpet. *BORIS BECKER: Wry, ruddy, noticeably lacking eyelash pigment, threw me one word: "No." (2.5).*

Mallory is back, out of breath. "Hide me," she begs, but it's too late. Cuba Gooding Jr. races up behind her and tries to grab her ass.

"That booty!" He's moving and dancing to a beat all his own. "*Mmm, mmm, mmm.*" Mallory moves away but he's undeterred. I move between them. A moment later, something distracts Cuba and he takes off.

Mallory is fine, unflappable. "Any A-list sightings?"

"Not yet," I say.

I set off to do my own circle. I see Morgan Freeman, tall and debonair in his tux. If I can get him to say anything it will be a win—I've got to hear that *voice*. I ask him about books, then sports.

"Love the Olympics, of course," he says. "Love NASCAR. Love basketball—watching it, not playing it."

Two minutes into our chat I can tell he doesn't want to be doing this. I'm not going to push my luck, but I want a *tad* more. "How often do people ask you to narrate their lives? Are you harassed all the time?"

"Young lady," he says. "What do *you* think?"

He is the president from *Deep Impact*, Lucius Fox from *Batman*, and God, of course. I smile, thank him, and leave him be. There are worse things than being mildly chastised by Morgan Freeman. I pass by Cuba Gooding again, grooving on the dance floor by himself. He doesn't lust after me or chase me. He doesn't even notice me. "Cuba," I say, approaching and tapping him on the arm. He whirls on me and opens his eyes wide.

"Yes?" he asks, looking me up and down.

"I'm Augusta with *CelebLife*. Got time for a few questions?"

He shakes his head, keeps dancing in place. "Uh-uh, nope. I don't do that anymore."

He turns away; this is clearly his final answer. I weave my way back to my ottoman and jot some notes. Morgan gets 8.9. Cuba gets a 0.2. *Biggest disappointment since Bon Jovi,* I write. I slide my pen and notebook into my handbag, then set off to find the big game I came for. I work my way to the bar and order a straight pineapple juice this time, and as I turn away and put the straw in my mouth, I see the A-listers of the night on the other side of the bar: It's David and Victoria. This is the celebrity equivalent of the elusive white tiger—and not just one. A *pair* of them. *Alone.* No entourage. No agent chattering away and giving the evil eye to anyone who might approach. No scowling bodyguard. No kids. There have been split rumors floating around them for years, but here they are, together and standing close. I set my juice on the bar and go in for the kill. As I approach the couple, David—strong chin held high, dashing in black tie and slicked-back hair—does not even look at me. He stares straight over his wife's head. I draw closer and see how hard they are working to appear like a connected couple, but their body language has a desperate feel. Victoria is gyrating against the taut body of her husband, literally dancing on him while he stands still and looks bored.

House music thumps around us, and it's hard to hear anything, so David pretends he doesn't; his chiseled jaw is set so hard it's twitching at the joint, and he is focusing on a pulsing strobe light in the distance. Victoria notices me, though, and lets go of her husband. She is tiny. Minuscule—and even thinner than she appears in photos. This compactness is rampant among celebrities. It's not just that they're fat free, it's that they're built on a smaller scale than we brutish plebes. Tonight Victoria is swallowed up by a flowing lime-green, flamenco-style dress with a slit up the side and a plunging neckline. Because of the loud music I have to lean in to avoid yelling at her, and she follows suit. She isn't wearing the mean pout you see in every photo of her. She knows *CelebLife*, knows we're huge but non-threatening, that we give lots of love her and her family.

"OK," she agrees amiably when I ask if I can ask her some fashion questions.

We chat about clothes and I let her do all the talking because I'm clueless about sartorial matters. I jot down every word as she talks and David stares into the distance. I'm dying to say something passive aggressive like, *Hey, buddy, I don't blame you for being skittish—those latest cheating rumors are outrageous!* But I think better of it, because I don't need the storm he could bring down on me. I did my research before I came, including asking Gillian about her experiences. Her face darkened as she told me David and his people are not the most popular among the reporters who cover him. When she was planning a quick sit-down with the soccer legend, his people banned just about every topic no matter how benign, until she finally inquired, "What *can* I ask?" Then she showed me the hacked emails supposedly written (badly) by David when he was seeking a knighthood (which he still doesn't have). In one, David called the honors committee "cunts" for not granting him the knighthood.

"Can you name a celebrity whose fashion sense you love?" I ask Victoria.

"Gwen Stefani's style is a favorite," she says. "Always showing those abs. I love her voice, too: so bubbly and vibrant."

"Let's get *you* showing your abs!" I insist. "You look incredible." Being skinny is always incredible at *CelebLife*. That is the way that we start all body conversations: *You look great. You look incredible. How do you stay so thin?*

She shakes her head, genuinely horrified. "Are you kidding? I've had four kids." She tells me her tummy is like crepe paper, "*so far* from a six pack." She makes an *ick* face and adds, "I never show my stomach."

I raise my eyebrows, tilt my head, look down at my own non-flat tummy. *What must she think of me?* She's come under fire for hiring very, very thin models to advertise her fashion brand. I can see why that irks some, but at she's not selling starvation diets, bragging about her food intake, or pushing Gwyneth Paltrow-style fasting. She is who she is.

David finally looks at me but doesn't smile. He is a gorgeous man. I thank Victoria and she smiles, waves, and wishes me a good night.

When I get back to my ottoman in the corner, I write, *Victoria Beckham: 8.4. It was awful to hear her put herself down. Option 1: She genuinely thinks she's gross. Option 2: She thinks she has to confess to being gross to make herself seem relatable. Option 3: She hates all fat people and I stupidly fell for her charms. Either way, it's time to stop the madness.* Then I write, not for the first time, *But how?*

Then I start to regret *not* talking to David. It was a case of Celebrity Stockholm Syndrome in action: David's glare and lack of even the most basic manners stifled me because I let them. *Never again*, I write, *will I let a celebrity intimidate me out of doing my job.* I add, *Stop coveting other people's relationships. The reality is too often the opposite of what you think you see.* Unlike Victoria's body insecurities, nothing about their relationship felt authentic to me.

I wander the party and check my phone for the five billionth time. No texts, calls, or emails from Alexander. I keep telling myself I have no chance with him, but the way I caught him looking at me more than once makes believe the opposite.

I set off to join Mallory, and eventually find her alone and shaking her head. "I missed the Beckhams," she moans. "I'm so totally screwed."

I sympathize more than she knows, and since I'm done for the night, I can relax and try to help her out. "Let's go get you another drink," I suggest, whipping around and then whispering in her ear, "I think I see Cuba coming this way."

17

I need to see Caroline. I'm nursing some serious wounds after getting lied to and then summarily dumped in the first month of junior year. I aimed high for my first boyfriend ever, which was a mistake; I skipped over the dorky Jonos and the lacrosse playing Billy Ronsons, and went straight for the older, ultra-cool, sexy rocker guy all the girls were after.

I'm not at school, Caroline emails me back, *but you can meet me in the city if you want.*

If I want.

I hop a bus over a long weekend in the spring and find her lounging in a tiny walkup she's sharing with Ginger.

"Band guy is over," I tell her when she throws open the scratched metal door. "He was screwing a sorority girl the entire time." I need a fierce Caroline hug.

"I warned you," she says, offering only a weak embrace and trying but failing to hide her *I told you so* attitude. She leads me to the kitchen. "You want a drink? We've got tap water and vodka." Their place smells like Patchouli and Parmesan.

"Let's go out," I suggest. "I can't stay in the city for long. There must be a fun place close by…I've got an ID."

"Eh," she mumbles, and grabs a couple glasses out of a cabinet. She pours us two neat vodkas, then pads barefoot into the small living room.

I drop my bag on the floor. "He hates sorority girls," I tell her, trying to behave like everything's normal, like my best friend isn't acting distant and detached for reasons I can't begin to guess. "He spent months talking about how shallow and pathetic they are."

"For a man," Caroline says, laying on the sofa and leaving no room for me, "none of that matters in the end."

This is news to me. "She put out on the first night they met," I inform her. "She's a total slut." I sit on a low ottoman and cradle my vodka in two hands.

"Well, well…" she says, "look who's slut-shaming now."

There's an edge to her today I've never seen. "Caroline," I ask carefully, "what's wrong?"

"You really want to know? Really? Because I doubt you'd understand."

"Try me."

"Not everyone has rich parents," she says, crossing her slim, pale legs. She's talking slowly and seems out of it. Her eyes are hooded, cold. "I couldn't come up with tuition for junior year, so Ginger said I could move in with her. She left school to model full-time."

I want to help her, but how can a broke college junior who just got dumped by a bass player help a gorgeous woman with a killer apartment in the Village and a supermodel sidekick? "If I could scrape the money together, I would," I tell her. "You know I would. As it is, I'm out of pocket money after this trip."

"Poor thing," she says sarcastically.

I throw back half my vodka and almost gag. It's cold and chemical and unsatisfying.

Who the hell is this person? She knows my parents are professors. They're not rich. I never thought of us as a different class from Caroline's family. Her parents always had jobs working for different causes and nonprofits and owned a home in the city. Neither Caroline nor I got cars of our own or more than a few bucks' spending money growing up. On top of that, she's living the cliché she always professed to loathe: There's cocaine residue on the coffee table and I noticed a bottle of Xanax in the kitchen cabinet. I'd like to have a few words with Ginger, but she's off on a shoot.

I see the same box of art supplies Caroline had in their dorm room cowering next to the sofa, covered in cigarette ash and old newspapers. "Have you made anything lately?" I ask. "I don't see any new pieces around the apartment."

She re-crosses her legs.

"Ginger should be encouraging you to go back to school, not quit and live your life partying," I try. "What are you going to do when she gets a boyfriend or moves or whatever? You have to finish college, Caro."

She levels a gaze at me that says, *You are naïve and childish and you don't get it.*

Don't say it. I know she's going to say it. *Don't, Caroline.*

"You've always been jealous of Ginger," she says, hurting me and committing the crime of unoriginality at the same time. "I've told you it's ridiculous, but, at this point if you can't accept she's my friend too, I don't know what to tell you. At some point you've got to let go, you know? Lead your own life. Stop clinging."

"*Clinging?* I never see you! What, twice over the summer and once sophomore year?"

"But you're always *there*," she waves a hand in the air as if shooing away a fly. "Calling me, being the victim: 'Why doesn't anyone like me?' I'll tell you why. Whatever happened to you after you moved away messed you up.

You say you're 'shy,' but maybe that's just an excuse for being *rude*. Even when you're at a party you never join in. *That's* why."

I am taking in everything she says, and thinking she must be right, because she was always the coolest person I ever knew. I don't bother saying, *But I did* try. *Every time I spoke up I was ignored. So I stopped speaking up.* Maybe this is why I love my work on the school paper so much: My subjects have to listen to me; they have to respond. Even if they don't like me, even if they're rude, they can't help but engage.

"You've got a lot going for you, Augusta, but when you get around people, you're…well, you can be a bit of a dud. You're white, blonde, and wealthy. You have every privilege but you still whine about everything."

"You're white, beautiful, and skinny," I reply. "That trumps everything and you don't even know it." The race thing is new.

"I'm sorry," Caroline says, using her abs to sit up on the sofa, swinging her legs over so they're on the floor, "but It's true. And please don't do that crying thing. You know, a little tough love might actually be exactly what you need."

"Don't you think I know all that?" I croak. "How would you feel if you were all those things and people still didn't like you?"

"Oh, grow up," she responds coldly. "Go back to Virginia and figure out who you are."

I see a flicker of my Caroline then, just for a second—the eyes give it away. "Look," she says. "I don't mean to sound harsh. But these things happen…our lives are going in different directions. *We're* going in different directions."

This doesn't feel like a fight. Not that we ever fought much—only about stuff like whether Belinda Carlisle was half-French or if raising a kid in the suburbs constitutes child cruelty. We never fell out about the usual friend stuff—never competed for boys, popularity, general life success—because we both knew she'd win every time.

Caroline walks to the front door and stands there expectantly. This is catastrophic. She is my safe harbor, my sounding board, my soft place to fall.

"We don't have to let the distance beat us," I say, blinking back tears.

"But it is," she replies. "That's just the way things are."

Don't cry, don't cry, don't cry.

"Different but always together." I choke the words out as I stand and pick up my bag.

I wait, but I know that this Caroline won't say it, so I do, on my way out.

"Best friends forever," I whisper as I exit.

She closes the door and I hear the bolt slide into the lock.

18

#22, #23, #24, #25, #26

I arrive back from the Portugal trip, drop my bags, and head straight for a nap. I'm exhausted and hung over. Just as I'm nestling my head into the pillow, Stanley calls. For the first time ever, I want to duck him with every fiber of my being. But you don't ignore Stanley.

"What's up?" I ask, rolling over to check the time.

"Leicester Square. Premiere tonight. Need you to cover."

His words come in a distracted staccato, and I can hear him tapping on his keyboard. I continue to wonder why everything with *CelebLife* is so last minute. Are they profoundly disorganized, or do they like to mess with me?

"Oh—and then," Stanley says, clearly thinking about something else, "can you travel next week?"

I don't care what it is. *Yes.* Yes, I can. I want to become even more tired and immersed in this world where work is *the* most important thing. The late nights and impossible assignments serve to keep my brain busy. The more I worry about celebrities, the less I panic over the police and Caroline and my future as a possible convicted felon.

When I agree to whatever he's throwing at me, Stanley says, "Great. Robbie will send you the premiere info. Liam Neeson tonight—the ladies seem to dig him. I'll get back to you about the travel thing. Have fun."

I manage to fall asleep, and thank goodness my mother's call wakes me up at three because I'm supposed to leave at four for the premiere.

"The contractor will be there to start working within the week," Jemima tells me. "I'm sorry to say, but as soon as those floors are done—"

"And the toilet. You have to flush twice when you go number two."

"—and the toilet. When that's all done, the estate agent will start showing the flat. She thinks it'll go fast. Will you be ready to come home by then?"

She still does not realize that I don't know where home is. "I've got a job," I remind her. "I'm staying." I force myself out of bed and pad slowly to the bathroom.

"Why are you yawning so much? Are you depressed? You're not in bed at this hour…?"

I imagine her gripping the phone until her knuckles turn white.

"Augusta," she says. "Are you OK? I mean, are you—"

"I'm fine. *CelebLife* is a great place to work and I'm making tons of new friends. Coming here is the best thing I ever did. And hey—the notebook's filling up," I say brightly as I use one hand to silently apply a layer of toothpaste to my toothbrush. "Lots of interesting anecdotes. You'd be so jealous…I'm meeting Emma Thompson tonight."

There is a pause and I picture her clenching her jaw. "Well, if it really is that great out there, with all those stars," a thoroughly unimpressed Jemima warns, "I hope the landing isn't too hard when you fall back to earth."

Earth being Cambridge, I assume. I don't know if I'm ever falling back there.

"Augusta." She clears her throat. "Have you— Look, honey. Maybe you should write that letter you've talked about. If you haven't already...have you?" More throat clearing. "Just *write* it, and then you can think about sending it. The act itself might help more than you think. I know Caroline forgave you. I *know* it. It might help you remember, too. You know what the doctors said..."

Not now. I have to be bright-eyed and sociable in less than two hours. I can't do this.

Jemima is choking up. "It's not your fault," she says for the millionth time. "It's *his* fault. You did everything you could. I talked to Caroline's mother—"

"*No*," I say. "I love you, Mom, but I gotta go."

"Please, honey. Go back to therapy, even if it's over the phone. I worry about you so much."

The heartbreak in her voice almost makes me crumble, but I can't let it. "I'm OK, Mom, really. But I have to go. I'm sorry."

I hang up and throw cold water on my face. I push everything to the back again and visualize six-foot-five Liam Neeson looking down at me; then I imagine Emma Thompson throwing her head back and cracking up at something I said.

It will be OK. I am calm. Breathe.

I circle Emma Thompson with a pomegranate martini in hand, waiting for people to get the hell out of my way. She is over-the-top popular. People respond to her like she's the Pope meets Mary Poppins meets Princess Diana. I check my watch. I've got nothing so far, and this opulent, large-scale after party—spread over three floors, signaling to everyone with a brain that there's a shitload of pressure on the big-name director's popcorn epic—is well underway.

I inch closer to Emma. My drink is gone and I'm getting hungry. The instant Emma says goodbye to one of the worshipping industry types, I break into her circle.

"Well hello, *CelebLife*!" she greets me, throwing her hands in the air. "I'm doing well. You?"

"I'm great," I tell her.

I seem to have Emma's full attention for at least a speed round. Her fetchingly crooked teeth and her penchant for extreme enunciation are utterly charming. When I ask about her happy family life, she regales me with a set piece about the cake at her wedding in 2004. "It was supposed to be Scotland's rolling hills, but it looked like a pair of glorious green tits!"

It's true love between Emma and me. I valiantly stop myself from asking for her number. She corrects me when I mention her daughter; "No, no; not GAY-a; it's GUY-a." She even shows true, loyal fondness for *Love Actually,* which everyone secretly adores even if some holdouts claim they don't. *Instant rating: 9.6.*

When I'm done with Emma, or should I say when she is done with me, I repair to a low-lit corner of Whitehall and scribble my heart out. *Ooh.* I see Julie Delpy—a resident of my teenage bedroom wall along with Ethan Hawke. I watched *Before Sunrise* on a loop over and over until I knew Vienna like the back of my hand, and then waited for my own shaggy, tortured Ethan Hawke to pluck me off a train and show me the world. Of course, Julie's a star *CelebLife* won't be interested in because she's actually *talented*, and she probably likes it that way.

"Hi!" Julie returns my greeting as if we are great friends. "Oh, my. *CelebLife*. Nice to meet you. What do you want with me?"

She has luscious red lips and young-looking skin. "I want to know how you write so well," I ask her. A bit fawning, perhaps, but with the weight of a major global publication behind me, I can get away with it.

She laughs, shakes her head. "Please. It is work—the hardest work. I never stop. I won't ever back down until the work is ready. You're a writer, right? You know what it's like."

Her lilting French accent makes me swoon. I think Oscar the Grouch could speak in a French accent and I would go knock-kneed. The night is getting away from me, and as much as I'd love to be talked to by Julie for hours, I have bigger stars to land. Anyway, I notice Jeremy Irons waiting to talk to her, so I doubt she'll feel abandoned. I thank her and head back to the wine-and-dessert bar. I make a quick note as I look out for Orlando Bloom, who arrived late to the red carpet and whizzed right past me. *Julie Delpy: 8.3. Inspiring (but no story :(). Note to self: start thinking about writing a book.*

I find the rep, who I am counting on to will help me find at least *one* of this movie's stars.

"Liam couldn't make it," he tells me over the twang of lute players strumming in the corner. "It's not his fault, of course. Something came up."

"I get it," I assure him. "But I didn't get to talk to Orlando on the red carpet. Is he around?"

"Tell you what," he says conspiratorially. "Orlando's doing a few select interviews. Head up to the fifth floor library in five minutes. I'll call ahead, but you can tell them Jago sent you."

I find the elevator and make my way to the library, where I put my ear to the door and hear nothing, so I push it open. Before I step inside, another rep—Orlando's? The studio's?—grabs my elbow. I rip it away but manage to stop myself from snarling *Get off me*. She hisses, "*CelebLife*, right? You weren't on the list, but OK, as long as you're here...five minutes. Just don't ask about his love life or his kid. Stick to the movie. Understood?"

"Sure," I say coldly. "I got you."

I enter the library and find it empty, so I sit down at a small table. Orlando lopes in, head down, and sits across from me. He spreads out his long legs so one knee is akimbo. He taps his fingers on the table, looks anywhere but at me, like a boy with ADD called to the principal's office. I wanted Legolas. I got a moody teenager. This takes me by surprise, as he's usually so refined and engaging on late-night TV.

Normally I'd shoehorn in a question relating to parenthood or romance, something like, *Does it affect you in real life to have to grieve your on-screen wife in this film?* But the grabby PR lady has spooked me, so I stick to the script for a few minutes, but that starts to get boring. At one point my spare pen rolls onto the floor. As he's still talking, I crawl under the table to grab it—and come face-to-face with his crotch, which the public got a great view of when he went paddle boarding nude in front of a pack of photographers. Partly because it's too dark down there to see much of anything, and partly because we (thankfully) live in a time where boundaries must be respected (except for reps who think they can physically accost you, apparently), I quickly pop back up and continue the interview. He continues to make no effort to charm me. I learn nothing from Orlando but this: If an actor really, *really* doesn't want you to crack his façade, you won't. *Score: 6.0*

Dragon Lady and another rep accompany me back down to the party as if they think I'm going to whip around and storm back up to bombard their defenseless celebrity with forbidden *personal questions.* I could never be a publicist. I do another circle of the gigantic party, and I'm beside myself to see Jason Bateman in a blue suit with a glass of clear liquid on ice in his hand. (In journalism, you never assume: Could be vodka soda, could be Pellegrino. *Technically.*) I shove the last of a mini hummus-pita into my mouth and prepare to approach, thinking fast. Jason Bateman wasn't on my list. What can I ask him that *CelebLife* would write about? He's married, two kids. No babies on the way, no known cheating. *Borrrrring.*

He's surrounded by three people, and they're all chatting away. I wait for an opening but when none comes, I barge in and introduce myself. I'm getting good at it.

"Hey," Jason drawls with that signature dimpled grin. He wasn't a poster on my wall, but he's a longtime crush. "How's it going?"

"Great," I smile back, surprisingly calm. He's taller than I thought, maybe six-foot-one, and slight underneath his suit.

We talk about how great the movie was (he's not in it, "just in town for another project and came along for fun"), how wild this party is ("one of the most extravagant I've been to"). None of this is a story. I'm flipping through my memory banks trying to envision Jason with any A-lister.

Think, think, think. Oh, right! Jen!

"Your old friend Jennifer Aniston's been in a lot of big movies lately," I say. "How is it starring alongside her? I mean, what's she really like?"

"Yeah…we were in Horrible Bosses together," he recalls. "She's, um…" He grins like the Cheshire Cat. "Let's just say even getting a root canal would be enjoyable if it came from her."

"So…you're not afraid of the dentist?" I try for a sly smile.

He sips his drink, then shrugs.

"Not if Ms. Jen is the one handling the drill."

Coming from anyone else, this might sound lewd or creepy, but not when it's cheeky Jason Bateman. This is a good story that will gain me kudos and many clicks for CelebLife.com—but it's not *the* story. I ask with great concern, "How's Jen doing these days? I mean, since the split…"

She's allegedly heading for her second divorce, and her fans continue to work themselves into an Anistonian lather about who she should date next (hint: His name rhymes with Vlad Mitt). I'm gritting my teeth under my relaxed smile. It's dark in here, but I think I see Jason's eyes cloud over. Luckily, he decides to play the game instead of run away.

"She's doing great," he says. "She's an amazingly strong person." And, *bam*—it may or may not be true that she's amazing *or* strong, but for *CelebLife*, this is a major headline. I suppress my excitement, though, because we're talking about a woman who's suffered great heartbreak. Jason and I part ways and I grab one more glass of wine and a chocolate cupcake and head out to grab a cab home. Just before I hit the street, I run into Tom Hanks.

"Hey, Tom," I say. "I'm Augusta with *CelebLife*. Having a good night?"

"Of course," he says.

After the requisite intro questions, I ask, "What were you like in school? And what was your favorite thing about growing up?"

"Well," he replies, "I was an average goofy doofus." He tells me summer camp was the best, and nighttime was his favorite time, and he makes me think of Camp Naked, and then, of course, Caroline. I force the thought away. A handler comes over and tugs at Tom, who smiles at me. "Gotta go," he says. "Enjoy the party."

This is the glamorous life, I think as I walk away. It's fun, but it's proven harder than I ever thought to burrow beneath the stars' carefully cultivated images. As I head for the exit, I find myself wondering if it ever gets any deeper than this.

Tom gets a respectable 8.5. No surprise there. Was he ever going to be anything but nice?

Lying in bed hours later, after I've filed everything and I'm too wired to sleep, I make my final notes. *Jason Bateman: 9.7 for star power and for giving me a Jen story that CelebLife.com will go apeshit over. And most of all, for that friendly, dimply smile. It costs nothing to be kind. Why can't more people manage it?*

All in all, a winning night. I can live with my disappointment in Orlando Bloom. But if the others—Emma, Jason, or Tom—hadn't lived up to expectations, it would've shaken my faith in the healing power of celebrities.

19

"Yes," Caroline finally admits, "this *is* the best brunch in the city."

"Told you. I dream about their strawberry butter." Which I'm currently slathering on house-made cinnamon bread.

"And their Bellinis." Caroline holds up her glass and I clink it with mine, then we both drink.

It is like old times, only better. We're all grown up, we have real jobs, we're technically single, and we live in Manhattan. There were never any apologies between us, just a two-year desert of communication after our heartbreaking confrontation junior year. Out of the blue, the day before I graduated college, I got an email from her: *I'd love to see you when you're next in Mass. I'll be back at Christmas. I've transferred to Berkeley where I'll finish undergrad and go for an MA in social work.*

I didn't ask her how she was paying for it and she didn't tell me, but the top suspect has always been Ginger. We kept up only written communication for several years, until we moved to New York in the same month, I for a junior reporter gig at *Newstime* and Caroline for a job as a social worker at New York Mercy Clinic. We never talked about that day, or that long gap in our friendship; someday I'll tell her she was right, that our time apart turned out to be a good thing—that without her I found my wings, my strength, myself. For now, I'm just glad to have her back in my life.

Caroline keeps turning to watch the door. It's not like her to be so nervous.

"He might be the *one*," she tells me, downing her Bellini. "I mean it, Augusta. He's the first guy I've ever dated who actually challenges me."

"What does he do again?"

She makes a face. "Hedge funds. Yes, I know. Don't look at me like that. He doesn't have to be *alternative* to be different, you know. Despite what my parents think, being poor doesn't make you a better person. And anyway, the guy volunteers reading to kids on Saturdays, holds the door for *everyone*, and has a black belt in Tai-Ka-McGraw or whatever."

"Does he know you don't have an athletic bone in your body?"

"Yep," she nods, buttering her bread. "He asked me once to try a class, I said no, and he kissed me and told me I was perfect. Know what else?"

"What?" I ask, wishing he would get here already so I could order my Spinach Eggs Benedict.

"He hates jazz."

I nod approvingly. "Why didn't you say so? It's official: You, my friend, have found a gem."

"There's more," she almost whispers, leaning in. "His parents live on Park Avenue. They're old money. My parents are going to disown me."

"Name?" I've got my phone out, ready to look him up.

"Lannells. Joe Lannells."

"Joe *Lannells*?" I look up from my phone. "Of the *Swiss chocolate* Lannells? Are you kidding me right now?" Whenever I'm in an airport I pick up a Lannells Bar for, like, eight bucks. I'm weak that way.

I tilt my head toward the entrance. "Speak of the Devil—I think he's here," I say as a thin guy with brown poufy hair, wearing jeans and a lilac button-down shirt, strides toward us, grinning like a lovesick teenager. I feel a pang. I'd give my custom-made reporter's notebook to have a great guy look at me like that for just one brunch.

"You must be the best friend," the guy says, extending a hand as I stand to greet him. I have mixed feelings. I just got Caroline back—I don't want some Wall Street bro taking her away. That said, he's cute, with shining eyes and a firm handshake.

"Hi, sweetie," he says, kissing Caroline lightly on the cheek.

We're already at sweetie?

"So, Augusta Noble," this Joe interloper person says as he sits and pulls his chair closer to the table. "You won't believe this, but I read your work before I ever met Caroline. How crazy is that? You wrote the piece on ethics in hedge funds in *Newstime* a few months back, right?"

"That was me," I nod. "So *you're* the one who read it."

I was forced by *Newstime*'s business editor to take the story over for one of his sick reporters. I studied all night to write it, and the boredom of it almost did me in. The editor tore it up and rewrote most of it; I refuse to ever cover the markets again.

Joe smiles at my lame joke. He's expressive and wants to impress me, which I always like in a man. His teeth are celebrity white and straight. "Hate to burst your bubble, but the whole firm read it—all ten of us. It's laminated and pinned to our wall."

Caroline is watching this back-and-forth with a look of bliss on her face. "I'm afraid that article was a bit of an exception, honey. Augusta's tastes run more to Chris Pine's wardrobe changes than finance," she says, winking at me. I never thought of Caroline as a winker. "But she puts on a good act at her serious magazine."

"Well," Joe says, smiling at the server who's arrived to take drink orders, "I think you have one of the coolest jobs on the planet. I'd love to do something like that."

"It's not as glamorous as it sounds," I say, "but thanks." We all order cappuccinos and more Bellinis, and Joe leads a toast. "To the two most beautiful women in all of Manhattan," he says, and we both roll our eyes semi-jokingly.

Caroline's glowing face falls abruptly. She closes her eyes as if whatever she sees might go away if she doesn't look at it. I swivel around to see what's the matter. Lincoln is at the window. He locks eyes on me, then on Caroline, then on Joe.

"What's going on?" Joe asks, concerned, following our eyes and noticing Lincoln. "Is this something I need to take care of?"

"No, no," Caroline says softly. "I haven't been fair to him." She sighs. "It's my fault."

"Bullshit," Joe argues, shaking his head, then thanking the server as our coffees arrive. "He's responsible for his own behavior. I'll go have a chat with him."

Caroline touches his hand, shakes her head vehemently. "Please don't. He's harmless—he's hurting, is all. Let him be."

"Trust me," Joe says evenly. "He can't be lurking around restaurants like this. There won't be any trouble, I promise. This is what I do."

Caroline shoots a look at me and I raise my eyebrows. Joe is already stalking out of the restaurant. We watch through the window as he approaches Lincoln with his hands out in a placating gesture. He doesn't get too close, but inches nearer as Lincoln appears to let his guard down. The two men stand in front of the windows as regular New Yorkers stroll by without a second look. Joe holds his hands out as if to say, *OK*? Lincoln looks at the ground, shakes his head, looks up. Joe keeps talking, nods his head, and Lincoln crosses his arms over his chest. I don't have a clue what's going on, but at the end of it, Lincoln looks at the ground again and walks away slowly, without a glance back.

"What did you say to him?" Caroline says when Joe returns looking slightly flushed.

"I told him the truth," Joe replies. "That's all. He won't be bothering you again."

"He's one of my oldest friends," Caroline says, shaking her head. "I don't want to lose him. I just want him to calm down."

Joe's reading the menu. "Better off without friends like that, Caro. The guy's a loose cannon. *Ooh*. How are the Eggs Benedict here?"

20

#27, #28, #29, #30

I'm snuggled under the covers reading Alexander's latest feature in the *International Post* when Robbie calls and asks me to zip out to Mayfair for a club opening.

"Not sure who's going," he tells me. "The rep is promising an A-lister or two, but so far the only names on the list are Val Kilmer, Kate Moss, and Robbie Williams, so it might end up being nothing."

"I'm on it," I tell him. I think better of adding, *But don't call Iceman "nothing."*

Val Kilmer was on my bedroom wall. He is one of my biggest crushes, but also one of greatest fears, because everyone's always reporting how "difficult" he is. Val was my everything after *Top Gun*, and then Caroline made me watch *Real Genius* and I thought, *Yes, this blond, jaw-snapping, hawk-eyed man with the kissable mouth is the one for me.* When I heard what a hard bastard he allegedly was during his nineties heyday, it made me all the more intrigued.

Flounce is not a nightclub so much as a palace decorated by some combination of a drunk sheik, Kelly Wearstler, and Liberace. I am welcomed through the towering doorway like a celebrity, but they're only giving out old-fashioneds at the door so I walk briskly toward the bar and run into Robbie Williams, whom Americans know from his days in the boy band Take That and his massive solo hit "Angels." He's leaning with one hip against the bar. It's still early, so there are only a handful of other important people around, all of whom are too cool to bother Robbie Williams.

I smile at Robbie, then the bartender, and order a cosmo, which is eighteen British pounds for civilians but free for VIPs like Robbie and me. As I wait for my drink, a young man in tight silver pants and a black vest swans up with a tray of weird hors d'oeuvres that look like rubbery cigars garnished with poison ivy. I help myself. Robbie, who looks his age and has left the deep laugh lines around his mouth alone, takes one and thanks the man.

"What *is* this?" I ask Robbie after the man walks away.

"I genuinely don't know," the singer replies, "but let's try it."

I take a small bite and sense pulverized entrails of cow or some other poor animal. I discreetly empty my mouth into my cocktail napkin, squeeze it into a ball, and place it on the bar. Thank God my cosmo has arrived; I down half of it in one.

"Don't like it?" Robbie's not smiling, but his eyes are twinkly. "Chef here's got two Michelin stars, you know."

I nod, and drink the rest of my (small) cosmo to wash the residue down.

"Can I get an espresso, mate?" Robbie asks the bartender.

The singer turns to me. "Another one?"

"Yes, please," I reply. "And a glass of water."

"Of course," the barman replies.

"*Coffee?*" I ask Robbie, as if we're at a frat party and all the cool kids are drinking booze.

Without missing a beat, he shrugs, "I'm sober."

He is serene as he is as he says this, but I also see sadness in those eyes.

"'Angels' is the most-requested song at American funerals," I blurt. I read that on the way here, but why I felt the need point it out, I do not know.

"Whatever works for people," he replies.

I shift back to his sobriety, a topic only slightly less sensitive than funerals. "I think you're brave for talking about your struggles," I say. He's been quite open in recent years about his substance abuse.

"I'm not. I've been scared plenty. When I was taking a handful of Vicodin in a night and waking myself up with Adderall—that was terrifying." He smiles. "Turns out I'm a sharer. Who would've thought it?"

"You have to say that because you're an overly modest English bloke," I joke, perhaps unwisely. "Plus, that's what courage *is*, right? Being scared and doing it anyway."

He laughs at that as my second cosmopolitan appears.

"This isn't the hard part," he says, gesturing with his espresso. "When I covered everything up, pretended it wasn't happening—that's when it got bad."

I feel a little jolt when I process what he's just said. That last line hits home for me in ways I'm not ready to think about. I recover quickly, though, and wish him a good night. Sadly, *CelebLife* will not print his wise words, not in the magazine or online, and perhaps he knows that, and it's why he was so open with me. Since I've been in England, he's been in the papers at least once a week. He's won a bajillion awards and is the most popular non-Latin musician in Latin America. But that's not enough for *CelebLife*'s reality-star-loving editors.

I wander the party and find the club's PR boss, who insists a mystery A-lister is *definitely probably* arriving shortly. "You understand I can't say who…but we're hopeful."

I make a show of looking at my non-existent watch. It's one a.m. No surprise A-listers are coming—he knows it and I know it. I check the entrance hall again, find no exciting stars, then turn back and almost bump into Val Kilmer. He appears to be heading for the exit, so it's now or never. The problem is, as soon as I register it's him, my chest tightens. I feel a wave coming; it squeezes my throat. My therapist calls this panicky version of me Ms. Unresolved Trauma, and that person never shares her calendar with me. I can never predict what will bring her out.

Breathe. Focus on one point in the room. Stop it before it starts.

I focus on Val, on the way he moves: slow and sure, as if he's just another guy. I manage to slow my breathing with thoughts of Iceman flying a MiG-28 through the clouds. It works—suddenly, my need for oxygen is overridden by my need to get to Val Kilmer. I move quickly through the crowd and cut him off at the pass, pretending I'm randomly bumping into him.

"Oh hey, Val," I say, holding my hand up for a little wave, a reporter's sign of peace. "I'm Augusta with *CelebLife* magazine. Do you have a minute for a quick chat?"

Of course he doesn't. He's a serious, difficult man with important things to do and no interest in a gossip magazine.

"Hi, Augusta," he says warmly, stopping dead in his tracks and lightly touching my arm to guide me out of the melee. We're perilously close to the front door. "What's up?"

Whoa—*what*? I wasn't prepared for this reaction. Then again, I'm constantly thrown off balance by unpredictable celebrities. Val, though, puts me instantly at ease. I ask him how he likes the club, and London, and he tells me he's delighted to be in town conducting some actorly business. His eternally dirty blond hair is just long enough to tuck behind his ears. He appears more fragile than I normally think of him, which is understandable; we know something has gone on with his health, but we don't know quite what at this point.

I can't inquire, *Dude, are you OK? What's going on with you? Tell me you're going to be around for a long time, or at least until* Top Gun II. I ask him about his beloved one-man show, which he worked on for years. "You put everything into *Citizen Twain* to bring Mark Twain alive on stage and screen. Has this been one of your most important roles?"

"Well," he says thoughtfully, "He's the oldest guy I've ever played, and the hardest in some ways. Like Twain said, 'I wonder if there's ever a day you don't forget you're old?' You know, old people don't *feel* old inside, but their bodies tell them they are, and people treat them differently. But you feel like you've always felt—like yourself, as if you were still young. I've felt this way my whole life…I don't feel older."

He's trying to make me understand. "I don't feel my age," he says. "I'm fifty-eight, but I feel the same way I've always felt, even at twenty eight."

"I get it," I nod, though I don't entirely understand. My thirtieth birthday is approaching, and I feel twenty-five; does that count?

I stand with him for a while, and we talk about Twain, but after a while his eyes flit toward the door, my cue to wrap it up. Not wanting to be annoying, I thank him and he heads out. I decide it's time for me to exit, too.

Out on the street, I bump into Rhys Ifans and Kate Moss, who appear to be hailing a cab.

"Hahhahahahahaaaa," they laugh in unison when I ask how their night was. They're laughing *at* me not *with* me. I know the difference. I got it all through school. When I ask Rhys if he'll answer a few questions he laughs again and says, "I don't do *interviews*," as if I've asked him to spank me in public. "I'm not talking to you."

Kate Moss cackles. I haven't liked her since she caused an uproar with her pro-anorexia slogan, "Nothing tastes as good as skinny feels." I'll give her this: she's thin as a rail.

I look at Rhys's back and at his wild, thinning hair as the two stumble off down the sidewalk and think, *You, my man, are no Val Kilmer.*

As my own taxi bumps along back to Wimbledon, I try not to dwell on the sting of their laughter, though it brings me back instantly to the powerless girl on the playground. Rhys and Kate know the score: They come to these events to help the venues get free publicity. I wasn't out of line for approaching them. The more I begin to loathe them, the more I love Val. It occurs to me my Celebrity Stockholm Syndrome is getting worse. I have at least forty minutes in the cab, so I make notes while the events are still fresh.

Robbie Williams: 8.6 (didn't get a story out of it).

Val Kilmer gets my highest rating to date, 9.7. *Beat that, other celebrities. I don't need to be so fearful of men. They're not all going to make fun of me. They're not all going to hurt me.*

Rhys and Kate get my first zeroes, noted mostly so I can remember in my dotage what happened on the streets of London this night. I'm sure I'll laugh about it one day.

I wake up at ten the next morning to the sound of banging on the front door. I fly out of bed and throw on a robe, peeking through the window to see a trio of people wielding claw hammers, paintbrushes, and power tools. I groan. The intrusion has begun. Time to start thinking seriously about getting my own flat. The workmen are actually two men and one woman from Poland; the woman is slight, maybe 115 pounds soaking wet, and introduces herself solemnly.

"I am Dagmara. Lead me to your kitchen floor, if you please."

I haven't had my coffee yet. After I show them in, I head to the bedroom and flop back on the bed, knowing there's no chance of more sleep, so I take the opportunity to Yammer the coke-snorting action star. I've been keeping tabs on him since our dramatic confrontation. Stanley hasn't said *boo* about it since Dublin, and Stanley's a tough guy to get an audience with unless *he's* doing the summoning. There are no fresh news stories, and the most recent Instagram pic of the action star shows him shirtless at an undisclosed beach, sand sticking to the coconut oil slathered on his body.

21

#31, #32, #33, #34, #35, #36

Clive Owen: *This one kills me. Not quite as slick, handsome, and charismatic in person as he is onscreen (I guess that's why they call it acting). His hair, perhaps for a role, is dyed a clumsy black. He's nice but not open. Polite but not revealing. Score: 8.8 out of guilt for me being so judgy.*

I finish my notes and close the book as a rep deposits Daniel Craig in front of me. We stand eye-to-eye on a freezing, rainy night in Chelsea, shielded by a flimsy plastic tunnel constructed over the red carpet. I ask him what it's like to be out on the town for charity with his wife. "It must be a great bonding experience," I observe.

He nods as if he's going to answer my question. "It's all very well to throw money around when you've got it, but you want to follow through with it as well," he says, not answering my question.

Um…uh…"What attracted you and Rachel to this event?"

Another nod. "It's helping less-fortunate kids get to college—but also, the most important thing is keeping them there." He speaks quickly, standing frozen in place, those juicy, pouty lips moving at speed but not actually offering answers to my questions.

I try one more, and get the same kind of off-topic result. This is a new one on me. I think it might be fun to inquire, "Can I shove a glazed donut up your bum?" or, "What does a puppy taste like?" just to see if he'd give equally practiced answers—but the game is over. A rep saves him from me, smiles, and I say, dutifully, "Thanks, Daniel." At that, Mr. Bond sidesteps to the next reporter and I hear him giving identical answers off a script he's clearly memorized. I have a grudging respect. He *so* didn't want to do this, but he did it for the kids. What can I say? I'm a sucker for celebrities using their fame to help the less fortunate, and my bar is now extremely low: Don't be blatantly rude or mean and you get a pass.

Here comes his Oscar-winning wife, Rachel Weisz. A bevy of frantic, wet handlers are holding an umbrella over her head, trying to give her a jacket, and fretting, "No, no, you don't have to do the interviews, you must be freezing, it's so *cold*."

"No," she protests, visibly shivering, "I can do it. Of course I will. I'm fine, it's fine."

When it's my turn, I see her lips have a blue tinge beneath her lip-gloss, and yet she's *with* me. It's as if she's making up for him. She's engaging, sweet, bright-eyed, listens. "We love doing this as a family," she replies to my first question. "It's something we feel really strongly about and it's so important."

This may not be a grand revelation, but it's enough. A-list couples out together are catnip to *CelebLife*. Rachel is prettier in person, a true English rose. I chat with her for a bit longer and realize she seems *nervous*, almost as if she's trying to impress me with her answers. What is it they say? It's not how nice you are when things are easy. It's how you hold it together when things are hard. Daniel did OK. He gets a 7.2 because he's James Bloody Bond. Rachel is awesome and gets a 9.2.

Here comes Christian Bale. Even though he's older than I am, I still feel like I watched him grow up, from *Newsies* to *Little Women* and on to his uber-hot phase around *American Psycho*, and now to his fully grown-up roles. I ask him how his latest performance was received— "and I *loved* it, but the way," I gush.

"I'm always flattered to hear that," he replies, smiling, nodding. "I adore it when people tell me I've touched them in some way with a performance. It's an honor."

He has an earnest way of speaking and uses firm, strong gestures and sharp nods of the head. Someone he knows passes by and says something to him, and Christian responds with a full, open-mouthed, dorky laugh. Well, slap me hard and call me Angelina Jolie. Christian Bale is a *goofball*. Shorter than I thought. Big head. And let's talk about that accent: London cabbie meets Welsh nobleman meets American dude. His wife, Sibi, stands several feet behind him beaming, tanned, and ultra fit—thin but defined and strong. *If only. That will never be me.* Christian gets an 8.5. (Loses points for not dumping Sibi and running away with me). I know he's not a saint. I mean, who doesn't remember those recordings of his temper tantrum on the *Terminator Salvation* set? Still, he apologized sincerely and completely, and I haven't heard anything bad since.

Time to head in to the party, thank God, because my fingers are numb. On the way in, I try to chat with press-shy Gillian Anderson, who's petite and strawberry blonde and skipped the red carpet interviews. She's not interested. I watch her greet Stellan Skarsgård with a full smooch on the mouth. He is a cool character and I can see why Paul Bettany, who I want to marry immediately if not sooner, and his wife Jennifer Connolly, who stole my man ages ago, named their kid after him. I grab a signature drink—a cucumber-gin deal—and immediately bump into Stellan.

"You've been in some controversial films," I observe after introductions. "You ever get any blowback for that?"

"Anything to do with sex is a bigger deal in the U.S.," he laughs. "Growing up, my parents were naked around the house. I walk naked around the house. I was born naked—I don't know about you…"

"Yes, as far as I know," I confirm. "As was your son, I assume?" *Your gigantic, hunky son?*

He doesn't bite. "You Americans are such prudes," he says in his thick Swedish accent and voice like sandpaper. He has bags under slightly blood-shot eyes and a smile that takes over his whole face. He looks like he's having a better time than anyone, all the time. He's relaxed and confident, and so at odds with what Hollywood seems to be about; as the night progresses, I watch all the stars gravitate to him and get the feeling he's the mayor of Hollywood.

I watch Rachel and Daniel, too, because Stanley will want copious notes on them. She rubs his back when they go on stage to accept an award from the charity. He appears intermittently grumpy and, tonight at least, stiff, while she cheerfully follows in his wake, doing what she can to lift them both up.

22

#37, #38, #39, #40, #41, #42, #43, #44, #45, #46, #47

I sip prosecco in the five-star Hotel Hassler, high atop Rome's Spanish Steps, and wonder what I've been doing with my life. We've got Italian antiques, we've got silk upholstery, marble floors, brass fittings, and gold-dipped accessories. We've got Tom Cruise, amazing coffee, Pellegrino, endless cocktails, and J. Lo. After sitting for six hours I've developed football-sized cankles.

Gillian floats back from her phone meeting with the bosses in her nine-hundred-euro-a-night room. "Tell me again how the celebrities are *not* supposed to know we're spying on them?" I ask when she slides into her seat across from me at the little round European café-style table. "Do they really think they're safe in here?" Frankly, I'm not convinced we've done the best job of playing Bored Tourists Who Sit a Lot and Drink Many Fluids.

Gillian picks up the diet soda she had me order for her. "Of course they know, silly girl," she says, shooting a lightning-fast glance toward the table of stars five feet away. "We have a deal. They pretend they don't know we're here, we keep our distance and don't report anything other than happy families, stunning outfits, and incredible bodies."

It's the first night of the "Fashion in Film" event we're here to cover, which so far looks to me like an excuse for actors to mix with models and call it work. I watch Tom Cruise cross one leg over the other, lean back, laugh at something Brooke Shields says. She strikes me as lovely to be around. Her hair falls in waves down her back and her face is perfectly symmetrical. She's one of the few celebrities I've been close to so far who is as big-boned as I am. As lesser stars chatter away, one of the world's top action heroes listens intently, but isn't generally the center of attention. Tom Cruise is not a natural raconteur—nor is he as short as the blogs say, even if he does allegedly wear lifts (I cannot confirm this).

Gillian, wearing this season's Dolce & Gabbana floral shift dress, says, "You're on the red carpet tonight, yes?"

I nod. She doesn't do red carpets. I've learned junior staff and interns do most of the celebrity interviewing at *CelebLife* and its ilk, which is weird, because you'd think the staff want to get to know the people they cover.

"OK…" Gillian scans a to-do list on her phone, "your other job was to get us reservations at Nino, Tom's drop-dead favorite restaurant, on the last night. For two." She looks up, eyebrows halfway up her forehead. "You did this before you came, right? Stanley said he told you…"

What? I have no memory of that. Oh, wait…right. *Shit.* "Of course," I nod. "All set."

"Really? That easy? Nice work." Gillian crosses that off her list. "We'll eat there and Hoover up any back-reporting. All the big stars will have been there at one point or another over the long weekend. We have to find out who canoodled, who fought, and who threw up in the bathroom after eating naughty pasta."

Will and Jada Smith stop by the table we're surveilling. They're quiet, so I don't get a taste of that joyful Will Smith laugh. Jada is polite but barely smiles. She is all sinew and angles, stunning in her small frame and defined jaw, though she appears to have inserted something into her cheeks to make them newly pillowy. I recall that she once told *Essence*, "I don't eat for pleasure." Considering the amount of truffle fettuccine and olive-oil-dipped bread I've already had since I've been in Rome, I wonder if I should be more like Jada.

I open my notebook under the table. *Would you rather have tens of millions in the bank, a tight body, and a miserable disposition; or, be poor, lost, and fat but free to eat olive oil linguine paired with a gorgeous Tuscan white?* This seems to be the choice women face. Maybe there are people who live in the in-between world. If so, I don't know them.

Jada and Will seem like old friends—close but no touching. Then again, do non-famous twenty-years-married couples touch all the livelong day? The mega couple doesn't stay long, and when they're gone, I ask Gillian for the real story.

Her face communicates volumes, but in the end she'll only hedge. "Let's say there are rumors that they don't have a traditional marriage," she says diplomatically. "Half of Hollywood doesn't. That's why we have to be careful writing that so-and-so 'cheated' on his wife when the guy's caught diddling a slinky blonde starlet or a burly young rapper. If you have an open marriage or even a bearding situation, it's not technically *cheating*." I never thought about it that way, but it makes perfect sense.

Now Gillian's settled in, I excuse myself to go to the bathroom, then sit in a stall and do my millionth search to see what Alexander's been up to. There's been nothing new for a week, but today a photo pops up in the society pages in which his arm is wrapped warmly, protectively around Belinda Oliver, the English actress who's had more than one minor comeback but never seems to burst out of her B/C-list constraints. She always seems to hang out with A-listers and had a public affair with one of their husbands. She's so pretty, thin, and rich, and so tucked into Alexander's protective embrace in this infuriating photo. *Shit.* What was I thinking? A *Viscount*? A gorgeous, funny, smart, talented member of the British aristocracy? Certain people are right—I *am* delusional.

I head back to the table to watch the celebs again. I'm testing my Prince Harry Theory this weekend, and in the *What are they really like?* stakes, the best I can say is, Tom Cruise is nice to the staff, friendly to the two fans he bumps into, smiles a lot, and has a classic conversation in the lobby with an elderly couple who've been married for a hundred years. "I'd love to have what you have someday," I hear him say, and they glow in return.

But Tom's got a mixed back-story. Leah Remini, who's spent a lot of time with him over the years and attended his wedding to Katie Holmes, says he's "diabolical" and *not* a good person. It's confusing.

I watch J. Lo on this spying mission, too, and she ignores the fans who try to talk to her, lets her staff deal with the waiter for her, and her bodyguards hang over her like bovine carcasses at a meatpacking plant. By contrast, Tom's bodyguards hang back and are barely noticeable. In general, being this close to such huge stars grows banal after a while; it starts to feel a little like being at a high school cafeteria. The stars are not exceptionally intelligent, interesting or charismatic. They speak not of their travels and museums and books, but of first dates and different kinds of beer, their favorite handbag, their kids. I check my watch. It's about time for me to get cleaned up for my event tonight.

The red carpet is at a real Italian castle outside Rome, one made of ancient stones lit with torches and buttressed by an imposing wall. As I wait for the stars to arrive, I try to subtly pull up my control-top hose, which have started to roll down over the smooth bodyshaper beneath. It's not working; there's no way to pull them up without publicly putting my hand up my dress. Leaving even for a few minutes is out of the question, lest I miss a big star. I gaze around innocently as I grab a handful of my stretchy Calvin Klein clearance dress at the hip, cock the hip casually and coolly, and yank. Half my short dress comes up with the hose, but at least I'm contained for the moment, as long as I don't shift too much.

My friend Mallory from Lisbon is here, too, far down in Red Carpet Siberia because she works for a dreaded tabloid. As I flash her a smile and a wave, Scott Eastwood walks in front of me. The cheekbones are real, the lips oh-so-slightly pouty, the flaxen mane coiffed like tamed angel hair. If he didn't have such an easy way about him and a killer smile, he'd be too vain and too pretty for me to stand it. He nods to me and smiles, and I'm ready with a question, but he's not doing press.

"Hey," he says to me. Then he is gone. This is one for the record books, perhaps my shortest interview ever, a one-act play and an ode to simplicity: *Hey,* by Scott Eastwood.

I'm seeing more and more stars drawn to cameras like magnets and repelled by pens and notebooks as if they're kryptonite, and Scott's no exception. He's got a handler sticking to him like tit-tape who steers the actor away from the print press like we're measles-ridden fans. I see someone better anyway. It's Joshua Jackson—Pacey Witter from *Dawson's Creek*—descended from my bedroom wall to entertain me. I'm ready, pen poised, professional face on, but then, suddenly, he sidesteps the red carpet and walks behind it. I don't see anyone else interesting coming down, so I ditch my spot and follow him.

"Joshua," I call out. "Can I just ask you a couple of questions? I'm with *CelebLife*."

And then...*oh, fuck*. My pantyhose are rolling down again. I knew they were a *tad* too small when I left tonight, but I had no other options and my pale legs aren't fit for public viewing this time of year. The elastic is stuck halfway down my hip, so there is no ledge to keep them in place. I grab at the waistband through my dress, bunching up the fabric in a most unsubtle fashion. Good thing Pacey's reluctant; better let him keep moving. But no, turns out he's one of the good ones.

The actor stops, turns back, makes a friendly *Why the hell not?* face. "Yes—sure," he replies brightly.

Dammit. On the flip side of the carpet where no one's looking, he stands in front of me and asks how I am. I am making deals with God. *Please, please, please let my pinching the elastic be enough. As soon as my real life starts, as soon as I'm settled, when I've done what I've set out to do in my career, I'll adopt an orphan.* The elastic shifts. I'm holding the left side up while the right is trying to roll all the way to my ankles, finding an easy, slippery path against the shiny bodyshaper beneath. *OK—TWO orphans. PLEASE don't let my pantyhose roll down to my ankles with every photographer in Europe standing by and Joshua Jackson in my face.*

God is not impressed. The pantyhose roll down over my hips in one quick rush, and I reach down and grab the waistband again through my dress, pretending to shift dramatically on my feet. I'm holding the ultra-tight elastic bunched with my dress in my left hand while holding the recorder near Joshua's mouth in my right. They're stuck at the crevice at the top of my legs with only two fingers keeping them from dropping to my ankles. As I try to act normal, Joshua gives me an exclusive interview. I tell him I'm a new expat and he congratulates me, and says it was scary at first, but he'll never regret his time living in Paris with Diane Kruger.

"Travel helps make you who you are," he says. "If you can, I highly recommend getting out of your comfort zone and seeing the world."

I ask him why he's skipping the red carpet; does he grow tired of people always wanting to be near him? His answer is refreshingly honest.

"Have you ever met an actor who doesn't love the adulation?" he jokes. "No, but really, I love people. And all this comes with the territory." His voice, dark and strident, is seductive. He insists that he happily basks in the attention that comes with his work, lately on Showtime's *The Affair*. Joshua has low-lidded eyes and a deep pinch of skin between his eyebrows. He's tall and solid. I ask him if he's in touch with Katie Holmes, his longtime pal from *Dawson's Creek*. "Yeah, yeah," he nods, entirely unruffled by such an impertinent question. "When we can, we check in. She's great."

Joshua Jackson: An extrovert, a talent, and a gentleman. 9.7.

I shuffle a few steps around to the velvet rope to catch the last celebrity of the night, who turns out to be Robert De Niro. Our interview goes something like this: "Hi,

Robert! What's your favorite thing about being here in Rome?"

"Mumble mumble yeah, grumble mumble. Yes, uh huh, it's great to be here. Yes, I'm enjoying Rome. Life is good." He's smiley but in a hurry, and gives off a hunted sort of feel, as if he's never been under the spotlight before. I want to reach out, pinch his cheeks, and call him grandpa.

And now I'm free, so I shuffle to the women's room with my hand stuck to my thigh as if I have a profound leg injury. I stand in a stall and consider my options. The smart choice is remove the hose entirely so as not to risk another emergency. But this will reveal painfully white, not-shaved-in-two-days legs, which is *not* an option. I sit on the toilet, take off my shoes, and tug the nylon from toes to calf, knee to thigh, until I get the waistband all the way up under my bra. The second I stand up, it falls back to my waist. I hold it there; if I have to spend the evening clutching my own hip, so be it. I need bigger clothes, or I need to shrink my body. Either one.

I take short, slow strides to the main salon, where there's a sit-down dinner at narrow tables that have no end. I am seated across from Dev Patel, who is fidgety and a fast-blinker. He introduces himself to me, then I meet his small entourage, and I'm taken aback because his accent is hard-core Londoner. He's a good-looking bloke, dark and thin, with curious eyes and impeccable manners. Dev takes an interest in me, asking me about living in London. He says he lives in L.A. now and that I might love it, then asks me how I got into journalism. Dinner is gorgeous, the wine flows, and for once in the longest time, I exhale and forget everything but the moment.

On the way into the after party, I pass something I've never seen before. Scott Eastwood is standing in a corner with a handler and a tablet, swiping photo after photo of himself. "That one," he points. "No, not that one. Yes—this one's good. Yes." This goes on for a while, and I'm reminded of a bible verse from English lit in high school. While pretending not to lurk, I look it up; it's from Ecclesiastes. "Vanity of vanities, says Qoheleth, vanity of vanities! All things are vanity!" To be fair to Scott Eastwood, Hollywood is full of all things vanity.

I wander into the after party for a bitter Campari cocktail and find Jeremy Renner, one of the first to arrive, dancing alone on the empty wooden floor, unbothered and unmolested as he performs white-man moves I saw in a movie once. The best way I can describe it is, if you slowed the Carlton Dance down to twenty-five percent, you'd have Jeremy Renner.

Gillian has ordered me to do her dirty work, so I'm back at the Hassler by one a.m., ready to pounce (politely) on Victoria Beckham, who is returning from the after party with her sister, while Gillian supervises. I ask how it was, and Victoria turns, smiles, and says, "It was great," then makes a quick getaway. It occurred to me to say, *Hey, Vicky! Remember me from Portugal?* But clearly she doesn't, so I played it straight.

Next up is Jennifer Lopez and entourage. "How was the event?" I ask her.

Ms. Lo speeds up and, as she passes in front of me, she *almost* I-think-she-kind-of-did spit with a fierce *Pss-fff-tsshh* in my direction. I am taken aback. As she swans away, her famous butt undulates under her silken baby-pink gown. To me now, she is ugly inside and out. I also realize the wrap she's wearing is fur. *Real fur.* What year is this? My mind flashes up an image of the animal being skinned alive so Jennifer Lopez can feel pretty, and I want to throw up. "Jenny from the Block," my ass. More like Jenny with a mansion and an attitude. In the same way I'll never forget that moment, I'm certain she'll never remember it. We are, most of us, beneath her.

Having pretty much served as a human spittoon, I run to the bathroom while Gillian keeps watch. On my way back, I notice a group I haven't seen before eyeing me up. A man shyly nods at me. He's a celebrity of some sort, though I can't quite place him. He's surrounded by an entourage, all men, including a few skinny pals and a couple of fridge-sized bodyguards, and they are taking note of me as I head to the front desk to get an early copy of my ever-growing bill. The shy guy is the center of attention. He is ducking his head, smiling, so bashful I swear he actually says *Aw, shucks* when I make eye contact, and then I lose him under his baseball cap. It's his entourage that goes nuts with the come-ons.

"Heyyy," one of them drawls in a husky voice, "my man wants to talk to you. Where you goin'? *Hey!*" I hear a couple more *My man this, that, ooh, ooh, where you goin'?!* The largest of the men reaches out to grab my arm and I pull it skyward, but not fast enough. He grips hard, yanks me toward him like I'm a rag doll, and I have to wriggle and push to extricate myself.

"Sorry," I say, rubbing my arm where he gripped it. Then, looking right at the celebrity, I say, "I don't know who you are." The star looks down at the floor; his entourage is all *Ooohh, snap!*

I throw them what I hope is a sly *better luck next time* look. I'm so bad at this. As I look back at the star, a light bulb goes off. *Ah*; it's Mr. Mac McMoney—as in multi-hyphenate rap star, actor, businessman, perpetually unmarried, globally famous McMoney. In a hotel full of models, I don't know why the hell he's turned his attention on me, but he's not bad looking. Those muscles, cut but not brutish…then again, still, I escape them, make it to reception, and get a five-page copy of my bill, which has line after line of ten-euro Diet Cokes and eighteen-euro glasses of prosecco. I end up passing the rowdy entourage again near the hotel's front door, as they wait for their limo.

"That's your bill?" one of the slavering refrigerators shouts as he rolls my way. "We can get her room number now! Yeah, let's get it. Come on, baby. Show me your room."

McMoney, who I can see now has a slight orange tinge from a fake tan gone wrong, is raising his eyebrows at his bodyguard in quiet encouragement of this plan.

"Ha, ha," I laugh, like, *you'll never get me*—but it is a nervous laugh. I get chills—not the good kind. The refrigerator reaches for the paperwork and I pull away, watch McMoney laughing. "Whoa—nope!" I say. Things go from flattering to sinister in the flap of a page and the grasp of a meaty hand. I hug my folio to my chest and stalk back to my table with one quiet, sobering thought in my mind: *I've escaped something.*

Still shaky, I find Gillian and beg her to let me off duty for the night.

"You did great," she nods. "Get out of here and get some sleep. After you file, of course." *Of course.*

"Oh, and it turns out I can't go to Nino with you tomorrow," she tells me. "I'm flying out in the morning. But New York is keen to get all the back reporting. They want the whole experience, what the stars ate, what the atmosphere is like there. I'm sure you can change your reservation to one without a problem. Or," she adds brightly, "take a friend."

"Right," I say. I have so many pals in Rome. *Crap.*

I check the time. It's two-thirty. Nino is closed, and doesn't open until five p.m. tomorrow. If I screw this up, Stanley might decide I'm not such a useful freelancer to have around after all.

23

Caroline is not the lighthearted bar buddy I was looking for tonight. "I don't think I'm cut out for monogamy," she moans. "I don't know what's wrong with me."

"Says the woman who has two gorgeous men fighting over her," I say, taking a sip of Vermouth's famous Raspberry Dream martini.

Caroline puts her head down and rests it in the crook of her arm.

"I thought Joe was the one," I say. "That you finally found the guy who 'thrills' you."

"I wouldn't say 'thrills,'" she says, lifting her head with great effort. She blows a piece of hair out of her eye. "He woke me up…at first. Now it's just like everything else that's ever been. A taste of *blah* leading to an endless stretch of boredom with average experiences for the rest of my life."

I am starting to realize we have the same affliction with two very different provenances. "Caroline…" I say. "Do you think you're…"

"What?"

I try to read her face. She's regarding me with droopy, glum eyes.

"Do you think maybe you're depressed? That you can't feel happy because there's something going on…I don't know…chemically?"

"Oh," she perks up and lets out a chuckle. "*No.* I'm not depressed. I thought you were going to ask me if I was gay."

"I was, but I lost my nerve. Are you, though? I mean, could you be?"

"I'm a confident, liberal woman," she says, twirling the stem of her glass. "However, the fact remains: I do not like vaginas. At all. Can't stand them. I tried to look at my own with a mirror once and almost threw up."

I laugh. "Yeah, I guess you'd know by now. Or maybe not. OK, so now what?"

"Who knows? Maybe I *still* haven't met the right guy. Maybe he's at a bar in Nairobi right now, drinking whatever they drink in bars in Nairobi. And we're destined to never meet because he lives in Africa and I live in New Fucking York."

I toss back the rest of my Raspberry Dream and set down the empty glass, continuing to act as if everything's normal as it hits me that I've had questions about Caroline's romantic inclinations in the back of my mind for years.

"Who says we need a guy, anyway? Because we *don't*," I say. "Just look at me—the majority of my life has been spent without a serious relationship and I'm entirely well-adjusted."

"*Mmm hmm*," Caroline mumbles sardonically, perusing Vermouth's endless martini menu. "Sure you are. You continue to well-adjustedly gravitate to 'relationships' you know will lead nowhere because you're terrified of intimacy, because once the guy gets to know the real you, he'll take off because no one has ever stuck around before."

"Let's order some more drinks," I suggest, because I can't argue with her.

"Oh, fuck it. I'll have another vodka martini—extra dirty, three blue-cheese-stuffed olives, stirred not shaken," Caroline says to the bartender.

"Another Raspberry Dream, please," I say. Turning to Caroline, I ask, "Does Mr. Perfect know that you're…feeling lukewarm all of a sudden?"

She lets out a dramatic Caroline sigh and picks at some germy nuts from the bowl on the bar. "I've actually told him I want to slow things down. He didn't take it well. He wants to take me out to the weekend house in Greenwich to meet the parents. I told him I thought it was too fast."

"Poor you," I say, rolling my eyes.

"Shut up," she snaps, and I can see she's truly upset.

"Hey…I was kidding. I know relationships are hard…no matter who they're with."

She nods absently, watches the bartender stir her martini.

"I have something that'll take our minds off all this crap," I tell her cheerfully. "A plus-one for a huge party tomorrow in Chelsea. With *celebrities*."

"You and celebrities." She shakes her head, tests her drink, swallows. "You're obsessed, yet you write for the most dryly serious newsmagazine in existence. I can't figure you out."

"Join the club. So. You coming or not?" It's not lost on me that she used to invite me to the cool parties, and now it's my turn.

"What about Mike, the Asexual Bond Trader?" she asks me. "You've been on, what, three dates? Don't you want to bring him as your plus-one?"

"Tempting," I smile, "but no."

She sucks an olive off her sword-shaped cocktail stick.

"Should we pick up some Ray's on the way home?" she asks.

"Absolutely. And I'll tell you more about the party."

At my apartment on the Upper West Side, we sit cross-legged on the living room floor, a gigantic pizza box between us.

"At least your love life is more normal than mine," I say. "I'm dating the one guy in Manhattan who tries to *avoid* going back to his place for 'coffee' at the end of the night and just *loooves* to talk on the phone like a teenage girl. So…what's going on with Big Linc?"

Caroline blots her pizza with a paper towel. "Lincoln's living in Brooklyn but still can't seem to hold down a job. He's not happy about Joe, but I've tried to tell him it's my life, and he needs to focus on his own now."

She's defended Lincoln her whole life, even when he showed his temper at times. *He has no stability*, she'd always tell me. *He's practically feral. You don't know what it's like.*

I used to be jealous of Caroline's hold over the male species. Now I realize it can be a burden, having had a taste of male predatory behavior since leaving high school.

"No wonder you're stressed," I observe, dropping my crust in the box and picking up my second slice. "Screw the guys. If you need a break, you can stay here. Neither of them knows where I live, right? Stay as long as you want until things cool down."

"Maybe I'll take you up on that," she replies thoughtfully.

24

I'm the last *CelebLife* person left in Rome. I spend the day sleeping in, fast-walking the Spanish Steps a few times, and thinking about how the hell to get into Nino. The restaurant doesn't even have a bar I can sidle up to. I don't speak Italian—I can't simply walk in and start covertly asking the staff probing questions about celebrities. I'm going to have to creatively humiliate myself by pretending to have a reservation, or be lost, or confused, or hold a waiter at penpoint until he talks. Failure is not an option. One of the foundational principles of journalism is not taking no for an answer.

I'm sitting on my hotel-room bed when I get a text from Mallory. *Ding dong, all the celebs are gone! Celebrating at six at Vineto. You in?*

I'm in. I could use a warm-up before my undoubtedly doomed trip to Nino. I race over to the bar, eager to shake off this entire Rome assignment.

At the packed bar, which has a domed ceiling painted in imitation Michelangelo, I find Mallory regaling another journo with a tale of following J. Lo through the streets of Rome in the middle of the night. She stops mid-sentence and gives me a cheek kiss. "Why don't I recognize any of these people?" I ask her, checking out the group of mostly British journalists.

"Most of them aren't here for the celebrities," she informs me. "A British girl's been murdered. Big case."

"Terribly tragic," a voice behind me says.

I freeze. In an instant I transmogrify from Augusta Noble, international magazine reporter, to seventh-grade Augusta who's terrified of boys. I turn to face him.

"You again," I say.

His eyes are determined, and they're only for me. I feel like I'm going to throw up—in a good way. "Me again," he confirms. I can feel Mallory staring at us.

"You coming to dinner with us?" she asks him, her voice chirpier than normal.

"Not tonight," Alexander tells her. "Have a good one, gang." He takes my hand and leads me wordlessly away, out of the bar and onto the quiet side street. I couldn't have stopped him if I'd tried; I'm made of jelly.

We walk toward the Spanish Steps. "Why did you leave me in Klosters?" Alexander asks. He's trimmed his dark hair so it's not so wavy. "You broke my heart."

I try to appear cynical, but my face starts to collapse into a shameless grin. "You could've called to ask me that question ages ago. You're a half-decent reporter, I've heard." Our fingers are intertwined.

"Half-decent? I'm flattered. High praise from the American journalist."

The ominous feeling I had on my way out of the Hassler has receded. I feel safe and confident with Alexander, though I don't know why. I've never come close to having this feeling about any man, let alone one I was wildly, fall-down-like-an-eighteenth-century-heroine-with-the-vapors attracted to.

"But really," I say, possibly not hiding my hurt, "you never called."

He squeezes my hand, then lets go. "It entered my mind. Then I thought, it's her place of work," he explains. "I decided creeping up to your colleagues, asking for your number, and leaving them thinking I'm trying to get into your knickers might not bode well for you professionally."

"Aren't you?" I ask. "Trying, I mean?"

"Absolutely," he says, stopping at the base of the storied steps, looking down at me as if I'm the most beautiful woman on earth, or at least in the general area.

Oh, dear god.

The arm goes around my waist, he presses against me, and plants a firm, quick kiss. Still holding me, he asks softly, "You hungry?"

"Very," I say. He lets go. "But I'm still working. I'd invite you to have dinner with me, but *I* don't even have a reservation at this place."

"Oh? What's on for tonight?"

"Nino," I say, dejected. "I have to—"

"*Nino?*" He smiles. "Say no more. Come with me."

He takes my hand and we zip across the palazzo and down an alley. Five minutes later, Alexander stops at a heavy wooden door with no sign and knocks three times.

The door swings open. "Oh! Ciao, Signore Matten," an Italian man greets us.

"Ciao, Luca," Alexander replies, then asks him something in Italian.

The man nods and leads us into the darkened, bustling restaurant. "We have a back table for you tonight. This is good?"

"Of course," Alexander nods. "Thank you for fitting me in."

"Always for you," Luca says. "How is your father?"

"Busy and grumpy as always," Alexander says, smiling. "He says to tell you hello."

Luca nods and rushes off. Seconds later, a waiter arrives with a bottle of prosecco and pours us two glasses.

"Grazie," Alexander says, then nods subtly in my direction. "*Per favore, noi siamo vegetariani.*"

"Si, si. Bene." The man nods and hurries away.

Alexander notes my expression. "What?"

"You remembered." I can't stop smiling.

Neither can he. "How could I forget the woman who nibbled carrots and worried about the polo horses while the rest of us shoved filet mignon down our gullets?"

A server arrives with a basket of hot bread, a small jug of olive oil, and a plate of antipasti including mushrooms, tomatoes, peppers, Burrata, and eggplant. We have not been given a menu. Alexander picks up a small plate in front of him, then gestures for me to go first. I stab at a deep red tomato and a piece of asparagus, then go back for a knob of soft Burrata. Another waiter arrives with a carafe of red wine and pours us each a glass.

"Are you OK with red?" Alexander asks. "They do a set pairing with the tasting menu. Everyone gets the same menu."

"Of course," I pick up my glass. "When in Rome…"

"Ha," Alexander responds to my hilarious quip wryly, piling some vegetables on his plate.

I ask, "How come you're such a VIP here?"

"My father has a flat in the city…this is his favorite place." He pauses, clears his throat. "Mia mentioned she told you about my family. She said you seemed genuinely shocked."

I watch him, and beneath the calm I see a hint of nervousness.

I spear a piece of fried eggplant. "She would be correct," I say. "So…you're not that guy who's looking for that *one elusive woman* who loves you for *you*, and not because you're a famous Earl or whatever—are you?"

He flinches ever so slightly, and I instantly regret my blunt response to an obviously sensitive issue. Alexander picks up a piece of zucchini, then meets my eyes. "You don't know what it's like," he says, holding his fork in mid-air. "Sometimes it's hard to tell."

"Of course I know what it's like," I reply. "It's called being a woman." He pops the grilled zucchini in his mouth and listens. "Let's say, hypothetically speaking, you're a tall, young, size-four blonde with big boobs. Weeding out the guys who want to road test you from those who want to get to know you is a Sisyphean task. But it's life, and we mustn't cry for the stunning blonde."

"Who exactly are we talking about?" he asks, eyes slightly narrowed.

"Any attractive woman," I shrug. I try to lighten things up. "If it makes you feel better, I fancied you long before I knew about your pedigree. It was your hot journalist moves that got me."

Alexander throws his head back, laughs, and seems to forgive me for my outspokenness. It's the pineapple thing again. My instinct is always to defend, to stay prickly. "And hey," I add, "Prince Harry and Meghan Markle are about as happy and sickeningly in love as two people can be. She knew exactly who he was when they got together, and they're working out just fine. I guess the key is making the guy *think* you don't know."

"Meghan said during her engagement interview that she hadn't a clue about Harry when they were set up," he argues, watching me inquisitively.

"She kept a book about his *mother* on her shelf. She knew," I say.

He nods. "She knew."

A different server comes by, takes the platter, and sets truffle risotto before us. He comes back seconds later and pours us glasses of white wine.

Alexander shifts in his seat and picks up his wine glass. "Tell me, Augusta Noble, how did you get mixed up in the world of celebrities?"

It's my turn to sort-of flinch. "I could ask you the same thing," I parry. "A photo came over the transom in the office the other day. It was you… with…what's her name again? Belinda Oliver?"

He clears his throat. "We're friends," he says. "She's lovely. And I'll tell you a secret—she's a wounded soul."

"A wounded soul with legs up to here," I say wryly.

"Nah," he says seriously. "She struggles with this bloody business. Just last week she was told she's too thin for a part. But three months ago, they told her that her thighs were too thick." He shakes his head almost angrily.

Ohhhh, I'm in trouble. Even my mother, a tougher nut to crack than I am, would fall for this man. "It's a messed-up business," I agree.

The night goes on with saffron fettuccini, more crisp white wine, salad, eggplant parmigiana. We talk about nothing or everything so easily that the time is over before it begins, and there is never an awkward, what-should-we-talk-about-next moment. After thick, sweet Vin Santo and chocolate layer cake, Luca checks on us and leaves bottles of grappa and Limoncello on our table. Before I take a shot of either one, I excuse myself. "Time to work," I say.

I follow Luca, coax him into a corner, and extract some fun details from him, promising not to release his name. There are no scandalous scoops, but I learn J. Lo likes pizza and Tom's assistant ordered his dinner for him, and his crust was gluten free. When I have enough detail to prove I've done my due diligence, I head back to the table.

Alexander has poured us each a finger of grappa and knocks his back. I have to fight not to spit mine out because it goes down like gasoline.

"I'm staying at my father's flat," he says. "You're welcome to come by for a night cap."

I don't hesitate.

His father's "flat" is more like an ornate Italian palace with ceilings up to the sky and a living room bigger than my entire place in London. Alexander, who also has an article due tonight about the murder he's here to cover, sets me up at a desk so I can get my story in. We write on our respective laptops at opposite ends of the room, his iPod softly playing the Beatles.

"Done!" I shout two hours later with an exhausted, muted glee. I swivel in my seat as he closes his laptop. "You done, too?"

"Nope," he says, then rises from his chair, strides over to me, and takes my hand. I stand, my heart pounding and my breath short. He takes me to his room, and I let this almost perfect night wash over me. I push every negative thought, every dark memory, every nagging voice away, and let in the light.

You deserve this. Enjoy it. Be happy.

In the middle of the night, as I'm reaching for a glass of water, he wakes. I drink, put the glass down, then lie back on my pillow and watch him unlocking his phone. "I'm not missing out again," he says in a sleepy, husky voice. "I want your phone number. *Now.*"

I lay back and recite the digits. Then he reaches for me, kisses me, and we do it again.

25

I'm running early. So is the guy striding alongside me looking lost. I stop outside the venue, which has two tinted-glass doors and no one outside to check me in. The guy watches me, then walks up to the door. He's got L.A. written all over him: He's fit, blonde, and looks like he should have a surfboard tucked under his arm.

"You going to the premiere party?" I smile.

"*Yes*. Is this it?" He shakes his head. "Man, New York is a zoo. I mean, it's cool and everything, but get me back to the sunshine. Get me back to my *car*, right?"

"I haven't owned a car in two years," I tell him. "It's incredibly freeing."

He pulls open the door for me and I step in. A suited man with a clipboard stops me with a gigantic, toothy smile.

"Augusta Noble," I say. "*Newstime* magazine."

"*Wonderful*," he says as if he's been waiting for me his whole life. "Have a great night!"

I stop inside the doorway to check out the scene, then do a casual half-turn and throw a look back at the guy.

"Oh! Mr. Snow. Welcome," Clipboard Guy enthuses. "You're in the VIP area, and when Mr. McGraw comes, you'll have your own server and bottle service."

Mr. Snow? It sounds like a made-up moniker for someone on the lam.

"Great," Mr. Snow says, then, "Hey," as he passes me. "See you around?"

"Yes," I nod, and set off to find the bar. There's no line yet, and I quickly discover they have a signature cocktail involving ginger, which I don't like, and vodka, which I do like. I order a cosmo and start working the party. It's sparsely populated. I hang by the door until I see Caroline, whose sense of style has always been the opposite of mine. Tonight she's wearing a distressed jean skirt with a shimmery grey tank top and gladiator sandals, and it simply *works*. Her hair is cut short in the back these days, with a light-brown and blonde-highlighted swoop in the front.

I hug her when she walks in. "Come on. I'll take you to the bar and we can check out the scene."

She nods and follows me.

"Hey! Blondie! Remember me?" Mr. Snow is leaning over the velvet rope cordoning off the raised VIP section.

"Of course," I say. "Lost Guy."

"Why don't you and your friend come up here?" He gestures to the soft, velvety sofas. "There's plenty of room."

I elbow Caroline. *VIP with bottle service*, I mouth.

She nods.

Mr. Snow has a word with the security guy, who unhooks the rope and lets us in. He's sitting with a few pals who completely ignore us. A server is on us immediately, though, and Caroline orders the ginger thing while I go for another cosmo.

"Tell me," Mr. Snow says, leaning in toward us. "What are your names and what brings you out tonight?"

His eyes light up when he hears I work for a national magazine. "Well," he says, "I'm Jim Snow. I'm a director."

"Oh?" I say. He's kind of cute, gives good eye contact, and is taller than I am, even in heels. "What's your latest movie?"

"*Millennial Blues*. The actor starring in this movie we're here to party for tonight is doing mine next. The minute promotion for this film ends, we start shooting in New Mexico."

Our drinks come, and Jim's friends start talking to him. I elbow Caroline, who's been too quiet.

"Everything OK?" I ask.

She nods. "I'm tired, that's all. I'll perk up. I see some food over there—come with?"

We mosey over to the VIP spread, and she picks at some stuffed mushroom caps and a couple of crab cakes. I don't want to eat, lest I risk bad breath and gook in my teeth. As we walk back from the buffet, I see a few models have joined Jim's posse. Two, to be exact. I give them the evil eye from a distance.

"I don't sleep with actresses," Jim is saying. "Unless they have *really* great tits." This cracks him and the girls up. Caroline doesn't smile.

"I'm liking the bottle service, but the guy seems like a douche," she says out of the corner of her mouth. "What do we need him for? The drinks are free."

"He's cute," I say. "And a soon-to-be-famous. You're the one who told me to get rid of Mike the Asexual Bond Trader. Here's me, moving on."

Annnd here comes the sigh. Caroline knits her brow and gives me one of her intense looks.

"After all this time, you still don't get it," she says. "There are a ton of nice guys out there who'll love you for your beauty *and* your brains. When will you realize how gorgeous you are?"

She's the one who doesn't get it. "It's quite possible," I tell her, saying it out loud for the first time in my life, "there is no one for me. I've accepted it. I go for whoever I like at the time."

Her face darkens, her body tenses, her glass shakes. "Shit," Caroline says through gritted teeth. "He's here."

"Who?"

Caroline doesn't answer me. "How did he get in? How did he know where I'd be?"

I glance over at the bar the commoners have to use. How did he get in, indeed? It's Lincoln, wearing the saggy, Army-green fatigues, the fashionably-yet-completely-real distressed black tee shirt with a tear in the shoulder, and the glowering frown. He's accessorized with muscles, hair shaved so short he's almost bald, and an art gallery of tattoos. Oh…*that's* how he got in. I could be describing Tyson Beckford, who would be let in easily, list or no list.

"Lincoln is one of your best friends," I say lamely. I know something's up, but she hasn't let me in on what it is. "What's wrong, Caro?"

Caroline looks exhausted and near tears. "He is. He was…he always has been. I still love him like a brother. He's always been there for me."

"So why are you so upset?" I ask gently. "What is it you're not telling me?"

"I know, I know. I don't blame you for being confused," she says. She clears her throat, stands up straight, seems to make a decision. "It's complicated. Lincoln's upset because he doesn't like Joe. He says Joe is bad for me—that he's 'not a good guy.'"

"Right, OK…" I cross my arms. "He also didn't like the last guy. Or the one before that."

"I know. I'll go talk to him."

"Don't. Let me find the rep and have him escorted out. He hasn't seen you yet. We can do this peacefully."

I leave Caroline on a sofa while I go find my clipboard-wielding contact.

"*That* guy?" the rep says, squinting to try to see Lincoln in the gloom far away. "I thought that was Tyson Beckford."

"Not Tyson Beckford."

"Gotcha. I'll check him out. Not to worry."

I head back and find Caroline on her second drink. We stand, sip, listen to the music. Caroline can't relax. A few minutes go by and the rep finds us.

"Your problem," clipboard man says, smiling proudly, "is solved. It was nothing—he left without issue."

"See?" I smile at Caroline. "All good."

We spend some more time in the VIP area, and Jim leaves the models once in a while to come hang out with us.

"Jim's not so bad," I tell Caroline when we're alone on a loveseat. "He has a suite at the Mandarin Oriental. There's talk of continuing the party over there."

She checks him out, trying to see what I see.

"I don't like him," Caroline says finally. "He winked at me earlier. It was creepy."

I close my eyes for a moment, but the patience I'm hoping for doesn't come. "You know," I say sharply, "I'm aware that every guy prefers you to me, OK? Just one time, can *I* be the one? He's got a flock of models circling him— but for some reason he's into *me*."

Her face crumples. I've hurt her. I'm sorry for that, but I'm hurt, too. She really has no idea. I am not someone who indulges in one-night stands. My usual M.O. is to keep things PG-13 unless I'm semi-seriously dating the guy. Tonight, I want to do what normal twenty-nine-year-olds do.

"I'm gonna take off," she says abruptly.

"Wait," I plead. "Don't go yet. Are you OK?"

"I'm fine. I need to sleep. You have fun, though." She gets up off the sofa.

"OK," I nod. "Promise me you'll cab it home, though? It's late."

"I'll cab it," she agrees wearily.

"Save the receipt—I can expense it." I pause, take a look at her. "Are you *sure* you're OK?"

"Are you sure *you* are?"

She turns and leaves, and I let her.

It's so late when we get back to Jim's hotel I barely get a glimpse of the big suite he bragged about earlier. He doesn't try to woo me with Champagne or pharmaceuticals. He kisses me as soon as we get close to the bed, pushes me back, and we roll around for a few minutes. He stops inexplicably and lays back, stares at the ceiling. I do the same. Then he sits up, twists toward the nightstand, and takes a sip of bottled water. The blinds are open and our view is of the moon.

The director turns back, hovers over me. "Do you want me to fuck you?"

What? This is what we women call a turnoff. Is he looking for consent, or for me to beg, or what? It's a mood-killer, but for lack of anything else to do, I say nothing, and after a while he does, and I let him.

Five minutes into it he says, inexplicably, "My last girlfriend looked like a young Cindy Crawford." Then he says it again, and thirty seconds later it's over. He passes out instantly. This is why I avoid one-night stands. I head to the bathroom and sit on the toilet. I text Caroline. *You get home OK?*

I'm so tired I'm about to pass out myself. I pad back to bed and fall asleep before I get an answer.

26

#48

I push the office door open slowly, but it creaks loudly. "You're late." Stanley is grouchy.

"You only called me an hour ago. I got here as fast as I could." I smile apologetically at the rest of the crew.

He gestures at the one empty chair in front of his desk. Everyone's here but Poppy, who's out in the pod going through the morning papers.

"Have a seat. You know our annual World's Hottest Human issue?" Stanley asks me.

"Of course," I reply. It breaks the Internet whenever it comes out, with half the population vehemently disagreeing with the choice of cover subject and the other half swooning over him/her/them. "Who's on the cover?"

"Ha," Barton says.

"What do you mean, 'ha'?" I ask.

Stanley takes over. "Seriously, Augusta? *We* don't even know who's on the cover until it comes out." He says it like I've just asked him to point out Atlantis on a map. "OK, maybe *I* know a week or so before, but not this early."

I force myself not to roll my eyes. "We're not talking about the cure for cancer," I point out. "It's a big, fat airbrushed face of whoever's desperate enough to pay for the cover."

"No, no, *no*," the boss shakes his head. "Our fearless leader Jack Barclay makes the final decision, and all he cares about is who will sell. If old Fish Sticks called him right now and promised him a shopping spree at GOOP plus access to her private diary, a look at her jade vagina eggs, and his own room in her house, it wouldn't matter."

I remind myself to Yammer "Fish Sticks." Never heard that nickname for Gwyneth before. Must be a British thing. Barton adds, "Lassie, only the desperate ones *ask* for the cover."

"Moving on," Stanley says. "This year's assignments are in."

He reads out Barton's, which will take him to Paris, London, and tentatively Cardiff. Gillian has four very glamorous ones, including Kit Harrington and Pierce Brosnan.

"Augusta," Stanley turns to me, "you've got two. Sting and Roger Federer." He doesn't ask; he tells. "Sting by phone Thursday, Roger in Switzerland next week. Let's have you work in the office for the next few days."

Barton asks, "Boss, anything new on the layoff rumors?"

I start to feel panicky. "Layoffs?"

"There's talk of it," Gillian says tightly, "even though we have the smallest staff by far. We can't spare anyone."

"Hey," Stanley interjects sharply. "There's been no direct mention of London. Let's think positive."

"Tell that to Uvula," Gillian pipes up.

"Who *is* this Uvula person I keep hearing about?" I finally ask.

"Legend has it," Robbie tells me in hushed, ghost-story tones, "if she looks you in the eye for more than three seconds, you'll be fired within the month."

Barton adds, "In New York, they say if you walk by her office and say 'Hi,' she'll look up at you and just stare. Like this." He does a zombie-like glare.

"She's a CelebLife Corp. stalwart," Stanley chimes in dutifully. She was second in command when Princess Diana got married—and when she died. Liz Taylor used to call her at home. She has an office in every bureau and she's not that bad."

"She sounds that bad," I say.

"Meeting dismissed," says Stanley. "Except you, Augusta."

My colleagues raise their eyebrows as they file out and I dutifully remain in my chair. When we're alone, Stanley says, "Well, it finally happened—we're breaking the coke-snorting action star story with a *huge* cover this week. We've got exclusive confirmation he's checking into rehab. And that," he says pointing right at me, "is largely thanks to you." He grins. "This was an L.A. story because he actor is based there, but London was the linchpin that allowed us to nail it down. So—congratulations."

I nod, relieved to be the hero of this tale when Ivan Deaver was so eager to take me down.

"What's the story, exactly?" I ask. Something's not making sense—including that nobody has asked me for a detailed description of what I saw in Dublin.

"The action star is giving us an exclusive quote and copping to 'substance abuse issues.' We get the scoop about rehab, and Deaver gets to shield his client from the ugly stain of hardcore street drugs. It's win-win," Stanley says, glowing with pride.

I think about that for a moment, and can't hide my distaste. "But we *have* the details. The full story—why protect an *actor*? Why not tell the truth?" *Like real journalists.*

Stanley shakes his head. "*CelebLife* is all about negotiation, Augusta. Jack Barclay worked directly with Ivan on this one—it's how we keep our access. It's a great cover, OK? Enjoy it!" He scoots his chair closer to his desk. "Speaking of which, since you're not on staff, they're not going to give you a bonus or a byline. You know how it goes at this place. But I'll tell you what, whatever day you don't work this week, bill an extra full day."

I sigh inwardly. It's better than nothing. "Thanks," I say, mustering a smile. "But what about Ivan Deaver? He's not going to come after me, is he?"

"Nah," Stanley shakes his head. "He doesn't know anything about you. We told him we had an *L.A.*-based sighting of his client snorting coke. He didn't even question it. You're safe."

I'm not so sure, but I nod, thank him, and leave with mixed feelings about how the head office is handling my "scoop"—and me. Back at my desk, I conduct an Internet search for Jack Barclay that brings up rows of photos of his grinning, dopey face. Jack is *CelebLife*'s flagship editor, and judging by how many available images there are of him, he's busier building his own brand than editing the magazine. His TV show on CelebLife.com, *Jack Talk*, verges on embarrassing. Watching a greying white man overestimate his own coolness while trying to interview Nicki Minaj is an exercise in full-body cringing. Next, I check out Uvula Garsh. She's got a wild gray wedge haircut parted in the middle, a pinched mouth, a bulbous nose, and dead eyes. She's clearly trying to smile, but the effect is more like a bad case of indigestion. I quickly click away.

Time to study up on my rock star and memorize the questions Stanley sent me.

Two days later, I lock myself in one of the free offices and calm myself before my Sting interview. I stare at the phone until it rings, right on time. The panel reads *private number*. Dammit. I go to answer and instantly panic; what do I call him? *Shit, shit, shit*. I can't call a grown man Sting. I just can't. I go with, "Hello! This is Augusta Noble."

"Hello," comes a husky, languid voice. "This is Sting."

The pleasantries are fairly standard, and I manage to choke out my side of things, though his voice is thick and low; he doesn't sound like he's *trying* to be suggestive. He just is.

"I'm drinking tea by the fire," he responds to my warm-up question. "What are *you* doing, Augusta?"

I take a look around. I think about telling the truth: *I'm in an office that used to belong to a hoarder who got fired and it smells of mildew from the stacks of rotting papers crammed in it.*

"I'm at work," I say instead, trying to adopt an adorable cutesy-voice but suspecting I've channeled Minnie Mouse. "In my office."

I ask him a bunch of the hot-man questions on my list, and every reply is in that same sexy British voice. I'm getting warm and could use a fan in here. My no-swooning policy is slipping badly.

"Back in the days when you were single, what were some of the pickup lines you used?"

He takes a moment, then tells me he used to have a great opening line about needing change for a ten-pound note. I figure he has a sense of humor, so I take a risk: "That's not the most seductive line I've ever heard. I mean, did it really…?"

"It works," he assures me. "It's all in the way you approach it."

I check the clock. *Uh oh;* we have three minutes left. "How are you doing on time?" I ask.

"I'm doing OK," Mr. Sting replies. "I think talking is an aphrodisiac, don't you, Augusta?"

I assume the query was rhetorical and reluctantly let it go, because every response that comes to mind is entirely inappropriate and would likely get me into trouble. I glance at my sheet. Here I am, trying to stay professional, and every single question is about sex, love, or romance. I choose one of the less racy ones. "What attracts you to a woman? What do you look for?"

He thinks for a moment then replies slowly, "I'm attracted to people who speak well. Camilla Parker Bowles is one—I sat next to her at an event once and she's absolutely lovely."

Thank you, Mr. Sting. I got some great quotes, and he made it fun, too. When we say our goodbyes and I hang up, I pick up a piece of paper and fold it into a fan. I need a minute before I can start writing up a story.

27

Film director Jim Snow, who's currently snoring like a rusted muffler, is not going to call me. I know this because during the night when I got up to use the bathroom, he rolled over and mumbled, "You're still here?"

Oh, how Caroline is going to laugh when she finds out how right she was about this guy.

I look at my phone: seven-thirty. I slip out of bed and head to the bathroom. Today is a bitch of a workday, actually, because I have an article due *and* I'm supposed to help Greta the senior writer research her big cover, which means I do the grunt work and she does the writing and gets the credit.

I sit on the toilet and check my texts. Still nothing from Caroline. It's Thursday, so she could be on her way to work, or maybe still asleep. But still…I want to be sure, so I call her. It rings and rings. If she were in the subway or out of power, it'd go straight to voicemail. I have a bad feeling, a nausea beyond the acid gurgling in my stomach from too many citrusy cocktails. I tell myself she is pointedly ignoring me to teach me a lesson. I type out one more text: *I'm worried. I'm coming over if you don't respond within five minutes. I know you don't want that (wink face).*

I get dressed and gather my things. This is the reason Caro and I exchanged keys the first month we both moved here—for times like these, when nothing is wrong, but we need to check up on each other anyway because if we don't, who will?

I call Caroline again on the walk from the 86th Street stop. It rings a bunch of times before cutting off. When I get to her building on East 90th, I fumble with the keys. I'm running through where she could be: not work, definitely not the gym. I race up to the fifth floor, my lungs stinging.

There is nothing wrong. You're being ridiculous.

There are only two other doors on her floor. The silence scares me. I knock on 5F, the sound echoing in the hallway. I bang harder. I put my ear to the door. Nothing.

I find the key and shake as I insert and turn it, then I tackle the sticky deadbolt. It takes a full minute of jiggling and two hands to slip it out of its bay.

I push open the door. Caroline's tiny living room is decorated to feel like a calming retreat: There's a ceramic Buddha on the mantle, a bamboo area rug, a faux-jade lamp, non-toxic cream candles. I scan the room. I'm a reporter; I observe for a living. Something is off, something is not right, but I cannot pin down what it is. There's a leftover wine glass on the coffee table with a splash of red pooled in the bottom—one glass, not two. The shoes in front of the sofa are the gladiator sandals she was wearing last night, the many straps unhooked and set free like little snakes. I move toward the bedroom and stop in the doorway, my eye going straight to Caroline's rosewood room divider. On the rice-paper panels there are dark markings, like something out of a horror movie, jagged slashes of what appear to be bloody letters. *L T I...*

No.... No. The letters are L I N C.

I step into the room, my hand fumbling for my phone, desperate to dial 911.

28

#49

While I'm waiting for Roger Federer to enter my corner penthouse hotel suite in Zurich to talk about sex and hotness, I'm thinking about Alexander—who then texts me right on cue: *Hello, beautiful. I'll be gone for a week with spotty reception. Don't forget about me. I want to see you as soon as I get back. I'm going to a dreadful party the day I land. Meet me. It'll be full of pointless inbred aristos but we can head over to Groucho if it gets too dire.*

Of *course* he belongs to the Groucho Club, one of London's most elite private venues for Fleet Street's top talent. I consider waiting until after the interview to text him back, but I suck at games *and* I'm over them. *Sounds glamorous,* I type. *Send me the time and place.* I consider some snappy jokes or racy innuendo, but think better of it.

I check the time; Roger's due any minute for my first big sit-down for *CelebLife*. There's a knock, so I spit my gum into a napkin, smile, and throw open the ultra-wide wooden door. I am both surprised and annoyed to see Roger's blonde wife standing beside him, looking past me into the room, which is packed with camera equipment and racks of clothes. Mirka—the wife—traipses in ahead of Roger, and my hopes for an intimate, open interview die a silent death. Mirka has a wavy, shoulder-length cut and young-looking skin. She is as naturally calm as I am high-strung, and moves and talks slowly.

Roger strides in behind her, and casts a heavy lidded glance at me. "Nice to meet you, Augusta."

I decide right then I'd like to work full time, permanently, on our World's Hottest Human issue. I'm not the only beneficiary of his politesse. Roger makes sure to greet every person in the room: makeup, stylist, photographer's assistant, and finally the photographer. *Smile, hello, handshake, nod, smile, hello, handshake, nod.* Roger moves like an athlete even off the court, i.e., more beautifully than the rest of us. He's long and lean and solid as a wall.

I show the happy couple to the spread I ordered up, which includes a silver service of tea, coffee, and juice, plus pastries, eggs, and toast. Mirka waves her hand in the air and drawls with a light Swiss German accent, "I'm sorry, but I *neeeed* my *cappucciiino.*"

I dutifully go to the phone and order her one posthaste, then turn back to find the couple hovering over the table where the interview will happen.

Mirka has my pink book in her hands. "What's this?"

My instinct is to lunge and tackle her to the ground to get it. I resist, grit my teeth, and walk slowly over. No sudden moves. "Oh, that's just an old keepsake," I say, panicking inside. "Something from my mother. I carry it so it feels like she's with me…God rest her soul." I half smile mournfully. *I'm going to hell.* I cross my fingers behind my back to try to keep my mother alive.

"It's pretty," Mirka says, rubbing the cover with her palm.

Dear God, I will never, ever, ever lie again if you please just make her drop the book. Please.

I draw closer to Mirka, then sit at the small table. Slowly, slowly, she lowers the book to the table and takes a

178

seat. I grab it and put it in my purse, which I then place in my lap. I am breathing heavily, and to cover it up I turn away and pretend to cough.

Roger speaks carefully and softly about hotness. I start to get used to Mirka hanging around. They talk about their first kiss—at the Sydney Olympics—and I can just picture two awkward kids fumbling around between tennis matches.

"When you burst onto the scene, you were a brat with a ponytail. What marked the turnaround for you—family, coaches, friends?"

"It's myself," he says, his eyes boring into mine. "Everybody told me I have to relax. But it was up to me to understand, to be able to make the change—and as long as I didn't get it, I wouldn't do it."

He sounds like Jemima Noble with her whole, *The answers are inside you, Augusta.* I hate when she's right.

"I think the important thing is I have both good and bad inside of myself," he goes on. "I accept both, and I try to make the right choice. It's not always the easy thing, but sometimes the right thing isn't the easy thing."

Roger's words hit me like one of his serves. *That* is where I have fallen down. I have not accepted the bad shots. I can't. Subconsciously or unconsciously, I am obsessed with stopping what happened. I'm living as if it's possible to go back in time if I will it hard enough.

To end the interview, I ask what he likes in a woman. He gives me a smoldering look.

"Nice curves," he replies.

Well played, Rog. I grin back at him and decide not to worry so much about having a little fun with these celebrities. That's what this game is about; the very purpose of this issue is to sell sex and romance. If I interview my subjects like a robot, the interviews will unfold accordingly. I decide I can sneak one final question in: "With your level of talent and fame, how do you stay grounded?" Translation: *Why are some celebrities dicks and you're so cool?*

"Well," he replies. "Someone once told me, 'It's nice to be important, but it's more important to be nice.' That's how I try to be all the time."

Pretty simple. He should teach spirituality and/or etiquette lessons in Hollywood. Roger gets a stellar 9.8. He's a gentleman who understands better than most the effect his fame has on people. Or perhaps others understand it fine, but Roger *cares* more about wielding the responsibility that comes with it. In the end, meeting Mirka served a purpose as well. It gave me a goal to aspire to: I hope someday to feel the kind of innate confidence that radiates the way hers does.

I write in my book the words Roger said about dealing with discomfort and pain, and what sticks out most to me is, *Sometimes the right thing isn't the easy thing.* I add, *Remember what the therapist said: You're uncomfortable. There is pain. Learn to sit with it. You are imperfect…and that's OK.*

As they leave, Mirka touches my arm and says, "I'm sorry about your mother, by the way."

I can only nod and wince. *Definitely going to hell.*

29

The day after I return from Zurich, Stanley walks into the office and strides past me without a word. Robbie is tense and barely looks at me as he rushes to his desk and logs on. Gillian and Barton are in their offices early, hunched over their computers.

At noon, there's a flurry of activity as Stanley tromps down the hall toward the pod. The elevator dings. Robbie says out of the corner of his mouth, "Big editors in town—Uvula Garsh and Jack Barclay's number-two guy, Darren Vagnesse. A last-minute thing. We have to act normal—you know, tidy, hard-working, polite—for one day."

Now that he's mentioned it, I see the pod has been neatened up, a week's worth of newspapers arranged in clean stacks, pens and pencils all in their rightful holders.

Stanley breaks into a welcoming grin as the two VIPs step off the elevator. I recognize both from my Internet research, though Uvula is even more sour looking in person and suffers from an awful case of resting bitch face.

"Long time no see. Welcome," Stanley says, leaning in for an air kiss with Uvula followed by a man-shake with Darren—a wiry, bowlegged man with slicked-back white hair. "Anything you need, let us know. Robbie will set you up for the day."

"No need," I hear Darren say. "Let's go straight to your office, Stanley."

They walk from the elevators to the hallway without so much as a look in our direction. Robbie has gone pale. Two long, tense minutes later, Robbie's mobile phone beeps and when he glances at it, he appears confused. He frantically beckons me to his desk and I rush over, crouching next to him. He puts the phone on speaker. Stanley's voice, thin and tinny, comes through.

"Darren, come on. This isn't right. You have to let me tell my own staff. Let me talk to them."

"That's not going to happen, Stanley."

"But…why shut down the whole bureau? We have enough work to keep us all busy and then some. We've produced the biggest covers of the year so far—"

I put my hand over my mouth in a reflexive self-soothing move, and Robbie's breath comes faster, harder, into the hyperventilation danger zone. This can't be happening. Magazines don't simply *shut down* a prolific, overworked news bureau out of the blue. *No, no, no.* Not when I was just getting my shit together.

"A lot of things are changing," Darren is saying coolly. "We have a new plan in place for Europe. It'll be an adjustment, but we'll be fully able to handle the load out of New York. That's what the European stringers are for, right?"

The smug, casual way he says *We'll be fully able* and *That's what stringers are for* makes me want to run down the hall and punch Darren Vagnesse in his phony-ass face. My stomach is in knots. I am overwhelmed with emotion, but I am acutely aware that this isn't my catastrophe; it belongs to the people here who've toiled for years to feed the celebrity beast that never sleeps. Robbie is rubbing his eyes, closing them, blinking, possibly trying not to cry. Stanley has been his mentor since Robbie dropped out of college to take care of his sick mum.

"What about keeping people on a contract basis?" Stanley is asking. "Giving them a chance?" His voice is growing higher pitched and more volatile. Uvula answers this one.

"You will all get a non-negotiable redundancy package, contingent upon each of you keeping calm and allowing us to do our job today. You and your people will stay in your offices until advised by security to leave, at which point you will file out calmly, with only your personal belongings. We thank you all for your years of service to *CelebLife*."

"What did we do wrong? What did *I* do…why didn't I get a warning?"

"You know, Stanley," Uvula says with a sinister inflection in her voice, "I would've thought after so long with us, you'd be more supportive of the cost-cutting measures we're required to make to keep *CelebLife* going. It's an institution, bigger than any one of us—or any one bureau."

The phone goes dead. Whatever Stanley is going to say next, he doesn't want us to hear. Robbie dashes away to warn Gillian and Barton. Poppy…*oh, Poppy*. She never came back from lunch. We gather up our things as quietly as we can, and I see Robbie grabbing binders and notebooks containing bureau secrets, shoving them into his backpack. Clever boy.

It happens fast. In a matter of minutes, a two-person elimination squad cuts a swath through the London bureau, slaying its inhabitants with a series of swift, merciless strokes. Each of the condemned cries out in pain, first a sharp yelp from Gillian, then a *No!* from Barton and a suggestion that Darren shove his layoffs up his bony arse, and then, finally, silence. They have no choice but to sit frozen in fear and take the blows. I dash to our closet-sized "library" to give Robbie his privacy as Darren and Uvula march down the hall in our direction.

That I can't be fired has already given me a bad case of survivor's guilt. I can stop being paid, but they can't fire someone they never thought worthy of hiring in the first place. When I can no longer hear voices, I emerge. Robbie looks shell-shocked but alive. Darren is surveying the area like a vulture, picking at magazines and papers, clearly mulling if he should be taking anything.

Darren side-eyes me and says, "You shouldn't have been here today," he says. "I'm sorry you were."

I can't tell if he is sorry for me, or for himself that an outsider witnessed the slaughter. He starts to head back to his loaner office, now with three security guards in tow, but turns back.

"You're welcome to send your resume in to New York," he tells me. "We'll be needing more stringers in London than ever—there's plenty of opportunity for good people."

"*Wanker,*" Robbie says under his breath, but he can't do more without risking his payoff. As Darren walks off, I give him the finger with both hands, jabbing angrily up to the skies, and Robbie rewards me with a weak smile.

There is no frantic texting among us, or confusion about what to do next. There is only one thing *to* do.

30

"The pub is the best treatment for this kind of shock," Robbie assures us.

"Did you know?" Barton asks Stanley, who's staring into his glass as if it's an oracle.

"I never imagined anything like this," he replies quietly. "I mean…when Chicago was shut down last year, and there's been talk about Miami, I couldn't think we were untouchable…but *this*?"

"We're all of Europe, though…how can they cover an entire continent without us?" Robbie says, but neither Stanley nor anybody else feels the need to answer. Poppy, who is slight and not a big drinker, is downing vodka cranberries like they're going out of style. She shakes as she tells us about coming back into the building with her tuna sandwich, at which point a security guard beckoned her over, demanded her pass, and ordered her to leave the premises. "I knew you'd all come to the Hog," she finishes.

"At least it's not cancer," Barton blurts.

"That's great, Barton," Gillian says. "I have a toddler at home. I'm the breadwinner. I'm absolutely fucked."

"I don't have a university degree," Robbie slurs. I think the shock has decimated him. That, or he's done some secret tequila shots.

"Life will go on, and so will *CelebLife*. It'll be fine. We all will."

Gillian, who has been crying, croaks, "Did they say why? Why they did this to us?"

Stanley gazes out the window. "Print is dying," he says. "That's the reality."

"*Our* bloody print revenue supports the entire company, and our readership is near forty million," Barton fumes. When he's drunk and upset, I can barely translate his heavy Scottish accent.

He's right, though. So is Stanley. It's only hitting me now that it's *really over*. For a few moments, it felt as if we were doing a bit of day drinking after a hard week, that we were just letting off steam and would be back at our desks tomorrow.

"Not anymore," Stanley argues. "It's shriveling up. Ads are way down. Content is king—but quality isn't."

Barton sighs. "They want the young ones now. Pay them pennies, get illiterate rubbish with no context or nuance. Fucking *listicles*." He glances at Robbie and Poppy. "No offense."

"Fucking listicles," I say, raising my crisp pint of Strongbow and Black.

"Fucking listicles!" everyone shouts, lifting their own glasses, and, having a laugh, which releases some of the tension. But my anxiety seems to bloom with the stimulation. Suddenly, I can't breathe. I grasp my drink hard. My chest feels like a piano is sitting on it.

Poppy elbows me, leans in, whispers, "Augusta? You OK?"

I nod and slip out of my chair, stride to the bathroom, pray it's open. I push the door and it gives way. I lock it behind me.

Learn how to handle your shit. Breathe. But I can't— that's the whole problem. It's a bullshit instruction, to breathe when your lungs are closed up, when your airway is constricted. It feels like someone is stepping on mine like a garden hose. There's a hard knock on the door, which I ignore. Next person says *breathe* to me is getting a smack to the face. After a couple of minutes trying to get a grip on myself, I manage to calm down. I exhale in a long, loud *whoosh*, then return to the table. Stanley takes care of two more rounds, but no one gets too drunk or loud. Gillian drains her shandy and says, "Well, I'd better get home and face the music."

"I have to go get pissed with my mates," Robbie adds. "Poppy, want to come along? One more for old time's sake?"

She nods, and starts to cry. "I love you all," she says, making eye contact with each one of us. "It's been an honor."

Gillian can't help but smile at the overwrought American intern, and even gives her a bony hug. "Sweetheart, you'll be fine. You go get 'em, OK? I expect to see your name *everywhere* in future." More tears, more hugs.

Barton offers one last melancholy smile. "Well, I'd better be off, too. Must break the news to Neville that his dreams of a detached house in Surrey just got further away. *C'est la vie.*"

I hug them all, too, promise to stay in touch, and on the way out Barton says, "I expect I'll see your byline in the magazine again. No reason for you to be cast out with the rest of us."

I shrug, shake my head, but I realize it is technically possible, if not utterly disloyal.

Stanley says nothing. His ex-wife and two kids are in New York, and I get the sense he has few good friends in London, largely because of his workaholic ways. The gang files out all at once, leaving behind foamy pint glasses, the last vestiges of their time at the Hog & Leaf, a place I fear we'll never visit again. I stay with Stanley and he insists on getting another round.

"Listen," he says as he sets my drink of the day in front of me. "*CelebLife* in London was decimated today, but L.A isn't going anywhere. There is work there, Augusta. I know the bureau chief…we started out in New York together thirteen years ago."

I shake my head. It feels like a copout, a betrayal. Like I'm running around the world to escape something, like I should eject myself from *CelebLife* in solidarity. I don't know how I can go from New York to London to Los Angeles and still have no home, no close friends around me, no real job, no health insurance.

"I thought L.A. and New York had too many freelancers as it is," I point out. "Do you think they'd really have enough work for me to survive?"

"They might," he says, "when I remind them you were responsible for the A-List Action Star drugs scoop. Without you, we'd be trailing behind that awful Nightcrawler Web site. I'll talk to the bureau chief out there—Maguire Carnaby is an old friend. You'd do a tryout and go from there."

Seriously? What does a journalist have to do to become immune to *the tryout*? What can the fluffy Los Angeles group throw me that I haven't already tackled? It's annoying, but it's possibly my only option. I am humbled by Stanley's grace in the face of the company's brutal betrayal. This man gave up his family, a social life, and normal blood pressure levels to keep readers entertained, only for the soulless corporate machine to sever him from his lifeblood, then perform only the most basic first aid as he lay dying. Yet in his last act, he focuses on making sure his team is taken care of.

"Go to L.A.," he says. "They could use some Augusta Noble out there."

I'm going to miss this guy. My eyes well up.

"Don't…"

"OK, Stanley," I say, blinking, beating back the sadness. I wasn't here long, but I'm mourning the loss of what I'd built up in my mind. London will never get old, never turn sour. "Maybe I'll give it a go." I clear my throat. "And thank you. For everything."

He nods. "And to you," he says. He drains his drink, which is two-thirds full.

"Are you going to be OK?" I ask dumbly as he glugs away. I've had enough and I think it's time to go.

"I'm always OK," he says.

Stanley is not a hugger, so I briefly squeeze his shoulder as I prepare to leave.

"We'll talk soon, yes?"

He nods. "You know…" he says as I walk toward the door.

I stop, turn, recall this moment in reverse that first day we met for British Mexican food.

"Thirteen years…a quarter of my life…and they never even said they were sorry."

I have to get out of there. It's too much. I smile through tears and bid him farewell.

31

LINC. The jagged scarlet letters are something out of a horror movie. My finger is on the *9* on my phone as I step into Caroline's bedroom. I can now hear water running; it's pelting the shower curtain in her tiny *en suite* bathroom. Then I see her: Caroline is on her bed, partially blocked by the rice-paper screen. It takes my mind a moment to reconcile what I'm seeing: Her head, covered in blood, the pillow with a ring of red around her, her face so covered in crimson I'm not sure if she has a face anymore. My heart feels like it's going to explode. I'm trying to get my phone to lie still in my hand, but it jumps and falls onto the floor. I am blind with panic.

"*Augusta*," a man calls. I scream, loud and long. It takes me a second to realize it's Joe Lannells emerging from the bathroom like a sinewy wraith in white boxers and a T-shirt stained with blood. "Hey, it's just me, OK? Thank *god* you're here."

His eyes are wide. He speaks in a stage whisper. "It's Lincoln." He points to the bathroom. "Caroline managed to call me without him knowing. Thank *god*." He is shaky, manic. "I came over right away." He holds up Caroline's phone with its jade-green cover.

"Is she dead?" I scream, inching over to Caroline, lying cold and silent and still. I turn away and throw up bile on her carpet.

Joe is across the bed from me now, standing over it.

"Why are you undressed? Why are you covered in blood? Why isn't the ambulance here? Is there a pulse?" I'm

190

terrified and sick all at once, and incapable of understanding what I'm seeing.

Joe makes a *slow down, calm down* motion with his hands. "Hey, hey…I've done everything I can. Of course I called 911 immediately. Caroline's still breathing—I think—and emergency services should be here any minute. The important thing is that Lincoln can't hurt her anymore."

"*No,*" I cry. "The important thing is that my best friend is dying here. I have to *do* something!"

Caroline is tucked under a blanket, arms by her sides, eyes closed, still as a corpse.

Joe closes his eyes for a moment, then kneels next to her. With his right hand he gently touches her forehead, then strokes her hair.

"Wait—Lincoln—you're saying *Lincoln* did this?" Through the sound of blood roaring in my ears, I hear something coming from the bathroom—some sort of grunting and thumping. The shower has been turned off.

"That's what I've been trying to tell you," Joe says in a quieter voice now. "I came in and found him stabbing her. I managed to overpower him and tie him up with some of Caroline's stockings. That's why I'm so bloody. That's why I took my clothes off."

In his wife-beater, I can see for the first time how cut he is, not bulky but muscular. Maybe he *could've* taken down Big Linc, knife and all. I recall Caroline mentioning a black belt in something.

My fingers are like icicles, numb and unable to manipulate my phone. "I'm calling 911." Everything I say comes out as a scream.

"I told you," Joe says, growing ever more calm, perhaps to help stop me from stroking out. My chest is heaving and adrenaline has invaded my body. "I've already called the police. I came in and found that *man* on top of her," he says. "He tried to run like a coward when I charged in."

"I don't hear any sirens. I'M CALLING 911 AGAIN—SHE'S DYING," I yell. "What about CPR?"

He shakes his head. "Too big a wound, too much blood." It's as if he's resigned to the fact she's not going to make it. I see no fight in him. "It's a waiting game now. I'm trying to hold it together, Augusta." He takes a few steps around the bed toward me. "OK? Can you help me keep it together until the EMTs get here?"

I hold up one hand while using the other to dial 911. "You stay back," I command. "I'm calling for help."

He bends over Caroline and lifts her limp arm to feel for a pulse. "It's thready," he confirms, his voice cracking. "But it's there." He takes another step toward me, hand out as if to take my phone. "Bothering them won't help Caroline."

"Stay *back*." I hold a hand up.

He looks at the floor. "Oh, gosh. I'm sorry, I'm so sorry. I've frightened you. It's just…" He seems to be blinking away tears. "This is so fucked up." He's started to sob, out of nowhere. He's making the noises, but I can't see any tears.

I start dialing. My hands are shaking so badly I start with 999, then 991…*delete delete.*

"Lincoln's going to pay for this," Joe growls, kneeling again next to my friend. "Don't you worry—he'll pay for what he did to my Caroline." He looks down at her. "They'll be here soon, baby. Hang on."

"Lincoln would never do this." My voice comes out as a croak now. "He loves her more than anyone in this world."

"*Augusta*," Joe says, meeting my eyes without blinking. "There are things you don't know. Caroline didn't tell you how bad it was getting, did she? His jealousy was out of control. I mean, the guy's been following us, making things up about me to pull her away, threatening her…he's not well. And he finally lost it."

I am watching Joe, and listening to the grunting and kicking coming from the bathroom, and I'm fumbling with my phone, and I'm watching Joe whispering to Caroline. I see a flash of *something,* but it is too late, and I feel a sharp pain on the back of my head like someone has shoved a hot poker through one ear and out the other, and everything goes black.

32

It's growing dark when I get back to Wimbledon, and thankfully Bohater, Dagmara, and Co. are gone. I sit on the sofa for a moment, staring into space. Bad idea. The thoughts rush in and the loneliness strangles me. I pick up the phone.

Jemima answers on the second ring. "Mom," I say, "everything's OK, but…" I break down then, ugly crying for five full minutes, my sobs so loud I worry the neighbors will hear.

My mom lets me go on, intermittently cooing, "Hey, honey, hey…it's OK…let it out…" When I run out of tears, I get the hiccups, and still she waits patiently. "What is it? Is it Caroline? Or did something happen?"

I hear my father pick up the extension in his study, and I fill them both in. I can practically hear my mother nodding on the other end of the line.

"Yes, yes. This is a huge blow, I know. But honey—it's a sign you should come *home*."

"Your place," I say as kindly as I can, "isn't my home, Mom."

"I'll move my elliptical, Dad will move his books… You can get back into therapy, look for a real job—"

I hear my father's voice. "Come on, Jem. If going to L.A. is what she needs to do, let her…shaking things up might actually work to jog her memory. Nothing else has."

My mother has her hand over the mouthpiece, but I can still hear her. "It's denial," she says to him. "All it does is delay the pain. She needs to face it."

Dad ignores that and says, "Whatever you need to do, Augusta, we'll support you. If this is how you want to do it, I say go for it. And remember, I love you."

He hasn't said that in a very, very long time. He is gone before I can say it back. I'm not sure if I was even going to. Those words don't come easily to me, either.

As soon as I'm off the phone, I fall back on the sofa, notebook on my lap. I run my hand over the still-shiny cover whose pristine pink has discolored from the passing years and its time living in my handbag. I flip it open and skim through, counting each star. I've reached Number 49. One cannot stop *one celebrity* before hitting the big 5-0. I'm almost halfway—how can I quit now?

Not that I don't have good reasons to stop. For starters, going to L.A. feels like selling out my London colleagues. But…*but*. There is my life to consider. If not L.A., then where? What will I do? I'd love to see if Jennifer Lawrence is as fun and real as some say, or arrogant and fake as others claim. I've got Julie Delpy, but she feels incomplete without Ethan Hawke.

I set the book on the coffee table, then pound ice water and the Internet. I force Alexander to the back of my mind, because if I think of him for even a hot second my resolve will collapse like a failed soufflé. I find a cheap one-way ticket to L.A., then discover a ton of temporary furnished sublets, which in New York is like finding a handsome rich guy dating a fat girl. It seems everyone's away on a shoot somewhere—camera people, makeup artists, actors—and they all need to pay the rent while they're gone. I like the look of West Hollywood because it's affordable, out of the path of the coming tsunami, and the closest thing to a walkable neighborhood besides Santa Monica. Before I lose my nerve, I send a note to the most promising landlord.

It's almost too much; tomorrow is my first real date with Alexander at the party he invited me to. It feels like a coming out of sorts, where he'll parade the American girl in front of the cameras, newspaper reporters and his friends. But now, the life I was starting to build here has been razed in one fell swoop.

The next morning, I start robotically packing, not really believing I'm going anywhere. At two, I go for a blowout at Wimbledon's finest salon. When it's time to get dressed for the party, I notice the past weeks of cutting down on pints and rich dinners out is working: I feel healthier and less bloated. I suck in, put on a classic little black dress with stretch, and decide I actually look presentable, kind of pretty even. I spring for a car to avoid the stench and delays of public transportation. I feel an odd sense of acceptance: What will happen, will happen. I don't know why—maybe it's the old-fashioned wannabe princess lurking inside—but part of me is hoping Alexander will have answers, that he'll guide me onto the correct path so I don't have to choose. I envision us lying in bed at his flat tonight, all of my life decisions tidily made.

My driver pulls up in front of the Four Seasons. The charity has laid out a small but lively red carpet where a handful of photographers are shouting for socialites, reality stars, and fame-hungry politicians to smile, pose, turn in front of the step-and-repeat, which has the name of a mental health organization all over it. As I approach, I'm smiling, a little high with anticipation. I almost feel like a celebrity.

When I get within a few feet of the action, though, I get a shock: Alexander is there, smiling and posing and looking incredible in a navy suit, but he's not alone—he's with Belinda Bloody Oliver. They're hugging; she kisses him on the cheek, he smiles down at her, she squeezes him. They make a stunning couple. She is a willowy goddess and everyone is screaming her name. Next to her, I'd look like a wandering cow with regular-people front teeth.

I can't look away. After another minute or so, they turn to go inside together, his hand on the small of her back, guiding her in like he did with me in Rome. Of course they're together. Why would he want me? It makes no sense. I'm a bit of fun, something to do when he's on the road playing the role of Normal Guy.

I turn back toward the street, but my car has pulled away. I walk toward the Tube. As it turns out, Alexander did provide answers tonight; he made it easy. I'm leaving for L.A. on the first affordable flight out.

I'm already back in Wimbledon, sitting on my couch staring into space, when Alexander texts.

Where are you? He has the nerve to write. *Are you OK? I'm here x*

I don't hesitate. *Saw you on the red carpet. Didn't want to intrude on your time with Belinda. She really is stunning.*

There is a long delay this time, and lots of ellipses as I picture him writing, erasing, writing, erasing. What finally arrives is, *What?? I was just posing for the charity. I thought I explained all this in Rome. Please come. I want to see you. She's a FRIEND :)*

I think it's best if I don't.

Please don't be mad. I want to see you. Desperately. x

I'm not mad, I text him. To get angry would be psycho. Women must not be psycho; it is unbecoming. *I'm taking myself out of the running, that's all,* I write. *Have a fun night.*

My throat is tight, and my eyes well up. I don't want to take myself out of the running. I want him to come get me, to beg me, to call me.

Later, as I'm dressing for bed, he does call. Three times, no message. As far as I know, he's not aware of my situation, that I might be gone soon, that my job has disappeared and I have no more immediate ties to London. There hasn't been much press yet about the London bureau's demise. I should answer his calls. I almost do once, but my self-protective instincts won't allow it. Much better to go out this way, on my terms.

Before I can change my mind, I book a nonrefundable flight to Los Angeles and put down a security deposit on the West Hollywood apartment.

33

#50, #51, #52

A hot wind blows grit into my eyes as it roars through like Mother Nature's hairdryer, pummeling palm trees and whipping my hair into a bird's nest of tangles. It's a thousand degrees on the Fox studio lot, and instead of the Patron margarita I deserve, I've been offered cheese in all its forms: cubed, melted over a hotdog, congealing on a pizza wallowing in the sun. Now, the star of this kids' movie, the glassy eyed "comedian" Andy Samberg, is talking at me on this orange carpet laid out over steaming pavement. Actually, "talking" is too generous; he is laughing at nothing and spouting toilet humor. Is he high as shit? I couldn't possibly speculate. Our conversation goes like this:

"Describe your worst dating disaster," I ask him, blinking to get a bit of dust off my eyeball.

"Sure! There was a time when I went on a date with a girl, and we both just barfed all over each other, and then we both farted."

This cracks him up. He looks like a shorter, bespecta-cled Greg Brady with his old-fashioned feathered hair and narrow hips. I'm an award-winning journalist, yet here I am on a Sunday at the premiere of *Rats on Roller Skates*. Am I being hazed by my new L.A. bureau colleagues? Somehow I don't think so. I have a hunch the ladies back in *CelebLife's* L.A. office think they're doing me a favor. It's money in my pocket, after all. It's work. I try to be grateful, but it's not taking. I served the magazine valiantly in Europe and came home to *Rats on Fucking Rollerskates.* To add insult to degradation, I've been ordered to send my file to a cutesy twenty-five-year-old staffer for "approval" before I email it to the editors. Everyone normal is at the beach today. Anyway, back to Andy.

"Seriously? How about a real example?" I'm no longer hiding my annoyance.

Andy, faux indignant: "If you're saying you don't believe me…are you saying you don't believe me? *I want to be in your magazine.*"

"Are you really insisting that is a true account of your worst date?"

"Oh, yeah. I had a date where we barfed all over each other and we both farted." More laughing.

I smile and say, "You're quite the funny little prick, aren't you?"

Andy says nothing, squints at me. "Um…What?"

I say, louder this time, "I said, you've got quite the funny shtick. You're hilarious!"

He shakes his head like he's confused and also sick of talking to me, then smiles, his brain finally seeming to catch up. "Yeah," he says weakly. "Thanks…"

"OK, thanks, Andy," I dismiss him, and he shuffles away to talk to the competition next to me. Good luck to her.

He's screwed me over with his infantile interview, because now I don't have a story—the magazine is not going to touch this scatological drivel, which I suspect is why he did it. I glance over at the hipster reporter on my right (man-bun, skinny jeans, dark-rimmed glasses) who is way too cool for this scene.

I ask him, "Why did Andy do that to me at his own premiere?"

"Because he hates you," the hipster replies without a trace of irony. "They all do. Don't kid yourself."

Hipster looks over my head for his next celebrity prey, and I see Bella Thorne, loopy and loose-limbed like spaghetti. I don't see anyone else coming down the line who could provide me with a story.

"Whiners. All of them," Hipster adds. "They want the millions and the accolades, but they don't want to do promotion." I check him out more closely. Struggling screenwriter, I decide.

The slender, ultra-goth reporter on my left gasps. "Oh god. Oh no. *Gah*. This is awkward."

"What?" I ask.

Big sigh. "It's Jeff Goldblum. He *totally* knows me, and he flirts like crazy." She lowers her voice to a loud whisper. "He has a thing for me."

He's coming closer. "Oh, lord," she says, straightening her leather mini-skirt and running her tongue over her upper teeth. "Watch this."

I watch. She juts out her left hip and trills "Hiiiii Jeffff," smiling coquettishly.

"Hey!" he replies. "How's it going?"

"I'm Lizzie with *Star Scene*," she breathes.

"Nice to meet you," purrs Jeff obliviously. He's genial, relaxed, exactly like his image and ninety percent of the roles he plays. Also, he's gigantic.

Out of the corner of my eye, I see the goth deflate, and I feel sorry for her. She's young, and it appears she's only now learning the hard lessons about actors and what they're best at.

When it's my turn with Jeff, he's equally friendly to me. I learn he's a big fan of a healthy Earth: "Our oceans are in trouble," he intones. "We have to do everything we can to preserve them." He also tells me how he stays so youthful: "It's not makeup—I don't wear any. I take lots of naps." Which sounds like a great idea to me. Jeff's getting a round 8.0.

He also makes me think back to Victoria Beckham, who I met in Lisbon—and again in Rome, where it was pretty clear she didn't remember me. I hereby institute the Goldblum Rule: *Never* assume a celebrity will remember you, because they probably won't.

Next, I speak to young Bella Thorne, her concave, alabaster tummy on show, her lips cracked and dry. She's cool, she's confident, she's sharp-eyed—but she has a vulnerability about her, too. I was impressed by her bravery in revealing horrendous abuse she suffered, but I've never seen her work. I didn't see her on the tip sheet, so I wasn't able to research her; I decide to keep it light today. Reception on the lot is terrible, so Yammering her is a no-go. I know she has a fondness for Coachella and a love life the tabloids find fascinating. I ask her vaguely about her "latest man" because I don't know who he is—if there is one.

"We're just hanging out," she assures me, pointing a friendly finger in my general direction. "It's fun…"

When she trails off, I ask, "What's your advice for coming out of Coachella alive?"

She laughs. "There's no way to survive Coachella," she tells me. "All I can say is, bring your phone charger."

"Thanks so much, Bella. Have fun at the party." She's a sweetheart—and, I suspect, smarter than she's given credit for.

Still, I don't see how any of what I've gleaned today makes a story. Stanley's parting advice was infuriatingly simple: *Don't screw up your first shot. Maguire's not known for second chances.*

This was my first shot.

Two hours later, I'm back at my one-bedroom sublet, which is tucked into a shabby replica of Melrose Place with a pool the size of a short school bus. I lay on the squishy mattress my "landlord"—a gaffer or grip or other *G*-related crewmember currently working on a cable show in Tulsa—left behind, and make my notes. I am entirely shell-shocked by this move. The Los Angeles in my head, where every road is Rodeo Drive, everyone is beautiful, and days are spent in the Malibu surf, is a bitter lie. The reality is a hot, dusty replica of a seventies bad dream. The streets you hear about in songs, like Santa Monica Boulevard, are lined with strip malls, pawnshops with dirty windows, and raggedy palms. I've learned in one week that everything is crowded, lightning fast, and always at a standstill.

I flip to a new page in my notebook. *ANDY SAMBERG: Is he a good guy? He married a talented woman, a world-renowned harpist. Cool points for that. But...no. Not a fan. Who behaves like that at work? Score: 5.2* (the points he gets are for not making it personal, at least, and for not being mean so much as obstructive and immature). Bella gets an 8.4.

Tracey, one of the reporters in L.A. who has never worked in a real newsroom (I've already Internet-stalked her), texts me: *I want your story immediately. Come in tomorrow. Maguire wants to talk to you.*

I type out, *What fucking story?* Then erase it.

I type, *Of course. On it. I'll be there by ten a.m.* I hit send.

I Yammer all my people from today again. Ah, *Bella*. It has to be her. She's dating someone CelebLife.com keeps speculating about but can't get confirmation—and I got a quote about him. This is surely the story Tracey wants, so I write up a brief, snappy, breathless piece around Bella's one sentence and send it in.

34

Maguire Carnaby's voluminous honey-brown hair is piled atop her head like a sleeping Chihuahua. She brings a dripping cheeseburger to her mouth as she returns an email. She wears little makeup and has fillers in her overstretched lips, but incongruously skipped the injections for the crows' feet and smile lines. She's wearing an oversized men's blue work shirt and wrinkled khakis. I'm sitting next to Tracey, L.A.'s Senior Celebrity Guru (whatever that means).

"So. You're from the London office. Stan likes you," Maguire says.

I am uncomfortable. Not just now—every minute I'm treading on this town's shaky, fault-lined ground. To make matters extra deadly, *CelebLife*'s offices sit precariously on the twenty-seventh floor.

"Clearly you can talk to celebrities," she adds. "And you can write. But what can you do for us here in L.A.?"

"I'm sorry?" She is shifting gears too fast for my jetlagged brain.

Tracey chimes in, "Do you have sources?"

"Sources?" I repeat the word the same way I echoed *Shifts?* at Stanley. I check out her office. It's decorated with Mexican textiles and what I'm pretty sure is a Day of the Dead-related skull.

"We need people with sources," Maguire presses, wiping her hands after finishing her last bite of burger. "What do you do when we're chasing a rumor that Zayn Malik is having a torrid affair with Julia Roberts? We need more than publicist comments—we need insider info. Do you know anyone in Zayn's camp? Do you have an *in* with Julia Roberts' circle?"

I want to burst out laughing from the absurdity of it all, but I force myself to deadpan, "I'm afraid not." *I just got here.* "I do know how to *build* sources, though. That's what I've been doing my entire career…it's how I've gotten my best scoops." She should remember this, but I say it anyway: "I also helped break that rehab story with my reporting out of Dublin…"

"Oh, right. Stanley reminded me. You stumbled on the action star doing coke. That helped us confirm a story we'd been working on for a year." Her words should be sarcastic and biting, but her tone is flat; it doesn't feel like a rebuke. I try not to be insulted.

Maguire couldn't look more bored. I can see the start of the sapphire Pacific from my chair, rolling out behind her until it stops with a thud against a wall of smog. I check out the portrait on her desk: Maguire linking arms with a woman with white-blonde hair, twin girls in their laps.

"Well," I say carefully, "I'm game for anything. Breaking news, events, staking out restaurants and clubs—"

Reflexively, without thought or consideration, Tracey half laughs, half sneers. "*You?* Oh, no. You won't be doing nightclubs. *No, no.* We have…other…um…people for that." By the way she says *people* I take her to mean younger, thinner, more fashionable women. Profoundly unglamorous herself, Tracey wears her tightly curled brown hair in two low ponytails. As she talks, she keeps glancing at her phone.

Maguire says, "I'm sure Stanley told you we have a loyal stable of stringers, and we have to keep them busy.

Still, it's possible Tracey and Tatiana can fit you in for the occasional event."

Possible? Occasional? Great. I'm *so* glad I just signed a six-month lease. And bought a 1999 SAAB convertible whose top doesn't go up from some guy in an Orange County parking lot. I haven't figured out what I'm going to do when it rains.

"However," Maguire adds, picking a front tooth with a fingernail, "you may know we just had our own round of layoffs. I could use an extra hand in the office now and then. Just know we can't hire you full-time, so don't ask."

No, I *didn't* know they'd had layoffs. No one's mentioned it, and nothing seems awry.

Tracey is wide-eyed, irritated. "Do you think hiring someone new is going to go over well with the staff, considering it just happened *Friday*?" she asks Maguire through gritted teeth. She has a point. It's only Monday.

Ignoring her, Maguire says, "We can always use freelancers. Why don't you introduce Augusta around the office, OK?" She waves us off while pushing buttons on her phone.

A fuming Tracey and a nonplussed me set off through the twisty halls, and I get a better look at the odd décor. I expected the entertainment mecca of the world's most influential celebrity magazine to have every available gloss. Once again, I was wrong. The place looks like someone took a rack of storm trooper costumes, turned them into furniture, skinned the abominable snowman and used his pelt for rugs and sofas, then left it all to stew for twenty years in spilled coffee and leaked mustard accented with Chinese-food drippings. We pass through a corridor lined with offices, some with people sitting behind desks, a couple with doors closed, and several empty other than dust balls and scraps of paper strewn about the floor. "That's where the more…um, *old-school,* non-celebrity-news reporters were," Tracey tells me, "until last week…"

As we round a corner, Tracey beckons me into an office and introduces me to Tatiana, who, she explains, assigns most of the events. "Tati also covers music," she says.

"Hey," Tatiana says, raising her head, giving me a flat, closed mouth smile.

"Hi," I say.

"Augusta used to work in the London office," Tracey adds.

"Oh." Tatiana talks like a chipmunk and looks like a poor man's Jessica Simpson.

"Let's move on," Tracey says. What the point of that encounter was, I'll never know. The whole experience feels like what a sorority rush must be like.

I am taken next door. "This is Esdee. She's our senior movies reporter." A plaque on her desk reads S.D. Ehrlanger. She is a woman of indeterminate age with smooth jet-black hair parted in the middle and flowing down her back.

"Augusta is a new stringer from London," Tracey intones as if she's introducing the vacuum cleaner repairwoman. "Maguire's going to try her out in the office tomorrow."

Esdee/S.D. nods hello. "You need anything, you come to me," she says in a deep, sure voice. "Great to have you on board."

Next, Tracey leads me down a hall of cubicles filled with twenty-one-year-olds who are either flinging rubber bands at each other, on their phones, or taking selfies. Tracey quickens her pace. "We call them the Children of CelebLife.com," she whispers. "It's low pay, high turnover, glorified shift work." She makes a face as if just *looking* at the digital team gives her the willies. "The *print* side is where you want to be. The Children don't have sources. They don't go to the *Oscars.*"

I must appear incredulous because she adds, "Trust me, print *is* best…well, apart from the all the layoffs, I mean."

When we've covered the entire floor—I estimate about twenty staffers still work here—Tracey walks me back to Maguire's office to meet her assistant, a nervous, petite woman of about twenty-five. "I'm June," she says. "Be here by nine-fifteen tomorrow and I'll get you a pass and set you up in a cubicle before the morning meeting. Oh, and don't be late. Maguire doesn't like it."

I change out of my interview clothes the minute I get home, then head out for a walk. When I get to the small park up the street, I settle on a bench in the sun. I spot a fallen avocado and take two long steps to grab it. It may not be salad-worthy, but for an east coast girl, naturally grown avocados and palm trees are beyond exotic.

After my visit to *CelebLife*'s L.A. bureau, I never want to go back. I want to go home—to *London*. L.A. does not feel glamorous, exciting or propitious to me. Where London seemed familiar right from the start, this city is frightening and foreign. *London.* It hits me like a falling avocado to the head. I found home there and didn't know it. I was building a foundation for a life, and—even considering it gets dark there at four p.m. and the Tube system is ancient and rickety—I loved it. I decide finding *home* isn't about a list of reasons why. It's an ungraspable wisp of a dream that floats by, and if you notice it in time, you can grab it and stop searching. I let it get away and now I'm lost again. My therapist was right. Whatever lies beneath consciousness—the unconscious, subconscious, uberconscious—is always hard at work concocting plans, philosophies, roadmaps, epiphanies.

I know I'm going to do that thing I shouldn't do. I toss the avocado in a bin a few feet away from my bench. Of course I'll do it. I Yammer *Alexander Matten* like I do every single day and, for the first time in a week, I find a brand-new result. It's a GQ feature about him with the headline: *Aristocrat on Fire: British Journalist Alexander Matten-Thorpe Takes us to the Andes for a New Look at the 'Alive' Plane Crash.* There's a photo of him sitting on a mountain in Argentina, his jawline defined and angular as he stares at the sky, his full head of dark hair set aglow by the sun. He's "brave," the story says; he's the "eligible" heir to his father's earldom, a top writer for Europe's "most respected broadsheet newspaper."

This article should silence the inner shrieks of *What the hell did I do, giving up on him so easily?* that have been plaguing me since I left London. The truth is, I never had a chance with Alexander, and now his status as one of the UK's most eligible bachelors has gone global. Time to let the dream of him fade away.

35

As instructed, I'm back at the L.A. office at nine the following morning. At nine-fifteen, June leads me to a lonesome cubicle far from the entrance and across from two empty cubes. I grab a notebook and discover I'm first in the meeting room, followed shortly after by a fifty-something man with skinny legs and a taut belly like half an exercise ball. He sets about arranging a projector screen and a laptop.

"Quinn Bayliss," he says by way of introduction. "You new?"

"Stringer," I say. "Augusta Noble. Leftover from London."

"Ah," he says, fiddling with a power cord. "Stanley's the man."

"He *is* the man," I agree. I miss him more than ever.

As people file in with coffees, bottled waters, and smoothies, I smile nervously and receive some waves, smiles, and *heys* in return, but no questions or *welcome*s. Maguire blows in at nine thirty-five in saggy khakis and a basic black tee, settles in her seat, and says crisply, "OK, folks, quiet down. Quinn, let's get the photo show up."

Tracey hits the lights. First up on the screen is Jennifer Garner and her kids. The comments start spewing.

"She looks fat."

"She's pregnant again! I've been saying this."

"*Nope*. She always has a tummy. That's how she's built."

She's a size four, max.

"God, those kids are cute."

"Shame about the dad…"

"Oh, come on…he's hot."

"Not anymore. He's kind of a dick. I told you what he said to my friend that one time about her tits…"

Maguire chooses this moment to cut in. "Enough. Where was this taken, Quinn?"

"Outside the school," Quinn replies.

Maguire nods. "Tracey, find out where Jennifer was going in this pic and where Ben was at this exact moment in time. *Next.*"

There's a click, and Bradley Cooper jogging with a hot guy lights up the screen. The room—which I'm realizing is mostly female—starts cooing and *Mmm hmmm*-ing.

"He's hot," Esdee pronounces. "I mean, they both are."

"Yummy," Tracey agrees.

"Who *is* that with him?" Maguire squints at the screen.

"I'll find out," Tracey replies.

This goes on for a while; pap shots of stars are projected on the wall, at which point they are declared "old," "bloated," "gorgeous," or some other colorful adjective. It strikes me as gruesome. But…these people are, after all, celebrities—they put themselves out there for us to consume and judge and aspire to, so they should expect this kind of thing. *Right?*

When the lights come back on, Maguire snaps, "Time to play 'Find the Celebrity.' Now, gang: Where is Brad Pitt? Where is he *right now?*"

After the meeting, Esdee calls me to her office and taps a folder on her desk with one French-manicured finger.

"Jennifer Aniston," she says, "is our bread and butter. The Kardashians are the occasional dessert, Reese is our dependable dinner salad, Angelina is the caviar. But Jen— she's our cover girl." She slides the folder across to me. The words *DOSSIER: Jennifer Aniston* are written on the translucent blue plastic in heavy black marker.

"From what I've seen since I've been at the magazine, she doesn't return the love," I observe carefully. "She doesn't give *CelebLife* too many interviews."

"Too true," Esdee admits. "We've had a long and checkered past with her and her reps. Never forget," she wags a finger at me, "the publicists' job is to prevent interviews with their clients. Ours is to get around them. And the game continues."

She opens the dossier and presses it flat like it's the schematics for North Korea's top nuclear facility. "Read this," she says. "You might meet her today. We need you to cover a huge junket that starts in, like, two hours. The original guy bailed last minute." She purses her lips. "We won't be calling him for more work anytime soon."

"Got it," I say. I take the folder, flip through it, close it, and make a move for the door.

"Oh, no, no," Esdee says, standing up. "It can't leave this office. Read it here."

"Seriously?"

"Seriously." She sits back down and turns to her monitor. "I've got to write *Five Reasons Cindy Crawford's Daughter Is Already Hotter Than Her* for the Web site." She gathers up her long black hair and throws it over one shoulder while I read.

1. OBSERVATIONS FROM THOSE WHO HAVE MET JEN

Super nice to me during our interview, but told me nothing. Mentioned her water company five times. Kind of brilliant in that way.

Likes vodka and white wine.

So, so tanned.

2. WHAT SOURCES ARE SAYING

A diva? Sources said she won't eat lunch with the rest of the cast and crew on some movie sets.

A real homebody—likes to get services at home. Dermatologist types have been seen pulling up with medical bags, plus yoga gurus and stuff.

A guy who spent a short time on the Friends *writing team said she and Lisa Kudrow were "the most horrible human beings in the world." (ed. Note: Is she a horrible human being? can we nail this down? Reporter note: No, we cannot).*

I look up at Esdee. "Is that true—about how horrible she is?"

She laughs. "I don't think so," she says. "I've met her. She's just hopelessly out of touch, in my opinion. When you're hunted like you're more valuable than diamonds, and when you can afford to *buy* all the diamonds, you can't help but believe your own hype. Her personal closet is the size of a four-car garage. She's a master at the non-answer answer, but she makes you like her."

"So…she's *nice?*"

"She's really smart about managing her image," Esdee replies, in a tone that says the conversation is over.

She hands me a tip sheet (PR-speak for guest list) for today's extravaganza and I scan it. There are a bunch of huge names. "Basically half the Hollywood A-list will be in one hotel at the same time," I observe.

"You could say that," Esdee replies. "Except don't call Ashton A-list. He's barely a B these days." I smile, but she doesn't. "You'll find," she says, "we each have our favorites here—and our nemeses. We don't always agree."

I hear that. "You sure you don't want this junket?" I ask.

"Are you kidding?" Esdee makes a face like I just farted. "No, thanks. I've paid my dues—I don't do press days."

Again with the reporters who don't want to meet the celebrities they cover. *Fascinating.*

"Go," Esdee says. "You don't have much time. I'll work on getting them to let you in. Security at these things is like the frigging UN—and they have the other stringer's name on their precious list."

36

#53, #54, #55, #56, #57, #58, #59, #60

I burst through the storied hotel's double doors, imagining myself swinging shopping bags and shouting *Big mistake. HUGE.* I'm about to hang with Julia Roberts at the Beverly Wilshire, which means my life has officially turned into *Pretty Woman.* I clip-clop across the blindingly shiny marble floors past the famous columns to find the elevators.

"You're late," one of the reps says when I arrive at the press suite. "You're supposed to be in place well before the talent." She asks for my I.D., copies it with a hand-held scanner, then stands. "Follow me."

She deposits me in a fancy suite decorated in beiges, creams, and muted yellows. I sit alone for ten minutes before two reps slip in to inform me that the stars are on the way. The Talent, aka Jennifer Garner and Ashton Kutcher, enter the hushed room. Jen sits at one end of the sofa, Ashton the other. After my warm-up movie question, he gets up and walks to the window, stares out, starts pacing. I pose a few more movie-related queries, then manage to steer the conversation to one of celebrity media's clickiest topics: body after baby.

"You've had so many babies, Jen (*ha ha*). What do you think about these high expectations for new moms?"

Jennifer bristles, but tamps it down immediately and answers me, admitting she always felt pressure to be thin and to drop her baby weight right after giving birth. "But," she adds, "I can't make it come off faster than it does. I can't seem to be pregnant without gaining forty-five pounds. I do feel the pressure and I do see the cameras." She's on a roll. "And it's the one time when having people follow you and take pictures is just excruciating."

The one time. Interesting—does that mean she eats it up the rest of the time? She seems annoyed (though works hard to hide it) to have to face questions like these. This makes me like her more, because frankly, leave women the hell alone about our bodies.

Ashton is exactly as he appears on camera, with the same dopey frat-boy manner. He's animated and paces, then stops at the giant picture window, turns, paces back. He talks *at* me more than with me. He refers to himself in the third person. I ask about what it's like to be a celebrity.

"You must get a ton of special treatment," I say. "It must be good for impressing the ladies." He tosses a bit of feathered hair back with the shake of his head.

"The profession does afford you the ability to be extraordinarily romantic," Ashton admits.

"You can make big gestures," Jen adds.

"You can make big gestures, but you can also get reservations at the restaurant," Ashton says. "Everything fell through with this dinner one time, so I'm calling around, I'm trying to pull every bit of juice I can, but I hate dropping my name. I'm like, 'yes, I'm calling from Mr. Kutcher's office. Mr. Kutcher would like a reservation'— and literally every place was booked. But I did it. The reservation pull is big."

Jennifer nods. "The reservation thing—you gotta do it."

"That's what our profession does."

"You can have a violinist," Jen chimes in.

"You can have an orchestra. We know people who know orchestras."

Thankfully, it's over quickly. The notes afterward are easy: *Ashton Kutcher: Knows orchestras. 7.5. Jennifer Garner: May or may not be part of Hollywood's women-must-look-a-certain-way problem. 8.0.*

My Day of Big Stars continues with a presser in Conference Room A. Jennifer Aniston and three other cast members take their places at a long table at the front of the room. Jen is confident, relaxed, and petite. She likes to toss her hair. I look around the room; turns out there are a lot of us misfits in this line of work. Not for the first time, I wonder if the celebrities keep notes on *us*, and if so, what do they say? If they did, I suspect they'd be quite dull. *Some plain chick who I'll never remember asked me a dumb question. Guy with B.O. got too close—ewww. Where's my limo?*

There is a stern woman in charge of walking the microphone around. I keep raising my hand but I'm never picked. What else is new? The microphone queen approaches one of the professional junketeers—the people who get travel and expenses paid for in exchange for writing about a movie. He proceeds to stand up and ask in a weak, nasal voice, "Um, Jennifer, do you think you're really the right actress for the role of a *mom* considering *you've never been a mother yourself?*"

I gasp audibly—for all we know, she's pregnant now, or was pregnant last week but lost the baby—but everyone else sits like good little junketeers. Jen heroically stops herself from rolling her eyes and/or leaping off her chair and wrapping her delicate hands around his pencil neck, as do I. I have to wonder, when George Clooney was cruising the Oscar campaign circuit for his role as a father in *The Descendants*, did anyone ask him about not being a father in real life? Pretty sure they didn't. Jennifer answers diplomatically, "Well, I certainly think so. It's my job to be able to take on all kinds of different roles, and I hope I've done this one justice."

I raise my hand, stand, gesture for the mic—and finally get it. "Hi Jen," I say, not identifying myself as I'm supposed to. "Just a quick one. Do you think Matt Damon should have been allowed to play an astronaut in *The Martian*, considering he's never been to Mars?"

This is Hollywood, where entertainment is deadly serious. No one thinks I'm funny. I get a few sniggers, but the studio minions are not happy I went off script. I see something in Jen's eyes, though; could it be appreciation? She gets it.

"Absolutely," she says. "He deserved every accolade he got for that performance. It was like he'd actually been to the red planet, you know?" That's as far as she'll go. She smiles, then expertly switches the topic to *her* movie. "I think everyone in this film has experiences they brought to their characters," she says. "It's why I love this one."

Next up in Conference Room C: The Big Daddy of press conferences. This movie is already getting terrible buzz, which is quite a feat given its epic star power. I lag behind the crowd, needing to stop in the bathroom, wanting a quick breather, but I can't get across the lobby. Is the President of the United States about to walk past me? Oh, wait, no, it's Bradley Cooper. He's mega-tall and holding a glass plate close to his face. He hunches his shoulders as he stabs at an avocado salad. He's followed by a phalanx of people in suits looking important, making urgent calls and typing furiously on their phones while looking around for threats. No wonder these Hollywood people lose themselves in a pervasive fog of ego. Who *wouldn't* believe they were gods if they were always treated like this? I'm not sure if I'll meet him officially today so I say, "Hi, Bradley." He shoots a glance at me and gives me a tight-lipped half-smile in case he's supposed to know me. He'll go in the book.

After a quick trip to the loo, I head to the next presser. I'm interested to see Julia Roberts, aka Mrs. Danny Moder, in the flesh. Her phony, stock movie laugh drives me bonkers, plus I've side-eyed her ever since the T-shirt incident back in the day, when I guess Danny's then-wife Vera wasn't giving up her husband fast enough because Julia, knowing she'd be photographed, went for a stroll with a hand-written *A Low Vera* on her shirt in the middle of the Moders' divorce. I shudder when I think of Julia bent over the white tee, cackling as she carefully drew out each letter. "It was private," she later told Oprah of her motives, and then added, "I stand by my T-shirt."

I'll keep an open mind, of course. This conference room is huge. They've set the celebrities up in stadium seating, with Julia as queen bee sitting above everyone. Below her are some of Hollywood's hottest men, including my new buddies Bradley and Ashton. On the lowest tier, Jessica Alba is flanked by a dimpled Jen Garner and the legendary Shirley MacLaine. We're still waiting for a couple of people as Julia banters with the cast.

Here comes Jessica Biel, who smiles shyly and takes her seat. I am not recording yet so I have to paraphrase what Julia says as Biel settles in: *LOOK at those cheekbones. Oh, wow. What a beauty. Are you seeing this? Isn't she gorgeous?*

Julia asks the room, forcing everyone in the bleachers and on the floor to agree with her. The other two American beauties, Alba and Garner, sit quietly, looking mildly embarrassed and nodding with frozen smiles. I cringe, then watch Julia. She knows exactly what she's doing and I believe she *loves* it.

As the presser gets underway, Julia sits above us all like a one-woman Statler & Waldorf, quipping and making charming cracks. She gives the room what they want: relief from boredom. It gets better when Shirley MacLaine looks over at uber-slim Jennifer Garner and Jessica Biel sitting next to each other, and says, "What do all the women up here *eat*? I'd like to have a rundown—do you diet all the time and is it worth it?"

Not one to let the spotlight veer off of her for long, Julia pipes up with a glint in her eye, "You girls *are* slim…" While Biel doesn't say much, Garner apologizes for being thin, saying breastfeeding keeps her fit and promising she'll "puff back up" soon enough.

I suddenly don't feel so messed up. These women have serious issues. Suddenly, giving out rankings seems gauche and unnecessary today. I don't know about the rest of them down the line, but for today, I don't have the stomach for it.

37

The balding detective's legs are spread wide, like one of those dickheads on the subway. He leans forward and rests his elbows on his thighs.

"I understand this is hard, but if you continue to be unable to remember, we'll be in a tight spot, OK?"

He's one of those people who ends every sentence with *OK?*

I've been crying for twenty-four hours, in between bouts of shock during which I get the giggles or feel an uncontrollable need to kick someone, preferably a male, preferably in the nuts. I've been out of the hospital for twelve hours and I've already driven my mother crazy.

"I've *tried*," I tell the detective again. "All I've done is try. I have a permanent splitting headache. No matter what, I can't remember what happened after I got hit over the head. My brain is constipated."

He tries on a sympathetic face. "No one hit you over the head, Miss Noble," Detective Barilla tells me for the tenth time. "The doctors say you don't have any head injuries, OK?"

"Then why do I still have a headache? Why do I remember a sudden pain? Why did I black out, and why do I have no idea how I got in that ambulance?"

The detective rubs his temples and closes his eyes. What he doesn't understand is that none of this will matter to me until I find out if Caroline is going to be all right. Not just alive, but *fine. Perfect.* Just as she was before I abandoned her to go fuck some prick of a director for kicks.

As of one hour ago, Caroline was in a coma and the prognosis was poor. They say the assailant slashed her from mouth to ear.

"Detective Barilla," I say, realizing now why his name sounds familiar. "Any relation to the pasta Barillas? Are you some kind of noodle heir?" I don't know any other way to deal with things this heavy other than snark and avoidance.

"I only wish." I can see now that he's exhausted, too, and I feel sorry for him in a way. "Let's go over this again, Miss Noble, OK?"

He opens the already thick file. "Lincoln Bray is seen entering Caroline Rain's apartment building at two-thirty-five a.m. He appears to have a key. Joe Lannells arrives thirty minutes later—he's buzzed in. At approximately eight a.m., surveillance cameras from the co-op next door show you entering, again with a key. You've told us that Joe had Lincoln tied up and gagged in the bathroom when you arrived. That certainly supports the timeline and Mr. Lannells' clam that he came in and caught Lincoln in the act of—"

"*No.*" I shake my head. "Not necessarily. Lincoln is a lurker. Couldn't he have been waiting in the service elevator, the stairway, even a corner of the lobby? He's always watched over Caroline; it's his main hobby. He once called it his 'job.'"

Barilla is unmoved.

"OK, what about the neighbors?" I press. The reporter in me sneaks out beneath the hard wall of shock. "Someone must've heard *something*."

"Nothing unusual," Barilla says. "Those pre-war buildings cover noise up real good. The apartment below was vacant. One couple seemed to think they heard some sounds that may have been…sex related."

"Wait," I say. "What about the 911 call? That should clear up everything. I kept trying to call, but Joe said not to because he already had. Did he?"

"Possibly." Barilla checks the folder. "A call came in at seven fifteen a.m. from Miss Rain's cell, but there was only interference and unintelligible yelling on the line, and it lasted less than thirty seconds. There's no way to tell whose voices they were or what they were trying to say—if anything. It took time to triangulate the location, which is why there was a delay with emergency services."

My instincts are failing me; I can't get a grip on this thing. "Can't Lincoln tell you what happened? Something that will match your evidence? If it does, he's innocent, right?"

A uniformed cop comes into the room and I see a flash of my mother's flowing, colorful jacket in the hallway. He's brought me some coffee in a paper cup, for which I thank him. It's lukewarm and tastes like sweetened cigarette ashes. "Yummy," I say, and set the cup down.

"The evidence so far can fit either narrative," Barilla explains somberly. "The knife near Joe's body was Lincoln's, and it had only Caroline's DNA on it. Mr. Lannells either subdued Lincoln to stop his rampage, or took him down because Lincoln caught *him* in the act."

It's interesting to me that Barilla keeps calling Linc by his first name, while Park Avenue Joe is "Mr. Lannells."

"Were there gloves found at the scene?" I ask.

Barilla shakes his head.

"OK. So whose fingerprints were on the knife?"

"Both men left prints on the handle, which would make sense if Mr. Lannells wrestled the knife from Lincoln as he indicated to you."

"Who wrote the bloody words?" I ask, my mind racing.

"We think Caroline was naming her assailant. Several letters were written in her own blood."

LINC.

"Caroline was—*is*—an artist. That's not her writing. It's a man's hand—long and messy and aggressive," I tell him. "Even if she were...even if she were in bad shape, that's not her. Her hands are so little..."

"We are investigating all possibilities," Barilla says.

"What about the fifth person?" I ask for the millionth time. "Doesn't it make sense that he or she knocked me out and then killed Joe?"

I did not kill someone. I did not take a human life.

"Can you bring in Miss Noble's mother, please?" Detective Barilla says wearily to Vito, whose only job seems to be guarding the door and fetching refreshments.

Barilla turns back to me. "It's time you accept that there is *zero* evidence of a fifth person in the apartment that day...OK?" he says slowly, firmly. "It was you, Lincoln, Caroline, and Mr. Lannells. That is a fact. It might be time to face the likelihood that the only person who could've killed Joe Lannells is you, Ms. Noble."

38

With no one in *CelebLife*'s L.A.'s bureau watching my back the way Stanley did, I decide to pull a Kramer and show up at the office every day until someone tells me not to. Esdee smiles and winks at me the following Monday, when I casually take a seat in the morning meeting. Afterward, she visits my cube with a stack of papers two inches thick.

"These are names of all below-the-line actors and crew on twelve different A-listers' last few films." Esdee slaps the pages on my desk. "Find them and call them."

"*All* of them?" I flip through the pages. There has to be a thousand names, and no contact information.

"All of them." Esdee winks at me again, then takes off.

I'd rather sell encyclopedias door-to-door, but I dive in as instructed, and after about fifteen mortifying cold-calls and emails, I get a hit. Then another, and another. I begin to enjoy speaking to the underlings nobody notices, but who watch everything. Throughout the week I start to learn the truth about celebrities from the faceless crewmembers who serve them: Jennifer Aniston keeps to herself and doesn't mix with others, brings in her own food and eats separately, and people do not like this. Below-the-line folks like working with Scott Eastwood, but not with Ben Stiller, who allegedly throws tantrums and treats certain people like crap. There is a wacky blonde actress who's drunk on Chardonnay one-hundred percent of the time on her TV show, and no one says a word to her about it. There is a franchise action-movie actor and family man who gets blowies in his trailer, and everyone knows about it, even giving him high fives when he walks out smiling. Johnny Depp is a chain smoker who's super nice, chatty, and inclusive of everyone from the floor-sweeper to the stunt double to the director. Every single person I speak to about him raves about him, which is weird because I can't forget that video of him slamming things around and shouting at then-wife Amber Heard. One person tries to explain how great he is to work with by comparing him to another star, a comic actor I have loved for ages who started in TV and then moved on to do tons of movies. As the source tells it, this actor—whom I will call "Tim Mellor"—was filming a movie in the Southwest, when the following took place:

There's a day off from shooting, and some of the crew decide to play golf, right? Everyone knows Tim loves golf, so one of the crew—a man respected in his field and an important part of the production—lets Tim know he is welcome to join them. Tim responds by running to the director and demanding the crewmember is fired for, and I quote, "Being too familiar." The guy is immediately let go and banned from the set. I'm still furious. The guy Tim got fired is known to be a great guy. But the talent always wins, right?

Tim, if you're reading this, you know who you are. Someone needs to tell you, so I'll do it: You're an asshole, Tim. An Ass. Hole. I'm sad to hear this; he's self-deprecating, relatable, and insightful in most of his work. I don't get how Hollywood does this to people. Or maybe that's just who "Tim" is; it's hard to tell in this town. I also learn there about a legend who still works a ton and has dementia, but people think his forgetfulness is funny but it's not, at all. And there is that short, "sober" Hollywood stalwart dependent on weed. I don't want to do these calls anymore; already my childhood fairy tale is shattered and I can't take too much more disappointment.

They were right when they said we should never meet our heroes. An addendum: We should never know the truth about them, either.

39

Tom Cruise is standing ten inches from my face, wearing that crooked aren't-I-charming-AF grin. I'm not spying from afar this time; I could reach out and tweak his fetchingly prominent nose, grab his package, stab him in the sternum, anything I want, really.

"Hello, Augusta," Tom—whom I listed as Number 37 back in Rome so can't count him this time—says in his best 'you *will* love me' tone. He wins. I *do* love him, and I dare say he had me at hello. "I'm Tom," he adds.

"Hi, Tom," I reply, going along with the farce and shaking his hand, probably with some palm-sweat. I'll never be sure, because I am hypnotized. It's one thing to like him from afar when he's hanging out in a hotel; it's another to bask in his attention. It's not that I'm weak, it's that the name-check is a rare maneuver employed by somewhere in the realm of two celebrities. But Tom is savvy; Tom *gets* it; perhaps Tom even enjoys seeing unglamorous journalists crumble beneath the weight of his charm.

"How are you?" he asks, as if he means it.

I am smart enough to answer briefly, because I know it's a trick. If he can get me talking, I'll have no time to pry information out of him, and then I'll have to cobble together a story out of movie posters and Tom Cruise grins instead of the zinging quotes I need.

"Great!" I almost yell. I'm afraid I'm batting my eyelashes. *Batting my eyelashes.* "And you?"

He opens his arms and raises them toward the heavens to let me know he's the happiest guy on planet Earth. We are standing eye to eye. My brain's neurons recommence firing and I ask him the standard movie-related questions in rapid succession. I have become deft at four-minute journalism: *Your own stunts? Wow! The worst injury you've ever suffered for your craft? What's your favorite moment in this movie?* After he shares some mildly amusing on-set anecdotes, I hit him with the question the magazine really cares about: *What've you got up your sleeve for your daughter's upcoming birthday?* Not exactly controversial, but a good answer will get us half a million clicks.

Instead of the generic *It's gonna be awesome, we're gonna yadda yadda,* or the icy *Not sure, next question* response we red-carpet types are used to, he gives me something special and new: "Oh, Augusta," Tom coos. "It's a big one, isn't it? What was *your* best birthday?"

He wants to know—he *really* wants to know all about my best birthday. I involuntarily raise my voice one octave and tell him about how my professor parents were always forgetting about me because they were too busy writing papers at their fancy college in Cambridge, and how my sweet sixteen was unforgettable because they actually put on a party and bought a cake that had *my name* on it, evidence of rare advanced planning. I don't add the part about how few people came.

When the last word is out of my mouth and Tom's face comes back into focus, I realize I have royally fucked up. It's not as if I wasn't warned. *Watch out,* Tracey had told me before I left. *You might find yourself getting weak in the knees. He's been known to make reporters turn to jelly— men and women.*

Puh leeze, I'd responded. *He's old and not my type.* But tonight Tom is a combo of cocky Maverick from *Top Gun* and peak Jerry Maguire, the loveable rogue with a heart of gold.

I make one last attempt to save myself. "But, Tom," I ask again, "what're *you* doing for *your* daughter's birthday?"

He answers with two lines that I barely hear and do not absorb. I'm just relieved he's talking about his personal life. I see the devil PR person coming at me. Just as she grabs me with her claw-hand, four crooked fingers winding under my armpit and digging into the flesh of my upper arm, Tom finishes. "So…ha, ha, you know what I mean? Nice talking to you, Augusta!" And he is gone.

I wrench my arm away from the sour PR woman and she glares at me. The hypnotist has snapped his fingers and my blind adoration washes away like a cleansing tide as Tom leaves me.

Hipster Reporter is next to me again, fanning his face with his press kit. "Another day, another interview where Mr. Charming gets away with murder," he drawls. "Tell me, Augusta, old chum: Why is it no one ever calls Tommy out on his shit? There's so much of it—yet it never seems to stick."

I've been thinking the same thing. This is not the kind of journalism they teach you in school. You're supposed to dig deep for the answers, watch your quarry squirm, never let up in the search for truth. Why do we give Tom a pass? Well, now I know. I watched him earlier, greeting every single fan who came to see him, then turning back for more against the wishes of handlers trying to coax him onto the carpet. He gets a pass because he might very well be the last great movie star. We're not *supposed* to see, vet, judge, or prod these sublime beings. *Now* I get it. I open the book and scribble a summary of my encounter with Tom. I've had an epiphany.

Tricked me, made me swoon. Possibly the most nuanced role of his life is acting like a normal human being.

To me, Tom represents the extremes of all the different faces celebrities put on—and the futility of trying to figure out who's behind them. It reminds me of one of the life lessons from *Into the Woods*. I write, *Nice is different than kind, right is different from good, and just because the wolf at the door is nice doesn't mean he's not still a wolf. Score: 7.9.*

Tom's rating is on the lower side for someone who treated me so well. He was good, all right—too good. His ruse to get me to talk about myself docked him points. *That man,* I think as I watch him go, late for his own movie screening, *is an enigma wrapped in a cliffhanger.*

I tuck my notebook into my handbag and wait for the carpet to officially wrap up before taking off. My phone beeps. A new email. I see who it's from, and shake as I open it. He writes like a man, in short sentences with only the most basic, necessary information.

I don't have your new American number. I know you're not happy with me but I want to see you. I'll be in town next week, and I don't know anyone in L.A. Show me around?

Again, I am tempted to wait a day, make him suffer, play the game. I've always sucked at that. I write back immediately.

Nice try. I know for a fact you know people here.

I wait, nod to Hipster Reporter who's getting ready to take off, clutch my phone like it's a defibrillator. It dings in under a minute.

OK, I know people. But they're bloody boring. I can almost hear his voice, low and deep and with a river of laughter bubbling just beneath it.

When? I respond.

Probably Tuesday. Setting up interview as we speak. Are you going to give me your American number or not? Don't worry, I won't drunkenly sext you. Unless you want me to…

I have never felt like this. My body *needs* him. I've been dreaming of him since I left London, but never dared acknowledge the thoughts as anything more than fantasies. That he could be a reality again, a warm body and a real smile, changes everything.

I let out an involuntary yelp of excitement and Hipster Reporter inquires wryly, "Let me guess. A boy?"

"Nope," I reply, patting him on the cheek. "Not a boy, my misguided young friend. A *man*."

40

#61, #62, #63

I am staring straight into Charlize Theron's light-green eyes. She's got an inch or two on me, so I'm gazing upward to avoid staring at her cleavage, which is spectacular in a plunging neckline. It's been a delightful afternoon at the Beverly Hilton, but also awful because of the terrible stories we've heard today. Charlize is preternaturally annoyed and giving me four-word answers. She looks past me a lot, and if she catches one of the photographers aiming at her, she whips up a friendly smile.

We're at an event raising awareness about violence against women. I am steeling myself against any sort of panic or trigger. *It's not about you. Keep it about the celebrities and the victims. Breathe.*

"Are you OK?" Charlize looks down at me quizzically.

"Yeah—sorry. Had some dust in my throat." I cough into my forearm for good measure.

Charlize has been open in the past about her family's tragedy, so I figure it's fair game. "This must be really close to your heart," I say gently. "Is this cause something you feel connected to?"

"I don't think people have to be victims to understand," she says testily.

I take the hint and try another tack. "Jessica Alba's reading was moving, wasn't it?" Charlize nods. "Not to mention Rosario's and Kerry's?"

Freeze. Nothing. Meanwhile, my phone is flashing with text after text.

"Would you say it was…"

"It was moving." *Freeze.* She's reticent and a bit snobby, but she's not *mean*.

I let her go and take a breather to check my phone. There are four texts from Alexander. I smile to myself like an idiot standing alone in the middle of the room.

I can't wait to see you.

What are you wearing?

Getting on the plane now; Estonia this time. Don't forget me—I'll be there soon.

I smile, write back, *I'm wearing combat boots. Have a safe flight x.*

I push thoughts of him out of my head and walk over to Anne Hathaway, who's pale and sports a mahogany bob and a slash of red lipstick. This is a woman who gets highly annoyed at press intrusion. Or maybe it's only the paps she doesn't like, which is fair because they aren't all photographers; some are criminals who carry cameras and stalk people, including children. I never gave much thought to Anne Hathaway the person, though I rolled my eyes with the rest of the world when she whispered inauthentically, *It came true* when she got her Oscar for *Les Misérables.*

After that, I didn't want to pile on the Hathaway hate, so I forgot about her.

Turns out she's not such a priss. "I was in *The Vagina Monologues* in college," she tells me, "so I was one of those girls who was really affected by the movement. My generation of girls, we remember what it was like when it wasn't OK to say the word *vagina*."

She's not done. "And now it's become something all of us can own, and being a part of seeing this change makes me passionate about things, including being able to say *vagina*. It makes me never want to go back."

Being forced to talk about vaginas makes me think about Caroline, who told me so vociferously how icky she found them. When Anne and I are done chatting, I frantically check the room for a distraction. I find one in the form of my dashing, onyx-haired pal from Ireland, Dylan McDermott. I want to run up to him and pronounce, *We'll always have Dublin*. But I wisely stop myself due to the Goldblum Rule. I keep an eye on him, but he slips out before I can catch him. Kerry Washington is next. She's composed and articulate and intent on getting her message across, which I take to be, *Don't try to make important issues more important by using celebrities*. "I'd rather not treat violence against women as petty gossip, but as a social illness that happens far and away outside Hollywood, too."

I don't say this about all actresses, but I get the distinct feeling she's one of the smartest people in this room.

41

I killed someone. That's what the detective is telling me. My palms are clammy, so I flatten them on the gray, scratched metal table to cool them down. The room is severe, barren, designed to remind its inhabitants they are powerless.

"Ms. Noble, we are left here with the same conundrum we started with," Barilla explains, leaning forward in his chair. "We need to know *why* this happened if we want to mitigate it, OK? We're really going to need you to remember what happened."

I am overcome with a chill like I've never felt. *If we want to mitigate.* I could not willfully kill a living creature. Not an animal, not a bug, not a human being.

Vito escorts my mother in. Jemima has her tough professor face on, but I see her hands shaking slightly. "Mrs. Noble," Barilla greets her. "Please have a seat. We're about finished for today, but I want you both to know how we'd like to proceed."

My mother has not yet mentioned a lawyer, and neither have I. I strongly suspect she had some secret talks with the cops while I was in the hospital. She sits in the third metal chair and the legs squeak loudly as she settles in.

"The doctors have confirmed that there is nothing physically—medically—wrong with Augusta, here." I can't blame him for addressing himself to my mother. When he tried to pry information out of me in the hospital, I was alternately screaming, crying, threatening, and catatonic.

My mother nods, turns to me. "Please, honey. If there's anything at all you can—"

"*Mom.*"

She holds up her hands. "OK, OK. I'm sorry. I'm just—I know it's your mind protecting you. We have to figure out a way around that."

She turns to Barilla. "How long do we have? Realistically? Before…"

Before. Before the shit hits the fan and I'm a suspect plastered on the front page of every New York newspaper.

"I can tell you the Lannells family is extremely motivated to keep this quiet until all the facts are known," Barilla says with a neutral expression. "Being who they are, they hold sway with the department, and with the District Attorney."

I *bet* they're motivated. They don't want their dead son branded a torturer and attempted murderer of women. If things stay as they are, if neither I nor Caroline remember what happened, Lincoln won't have a chance against the prodigal son.

"That said," Barilla adds, his tired voice croaking now, "the Lannells family is not going to wait forever to clear their son's name and seek justice. Nor is the DA's office."

My mother nods. "We understand."

"If and when Miss Rain wakes up, the doctors believe there is every chance she will have a catastrophic and possibly permanent memory loss," Barilla says. "And that's a lot of 'ifs.'"

I've reached my emotional limit for today. The tears spill over once again, and then I am sobbing. Vito leaves, I hope to get some tissues because my sleeves are already wet.

Barilla lets me cry for a minute, then clears his throat. "All that is left," he says, "is for you to remember. OK? To help you, we're going to give you some time to let the shock wear off, to get back to your normal life, and to spend some time with Ms. Rain."

The tears fall silently now. Vito returns with tissues, and I blow.

"So," my mother says, "you're saying my daughter will get the time she needs to grieve, heal, and get her memory back without fear of interference or pressure from the police?"

Barilla nods slowly and convincingly. "Correct—but it won't be forever. There's only so long we can stall this. And there's one condition." He turns to me. "You need to get into intensive therapy to help jog your memory, starting immediately."

"Done," my mother answers for me, then asks, "What about the media?"

Barilla nods. "Right. We're not releasing any names related to this case for now, save for the deceased. There are rape shield laws that will protect Caroline, and you as well"—he meets my eyes—"because the investigation is ongoing." Bile rises in my throat. "Anyway, you'd be surprised how much the press misses these days. In the old days, they'd scour the blotter and interrogate us if a raccoon knocked down a garbage can. Now, if we don't give them everything on a silver platter, stuff gets missed."

I've covered cops. Not once was I given anything on any platter, silver or otherwise. I take this to mean the blue wall is blocking even more these days, which in this case is a good thing.

"What about Lincoln?" My mother asks. Caroline's parents treated him like a foster son, and my mother met him more than a few times over the years. "What will it take to clear his name?"

"Lincoln Bray does not have a record of violent crime," Barilla tells us. "One count of possession of marijuana. There is nothing in his history that would suggest any propensity for violence. However, there will be no clearing of any names until we find out *exactly* what happened. Is that understood?"

42

#64, #65, #66, #67, #68

It's George Clooney Day, otherwise known as Three Days to Alexander. First up is the junket presser. Conference Room D at yet another five-star hotel is pulsing with the anticipation of seeing the greying star in the flesh. A half hour after forty reporters and photographers are seated, George walks in, followed by the film's director and three co-stars no one cares about. They take their seats at a heavy wooden table on a platform looking down on the rest of us.

George shows no signs of anxiety or self-consciousness. His skin appears yellow-orange in a white polo shirt; he's flashing a row of bleached Chiclets. He greets us, cracks a quick joke, winks at a co-star. He's been here a thousand times before; he does this the same way the rest of the working public yawns through PowerPoint presentations in the Wednesday-morning meeting.

After a snoozefest of questions about the movie and what a wacky prankster George is on set, a young reporter stands up to face the stage. In a soft voice, the reporter throws George a softball hybrid question about the difficulty of working in Hollywood while having a personal life that's endlessly spun into tabloid fodder. George waits a beat; then he laughs at this reporter in the same way that boys used to laugh at me on the playground. The Oscar-winner scolds, "I'm very disappointed in you. I mean, everyone is a little ashamed of you right now."

The reporter appears shocked. George asks the reporter's name, further singling this person out in a room that's fallen deadly silent. I feel my blood pressure climbing. "Everybody remember that name," George mocks. "Great interview. You should be proud."

My mouth is agape. There is some nervous chuckling, but ultimately Clooney's outburst does its job. No one else asks anything other than film-related questions the rest of the conference, and I don't even bother trying. On the way out, I ask myself, why didn't I stick up for that reporter? Same reason as everyone else. Because I need this job. I think about what Caroline would've done, and I am ashamed. This is why the bullies win.

I spend the next three hours in the lobby bar typing out my transcript of the press conference. When I'm done filing, I do some people watching and hope George is in a kinder headspace at the charity gala this evening. The more I think about his performance, the more I wonder why he singled out this one reporter for asking a perfectly reasonable question. I Yammer George's recent interviews, and whaddaya know: He's given tons of quotes about his personal life. At a recent premiere, for example, he expounded about his wife breastfeeding the kids. What does this say about him? To me, it says he demands control. *He* decides who gets to ask what, and when.

After freshening up and applying my evening makeup, I head to the function room to claim my spot on the red carpet. The children come through first: a girl in a wheelchair, a boy on crutches, a little one wearing leg braces and a gargantuan grin. They are glowing, wide-eyed, giggling, and I am as excited as they are; happy tears threaten to interfere with my professionalism.

Danny DeVito struts out next, cackling and spewing a fine spittle as that voice we all know blasts through the chaotic room. His wild black hair rings his head like he's been struck by lightning. He gives everything to the moment. Each word he says makes the kids laugh, and it helps that he's not much taller than they are. Only when I take my eyes off Danny for a second do I see George walking stiffly behind him, carried in the wake of his friend as if Danny's the bigger star.

George stops right in front of me so I have a close-up of his profile. The cocky face is gone. He's got a sallow complexion. He's slighter than he appears onscreen and looks his age, which isn't far off sixty. His smile is fragile, and it wavers as the kids are drawn to Danny, who points to his old pal and growls an introduction. "Everyone—this is Geooorrrrge!"

Everyone looks at George and they all crack up. He is doing the penguin, arms stiffly by his sides, unsure how to connect with the kids. He's nice; he asks one boy if he likes snow. Danny is a natural, the pied piper leading everyone to joy, but George has to make a herculean effort. The first fully relaxed smile I see from him is when the event rep beckons him over to pose for photos.

I interview one of the kids and she's by far my favorite encounter of all time. "I'm gonna kick butt on the stage," she says in a six-year-old's sweet voice. "Make sure you watch!"

"I wouldn't miss it," I tell her, holding back more happy tears.

Meryl Streep swings by. Her blonde hair is set in a relaxed chignon and she wears fetching spectacles. After she poses for photos, she gives print reporters a couple of lines about "a worthy cause" and "how much fun this is!" She's nice enough, but has little use for red-carpet reporters.

George does a quick TV interview. When he passes by me afterward, I call out to him: *George….Geoooorrrgggeee,* but he flits his eyes away, apparently displeased with what he sees. "Nah," he says, and keeps walking. Four reporters down, on my left, a pretty, petite platinum blonde with an angora turtleneck calls out to him.

He stops short. "Yes," he says to the pretty blonde.

"After this" —she waves her arms in the kids' direction— "do you want more children of your own?"

He doesn't miss a beat. "Nice try," he replies, turns on his heel, and disappears.

George is at his best on stage. Even as he stutters through a fuckup—he announces there are five hundred countries on earth—he draws hearty laughs. I have a prime seat in the small theater, stage left, second row; I can see deep into the wings. When it's time for the music, a multitalented R&B legend treats the audience to a once-in-a-lifetime performance of her best songs while George and Meryl stand tucked away in a dark corner in the wings. I watch them clap, sway and sing along; Meryl looks euphoric. George stands close to her, occasionally attempting a sway and looking as if he might topple over. Meryl grabs George's arm with excitement more than once. The legend bows at the end of her final song, drops the mic, and strides offstage. Meryl's face is like a kid at Christmas. She holds out both arms, bends her knees slightly, ready to catch the Legend in a giant hug. *I am Meryl Streep. Come to me.* George nods and smiles.

The Legend brushes past them both without a flicker of recognition. I watch Meryl's arms fall back by her sides slowly, her face turning from joy to shock to hurt. I want to run up and tell her it's all going to be OK, that the Legend probably didn't see her clearly as she waited in the shadows. The tiniest part of me—an atom-sized bit, really—feels a blip of *schadenfreude* that even Meryl Streep gets humbled sometimes.

When the show's over I head to the bar, on the look-out for George. I'm deciding what to order when I realize Parker Posey, the talented and ultra-cool muse of nineties indie films, is next to me with an empty glass. The bartender raises his eyebrows.

"You need another?" I ask Parker.

"Grey Goose, rocks," she nods. "Thanks."

"Same," I say, "but add some olive juice and make it a dirty martini."

We get our drinks and I introduce myself to her. She nods agreeably.

"I'll give you quotes," she says. "I'm not going to mess around. I know you're *working*. I mean, sometimes I do evade and avoid, but I know it's a job and I'll give you good quotes."

Obviously, I love her immediately. I ask what she's been up to lately.

"I love reading great writers," she says. "Standing on stage and doing readings. I could do that 'til the cows come home. This is what I do since my movie and TV career are gone."

"*Whoa*. What? No," I say, shaking my head violently. "You were just in a movie with Nicole Kidman!"

She shrugs, waves me away. "I was supposed to do a reading in New York Wednesday night, but I wasn't feeling well. I fainted on Tuesday."

"*Wait*. You fainted? Are you OK?" *Is this a story?*

"It's not a huge deal." She shrugs. "It's just vasovagal syncope."

"Poor you," I say. We finish our drinks and I thank her and set off again to find George and look up "vasovagal syncope." *Parker Posey: 10.0, obviously.*

I don't find Big G, but I do see Kevin Kline, and why the hell not. He's standing with a man who has *fan* written all over him. Kevin is nodding and agreeing with whatever the guy is saying, but glancing around at the same time. I catch his eye and hold up my notebook to prove my officialness.

"Hi, Kevin. I'm Augusta with *CelebLife*. Do you have time for an interview?"

"Of course," he booms as if he's on stage doing Shakespeare.

The fan thanks him and bids him adieu as I muscle in. We exchange pleasantries, and I find I could bask in Kevin's grand theatrical delivery forever. I eventually ask him what he does to relax. He stares off into the distance, presumably considering my question.

"Beaches can be tranquil," I prod after a few moments of silence.

"What?" He pretends to be confused.

"What I'm getting at is, do you have a favorite beach?"

"You're writing a story about beaches?" He leans in to take a peek at my notebook. "What've you got so far?"

"Orient Bay nude beach in St Martin," I say. "Just kidding. You're the first I've asked."

Crap, I've done it again. Stanley's voice echoes in my mind from the past: *Don't piss off the celebrities. Stay classy.*

"There's a nude beach in St. Martin?"

"Yes, but the nude people there are not the ones you want to see naked."

We're standing close because the party is packed. I try not to invade his space.

"They never are," he nods in agreement.

There is a pause, during which he appears to be thinking very hard.

"My favorite beach…"

Pause.

"You know, I've been to so many."

Twenty-second pause.

"You don't have to be anywhere, do you?" His grey-blue eyes meet mine.

I can't help it. I burst out laughing until I cry. Normally I'd own up to the fact that I'd asked a dud of a question and move on. But, in his own way, Kevin's not letting me.

"OK," I say, cringing visibly, "You really don't have to answer if you don't want to. But—*but*. Who doesn't love beaches?"

"People who have fair skin and have to slather on inches of high powered SPF sunscreen," he informs me, "and for whom it takes an hour to find the shade under which to hide or put sunscreen on and you're all greased down. 'Isn't this wonderful?' I *do* love the ocean, though."

"What's your favorite ocean?"

"I'm glad you asked." He's not.

He pauses to sign an autograph, then turns back to me and makes a great show of pretending to think about my question.

"Come on. What's your favorite ocean?"

"That would be, hands down…" He rubs his temple. "Name a few oceans."

"Who doesn't like the Pacific?"

Long pause.

"The Caribbean's beautiful."

Pause.

"Or is that a sea?"

"I believe so," he agrees. "I like the ocean Freud talked about," Kevin says. "I like oceanic feelings. You'll have to do an Internet search for that one."

"It sounds made up," I say.

"Oh, no no *no*," Kevin chastises me. "Freud wrote at length about an oceanic feeling. I like all the oceans, actually. I like the idea of oceans, I think we need more of them. I'm all for oceans."

I nod along with him, make a show of taking notes. "You're clearly pro-ocean."

"They're an unstoppable trend…they're here to stay," he says. "When they overflow because of the ice caps, all the science-doubters can put on their little water wings and float about saying, 'Isn't the ocean wonderful? Right here in my backyard.'"

There are tears of laughter rolling down my cheeks. Unfortunately, some official-looking people, probably heads of the charity, interrupt us. "I'd better let you get back to your fans," I say, smiling and wiping my eyes. "Thank you—really."

His eyes are wide. "Stay." He keeps eye contact. "Come on."

He's an actor and a gentleman, but I have to leave because Stanley is in my ear again: *He's an actor. Let him be.*

I'm suddenly giving out tens like they're Junior Mints. So what? Kevin's a ten, Parker's a ten.

Over a cosmo in a dark corner of the cocktail party, I write, *Entertainment is supposed to be about telling stories of our lives; of community and fun and connection; something sweet to escape this cruel life that slams you from wall to wall like a battered racquetball. The George Clooneys have forgotten that. They have lost their way.*

I needed some Parker and Kevin tonight. I needed them bad.

43

#69, #71, #72, #73

I'm early to the Thursday morning meeting, so I chat with Quinn about how we haven't heard from Stanley since the London layoffs. As the gang files in, I'm shocked to see an old nemesis: Uvula Garsh. She shuffles in and sits next to Maguire, who introduces her with a chilly wave of the hand.

"Everyone, say hello to Uvula. She'll be in the office for the next few weeks, to get us through awards season." Everyone nods, smiles, pretends to be happy to see her, but I feel the trepidation. I hear she conducted the layoffs here a couple weeks ago.

Tracey hits the lights, and Quinn puts a photo show up. It's international sex symbol, talented musician and successful businesswoman Beyoncé, and *uh oh*—we've got cellulite, people.

"She may have a yacht, but her thighs look like cottage cheese," observes one CelebLife.com writer.

Next up: Justin Timberlake doing jazz hands.

"I *loooveee himmm*," Tatiana squeals.

"He's the worst. And he looks like a mole chewing a firecracker," Esdee hits back.

"We have a shoot with him next week," Maguire says flatly. "I guess we know who we're *not* sending to that."

"I hope you rented a space with a big door," says one of the boys of CelebLife.com, a young guy with a mess of a man bun I want to douse in hornet spray. Half the room looks at him. "So his head can fit through," he explains. "I did an event with him a few months ago. Let's just say he is deeply enamored with himself. Not the nicest fellow you'll ever meet."

I don't mean to, but I exhale loudly, then laugh nervously. "I thought this was the *nice* magazine." *Ha ha.* Laugh it off, and you can still be one of them.

"It's not bullying when you do it in private," Esdee informs me. "They put themselves out there for our consumption. Blame *them* for airbrushing everything, so that when we actually see their *real* selves, it's a shock. It's bad for girls, teens, and women when they make us believe Angelina Jolie has great skin or any one of them on Insta has a waist that's *actually that small* or there's anything of Kim Kardashian's original face left. Sorry," she holds her hands up. "But they're fair game."

"Totally," I agree. She is right in a way, and I'm complicit too. I'm self-aware enough to know that. Jemima raised me to look inward at every opportunity, which is part of the reason I'm half insane, but anyway.

"Moving ON," Maguire booms.

Quinn clicks a button and up goes someone I once met, a lanky boy with innocent eyes, freckled cheeks, and a shy smile.

"Tristan Catlin," Tracey narrates. "What the hell happened to him?"

I don't know. The shy, lanky boy I met on the ice that day no longer exists, and I don't know what did it to him, Hollywood or life. His eyes are puffy, he's got a hint of alcohol bloat (I know from bloating), and he's had his normal-looking nose whittled down to please the cameras. Tristan became the darling of independent film a few years after I interviewed him. The world was introduced to "Tristan Tears" when he cried in every other scene in *And She Played On,* a movie in which his piano-genius dying wife threw herself in front of a car to save his life. It earned him an Oscar nod but no award. Marrying America's sweetheart, Josephine Jansen, put him on the A-list and got him a role in an action franchise—at which point his marriage to Josephine began to crumble. She held on for a long time, after co-star affairs and rumors of various addictions, but now they're embroiled in a messy split.

"We're hearing Tristan is still living at the house. He's been seen there," Esdee says.

"Great," Maguire nods to Tracey. "Is Ivan confirming?"

"Does he ever?"

I get a hit of nausea. Hyper-controlling powerhouse publicist Ivan "The Deceiver" Deaver is both a thorn in the L.A. bureau's side and a mythical beast they speak of in hushed tones. He's also someone who might remember me; I'm still not sure if he got a good look before I ran out on his client's coke-doused hundred-dollar bill.

"Right. So how's he doing?" Maguire asks.

"I'm still hearing from sources that Tristan's pulling away from Josephine for good this time, but still wants to be seen as a family man. He can't be the guy who leaves his family, you know? I tell you," Esdee says, "Josephine Jansen's a saint."

"A doormat, you mean," someone mumbles.

"Look," Maguire says, "this couple is priority Number One. His big premiere is Thursday. Augusta's doing the red carpet."

"He's not going to talk on the *carpet*," Uvula sniffs. "If he even shows up."

"We know that," Maguire snaps. "Tracey's inside the after party and Esdee's on sources. We're covered."

"Let me know if you need anything else," I chime in. "I'm happy to pitch in."

"Do you have sources?" Maguire turns an icy gaze on me.

I have to shake my head.

"Didn't think so," she replies. "Stick to the carpet and get all the color you can. If Tristan so much as looks at a female for more than two seconds, report back. That said, he might skip the entire thing. But we need to be ready. OK. Assignments for the day, Esdee?"

Esdee nods. "I need someone good for this sexual abuse charity gala tonight. It's a sensitive thing—we need someone who can handle real news. In other words, no cub reporters." She throws a look my way. "Augusta, you free?"

I nod. "Sure."

"Speaking of events," Tatiana says to Maguire, "I've been getting complaints from stringers. They need more work—apparently, we've been doling out too many events in-house."

I want to crawl under the table.

Maguire looks at me. "I'll take that under advisement," she says.

On the way out of the meeting, Maguire waits for me at the door. "Walk with me," she says without looking up from her phone. She strides down the hall alongside Uvula while I nip at their heels. "You're doing a decent job in the office," Maguire says tightly. "But if you can't start producing sources, I'm not sure how much more I can use you."

Use you. Such an apt turn of phrase. She works her thumbs on her phone. "Everyone's on the same footing in this bureau, Augusta. No sources, no spot. That's how it works."

She looks up. I see a glint of enjoyment in her eyes as I squirm. "If our loyal stringers—we've known these people for *years*—don't have enough assignments to keep them busy, that doesn't work," she says.

We're at her office door. Uvula walks into the office next to hers, not even noticing me, let alone remembering me from London.

"I get it," I lie. "That's why I volunteer to go out so much at night. I'm always working on building sources."

"*Mmm hmm,*" she responds mildly. "Talk to me when you have actual quotes, 'kay?" The sarcasm zings off her. With that, I am dismissed.

Great. I'll just sidle up to Lady Gaga's gardener and try to get some intel without her calling the cops on me. I head back to my cubicle. London seems farther away than ever, and in between my worries about how I'll reach my goal— unbelievably, I'm nearing 70 stars—is a nagging thought I keep beating back: *What if I DO make it? What then?* Because as much as Maguire doesn't want me, I don't want her, either. Without this goal, what do I have? I never thought I'd do it, not really, but once I hit 50, there was no chance I'd give up. I have to remember it was supposed to change things—and it will. *It has to.*

In the meantime, with three days until Alexander, the beautification process is well underway: I'm waxed, pedicured, and spray tanned. I've been planning how I'm going to punish him, make him earn me back: *This doesn't mean you're forgiven. Don't think this can go anywhere, because it can't. We're both too transient, unstable.* All of this is preferably said between make-out sessions. I bought new pink satin lingerie and told Esdee and June I'd be at the doctor that day. It's time to grow up. The guy, a fun, gorgeous, talented guy, likes *me*. Time to embrace it.

Elsa Pataky, actress and wife of Thor, is routinely called "thirsty" on celebrity blogs. They say the petite Spanish beauty clawed at fame's door begging to be let in, and now that she's inside it's still not enough for her. If you read blind items, she's castigated for being phony, a user, and worse. From where I'm standing on this charity gala's red carpet, Elsa is something else: Cooperative, fun and helpful. Not to mention stunning and happy.

Pose, Elsa! Now turn! Hug Chris. Wonderful—brilliant. Good girl. Thank you!

Is she harming anyone by playing the game they've all signed up for? In contrast, her six-foot-three husband Chris Hemsworth looks like he's about to cry. He's utterly concerned because we reporters are not asking him the right questions. He's careful not to come off angry; instead, he tries to connect with us, bring us in on it: *Guys, come on. We're here for a good cause. We're here to talk about making the world a better place!*

When he's asked about Miley Cyrus, Elsa takes over. "We love her. She's wonderful, and as long as Liam is happy, we're happy." She radiates joy.

Chris is the first and only celebrity I've met who I believe genuinely wishes fame and worship didn't accompany the money and the craft. In part because he's said as much, and also because he's the first superstar I've met—I mean, come on, he's *Thor*—who's balanced respect and empathy toward reporters with his annoyance and disappointment in us. Anyway, Chris ends up giving us some of what we want, and I absorb a few minutes of his attention as his man-musk drizzles down on me from above, his blond hair in a low ponytail that works on him, those sad blue eyes pleading for me to ask about the charity, not his brother or his kids. I semi-comply by asking him what's most important in this life. "This cause matters so much to me," he tells me. "The environment, too. Our children deserve a clean planet. They need a *live* planet."

"And fatherhood," I say, "that's important, too?"

"It's amazing," he tells me. "It's everything." And *boom*—I've got a story.

When the smoking-hot couple leaves the carpet, I zoom over and privately ask Elsa how she's doing. "Great," she says, either excited to meet me or faking it very well.

"What's it like being in the spotlight? It seems to me that for every compliment there's a bunch of abuse that follows…"

"I don't know," she replies, thinking about it for a moment. "I am just myself. I am very, very happy, and maybe that bothers some people."

Her Spanish accent is adorable and she's beyond stunning and I want us to be friends. Chris takes her hand, and she crinkles up her eyes, smiles at me, waves…and I think, *There is no photo or movie screen that does them justice.* I don't know who's cheated or who's fame hungry, but one thing is for sure: They are by far the hottest couple I've ever been in the same room with.

I write in my notebook, *The most jealous you'll ever feel is of a person who's truly at peace and happy. No matter what they own, where they live, what they look like. True happiness is so rare, and it's the one thing celebrities can't find. They try harder than any of us to fill the hole, and when they realize they're finally famous but still miserable, it's enough to send them into an incurable depression.* Fuck it. I give them each a 10.0.

Next up is Patton Oswalt. I catch him off the carpet, when it's quiet, and he tells me he's only here and awake thanks to "four Diet Cokes. Life is busy. I'm grateful." *Even after what he's been through?* Life as a dad "is incredible and one of the hardest things you'll do," he responds. All you have to do is read his accounts of pushing through the grief of losing his wife to know what kind of a guy he is. When I say I'm sorry and that I'll let him go, he does a quick semi-bow of the head and says, "Of course! It's an honor."

He makes me feel good; he makes me smile. I scribble in my book as I wait for the next star: *We know how easily one small kindness can change things. We know better than to be stingy with our compliments. Why is it so hard to remember?*

I stand on tiptoes and see Hilary Swank posing for photos. I doubt she'll talk. Surely she thinks we're fluff. I am thoroughly unprepared when, seconds later, Hilary stops before me with a bright, expectant expression. She's in a white sleeveless dress, and her long hair parted in the middle, wavy at the bottom and slick at the top, like she hasn't washed it in days. I let her expound on how great a job this sexual abuse prevention charity has done. She stares earnestly into my eyes.

"This work is so necessary," Hilary raves. "The people who run it are an inspiration."

After gamely answering a few more questions, she says, "Thanks so much for being here. It's so important."

I never thought of myself as a Hilary Swank fan, but I'm one now.

The lights flicker, indicating cocktail hour is ending and it's time for dinner. I make my way through Scapollini, a gigantic restaurant and event space known for its reliable and grossly overpriced Italian fare. The place looks like a 1920s disused bank (which it is), with majestic columns and vaulted ceilings. I find my table, which is near the center, close to the front. Table Six—pride of place. I take a seat, then look to my right and spot one of my all-time favorites, Mr. Kyle MacLachlan. I stiffen, rework my posture, run my tongue over my teeth, and turn to the man you never hear a bad whisper about. With my luck, he's a dick who'll hate me simply because I adore him and we'll be stuck with each other for three long gala hours.

He smiles, holds out his hand. "Hello," he says. "I'm Kyle."

"Nice to meet you," I say, shaking his hand firmly. "I'm Augusta. With *CelebLife* magazine."

"Oh! Nice to meet you. It's great you're covering this."

Kyle, whose image appears under the word *dashing* in any dictionary I'd want to use, introduces me to the glamorous Spanish artist to his right, whom he's just met, and I reach across him to shake her hand. I sense someone hovering to my left who drops a phone on the empty seat. I look up to see Hilary Swank grinning widely at me. I smile back; she gives me a tight little wave and takes off. Her phone, in a white case, sits alone on the chair.

I reach across the table and grab a breadstick. I notice wine is sitting open in the center of the table, so I pour myself some Pinot Grigio, which I don't like much, but which I will tolerate. My hand twitches in the direction of the phone, orphaned and ripe on Hilary's seat. I want to grab it and protect it for her, but I know how that would look. I take a sip of wine as Hilary returns, chirping, "Hello, hello!" to us. There are now six of us and two empty place settings.

Once she's seated, I turn and mock-chastise her: "Hilary Swank," I say, as if she's a naughty teenager, "you left your phone *alone.* There are people everywhere waiting to steal your stuff—I wouldn't risk it."

She makes a sheepish and thankful face, then giggles at me.

"Oh, you're right," she breathes. "I shouldn't do that. Thanks for looking out for it!"

She's so nice. So open. She must've enjoyed my interview questions. Kyle leans across me and introduces himself to Hilary. They chat briefly before she turns back to her left, where some of the charity's staff are sitting. They're talking about sexual assault. The number of people who report their assaults—the numbers are too low. The actual number of rapes is sky-high. In this new world of #ItHappenedToMe and #NoMore, I note a disconnect between what we're talking about—regular people, big cities, small town America—and what women in Hollywood have gone through. I say nothing as we all eat our salads and buttered rolls they bemoan the terrible state of women's safety in this world, and I am triggered six ways to Sunday.

"Chances are," I say quietly after a while, "if you look at the numbers, now there are eight of us, someone at this table has been a victim of sexual assault."

Hilary nods passionately. "Yes, *yes*. That's true!"

"You know," I say, breaking the silence, "When I wrote about this issue when I was just starting out, it was something to be whispered about. It's harrowing the hear the stories, but so important to—"

And with that, Hilary changes; her face is now twisted into an angry mask. "You're from *CelebLife*! I just realized it," she snarls. "I just got all sweaty under the armpits."

I am rendered speechless. I tighten my grip on the wineglass. I am resetting, trying to recognize this new Hilary. I don't really want to know about her armpits, frankly.

She softens her expression slightly and pleads, "*Please* don't write about anything I've said. I really didn't mean for this to be written about. *Really*."

Don't write what? That Hilary Swank appears engaged, empathetic, totally against sexual abuse, and works to educate herself further? "I'm here for the presentation," I assure her. "For the charity. There's nothing to worry about."

"You don't understand. The tabloids have been *terrible* to me, OK? *OK*?!"

She's *mad* at me for being here, though we had a nice interview just fifteen minutes ago.

She shakes her head as if to loosen the bad thoughts. "I THOUGHT YOU WERE WITH THE CHARITY. I meet so many people. I didn't recognize you, OK? I've talked to a lot of people since then."

What? I'm guessing it's occurred to her she's only making things worse, because she turns away and stops speaking. A guy shows up late and drags a chair between me and Hilary. They start chattering away; he's a TV producer. Hilary whips out her phone and starts showing him pictures of her pets. I always admired her for her hands-on animal rescue efforts on the streets of L.A.

She shoots me looks, covers her phone with her hand, says loud enough for me to hear, "Don't let her see." (*Snotty look*). "Oh, just kidding!" She narrows her eyes. *Not kidding.*

I don't give a shit about our magazine's don't-upset-the-celebrity rule right now. I'm not going to be bullied by this woman. I level a calm gaze at her. "You're mean," I say simply, effectively, and loud enough for her to hear.

She recoils as if slapped, then recovers quickly and goes back to showing off her photos.

"Are you enjoying the evening?" Kyle says, blissfully unaware of my Hilary drama. The first part of the presentation has concluded and my tablemates start cutting into their chicken while I munch on a roll. I notice Hilary hasn't touched her food.

"I am," I smile. "It's a beautiful event. But I don't think everyone is as thrilled as you are to be seated next to a reporter."

"Oh?" Kyle keeps his face neutral. "Well. You can write anything you want about me. I'm happy to provide you with a scandal if you need one."

"I'll keep that in mind," I say, and finally start to relax.

He nods, then turns to listen to something the artist is saying. She's gorgeous and fascinating, so I join in in and manage to enjoy the rest of the dinner. I will forever love Kyle MacLachlan, dashing and diplomatic 'til the end: *10.0.*

I always have to know *why* about everything, such as, why did Hilary get so spooked? Back at my apartment, I search the Internet for *Hilary Swank + controversy*. Results burst onto the screen. *The Independent*'s headline reads, *So, what first attracted Hilary Swank to Chechnya's brutal tyrant?* Beneath that is an article outlining how she reportedly took hundreds of thousands of dollars to attend the thirty-fifth birthday party of despot Ramzan Kadyrov. After Hilary's manager Jason Weinberg assured Human Rights Watch that his client had no plans to attend, the *Independent*'s reporter wrote, *Fast forward exactly nine days, and, well, I think you can guess what happened. Dressed to the nines, and watched by this newspaper's Moscow correspondent, Ms. Swank sauntered up Mr. Kadyrov's red carpet before delivering a charming speech about how much she had already enjoyed her stay in Grozny. "I could feel the spirit of the people, and I could see that everyone was so happy," she said. "Happy birthday, Mr. President!"*

It's not just Hilary, to be fair. Fur-wearing diva Jennifer Lopez has reportedly been given money by "dictators and crooks" to perform, according to Human Rights Watch. Beyoncé sang for the Gaddafi family, allegedly for upwards of a cool million. (She insists she gave the proceeds to charity.) Sting played at the behest of an Uzbekistan dictator's family.

This is some ugly shit I did *not* know about. It's interesting that Hilary seems to blame "the tabloids" for it all. Here's an idea: If you don't want the media reporting your shitty behavior, don't act like a shit. They say narcissists are drawn to Hollywood. If you ask me, masochists are drawn to celebrity journalism. In the end, as I lay my head on the pillow, I'm hit with a realization: I owe Hilary a debt of gratitude. I was going to lose it about the sexual assault talk until she got weird. After that, her bizarre turn was all I focused on, and if I see her again, I will thank her for that.

44

#74, #75, #76, #77

I yawn, roll over, and grab my phone to check Cele-bLife.com. My story about Thor and Elsa is number two, under breaking news about Zac Efron's love life—which is great, but I still don't have the magical *sources* that will secure my place at the magazine. From what I can tell, Maguire is not one for idle threats, and I know I'm in danger of being jettisoned from the only gig that can get me to my goal. I also have one voicemail, which is unsettling. Who calls anyone anymore? I hit play, close my eyes, and fall back on the pillow.

My therapist's voice in the message is calm, but her words are not. She pierces my glamorous Hollywood bubble with news from Planet Reality. *Please call me back, Augusta. Your mother says she can't get ahold of you, either. We really need to talk.*

Busted—I haven't called my mom back in at least a week. I've been busy working nights, then showing up at nine-thirty meetings. She never said it was urgent, never left a message. I'd given all my contact information to Detective Barilla, but almost as soon as I left him, my numbers all changed and I made a point of not updating any of them with the police. If my therapist has been called in, it must be serious. I hit delete and head out for a hike around Runyon Canyon. Two days to Alexander, and still a chance to drop a few more pounds of water weight.

I'm at this music event but I'm not *here*. Breathing loudly and often isn't going to cut it this time. There are too many stressors fighting for space in my mind. Oh, look: Here comes Taylor Swift, who successfully pushes out thoughts of mom, the therapist, Caroline, violence.

"Taylor! *Tayyyllooorr*," I call out like a discarded friend begging for another chance. She's getting closer and says hello to a few music journos on her way to me, but doesn't give any interviews. She's taller than I am, but she hunches, making me want to adjust her shoulders with two firm hands—but I don't, because security is on us like white on Ryan Reynolds' teeth. Here's the thing about Taylor: You hear she's a de facto music mogul, not just a pop-singer/songwriter, but she *really is*. I watch the aging, wrinkling, non-skinny record execs who are always around these events guarding their assets, and here, Taylor is the boss of *them*. You can see it in the body language, in the way she walks ahead of them and they stop when she stops. I am starting to not believe in the wailing lovelorn waif I see in her videos. When I ask one of the execs how Taylor keeps churning out the hits without a hitch, he says, "You have to ask Taylor. It's all her."

She's about to pass me by and I don't have time to ask her about her music. "How's everything going with your man? We're so happy for you!"

She stops, hand on hip, turns halfway like it's a cat-walk, and throws me two headline-grabbing words with those heart-shaped lips: "It's good." Then she flounces off.

In a world infected with Celebrity Stockholm Syndrome, in which I am Patient Zero, this counts as a journalistic coup. I watch Taylor go, crafting my headline as she moves away: *EXCLUSIVE: Taylor Swift Speaks out to CelebLife About her 'Good' Love.*

There is a kerfuffle and I can see the cause is worth ditching the carpet for. Two titans are about to converge in the lobby. I click on my video recorder. The world stops. We mortals stand with gaping mouths, expecting the seas to rise and the mountains to tremble as Beyoncé and Taylor come face to face. The smiling women move in for a hug. The room vibrates with the bigness of it all. They pull slightly apart, and in sharing a quick word and a laugh, they put on a show we're all lapping up, selling us a story we believe because we're heavily invested in it. I can see behind the curtain when they part ways, when the faces fall, when orders are barked, when Beyoncé sneaks out with a team of security that would put the President's to shame, when she nearly trips from walking so fast in spiked heels, frowns, then glares. I am left feeling empty. I'm growing weary of the narratives shoved down my throat, of images tightly contorted into what amounts to fiction.

Ahhhh. I exhale. Here's Aretha Franklin. Someone real. She's stuck in a scrum of stars and handlers congregating around print reporters. A few call out to her but she doesn't stop, and no one accosts her. I ask her very nicely for a chat, and she stops for me. Aretha—the living legend—brings me back down to earth. She's like a grouchy grandma with preternatural talent who's not putting up with your shit. She's not fooled by any of it. I tell her she's an icon and she can't deny it since everyone in this event space today has proclaimed it so.

"I'm just some lady next door," she tells me, "but I'm honored to be called an icon today, and I just hope I've set a good example for younger artists."

Yes, she has, I affirm, and she moves on to cocktail hour. I'm not invited, but I crash it and see one more legend I can't ignore: Barbra Streisand. I observe her for a bit before I approach. James Brolin watches over her as a few brave people move in to say hello. He rests a comfortable, light arm on her lower back for a moment; she leans in to whisper something in his ear. I decide to grab a drink before going in. I did my research, and she is irrefutably difficult, oversensitive, and rude. One writer summed her up this way: *Not even the most worshipful of her biographers can disguise the fact that she's a pain in the ass.*

I finish my drink, set it on the bar, and squirt some breath spray into my mouth. I exhale, steel myself, and walk up to Barbra. I'm ready to be abused by her. It could be fun. *Bring it, Babs.*

I introduce myself. Her response is along the lines of, "Oh, fine. What? Yes…"

I shoot a look to Mr. Brolin. He's waving to someone across the room.

"Do you ever break into song around the house?" I ask her. *Silence.* Someone bumps into me, but I stop myself from falling on Barbra.

"Do you sing at home?" I turn to James. "Does she sing at home?"

She makes a face like I have just flashed my boobs at her. "*Never.*"

A one-word answer means change the subject. "What are you going to do if you get the munchies during the show tonight? Some big names are performing."

She squints at me. "I can be a very bad girl," she replies. "Sometimes I'll even bring my own popcorn to the movies—there's so much butter on the stuff you have to buy there."

"I hear you," I nod. I figure I have one more question. I decide to make it about me. An important-looking man with grey hair, a stern face, and a designer suit has approached and is trying to get her attention.

"You live in Malibu, right?" I ask Barbra.

"Right…." She says suspiciously.

"No, I'm not going to come to your house," I laugh, and she half-smiles, half shakes her head at me. She flips her hair with one hand. "What I want to know is, are you afraid of climate change?" She pauses, so I ask the question I *really* want to know the answer to. "I mean, they say the tsunami is coming… are you scared? Ever since I moved to L.A.," I add, "I've been terrified. It's a matter of when, not if, they say."

I have made Barbra laugh. She waves a hand at me like I'm the help. "*Please*," she says. "We live on a cliff. The water would have to come up ninety-five feet to get us. Don't worry about things you can't control," she advises me. "It's not worth it."

Suit guy steps in, so I thank Barbra and move aside, standing in a corner to make notes in my book. I never thought I'd learn anything from a legendary diva who will never know my name, but I did: *Don't worry about things you can't control.* Everyone knows it; few of us live it. Because it's straight from Babs, I listen.

As I'm about the leave the venue, Hipster Reporter rushes up to me. "I hear Taylor's staying here tonight. I'm gonna go check out her floor. Wanna come?" I nod. I'm not missing a chance to spy on Taylor in any hotel-related situation.

"Great," Hipsters says. "If we pretend we're a couple, there's less chance of getting caught."

I follow him down a gray hallway toward the elevators. We ride up to the fifth floor, step out, and are instantly hit with a foul stench that pierces the nostrils like a nuclear sewer.

"What the *hell?*" Hipster yells. "That *smell*—it's burrowing into my *brain.* Oh my *god.*"

"I *know*," I screech, bending over and turning in the other direction as I gag. "I think I'm going to throw up. Look away!"

I don't vomit, though, and when I straighten up I make sure to breathe through my mouth. Hipster is pressing the elevator button repeatedly with two fingers. Two maids, impeccably dressed to luxury hotel standards, are getting closer to us. They're carrying a bunch of sheets between them, both holding on at arm's length. A third maid emerges from a room, presumably working on turndown service at this hour.

"*Qué es esto?*" she shrieks.

"*Agggg*," growls one maid hopelessly, then speaks in rapid Spanish, of which I understand a few words: *El cantante* is singer, and I think *otra vez* is again. But I don't understand others, like *cago.*

"Shit," I say. "*What* is going on?"

"Exactly," Hipster tells me nasally; he's not breathing through his nose either.

"*What?*"

"*Poop.* I speak Spanish fluently. The maids—they said, 'That singer pooped the bed again. He always does that when he's here.'" I just stare at Hipster. "I've heard about this. It's a sex thing apparently," he clarifies helpfully.

"Are you effing kidding me? What the *hell* is going on?" *And who is this deviant singer?* "I'll tell you this much," I add, "if I don't get out of here immediately, there's going to be more than poop in this hallway." I gag again.

Hipster slams the elevator button and I cover my mouth and nose, hoping I can hold on. It's *that strong* in this enclosed space, even though the maids have passed us now. Finally, the elevator opens. A singer stands before us. He's tall, sad-eyed and alone. He walks out, and I watch him move toward the room the poop maids came out of. *Wow.* His music is *almost* easy listening at this point, but he hangs out with a lot of cool people, so he's still a tabloid darling.

Hipster steps into the lift. "We'll never speak of this again," he hisses.

"Agreed," I say. "*Never,* ever."

The elevator opens five floors down and we go our separate ways. I still want to throw up.

Back at the apartment, I file my reporting minus the literal crap, then start to grow nervous about returning to the office tomorrow. If they see my face, it'll remind them they don't want me around anymore. I practice what Barbra preached, though, and fall asleep telling myself not to worry.

45

I'm hunched in my cubicle in the New York bureau of *Newstime*, staring at my monitor and typing one number over and over: *107…107…107.* The idea came to me in today's therapy session, after which I took a few minutes to gather my courage, then made a move for the exit. The therapist tried to talk me out of going—I think she sensed I wasn't planning on coming back—but when she couldn't stop me, she issued a chilling warning as I stood at the door, a clammy palm grasping the handle: "I can keep the police at bay for now. But don't fall off the radar," she said. "Sooner or later, they're going to come for you. My bet is on sooner."

I thanked her for her concern, then bolted and fast-walked the ten blocks back to *Newstime*'s offices, where I am right now, trying to figure out how this brilliant plan will actually work. It was that famous Schweitzer quote my mother loves so much that set it all in motion: *In everyone's life, at some time, our inner fire goes out. It is then burst into flame by an encounter with another human being.* Well, my flame has gone out. I'm lost, listless, ruined. In the two months since the Horror happened, I've tried hypnosis (they told me I was resisting), meditation, going to the gym too much, walking the length of Manhattan, Ambien, Xanax, vodka, binge eating, and writing. I still can't remember everything that happened in Caroline's room.

I need those celebrities—the exact number of faces that adorned my walls as a teenager— to relight my fire. But how can I possibly get close to that many famous people? I type out another number: 103. That's how many stars are left after JFK Jr., Matthew, Jason, and Tristan Catlin, who's done quite well for himself since our hockey meeting. *I can do this. I WILL do this.*

At three-thirty, Jeff, *Newstime*'s associate editor of finance, carries in two large cheese pizzas. "For the afternoon lull," he says, laying the pies on the table in the common area behind my cubicle. He leans over and opens a box, releasing a smell of oregano and melted mozzarella that lures the staff from their offices one by one, attracted like bears to garbage.

Before I can reach for a slice, I start shaking. The tears come instantly, as if someone turned on a faucet. I turn and run to the bathroom. It takes a few minutes, but I manage to force myself to stop bawling, blow my nose, wipe my face, reapply some makeup. I make my way to my desk.

"Hey, there she is!" Jeff says too brightly, like I just got back from the asylum.

Gerry, our boss, nods to me as he stuffs pizza in his face.

"I quit," I find myself saying to him, as he works on a large bite.

He tries to swallow too soon and almost chokes.

"You *quit*?" Bits of mozzarella fly out of his mouth.

"Yes."

"Are you…OK?"

"I'm OK," I say. "I'm just—"

"Is this some kind of joke? Is this about the promotion? Because, frankly, you're just not ready. I thought I made that clear. I mean…you *know* how many writers beg me for a job every week, right?"

Gerry is relatively new. My last boss, a fierce, brilliant chief of correspondents, was "let go" four months ago for being old and having cancer. If I'd quit on his watch, he'd have told me to walk to Vermouth, order an oversized martini, and "get my head straight."

"No joke, Gerry," I say calmly. "I'm leaving."

Everyone has gone quiet. No one intervenes.

"You're aware that your contract requires two weeks' notice?" Gerry says. "So, um, yeah, I'm gonna need that before you go. And, um…let's take this offline, OK?"

I gather up some pens, a couple half-used notebooks, a book. "I'll be leaving now," I tell him. It's odd; I'd started carting personal stuff away over the past few weeks in a sort of unconscious preparation.

Greta, one of our senior writers, steps in, touches Gerry's arm, says in her softest yoga-instructor voice, "Let her go. She's clearly going through something. Give her a pass—maybe she'll come in tomorrow like this never happened."

He doesn't answer her. "Hey," he says to me as I hike my purse onto my shoulder, "those notebooks are company property."

For once, I don't cry. I burst out laughing, give him the finger, and fast-walk out of there.

When I make it back to my apartment, I calm down and figure out what sent me into a panic: We'd ordered pizza the night before it happened, Caroline and I. We'd wolfed down huge, greasy slices from Ray's. I am living a bad Off-

Broadway play called *Pizza: A trigger*. And now I'm unceremoniously unemployed. I sit cross-legged on my bed, computer on my lap, and go through my options. There's one particular magazine that has to be the one—the one stars seem to trust most, that vaunted, long-lived American institution called *CelebLife*. No other publication has their kind of access. Jennifer Lawrence doesn't do sit-down interviews with *Star Scene*. Tom Cruise doesn't stop for a red-carpet chat with *We Now! CelebLife* was created for people who want out of the real world; its pages were made for redemption.

I find contact information for *CelebLife* editors in New York and L.A. and write to them. I tell them about my six years of experience interviewing all kinds of people (including JFK Jr., of course), and my Ukee Award for excellence in New England journalism. I attach my biggest features for *Newstime*. I have two months' savings. After that, it's back to the parents' townhouse, in which case, kill me. I entertain the thought that maybe I should've waited to quit *Newstime* until I'd landed another gig, but I push the thought away. What's done is done.

46

#78, #79, #80, #81

Matthew McConaughey: *Has what we call in the writing biz "piercing blue eyes." Talked about losing weight for roles—sticks to "a few ounces of fish, some steamed vegetables," then chows down on cheeseburgers when it's over. Sometimes uses big words like he's practiced them at home. Talked about parenting in general, but when I asked about the kids, chided me somewhat opaquely. "Hey…what happens in our house, happens in our house." Um…OK…* **Camila Alves:** *Someone you automatically hate—curvy and skinny at the same time, with skin like body butter. She came out of a factory. I brought up Matt's draconian diets. Shrugged, "We like it. We're quite disciplined anyway…it's fun." FUN?! Are these people for real? There she is, in her Malibu mansion with her shirtless husband and their brood, and she's serving up a can of plain tuna for lunch and loving it? 8.0 for both.*

After finishing my diary notes from my one-on-one with Matthew, I sit in the pressroom and munch a mini-veggie croissant, carbs and all, figuring out how long I should drag out transcribing Matthew's wise words. I plan to skip going back to the office, go home instead, and get ready for Alexander's visit tomorrow. I'm *almost* relaxed when Tatiana shoots me an "urgent" email demanding I cover a premiere tonight. She doesn't give me the option of no.

Just as I'm tensing up about that, my phone rings—Mom again, but I'm too overwhelmed to speak to her. I hit cancel and send her a text. *Working, will get back to you when I can. xo.*

The reply comes swiftly. *I REALLY NEED TO TALK TO YOU*

She doesn't know how to get out of caps lock or use punctuation. I'm sure it's fine. I grab a miniscule brownie and a diet soda from the buffet and settle in to type out Matthew's interview.

Four hours later I arrive at the premiere, where everything is an eye-watering shade of electric blue. I don't know what this movie's about, but I'm standing in an anti-freeze-soaked world as I wait for Ryan Reynolds on the blueberry carpet behind an azure velvet rope.

Packs of reporters and photographers wait like cattle, listless and thirsty, for an hour before the first notables wind their way down the carpet. I check my assignment sheet again. This week, the editors are obsessed with what they call "health" questions, which are in fact more like roadmaps to the nearest eating disorder. *How do you stay so thin (if any give you their lowest weight ever = bonus)? What's the lowest number of calories you'll eat in a day when preparing to go on camera? (make sure to ask their tips for readers who want to drop weight quickly!) What are your red-carpet-ready diet tips (get specifics: Star Caps? Protein shakes? Gwyneth Paltrow's detox regime? Enemas?).*

"Ryan's never going to stop for me," moans a reporter three down from me.

"It's his movie," says an entertainment-TV reporter. "He'll talk."

"Maybe to you. He's a moody one, and I can't put him on TV."

I've heard chatter in the office and around town about the different facets of Ryan's personality. He's popular on social media for pics of himself in the gym and his wry wit...like when he posted a photo of himself on his wife's birthday as a joke, *ha ha*. Somehow it was still all about Ryan Reynolds. Anyway, it's Blake Lively who comes down first—alone. When she finishes with the photographers, she whooshes by the rest of us in a flounce of taffeta.

"*Blake! Blaaaakeee*," I yell out wistfully. She turns to look, then ignores me. I hear a roar from the photographers, and here comes Ryan, posing and causing mayhem simply by standing there in a fancy suit. As he draws closer to me, I see the teeth first. They look new and whiter than snow. There's one rep carrying his stuff, one guarding him, and one buffering him from the minions who want to give his movie free publicity. When Ryan appears unhappy with something—the noise? The weather?—someone pats him on the arm and talks him down.

Ryan's turning it on for the TV reporters to my left, gnashers glowing. He's wry, sharp, and finds it a challenge to smile, but seems to enjoy watching others react to his humor. Unlike some actors, there are no immediate surprises with IRL Ryan: He's as tall, lean, and healthy as he looks onscreen. Up close, though, his nose looks much different than it did on that sitcom I used to love about the pizza place. (I've noticed there seems to be only one nose allowed in Hollywood these days: straight and delicately tipped. Not even the likes of Scarlett Johansson, Robert Downey Jr., Ryan Gosling, or Angelina Jolie got away with the schnozzes they were born with. Ryan didn't have a prayer.) When he gets to the print journos, he gives a couple lines to *The Hollywood Reporter.*

I'm next. Ryan locates his handler, who nods down the line in my direction, and Ryan glances over. I click on my recorder. As the rep hangs back, holding his stuff, Ryan stops a few feet away from me. One more big step and he'll be in my face, primed for an interview. He looks at me. I smile. I'm opening my mouth to speak. He makes a face when he looks at the *CelebLife* placard taped to the ground. If I had to say what the expression is, I'd label it Dead Eyes and Disdain.

"Ryan! Ryan, I'm Augusta Noble with *CelebLife* magazine. Just a couple questions!" I call out. He stops three inches to my right, smack in front of the reporter after me, smirking.

It takes me a moment to adjust to being dissed. *So you don't want to talk to me? The biggest celebrity magazine in the world? Fine.* I'm in a huff.

When he's done, he moves down the line, out of sight. *Oh hell, no,* a little voice says. He's not robbing me, not tonight. I slip out of my spot, skipping potential interviews with any straggling actors and drawing glares as I push my way toward Ryan, stepping over photography equipment, bored producers, handbags. I catch up to my prey when he stops for some foreign TV reporters yelling out to him in cute accents. Like so many stars, Ryan appears to prefer the camera to the pen. I am hiding behind the fray, recording the group interview he's giving.

I shout above the foreign press, "Are you loving being a dad?" Ryan glares, then peers over heads and equipment to see who dared ask such a question, but doesn't ID me. Defeated, he breathes something very close to, "Uh huh," then walks off. I'll take it. I got my story; in my hands, it will be brilliant journalism. Headline: *Ryan Reynolds Confirms to* CelebLife *he Loves Being a Dad.* It won't have an EXCLUSIVE banner above it, but beggars can't be choosers, and Ryan will hate it.

As soon as I file my story, the emails fly. The chief CelebLife.com editor writes, *Thanks for this, Augusta! It's a really cute story!*

I glow for exactly five minutes, at which point Uvula Garsh chimes in with her blasting caps: *WHAT are you TALKING ABOUT? This is a "quote" with NO WORDS IN IT.*

It makes a story, though, the film editor, whom I've never met, adds from New York. *Let's post.*

THIS IS NOT A STORY. We have to have SOME standards, Uvula shoots back.

Starting when? I want to type, but don't. I write instead, *Ryan did speak to me and it was a really big premiere…everyone's posting about it…*

Who are you again? Uvula writes on a chain that goes to literally twenty-five staffers.

I clench my teeth and my fists. This woman appears to exist only to bully and fire people. *I only have about two hundred bylines at your magazine and met you in London, you raving cow.* Before I can get myself blacklisted, Maguire jumps in.

Augusta is one of our stringers. Yes, she should've gotten more. But let's go with what we have.

There is a deafening pause during which I receive no emails. Just when I think it's over, I get a private note from

Esdee.

Hey, we've loved your event coverage and your time in the office, but from now on we'll call ya if we need ya, OK? Enjoy some much-deserved time off (smiley face). I'll be in touch. x S.D.

The false chirpiness is as infuriating as the message. I should've known this was coming, that someone was going to notice me squatting in the office. Also, I billed for almost sixty hours last week, and with the axe always hanging over the staff I'm sure that didn't go over well. Still, the email is a gut-punch. It's all crumbling and I have no control over any of it.

I understand, I reply, *but can someone tell me what Maguire has against me? What's this really about?*

My phone rings. It's Esdee. No one ever talks to anyone at this magazine, so I know I've hit a nerve. "First rule of *CelebLife*," she blasts in my ear when I answer, "don't put anything in writing."

"OK," I say. "Fine. While I have you on the phone, then, what could I *possibly* have done to make Maguire dislike me so much?"

"Look," Esdee replies slowly, as if thinking of a way to spare my feelings. "Don't take it personally. You don't *know* anyone, is all. You were let in because of Stanley, and he's out of the game, so that shine's wearing off fast."

Finally, a real answer. I go for broke. "Fair enough," I lie, because it's bullshit. "So what about this Uvula person? What's her problem?"

Esdee lets out a sardonic chuckle. "That woman is a stone-cold bitch on wheels. I told you—we love your work. We're just going to have to calm it down for a while. That's all."

"Am I still on the Tristan Catlin premiere tomorrow?"

I ask flatly.

"Oh—of course," Esdee squeaks. "Definitely go to that."

I hear what she doesn't say: *Then we're done with you.*

After we hang up, I crawl under the covers and try to dream about Alexander and forget everything else, but the final text of the night does me in.

Good night, beautiful. Turns out I have to travel for a story in Madagascar, so I had to cancel my Tuesday interview in L.A. You're off the hook. I'll be in town soon, though…rain check? x

I feel like throwing up. The *x* is something, the *rain check* is promising, but really, this decimates the hope I'd clung to. It strips away the thin veil of denial I've been hiding behind; the promise of what could've been, how we might've moved forward if he'd come, is gone. All my recent failures fall into sharp relief. I can't ignore the therapist's calls or my mother's voicemails and emails anymore: They're in my face, staring at me, urging me to take action. Furthermore, celebrities don't fix anything, they're not special, and quite a few are offensive or dimwitted, two qualities I try to avoid in life. I wish I had some pills, a lot of pills. I discard the idea. OK, so *what?* As the therapist predicted months ago, alcohol has indeed turned out to be a slick, conniving, and phony friend who presents as sweet and helpful but turns toxic as soon as you start to count on him. I am out of coping mechanisms and yearning for oblivion. Lacking health insurance, the strongest thing I own besides tequila is Benadryl, so I down a couple antihistamines and let the drowsiness take me away, at least for a few hours.

47

#82

I wake up the morning after the Ryan Reynolds event with a renewed sense of purpose. Alexander is but a distraction. The goal is what matters. Finishing it, lighting the fire, gathering the strength to face what I've been avoiding, finding the answers that have eluded me. Which means I *have* to find a way back in to *CelebLife*. If these months have shown me anything, it's that my assumption was spot-on: No other publication would give me the access I need.

I dress like it's the Oscars for the Tristan Catlin premiere, donning my prettiest, most painful un-scuffed heels, two layers of bodyshapers, and a flattering black dress. I had a head start on the beautifying thanks to my preparations for Alexander's aborted visit.

On the red carpet, I get a bad crick in my neck from swiveling around every couple of minutes to look for Tristan. He's the key to clinging on at *CelebLife*—if I can get him. The young Tristan liked the teenage me, but I'm doubtful he'll even notice me tonight. *Remember the Goldblum Rule*, I remind myself, but a part of me is desperate for him to recall catching me on the ice.

First up in the line is one of my poster boys. I had Ethan Hawke from *Before Sunrise* on my wall, and, although I've since gotten over him for various reasons, it's still cool when he actually stops for me, sans publicist. He makes big eyes when I tell him who I work for. I wait.

Thumbs up, or thumbs down? Will he be a Grouchy Bon Jovi or a Cheeky Jason Bateman?

"You liked my movie this week," Ethan says. "Today, I love you."

Ding ding ding. Well, *I* didn't, but I'm assuming our film critic did. It's the first time a star has used the L word with me. Before I can even ask a question, he launches into an explanation of his latest movie, talking about it as if it's life or death. He's growing a bit craggy in his forties, and has a mouth like a Claymation Christmas character: supple, twitchy, and expressive, topped with dirty blond scruff. I picture him with a pipe in one hand as the other goes mad gesticulating. When I shoot for the golden ticket—fatherhood and children—he does not punish me.

"Everything about my life as a dad goes into these roles," he tells me, remaining passionate and earnest. "To pour those experiences into a creative entity is a luxury—it is awesome."

I smile and thank him, and he moves on. I strain again to check for Tristan, but Hipster Reporter (here he is again) shakes his head. He's got his most hipstery specs on today.

"Not yet. You'll know," he assures me.

I yawn, stretch my legs, check my phone. Out of boredom, I tap Hipster on the shoulder. "I'm Augusta, by the way," I smile. "I don't think we've properly met."

He smiles back and offers his hand for me to shake. "I'm Lance," he says. "And you're right—it's about time."

A few minutes go by, and then a roar builds in the crowd. The photographers go ape shit, screaming and competing for a nugget or a smile. "Over here! This way! Tristan—to your right!"

All eyes are turned toward the head of the carpet. Here he comes, cossetted by suited men and hurried women, and I'm shocked by how much smaller he is than I remember—without the skates and the pads, he's more Scott Eastwood-sized than Chris Hemsworth. *Aaaand* there he goes. He's fast. He's staring straight ahead, stone-faced. I am screwed. I was holding out a flicker of hope he might recognize me, whisk me away, save my gig at *CelebLife*. No one's going to be impressed with my reporting tonight: *Tristan walked by me in five seconds flat. He looked mad. The end.*

"Fuck," says Hipster Reporter, I mean Lance, as Tristan's entourage disappears into the venue. "That sucked. Literally one word from Tristan and we'd have a cover." He stares after the actor and sighs, "At least I'll have another chance inside the party."

"Exactly," H. Mark Liu, a red-carpet veteran I'm planted next to now and then, nods. "I know this club well. The VIP section is relatively accessible."

Not for me, it's not. Tracey's covering the party, and, speak of the devil, a familiar figure in a red knockoff bandage dress is sashaying toward the party entrance. Tracey is showing mountains of cleavage and carrying the one fancy clutch she owns, a baby pink Lally Lamay she pretends she bought but which everyone knows the designer comped her after Tracey wrote a positive story about her line, which is a no-no, but there it is. Anyway, Tracey's in and I'm not. The photographers start dismantling their equipment and Lance and H. Mark start walking away. H. Mark turns back. "You coming?"

"I'm not inside." I shrug like I don't care.

"Aw, sorry," he says. "I'm sure it will be lame, anyway. Have a good night!"

I wave, then decide I'm happier getting off my feet and back to my own bed anyway. I hike my handbag over my shoulder, step over someone's camera bag, and jump when I hear my name.

"Augusta Noble," a firm, silky female voice says. "*CelebLife* magazine?"

I turn back. "Yes?"

A short, stocky woman with a tight orange ponytail streaked with white like a creamsicle is standing calmly in my red carpet spot. She extends a sparkling wristband.

"Put this on," she says, then bobs her head toward the party entrance. "Go inside, wait an hour, and I'll find you."

"I'm sorry? Do I know you?" A bit of wind comes up and whips her ponytail.

"Go in, or don't," she shrugs, her voice like honey. "If you do, I'll see you in an hour." Naturally, I take the wristband. I love a good mystery. She turns and walks away.

I freshen up, check my teeth, brush my hair, reapply my makeup while I'm waiting in line. I wait a few moments before a staffer notes my sparkling wristband and waves me in with a smile. The club is packed, because they've clearly let too many people in. I check my watch: fifty-five minutes to go. I have to dodge Tracey while scanning for Tristan and trying to figure out who Ms. Creamsicle is. I beat my way through the hot crowd to find one of only two bars in the place, and it's clear I'll be spending my remaining fifty-something minutes in line waiting for a drink. I check my phone, fending off people pushing past and trying to cut the line.

Who's the angel who got me in tonight? Lance? H. Mark? Who else could it be? Of course, another fantasy option has occurred to me, but I don't dare acknowledge it. I get to the front of the line and shout my order for a Love-tini, tonight's signature drink that sounds suspiciously like a glorified Cape Codder, but whatever. I am on my first sip when I see Tracey. She's standing alone in a corner looking like a frightened bunny, holding her own Love-tini up to her face like a security blanket. She's supposed to find Tristan and watch his every move, and from what I can see, she's doing no such thing. *Interesting.* Lance and H. Mark burst into view, sweaty and grouchy.

"I literally would take *one detail* at this point," growls Lance. "Tristan's shit-hot right now, he's not talking, OK, fine. But can't he, like, talk to a girl in public or fall down drunk or something, where I can see?" He looks around frantically. "He's not even *here*, is he, at his own premiere party?"

"Don't sweat it," H. Mark yells over the din. "This is the reality of Hollywood reporting. As glamorous as a Port-a-Potty at a rodeo."

As I watch them disappear into the crowd, the mystery redhead appears by my side like a ghost. "Miss Noble. If you'd like to come with me."

I would like. As I stick close behind her, I see why it was so easy for her to sidle up to me—she's got a Mini-Cooper-sized security guy breaking the waves. We're approaching the VIP section, which is set on a raised platform surrounded by ropes and guards. There's Ethan Hawke, talking again. Jamie Foxx is lounging on a couch, and, wait, is that Cara Delevingne talking to Adam Levine? If they got married, she'd be Cara Delevingne-Levine.

I take a sidestep toward the rope, but my escort keeps walking forward. *OK, I'll play.* She leads me to the back wall, which, to my surprise, swings open. We're checked out by a stunning six-foot-tall drag queen before the wall/door slams shut behind us. Creamsicle leads me down a dark hallway to a velvet paradise of bottle service, waiters, food, and big-screen TVs. The film's director is here, and he's seated on a corner sofa talking to my old friend Tristan Catlin. Tristan's light brown hair is cut in a short, tousled style like Brad Pitt's in *Fight Club*. I feel all tingly, just as I did when I first met him as a teenage girl, but now Tristan's a global mega-star and I'm a tormented freelance reporter of frivolous things.

Ben Affleck is here, as is a dead-eyed and revolting Tobey "Bark like a seal" Maguire and a perky Drew Barrymore. Ben is trying to make it look like he's drinking Coke, but I smell alcohol when I get close. I swear I hear him say, "Nice tits" as I walk by, but maybe I imagine it. Mystery woman brings me straight to Tristan, who's in a tailored tux, surrounded by four ear-piece-wearing guards. He's sipping an old-fashioned and stands as I approach.

I should've known. I *did* know, but didn't dare believe it. His eyes didn't even dart in my general direction on the carpet.

"I can't believe it's you," he grins, shaking his head then holding out his arms wide. "I always hoped this day would come."

48

Tristan Catlin envelops me in a bear hug that squeezes the breath out of me.

"I would've contacted you sooner, Augusta Noble," he says when he lets go, regarding me with sparkling emerald eyes that are puffier now than when we first met and ringed by a few shallow crows' feet. "But I never knew your name, and I forgot which newspaper you worked for. My assistant found out for me when I pointed you out tonight. Thanks, Liv." He nods to Creamsicle, who nods back then disappears.

I'm speechless.

"Sit, sit," Tristan insists, pointing to the cushion next to his. The director of his film, a bored-looking fellow with a pretentious mustache and no muscle tone who dates A-list actresses, is forced to scoot over to make room for me. I see Liv talking to the guards and it looks a lot like, *Keep people away from my boss.*

"You have no idea what it's like getting started in this business," Tristan says. I watch his lips. They're less of a Channing Tatum bee-stung pout, more of a thin, Christian Bale sexy snarl. "When you made a point of wanting to interview me that day, I was at my lowest point. My confidence was in the gutter and my own agent assured me my pilot was going to flop…and it did. Can you believe that shit? *My own agent.* But you—" he's clasping his hands together, enunciating, sitting close to me—"you made me feel like *somebody.* It would've been my first interview…my first *respect,* you know? I never forgot it."

I force words out of my mouth. "I'm the one who owes *you*," I say. "I would've cracked my skull if you hadn't saved me that day."

"You haven't changed a bit," he smiles. "Same blue-green eyes, same blonde, simple look."

Simple?

He sees my face fall and shakes his head apologetically. "*Natural*, I mean," he corrects himself. "Not like every other girl in this business. I mean, *woman*. Back then, you were this cute high school kid who stood up for me, and for some reason, I never forgot you."

A server hurries up to us. "What'll you have?" Tristan asks me. "Seriously—anything."

I'm frozen, trying to think of the most celebrity-esque drink I can order.

"We'll have a bottle of Dom," Tristan tells the server. "Thanks so much, buddy."

I take a look around. Everyone wants a piece of Tristan, but none of them can get near him; he doesn't leave my side, keeps an arm draped protectively over the sofa behind me, and I lean back into it, though we don't touch. The Champagne comes in a silver ice bucket and the server pops the cork and pours it into two frosted flutes.

"To the good ones who keep your feet on the ground," he says when our glasses are full.

"To the brave ones who catch you when you fall," I add.

We clink glasses and reminisce about that day, and I pretend I'm talking to the kid on the ice, not the man I've seen in at least three huge movies, the guy who's been in every magazine including my own.

When there is a lull and it becomes clear I'm going to have to give him up before too long, I say, "You know, I'm still on the clock." I make a show of checking the non-existent watch on my wrist. "Anything you say to me is on the record."

"Oh?" He raises his eyebrows. "Well, then." He sits up straighter. "Let's do this for real. Let's have that interview we never got to do back in Falmouth."

"Farnsboro," I correct him. "And don't joke, because you know I'll take you up on it. We're working on a cover story about you this week."

"Of course you are," he says without a hint of irony or modesty. "It's only going to get worse when I file for divorce." He checks his phone. "In exactly…three days and nine hours."

"You're getting *divorced*?" I click my phone recorder on and cross one fake-tanned leg over the other.

"I thought everyone knew that," he replies, cocking his head.

"Well, no…I guess we kind of thought there was a chance for you two. The perfect family, the kids, the beauty and Hollywood's most sensitive hunk…"

He shakes his head. "No chance. She's not well. There's nothing I can do to help her, so…"

"What do you mean, not well?" *Act like a friend, not a reporter. Don't spook him.*

Tristan pauses for a moment. "I've already said too much. I can talk about me, but I don't want to invade Jo's privacy that way. Other than that," he offers, "ask me anything."

I'm weak, I'm too nice, I'm no longer a proper, real journalist. I can't help myself. "You can't do this on the record," I tell him. "Ivan would kill you. And me." I don't want to get back on Deaver the Deceiver's radar.

Tristan picks up his Champagne, finishes it, and sets the glass back on the table with a *clink*. "You," he says, "are right. He'd boil me in oil and invite Sandra Bullock over to watch. Tell you what—I've always wanted to do this—can you quote me as 'a source?' I'll tell you anything you want to know, and you say it came from 'a source close to Tristan Catlin.'"

"That's bad journalism," I say. "But in this case I'll make an exception."

CelebLife reporters do stuff like this all the time. Their favorite trick is writing: *Celebrity X's rep had no comment.* Then, in the same story, they quote a "source" who is, of course, Celebrity X's rep. Which to me is what you call a *lie*, but whatever.

I set my phone at the edge of the table with the audio recorder running, then ask Tristan absolutely everything the celebrity team in L.A has wrung their hands over for weeks. "So," I breathe in my most sympathetic talk-show-host manner, "how are you really doing?"

He exhales, suddenly seeming to realize this is going to hurt. "I'm sad for the kids," he says quietly. "It's sadder for them to grow up in a toxic home, but this isn't a great outcome either."

I nod, doing the sympathetic head tilt. I've never been close to marriage, but all I can think is, *I don't ever want to get a divorce. It sounds like hell on earth.*

"Are you seeing anyone new?" I ask as gently as I can.

He quickly shakes his head. "Nah." The way his eyes flit away makes me not believe him.

"Really? So rumors of a new woman are false?"

"There's no one serious." He looks me straight in the eye, flashing back into spin mode. "I don't want to say any more on that…you know, to protect the kids."

"I totally understand," I say. "They are adorable, by the way. What little cuties." I don't think I've ever called a kid a "little cutie," mostly because I don't know a lot of kids.

It's time for the big question. "Tristan," I say, "what happened? What led to this heartbreaking ending?"

He sighs. "It's personal, and it's messy, and it's hard to explain. You could say different values and growing apart were the major culprits. We've both changed."

"I totally get it," I say, although I don't, not really; my most serious relationship lasted a few months. I can see people rallying to get to him, so I squeeze in a few more questions: Is he claiming it's not alcohol and a desire to be single that caused it, like the tabloids claim? *Fuck no. No, no, no.*

Definitely divorcing?

Yes.

America's sweethearts are really, truly over? *Yes, yes and yes.*

I feel an odd sadness as he tells me all this. Meanwhile, Maguire & Co. are going to lose their minds. Yes, I'll be showing up to the office again whether invited or not, and this time I'll be welcomed with open arms. I can picture the cover line now: IT'S OVER.

Liv appears out of nowhere and makes a *wrap it up* motion to Tristan, who gives her an almost imperceptible nod. No one's bringing any more drinks, Ben Affleck is gone, and our silver bucket has disappeared. This last hour has been the first time in years I've been utterly present and forgotten all the flying detritus coming at me from every direction.

My all-time favorite 10.0+++ celebrity gives me a polite smile, stands, and holds out a hand to help me up. "I have to go say some goodbyes," he tells me.

"It's been great catching up," I say, praying he wants to exchange numbers.

He's shaking hands and doing half-hearted man-hugs with industry types, a model, the director, a co-star, another A-list actor I never liked. I'm waiting for a goodbye hug, but none comes.

"OK, well...bye," I say quietly, ready to slip away to write my insane story.

"Whoa, wait." Tristan grabs my arm, says in my ear, "You're coming, right? To the *after after* party at my place?"

Liv appears by my side. "Go out the back door. A car will be waiting."

49

The wine cellar at Tristan Catlin's Hollywood Hills home is like a trendy nightclub inside a French winery. I'm sunken into a deep armchair trying not to be shocked by the endless rows of vintage wine in his collection. I lean back and try the red Tristan suggested.

"Brad's obsessed with Burgundy," he says, twirling the glass while examining it as if it's a snow globe. "We've had many deep discussions about it. Well, we used to, anyway. I haven't talked to him since everything happened with Ange. You know…giving him space and stuff."

I'm enjoying his attention, though I'm also interested in the celebs he's brought home: a big-haired young music phenom, several female models (and a female singer I think is getting flirty with one of them), and some forty-somethings who appear to be reps and handlers. "Are you sure you don't need to tend to your guests upstairs?"

He shakes his head. "There are plenty of people up there to handle hosting. Don't worry about that."

I hope to get the full tour later. His place is not the Spanish-style ranch you often see up here, but rather a two-story glass museum with platinum, silver, stainless steel, and soapstone everywhere. I caught a glimpse of his infinity pool and its slate-gray decking and thought, with all the hard lines and absence of personal touches, a serial killer could live here. Or someone who doesn't view the property as *home*.

"So," Tristan says. "Did you get everything you needed for your cover story?"

"For now," I reply, thinking about asking for some fancy *white* wine.

I jab my index finger toward the ceiling. "I noticed that none of these people are ever photographed with you, or even mentioned it in the same breath."

"My real friends are lying low to see how the divorce plays out," he replies. "They haven't chosen sides yet."

"Oh? I'm not sure 'real friends' means what you think it means."

"Touché," Tristan says with a melancholy smile.

We're silent for a moment and I think, *Burgundy is good.* If Brad loves it, maybe I should give it a chance. "That couple of the moment upstairs—the model and the singer—*CelebLife* just did two full pages on their romance, but they don't seem lovey-dovey. At all."

"Them?" Tristan rolls his eyes. "They barely know each other. She's dating a chick and he fucks every groupie. You'd definitely have a shot."

Wonderful. "It all seems so cynical…the fake romances, the bearding…" I never liked being sold a bullshit fairytale. It's insulting.

"Hey," Tristan points an index finger at me. "The straights do showmances as well as anyone. It's all smoke and mirrors—and people *want* to buy into the fantasy. And now," he says, "you're one of us."

No. No, I'm not. That's when it hits me: I'm really, really not meant to be here. These are not my people and this isn't my life. I'm just a visitor here, and I get the feeling my trip is ending soon.

Tristan rises, holds out his hand. I take it and he pulls me up.

"You know why so many celebrities have dogs?" he asks out of nowhere. He stands so close to me that my breasts are nearly touching his chest.

"Because it's one more being in their life they can boss around?"

He narrows his eyes. I've hit a nerve. "*No*," he replies. "Because post-fame, dogs are the only ones in our lives who give us unconditional love. We don't have to question their motives, wonder if they're going to sell us out to *The National Enquirer*, extort us, blackmail or use us. A pit bull is the most loyal creature you'll ever love."

"Oh? Where's yours?"

"Josephine got him in the split," he says, and I feel terrible for questioning him. I see an errant tear glistening in his eye.

Post-fame. That's a new one on me. Anyway, Tristan recovers quickly, just like in the movies, and asks me if I want to see his room. I heroically stop myself from laughing. I'm transported back to college. *Do you want to see my mix tapes? Come up to my dorm and I'll show you...*

"Or not," he says, his voice low now, his eyes staring into mine. He pulls me in, lowers his lips to mine, and I feel like I'm in a movie, the way it's so practiced and perfect. We make out for a time, then I pull away. Everything in my head and heart is telling me this is wrong—which contradicts what my body is saying. I feel a pang about Alexander, then slap it away because he abandoned me again and I can't wait around for him.

I pull away.

"Really?" Tristan seems genuinely shocked. "But..." He kisses my neck, presses hard into me, his warm body comforting, until his hands find the bottom of my short black dress and start creeping dangerously close to my body-shaping underwear.

I gently but firmly push him away.

"How about some X? I guarantee that'll loosen you up." He pushes me against the wall. He's warm and strong and smells like expensive cologne. Jono the prom nerd pops into my head, followed by Billy Ronson and Amanda McJean, who made sure I never made it to the end-of-high-school party. But, as Tristan starts breathing harder, I'm finding the idea of avenging high school unsatisfying. I don't need it. I've already won. I'm loving Tristan's mouth on mine, but for many reasons, including whispers I've heard about how many cases of herpes are raging throughout Hollywood, I pull away one final time.

"OK," Tristan nods. "OK." He holds up his hands, backs away, rubs his eyes, adjusts his crotch and yawns. He moves back to his chair and plays on his phone.

"Another drink?" he asks. "I think they're doing frozen Bailey's shots upstairs."

It's turned weird. Someone is descending the stairs. *Click, click, click.* One of the lingerie models, the curve of her back slim, tanned and braless, appears. Her jet-black hair falls like a satin curtain halfway to her waist.

Tristan smiles at her, then turns to me and says, "Make yourself at home." Then he disappears up the winding staircase with the model.

I wait a couple minutes, then walk upstairs. I see the R&B artist/rapper on a sun lounger alone, and his model "girlfriend" on another, holding hands with the pop star—both women. There are a dozen other beautiful people I don't immediately recognize. I cradle my expensive wine and watch the valley of lights below for about half an hour, until Tristan returns and slips onto the lounge chair with me. We watch the sun begin to rise over his infinity pool.

I didn't realize I'd fallen asleep until Tristan nudges me gently with one hand. "Hey," he says. "It's seven. It's my day to take the kids to school. You ready to go?"

"I have to go to work," I mumble.

"No worries. My driver will take you."

50

Tristan's driver drops me on a side street off Wilshire Boulevard. I cleaned up best I could, but there's no doubt I'm on a long walk of shame, minus the shame. I totter across the parking lot and through our building's huge lobby in my form-fitting stretchy black dress, the straps of my heels digging into my ankles. I take the frightening elevator up to the twenty-seventh floor and rifle through to find my pass. I place it on the card reader. There's a long, red *beeeep*.

I flip the card over and try again. *Beeeep*.

I shouldn't be surprised. I don't know which one of these bitches took time out of their day to shut off a perfectly nice freelancer's access, but I plan to find out. I miss Stanley. I miss London.

I call June on her cubicle phone. "Yes?" She knows it's me.

"It's Augusta. I'm outside. Can you let me in?"

There is a silence during which I hope she is very uncomfortable. "I really shouldn't…"

"Big mistake, June. *Huge*." I'm finding this particular movie quote useful in many situations. But look—Roy the recently graduated CelebLife.com fashion blogger is here and opening the door.

I need these clowns for *twenty-five* more celebrities. That is all. After that, I'm free to decide. I'm out of here, or I'm not. Whatever happens, it'll be on my terms.

I'm early to the meeting and it feels like old times, as in three days ago. Quinn breaks out in a wide grin when he sees me. "Welcome back," he says. I shouldn't be surprised he knows I was cast out—the back channeling and gossip around here is epic.

Maguire and Esdee arrive late and won't look at me. Uvula, sour as ever, trundles in behind them and appears blissfully unaware of the office politics. Quinn reaches for the light switch to prepare for the photo show, but Maguire stops him with an open palm.

"Let's start with updates," she says, looking sideways at me.

I don't mind if I do. I flip through my notebook—the disposable one I used last night, not *the* notebook, of course. "Sure, I'll go."

"I should hope you have something good," Maguire snaps, "since no one got a file from last night's premiere and we close the magazine *today*."

"As you know, I recently moved here from London," I begin. "So it took me a couple months to build some good sources. But my nights out really paid off."

I turn to Maguire. "You're doing a Tristan Catlin cover this week, correct?"

"Yes," she says. "The issue closes tonight, which gives us about five hours to add any additional reporting to the story."

I review the quotes I wrote down. Most of the interview is on my phone and in the Cloud for safekeeping.

"Are you drunk?" Tracey, sitting next to me, asks loudly, sniffing the air.

"Possibly," I admit. "It's OK, though, because I'm not driving."

I smile brightly while they hypocritically clutch their metaphorical pearls. I know the stories of *CelebLife* reporters doing blow at Chateau Marmont with Heath Ledger and other stars, of going to DWI jail after covering a party and filing their stories from behind bars, of editors giving space in the magazine to certain brands in exchange for tips on celebrities or free stuff. You'd be surprised what juicy emails people accidentally forward.

"Anyway," I continue, "I've got a killer source *extremely* close to Tristan. He's on the record, but NFA. We cannot name him." I watch Maguire and Esdee, both of whom are trying to appear indifferent. "This source tells me Tristan will be filing for divorce in exactly two days. Well, at four fifty-nine p.m., I mean, so that other outlets won't be able to confirm it until the following day."

"*What*? Is this exclusive?" Esdee asks, leaning forward, arms flat on the table reaching toward me.

"Yes," I say. "I have this from an impeccable source."

Maguire is sizing me up. She doesn't believe me. "We've heard Josephine is giving him another chance and they're determined to give it another try for the kids."

"Oh?" I inquire innocently. "Whose camp is your source in?"

Maguire doesn't answer.

"Josephine's," Tracey blurts.

"Well," I reply, "She wouldn't know Tristan's plans, now, would she?"

"That's enough." Maguire waves at me like, *shut up.* "We'll talk about this privately. This discussion isn't appropriate for the general meeting. What else?" She asks the room while typing something on her phone.

"Awards season is around the corner," Esdee pipes up, shaking a sheaf of papers at us. "You all know what this means."

She deals out the pages to the print team, hesitates when she gets to me, then seems to realize everyone's watching, and flicks one my way. "New York has started sending in the drop-dead questions you *must* ask at awards shows and parties. By now everyone knows about this latest hashtag, #WomenAreMoreThanClothes."

There is snickering, grumbling, and eye rolling as Esdee reads aloud from the sheet.

"FOR ALL YOUNG, COOL FEMALE CELEBS:

Along with #ItHappenedToMe and #NoMore, #WomenAreMoreThanClothes is SO important (girl power!). However, we really need the fashion IDs and all the questions below asked. PLEASE DO NOT COME BACK WITHOUT DETAILS ABOUT EACH DRESS AND LOOK."

Esdee looks around the room. "OK?"

Tracey's leaning back in her chair with a frown, arms crossed over her chest. "Do you know what? This is out of hand. I remember Blake Lively ripping a reporter a new one for asking about her outfit at a women's luncheon. The same Blake Lively who, a couple months later, changed her outfit *seven times* in one day for a press tour, Instagrammed every look, and—well, what I'm saying is, we can't win. I mean, when we asked Lupita at that same luncheon a year before what she thinks of the upcoming election and the candidates, and she glared and snapped, 'Next question.'"

There is much nodding among the staff. Tracey crosses her arms angrily over her chest. "Celebrities are using this as another way to control interviews. Here's an idea: If you don't want to be *asked* about fashion, don't *lead* with fashion."

I didn't know Tracey had it in her. She's not wrong. *Who are you wearing?* may be a boring, insulting throwback, but when red-carpet reporters *do* try to ask meaningful questions, the reps often snap back faster than you can say Reese Witherspoon.

"That's enough," Uvula booms. "These stars are our bread and butter. If you'd rather knock them down instead of cooperate with them, go work for the *Enquirer*."

That shuts everyone up. On the way out of the meeting, Maguire snarls, "My office. Now."

Uvula, wearing the same heather-gray suit she wore for the London firings, something I'll never forget due to its bad fit and deep wedgie, says in her awkwardly sharp voice, "I'll come along too. I'd like to know more about your source."

Oh hell, no. I smile to myself. Do your worst, Uvula Harsh. I'm not talking. Maguire throws open her door and plops down in her leather swivel chair. I grab the comfy guest chair, leaving Uvula to take the hard rattan spare.

"It's interesting," Maguire says to me languidly, leaning back in her seat, "that a day after you're told not to come back to the office, you suddenly appear with this incredible source who's telling you everything about the movie star no one can get to."

I nod energetically. "I know, right? It's crazy timing."

She glares at me.

"Who, exactly, is this person you're talking to?" Uvula inches her chair closer, invading my space and providing me with a close-up of the mole on her cheek.

Funny, they never question Tracey, Tatiana, or Maguire's magical anonymous sources. "I can't tell you that, but let's just say Tristan was out last night with his entire entourage."

Uvula looks me up and down. There's a beep from Maguire's phone. She clicks on something and starts reading. Her eyebrows shoot up, wrinkling her forehead in several deep rows.

"Well," she says. "Ivan Deaver confirms what you've told us so far. He's not happy about it, but he admits your reporting is legit." She crosses her arms. "He wonders how you got it."

There's no chance I'm answering.

"I'm very impressed with your reporting, Andrea," Uvula nods in my direction.

I'm starting to feel sorry for her. Stanley said she lives with four rescue cats and has nothing to live for but her work at *CelebLife*.

"Tell us more," Maguire demands, reminding me of Cruella de Vil. "Tell us *everything*."

I sum up my reporting for them, and when I'm done, Uvula starts talking fast.

"Get a file together, and I mean *right now*, and send it in ASAP. Lila in the New York office is writing the story. I'll call her as soon as we're done here."

Little do they know I'm giving them about a third of what I got last night and holding back the rest, including Tristan's denials of substance abuse and some first-hand observational quotes from me. That'll drag my time out here as I "call my source" once a week to get "fresh" reporting.

I reply with some indifference, "Well, I mean, you guys had said I shouldn't come back into the office…I guess I shouldn't even be here…I might just head home if that's OK. I'll go through my notes there and send you some quotes later today."

"*No*," Uvula yells with a look of horror. "What? This closes today. Do you *get* that?"

Maguire's eyes are low-lidded. She understands. "What do you want?" she inquires wearily.

"It's awards season," I observe. "I'd love to be included in the fun stuff." *For starters.*

"You want to cover parties for us? At awards season? That's it?"

"Well, yes—and until the season is over, I assume you can still use me in the office every day…?" I'll rack up the hours and save the cash to live on after I hit my number, which is so close I can almost reach out and touch it.

Maguire raises one eyebrow. "Sure, Augusta. We can do that. Consider yourself a part of the Golden Globes and Oscars team."

"OK, then." I stand up and move toward the door. "I'll get filing."

I write for hours, fueled by coffee, ambition, and revenge fantasies. Uvula and Maguire have purposely made a tough transition to a new city—alone—even tougher, and having some control gives me a shot of satisfaction.

I consider other ways I can make them suffer. There's always the possibility of saving all the best Tristan reporting until I complete my mission, then selling it to the competition. This is all beneath me, of course, but I'm too tired to check my morality. By four, I can barely see straight. I head out to the parking garage before I remember I didn't drive here, and, rather than stagger back to the office and hope someone can give me a ride, I call a Lyft and wait in the lobby.

51

I am in a virtual dream state after staying awake for thirty-six hours for the first time in my life, so when someone starts banging on my door just before I'm about to fall into bed, it is only mildly alarming. I don't have a peephole. I stand at the locked door and consider pretending I'm not home.

"I know you're there, Augusta—I watched you walk in."

"That's not creepy at *all*," I hit back, then throw open the door. "Hello, Lincoln."

He looms in the doorway, tattoos on show around the collar and his arms poking out of his white tee. He's wearing the same kind of army-green cargo pants he's had since I've known him. His eyes stare into mine. I shiver.

"Hello, Augusta."

I turn and walk to the kitchen. He follows, and I hear the door shut behind him. I slide onto a stool and grip the glass of water I was going to take to bed with me; he stands opposite.

"You're not afraid of me," he observes. "Even after what they've said about me."

"Should I be?" I can only think of him as Big Linc. Not a killer, not violent, not anything but a friend.

"Look," he says, flattening his hands on the chipped linoleum counter, "I don't want to pressure you. But it's getting down to the wire and…well, Augusta, you know what could happen if they don't get the full story. They're talking about murder charges."

I take a sharp breath. For him, for me, for both? He doesn't specify. I feel a stab of fear.

When I don't answer, he raises his eyebrows. "No one's told you? It's all going down."

It can't be. Not yet. I'm not ready.

"My lawyer says it's a matter of weeks now. They haven't contacted you? *Really*?"

"Well…my mother's been calling but sometimes I don't answer…I can't deal with her non-pushy pushiness. She's beside herself about all of this."

"You're lucky to have a mother like that," Lincoln says. "You know, she offered to pay for a lawyer for me."

"Wow," I say. "I can't even get her to pay for my health insurance."

"I turned her down. I can take care of myself. I started a mobile motorcycle repair company a couple years ago. Who knew New York was so full of rich bike enthusiasts," he shrugs.

"Good for you," I reply lamely. I force myself to look at him and blurt the question before I have time to chicken out: "Did you do it, Lincoln? Did you hurt her?"

"God, *no*," he cries. "No, no, no. I hate that you could even think that."

I exhale long and slow. I hadn't realized I was holding my breath. "You know, Linc—you know you were crossing some boundaries. You were following her, you were showing up at her place uninvited at three in the morning…"

He closes his eyes, swallows again. "I know I went a little overboard…I get that now. But you have to understand, I'd do anything to protect her. That guy was bad news, but he had everyone fooled—*everyone*." His eyes lock on mine for a second, then he looks down at his hands. "Caroline was home to me, do you understand that?"

I'm trying hard.

"Please, Augusta." He leans forward slightly over the counter. "You have to remember what happened." When I don't reply, he says, "Do you know what Joe said to me outside the restaurant that day? He said, 'I'm in charge now. You're not needed anymore.' Who says that? Who says that to the best friend of a woman he's been dating for less than a month?"

That stings, because it reminds me how I failed to look out for my best friend.

"You know what they're saying, right?" Lincoln goes on, his voice rising in pitch. "That *I* could've killed him—somehow untied myself, killed Joe, then re-tied myself and waited for the police. It makes no sense, Augusta. You were there—you know. I need you to tell them, OK? Tell them I could never have done this. I tried to *save* her. Joe got the drop on me—he's some kind Muay Thai champion."

Lincoln is relentless; he won't let me look away. "One of us killed him," he pleads, gesturing to me, then back to himself, "and I know it wasn't me. *Please*, Augusta. Save my life. Tell the cops what happened."

"Have you spoken to"—the name sticks in my throat, and I can't get it out—"her since it happened?"

"No, no," he says, shaking his head. "My lawyer said if I attempted to have any contact with her, it would look very bad." He stares out the window, takes a deep breath, meets my eyes again with his light brown ones. "Have you?"

"No." My brain is fuzzy. I'm not afraid of him; I'm ashamed. I heard through the grapevine Caroline's parents and Ginger are by her side constantly as she heals from plastic surgery and goes through rehab for the arm they say sustained deep defensive wounds. "She wouldn't want to hear from me. It's my fault this happened." My tongue, thick and slow, gets in the way of forming words.

"*Your fault?* What are you talking about?"

"I let her go home that night." I'm whispering without meaning to. "She left the party early and I *let her go alone.* I knew she was upset, knew something was wrong, but I let her go anyway. Then I never checked on her…not really. One text, then I passed out."

I'm woozy all of a sudden, almost as if the memory is coming to life.

"Are you OK?" Lincoln squints at me, takes a step closer.

"I'm OK," I tell him, though I feel as if I'm floating out of my own body. I haven't talked about this…not ever. This conversation has only ever taken place inside my own head.

"Is that what you've been thinking all this time?" he asks softly, leaning his forearms on the counter. "Caroline is a grown woman, Augusta—you both are. This has nothing to do with you. This was *Joe.* We need to make sure this is pinned on Joe Lannells. Not me and not you. You saved all of our lives, Augusta. Do you understand that? You saved us."

No. I caused this. We are silent for a moment, then I get up. He sighs and we both head toward the door. He's whispering to me now, as if someone might overhear him.

"Don't tell anyone I was here, OK? I'd get in real trouble. I was *never here*."

I nod, choking up as I do. "I'm so sorry, Linc," I say, fighting the urge to break down and fall into his strong arms like the unapologetic heroine of a good bodice-ripper. "I just can't remember anything about that night. I'm trying—I promise you, I'm trying. And I'll keep working at it. Trust me, OK?" My urge is to tell him it's going to be OK and that I know he's innocent. If only I was sure about that.

When he's gone, I fall onto the scratchy futon whose dusty mildew smell I've grown used to, close my eyes, and think about the lies I've told. I lied to everyone—starting with myself. Denial really is as powerful as they say. All along, I knew; I must have. During tonight's dreamlike encounter, one horrendously clear memory came into focus: I killed a human being. I killed Joe Lannells. *I did it.* I can suddenly recall every detail, every smell, every aspect of making the decision to do it—and then I did it, hitting him as hard as I could. I expected any returning memories to introduce themselves like an anvil to the gut, sending me into a frenzy leading to the world's most epic panic attack. But no…the images have just slipped back in tonight as if they were never gone.

I remember the elephant, from its carefully crafted tail to its curved tusks. I fought to lift the heavy jade sculpture without making a sound, then brought it down on Joe's skull with a force I didn't know I had in me. I remember the sickening crack, then Joe collapsing beside the bed, bleeding, one arm still on the low mattress, almost touching

Caroline, and then me kicking his hand away from her. I remember that he had no time to do or say anything before crumpling like a bloody rag doll. I remember looking up in horror when the authorities burst in.

And that is all; it is enough to brand me a killer, but not enough to help Lincoln. This information, in fact, is almost meaningless in a legal sense. I can't remember the most important details of all: *why* I did it. I know I killed Joe, but I don't know what prompted me to attack him. Was I *sure*—or was I *gambling* that Joe was the perpetrator? What if Lincoln really was the unstable torturer of my friend Caroline, and Joe her savior? *What if I killed the wrong person?*

I wake up at two in the morning on the futon, cold and fully clothed, and stumble to bed where I shiver violently until I fall back to sleep.

52

#83, #84

Alexander has written to me almost every day since he cancelled his L.A. trip. Two days before Christmas, he sends a doozy: *I'm on Reunion Island, swimming while avoiding sharks—did you know this is where the deadliest maneaters in the world live?*

Lucky bastard. I've decided if I can't be with him, I want to *be* him. I'm sitting on someone else's futon in holey shorts watching reruns of *Psych*.

Wrong, I write back. *That place is Hollywood.*

Ha. Oh, how I miss your wit. I'll come for a visit soon, I promise. How was your event tonight?

Weird. Met Michael Stipe and Michael Shannon. The magazine won't care about the interviews, though, even though they're more interesting than ninety-nine percent of the "stars" we cover.

What are the Michaels like?

Stipe is painfully earnest and super sweet. Shannon is a little disheveled. VERY dry wit. Kind of like you, but grumpier.

What are you doing for the holidays?

Nothing.

In the Noble household, Christmas is a sacred time when family converges from their corners around the globe, my mother has an excuse to bake buttery sugar cookies with her secret recipe, and all thoughts of eco-responsibility evaporate as every inch of the house—inside and out—is strung with fairy lights. At *CelebLife*, Christmas is something that happens between awards shows. I'm willing to do anything to avoid going to my parents' this year, so I can't complain when Maguire blasts an email threatening to draft two staffers if no one steps up to work over the holiday. In fact, I am (secretly) thrilled to volunteer.

Alexander texts back, *You can't be alone on Christmas. Come to London for the holidays.*

Actually…come to London for good.

Whoa. *What?* He has to be kidding, though there's no laughing emoji alongside his words. I pretend he never said it. *I'll be fine. It'll be relaxing. I'm looking forward to a quiet one.*

Absolutely not. I'll call or text you in between my two dreadful family dinners. My father has a new girlfriend. Well, she's not a girl, thankfully. She's forty-five.

I laugh out loud at his text, then put the phone down. I can't quite get a grip on this global romance. It's like nothing I've experienced before, not least because of its intensity. Who meets a new man a grand total of three times, in three different countries, and decides she's in a *relationship*? Who sleeps with aristocracy in Rome, only to flee to L.A. and commence an electronic relationship with occasional FaceTime, tons of texting, and endless emails that cross in the night? Still, I have learned a few things about him; he confessed the English socialite he almost proposed to was having an affair, so he had to end it despite both families pushing for a wedding. When he talks about spending time with me—even virtually—on Christmas day, it feels intimate, promising, and a little scary. Then again, maybe he *won't* contact me, at which point I'll surely be utterly depressed. Like I said—it's a weird situation.

On Christmas day, I dutifully call home, at which point my mother chit-chats about presents and sugarplum fairies, then blindsides me with some fresh bad news. *I spoke to Detective Barilla,* she said, *and we have the holidays to regroup. Then…then you have to come back. And honey, he means it this time. Something's different. You really are out of time. Come home.*

I'm keeping news of my recovered memories to myself. I figure both mom and Barilla have known all along I did it, even if *I* wasn't ready to face it. An admission would just up the pressure on me to figure out why—and give the cops more reason to decide it was *murder*.

Later in the day, I take a trip to Santa Monica and walk along the beach with my headphones on, and it is, despite what some might think of a solitary Christmas, utterly peaceful. As I'm making my way back to my car along the boardwalk, Alexander calls—from bed, he reports. "I was thinking about what I said over text the other day," he says. "You don't seem to like L.A. at all, but you were thriving in London." I almost get knocked down by a rollerblader wondering what Alexander is getting at. "It makes me think you should move back here. I mean, there's a ton of work for writers—you could get back to hard news like you said you wanted."

I think he's had too much of whatever the British equivalent of eggnog is. I laugh nervously.

"I'd need a job for that," I say, even though it's a lie. I've thought more than once about trying to drum up some freelance work back in England. "And even if you were in the same city, why do I feel like I'd never see you?"

"Oh, you'd see me," he replies suggestively, causing me to catch my breath. I've made it to my Saab, which is in the beach parking lot, and I lean on it for stability.

As we're about to say goodnight, he says, "I know I've been rubbish about showing up so far. But I'm going to come get you. Don't doubt that for a second, Augusta."

53

#85, #86, #87

I recommend being present in the moment when alone with Peter Dinklage—but I'm too distracted to follow my own advice. He's been brought into one of those beige junket rooms to talk to me, just hours after I've delivered my biggest *CelebLife* scoop to date.

The court filing to dissolve the marriage of Josephine Jansen and Tristan Catlin happened at the precise moment he said it would. I camped out at the courthouse and retrieved the papers ten minutes before closing time, called it in, and editors posted my pre-written story fifteen minutes later, with one addition: Now we know that Tristan's grounds are "irreconcilable differences." I had to fight for the sole byline. They treat those like Skittles around here—one for you, two for me, a handful for her. Maguire tried to cram her name next to mine because she sent one email to Ivan, who promptly responded with a standard Deaver the Deceiver lie: *Nope. Not true.* I pushed, using my new Tristan leverage, until they agreed to put Maguire's name at the bottom of the story.

Peter introduces himself, instantly hypnotizing me with *that voice.* He's got great hair. He looks sad to me. I'm not saying he is sad, just that his seriousness and knitted eyebrows and concerned eyes affect me. After some small talk, I ask him what worries him, if anything, considering the incredible success he's found.

He thinks about my question. "I worried a lot when I was younger," he tells me. "I was never sure if it would all work out for me. I wish I hadn't taken everything so seriously. I trusted my instincts, in the end; it took me a long time, but it all worked out. I would tell young people that worry is suffering future pain, and that it is not necessary."

I decide Peter could be a doctor, convenience store clerk, stay-at-home dad or the president—he'd be equally mesmerizing and effective in any of those roles.

"Everyone is obsessed with your show," I say. "What's that like?"

He has an answer ready. "I understand why. It is an astounding piece of art. I'm excited for my new project, too, and for the future."

He is intense, earnest, authentic. He meets my eyes, frowns, waits for my next question. When we finish up and I thank him, he shakes my hand. "You are very welcome."

Peter Dinklage: 10.0.

When he's gone, I start thinking about Jennifer Lawrence. Who *doesn't* think about Jennifer? She's falling at the Oscars, making history by winning one at twenty-two; she's got a butt and an attitude. Some people don't like her. A British blog commented that if she were made of chocolate she'd lick herself. They say she's faux-down-to-earth, that she fakes being relatable to gain fans (I admit she almost lost me when she called the cosmetic-procedure-crazy, probably near-billionaires Kardashian Klan "grounded." Chloe Sevigny called her crass and annoying, but I've met people who think Chloe is crass and annoying. Time to see for myself.

The rep scurries in. They really do scurry a lot. "I'm sorry," she says, tugging on a piece of her own hair. "You'll have to catch Jennifer and Hugh on the carpet. We're out of time." I open my mouth to protest, but she is already gone.

It's a grey carpet this time, extra wide and soft, laid out indoors in a football-field-sized conference space. Behind the reporters and photographers, the studio has stacked bleachers with screaming fans. First up for me is Hugh Jackman—Wolverine in the flesh—jauntily strolling along the carpet, joking and laughing with reporters. He towers over me in a charcoal suit with a white shirt underneath and no tie.

"I'm Hugh," he says, offering me his hand.

Crap. I have to quickly wipe the sweat off my palm. I can't give this guy the clammy hand. James Franco, maybe. Hugh Jackman, no. I run my hand down my hip in one swift move, then take his hand and wince. *Yep.* Still moist.

"What's your name?"

"Augusta," I say too loud.

"Well, Augusta, how are you tonight?"

We chat for a bit, and I'm thrown by how he's able to tune out the chaos and focus only on me. I decide on a little joke. "So. Tell me—who are you wearing, Hugh?"

He bends over with laughter, then straightens up. "I don't bloody *know*, Augusta."

I must look horrified because he laughs and adds, "I'm *kidding*! I'm playing with you. Nah—I'm wearin' Tom Ford. I think so, anyway." He does a half-turn. "Do you approve?"

"Meh," I shrug. Two can play this game. I've heard a million stories from journalists about how awesome he is, how wonderful to each person he meets, from the valet to the president of whatever nation he's currently in, and only *one* anecdote where he was allegedly snappish and rude, and it was *years* ago in his native Australia. He would be a case of a celeb legitimately using the Bad Day Defense.

"Ask me anything, Augusta—I'm ready."

We chat for a bit about his bouts with skin cancer, and he implores me and my readers to use sunscreen and get checked—*don't be lazy or afraid*. I ask him about all the hoopla around his very presence, and he goes straight to his close-knit family: "I'm well aware that one day this might be over, but we'll all be together. We're always together as a family. That's what matters."

It's time for him to go. I thank him, and I'm rewarded with a beaming smile and a wave. Which is fine, because Jen's coming.

Here she is…and there she goes. *Wait, whoa.* "Jen! I'm with *CelebLife*."

She keeps walking, but I can see her hesitate. Good lord, it's exhausting trying to help stars promote their own movies. I don't even get panicky about it anymore—I'm simply *tired* of all the chasing and begging. "Just a quick chat? *CelebLife* readers adore you…"

Jennifer, in a floor-length crushed-velvet dress, stops, pivots, then walks back to me.

"How's your man? Can you tell us what makes him special?"

"He's great. Best friend, brilliant man, great guy. We're having a great time."

"You've had a rocky go of it with some bad press lately, in between all the accolades and fan-love. How do you handle it?"

"How do I handle it? I'm myself," she says. "Sometimes you have to do what you have to do—you can't live in fear of pissing people off."

That's all I'm getting, but it's more than enough. Jen's handlers guide her as she walks quickly away. The screening is about to start. But no; she's not ready. Jennifer tears away from all of them and turns like she's in a movie's last climactic scene. Her gown swishes as she glides over to a woman in a wheelchair who's been calling her name. Jennifer kneels, takes the woman's T-shirt, signs it, hugs her, takes a selfie, all while her fuming handlers stand in utter horror. I've seen this before—usually handlers love all good PR, but not when their star is delaying things. *You go, Jen.*

On my way back to my car, I get an email from Stanley: *Been seeing your name on the Tristan stories, usually with, like, seven other reporters. But why do I get the sense that's all you? Anyway, I'm starting a new enterprise in London. I want you to come work for me. Full time, benefits, vacations, and Prince Harry. No Bon Jovi—I promise.*

Wow. How's that for a plot twist just when I need one? London is calling, but I have no answer yet. Not until my case is settled. *Sorry, Stanley.*

I don't reply.

54

#93, #94, #95, #96, #97, #98

Jack Black bows his head and thanks me for interviewing him. He'll be getting a 10.0, partly because he's witty, kind, and hilarious, but also because he managed to help me forget my therapist called in the middle of my (*gasp!*) Oprah interview. As Jack moves on, however, I recommence freaking out. Apparently my choices are to a) call the therapist back, or b) face terrible, unspecified consequences.

*Ooh…*not yet, though. Here comes Tyra Banks. Clad in a shiny gold mermaid gown, she greets me with a serious face and a crisp, deep hello. My mouth opens but no words come out—I've been a fan since her fierce, teary "kiss-my-fat-ass" monologue on her eponymous talk show years ago. Tyra went on blast after she was papped in a one-piece bathing suit, slammed in the media because she wasn't thin as a pencil, and had to endure such headlines as "Thigh-ra Banks." Her response shot a new truth into my brain: I truly must *not* care what other people think of my body—good *or* bad. I repeated her battle cry to myself that day: *Kiss MY fat ass.*

I get a grip and ease in by asking Tyra about her charitable foundation. She nods and offers a quick smile. "My goal is to mentor young girls and boost their self-esteem. I don't just give money—I'm here for these girls, and I talk to them all the time."

"But how do you change their thinking?" I follow up. "In a world where the default reaction to female bodies is 'not good enough,' how do you get through to them?"

"Yep, it's hard," she nods, "but I don't tell them they have to be a certain size or look like anyone else. I talk to them about becoming the best *they* can be." She pauses and takes a hard look at me. I'm suddenly aware I'm fidgeting, adjusting my waistband, running my thumb under my straining bra strap, shifting on my feet.

"You know what *doesn't* work?" Tyra goes on. "Telling them in the moment they look great, they're fine, they're OK. Then they go out and face the world and feel terrible again." She's passionate, verging on angry (join the club). "A close friend of mine is a size 18—and she is *fierce*. She lifts, she runs, she's fit, she's happy, she's healthy. I tell the girls I've been slammed for being too fat—*and* for being too thin, when I was younger. That stuff's never OK. I tell them to get out there and be *their* best selves. You know what I mean?"

Funny she should ask. "I do," I nod, and soon after we part ways.

The carpet is starting to wind down, but I'm thinking I can stay awhile longer and *not* call the therapist back. There's no point—I have nothing new to share with her.

They won't leave me alone. A few days later, Mom calls four times in a row while I'm getting ready for the Golden Globes, for which I've had to trawl bargain stores for last season's fashions. To my shock and disgust, *CelebLife* expects its reporters to dress and primp like the stars, but won't pay for any of it. Jemima calls a fifth time. In case someone has died, I answer.

"Hi," I say. "What's up?"

"Augusta!" Jemima is almost yelling. "Return my calls. It's so…*really*. Not to return people's calls—it's rude."

"Mom, I emailed and texted you back every time. You never responded. That's usually how people—"

"You're out of time," she says. "*We're* out of time. Joe's family is threatening to pressure the DA to bring you up on charges. I'm sorry to sound so harsh, but things are getting serious. Whether you remember or not, you need to be ready to come back, meet with your therapist, and then…well, then we have to consider talking to a lawyer."

I sink down onto my bed and close my eyes.

"Augusta? Are you there?"

"Mom, I know. Give me a few days to regroup and think about things, and I promise I'll call you before the week is up."

Jemima lets out one of her famous sighs. "I'll try to stall them for a few more days—but then we *have* to deal with this, Augusta. We have no choice."

Security at the Beverly Hilton is worse than at the airport, and it takes me half an hour to get through the line. As I wait for the stars to filter into the after party, I check my email and am entertained by a *CelebLife* chain with a thousand names on it, flowing from the four staffers allowed backstage. *George Clooney just took a sip of his beer—and then put it down! OMG: BRAD IS SMILNG AT A YOUNG BLONDE. Who is she? Did we know Sandra Bullock is BFFs with Amy Schumer? They're hugging!!! I can't believe this—Channing Tatum has a booger! Reese looks pensive. Octavia sneezes.*

As the stars flow in, I see every single actor from every network TV show and all the movies from last year, along with every kind of food: a mashed potato volcano with gravy lava, a sushi bar attended by a chef, roast beast of every description, baskets of naughty carbs and bowls of colorful salads. I grab a quick bite while scanning the crowd for a victim.

Olivia Wilde is by the door. I head over for a chat. She is brilliantly authentic—I want to take her home and force her be my best friend. She smiles, holds out her arms when I approach, puts a hand on my shoulder.

"How's it going?" She's perpetually laughing or smiling. Doesn't matter what I ask her, she's game. Her skin is like a baby's bottom and her face is chiseled from stone.

I bump into Jason Bateman again and it takes everything I have to stick to the Goldblum Rule, but I do it, greeting him like we've never met. He gives me an enthusiastic "Hey, you," and we sip our drinks and chat for a bit about his next movie. Once again, I find I have to extract myself from the conversation before I overstay my welcome; he doesn't give out obvious *go away* vibes.

Quinn texts about the HBO party out by the pool because it's the coolest of all the Globes soirees scattered about the Hilton. I do one more circle and there, leaning up against a VIP booth with some friends, is a famous TV actress who used to do movies. I think of her as ultra-anal but likeable and cute, though she's gone heavy on the cosmetic procedures over the years. Her husband is with her, and *he* is the fuckup, the flighty one who allegedly can't beat his own goofy, substance-abusing demons. I approach gingerly with a basic "Hi."

She steps toward me, blue eyes wide open, and offers an excited "Hi!" She thinks she knows me. She lifts up her right hand as if swearing allegiance to the flag, frozen in place and grinning as if she's genuinely happy to see me. Her hand stays in the air for a moment, flat palm facing me.

"I'm with *CelebLife* magazine. You look great. Are you enjoying the party? Great food…"

"Yes! Hi!"

She thinks we are friends. I should be leaving now, out of respect. Her eyes are huge and unfocused. I have never seen anything like this, not even at Tristan Catlin's house. This is not pot or even prescription drugs, unless she way overdosed. Meth, perhaps? Crack? It feels extreme. The husband is the sober one. He nods calmly, smiles at me, and steps in. He is her ventriloquist. It's too late to get out of this gracefully.

"Can you give us your favorite health tip?" I ask her. "You've stayed so fit over the years, our readers want to know how you do it."

Her husband stands in front of her and coherently and thoughtfully answers for her, as if this is entirely normal. *She sticks with healthy whole foods, lean meats, and plenty of exercise.* He is propping her up as she sways and stares at the air. It's time to back away slowly and leave them to it. She is the last person I would've expected to find in this state.

I head for the exit and find that the line to get into the HBO party is about a hundred people long. I text Quinn, who strides out, finds me, and whisks me straight in the door, then heads back to his photo booth as I make a beeline for the bar. Drink in hand, I step back into the fray, and *ooh*, there's Leo. I get close and watch him for a while. What can I say about Leonardo DiCaprio? That he's an overgrown, modelizing mama's boy with puffy eyes who's taken private jets to environmental galas? Maybe he's decided that the millions his foundation gives out to save animals from extinction minimizes his personal footprint.

I decide he's no Tom Cruise. He's more of a bro than a slick movie star, and that's not entirely a bad thing. People seem to like him. He exchanges an affectionate hug and cheek-kisses with Laura Linney. He's relaxed and laughs a lot, and no one is stiff around him or has to babysit him. On the downside, he hangs with Tobey Maguire. Security is hovering so I decide not to approach, mostly because I am not authorized by *CelebLife* to cover this party, but I will count Leo because of all my close-up spying.

I run into Marisa Tomei, who has always touched me with her performances, and ask a tame warm-up question we tend to unleash on pretty much every nominee.

"I know you've been through the Oscar nomination game more than once. How do you and your fellow actors prepare for the big night?"

She makes a face and cocks her head, then laughs as if I've uttered the world's most obnoxious query. "You say it as if it's, like, a triathlon!" She's shrill, eyes narrowed. "The way I'm preparing is trying to stay in the moment." She walks away with her handler. I'm deflated.

There, up ahead: another chance. It's a cute sandy-haired guy of about forty I recognize instantly from *Chicago Fire* and, years ago, *House*. I stand back and Yammer those shows, and find his name: Jesse Spencer, Australian import.

"Hey, Jesse," I say, walking up to him and his date. "Great party, right?"

Jesse smiles, ready to welcome me. Then his expression morphs into something resembling determination. He walks at me. He is in my face. I pull back slightly, but he reaches his hand out so quickly I can't stop it, unfurls his right index finger, and commands, "Go like this."

His mouth is open in a garish smile as he bares his teeth. His exquisite date is giggling.

"Open ya mouth." Despite his long Hollywood career, he retains a thick Aussie accent.

I do as ordered. I could get in trouble for disobeying a celebrity. Then, here it comes: His I-don't-know-where-it's-been fingernail scrapes against my front tooth. He pulls his finger back and shows me a disgusting fleck of green. "Ya got spinach in ya teeth. It's OK. Don't be embarrassed. Someone's gotta tell ya."

He smiles, but it is only partially for my benefit. This, I suspect, was more for his own entertainment than to save me from the humiliation of approaching Robert Downey Jr. with a slick of emerald slime in my mouth.

The interview itself, which I feel I have to conduct to save face, is unremarkable because I can't get over the sensation of his finger in my mouth. I find the ladies' room and rinse for a few minutes with a vodka martini after, gargling and spitting into the sink.

55

I can't read any more. And anyway, they got it wrong. There is a difference between murder, homicide, and death. Any decent journalist knows this. It should read the *death* of Joe Lannells, not the *murder*. I killed him, yes; but if it's determined to be in self-defense, it's not murder.

If.

I'm lying on top of the covers after a brisk walk around Runyon Canyon, where I almost ran over Claire Danes on my way down. I read the article again. There hasn't been a fresh story in months, and this one is devastating. I see my name in the piece as if *Augusta Noble* is written in invisible ink on every line, ready to emerge at any point and expose me to everyone—to Stanley, to past colleagues, to Maguire, to *Alexander*—as the murderer I possibly am.

It's only a matter of time, but I need the cops, the DA, the therapist, all of them—to hang on just a little bit longer. The Academy Awards are tomorrow, and I'm planning to reach 107.

I set my phone on the nightstand and close my eyes. I don't have the luxury of letting this weigh on me. Peter Dinklage said it best: *Don't suffer future pain.* My mother has a saying, too—*Denial ain't just a river in Egypt*—but I'm going with Peter's.

Later that afternoon, I stop in the office. If I reach my goal at the Oscars, I'll quite possibly quit for good, so I want to say goodbye to Quinn and scrub any errant personal scribblings from my computer. When I step into the main corridor, I'm hit with an eerie silence. As I walk slowly toward Maguire's office, passing empty offices and cubicles, I imagine a harmonica crying the blues and wind whistling by my ear, blowing tumbleweed across the worn carpeting. I make it to Maguire's office and stop short. Esdee is in the barren room, cleaning the boss's empty desk with antibacterial wipes.

She looks up at me with red-rimmed eyes. "I'm your new bureau chief," she says thinly. "Maguire and Uvula are gone."

"What happened?"

Esdee stops wiping. The smell of bleach has taken over the room. "Maguire was caught accepting freebies. Uvula was too old and too expensive, plus, she didn't have any sources. She was a throwback, frankly."

The reasons those two were let go don't surprise me—but both of them being stone-cold *fired* is a shock nonetheless.

"New York lost three as well," she adds.

"The Oscars are *tomorrow*," I say pointlessly. "How can they do this now?"

"We'll make it work, like we always do," she shrugs and sighs at the same time. "Everyone is dispensable. The sooner people realize that, the more they'll work together as a team. We need you, Augusta—*I* need you to kick ass tomorrow, and to stay on your Tristan source indefinitely. It's you and me now, kid."

I'm not a kid and I'm leaving soon, but I don't tell her that. I've never trusted any of these people. "Where's everyone else?" I ask.

"Across the street getting blue margaritas," she says, rubbing hard at one spot on the desktop. She stops and makes a show of checking her watch. "The news should be on Twitter in three, two, one…"

All my thoughts of getting back at Maguire, of telling Uvula what a horrible person she is, of throwing Tristan in their face, of asking them *why*—why they wield their power so irresponsibly—have disappeared in a *poof*. The targets I'd fixated on are gone, leaving a vacuum where anger and resentment used to be. I feel nothing. The changing times are eating away at our business in big chunks, faster than we thought, without mercy or favor, like the Great Nothing.

I clean out my cubicle and erase everything on my computer as best I can, then stop by Quinn's office on my way out. The Great Nothing got him, too. All that's left of a twenty-five year career is a stray pencil, dust bunnies, wires, and scraps of paper where a vibrant talent with institutional memory used to be.

56

#99, #100, #101, #102, #103, #104, #105

The Oscars finally arrive, and the usual celebrity-related emails fly between New York and L.A. as if nothing has changed. But it has; everything feels like it's coming to a conclusion. With *eight* celebrities left to speak to, I know one of them will hold the key—I know it as surely as I exist.

As I wait outside for my Lyft, dressed in a Calvin Klein black number (I also sprang for a blowout and professional makeup), text messages start flying at me like slaps to the face. Apparently my mother has given up on phone calls.

WE ARE OUT OF TIME MEETING TUESDAY WITH BARILLA AND DA

Next, a link comes through. My mother still can't write in lower case or use punctuation, but she's learned how to send links. It's a plane ticket to New York in my name, leaving in the morning. Oh, hell, no. *No, no, no.*

I write back, shaking my head as if she can see me: *I can't—Oscars tonight! Then editing stories all day tomorrow.*

YOU HAVE NO CHOICE THEY WILL ARREST YOU IF YOU DONT RETURN BY TUESDAY

They can't do that—can they? They can't just force me back so abruptly!

NOT ABRUPT WE HAVE BEEN TRYING TO REACH YOU FOR SIX WEEKS GET ON THAT PLANE AUGUSTA

But I don't remember it all—not yet. A single tear forms in the corner of my eye.

IM SO SORRY SEE YOU TOMORROW HONEY TRY NOT TO WORRY JUST COME HOME

My Lyft arrives and I pause for a moment before getting into the not-so-new Honda, fearing I might throw up. *This can't be happening; I won't let it.* I push it all out of my mind as we crawl toward Hollywood Boulevard. I read over my notes, saying the names of the stars in my mind over and over to replace the dark thoughts. *Angelina. Taraji. Ryan. The Rock. Reese.*

The Academy Awards red carpet is like a two-lane road covered in crimson, but I'm not on it—I'm relegated to bleacher seats, backing up Tatiana and Tracey. This affair is exactly what you see on TV: A traffic jam of beautiful people trying to pretend they're not jockeying for attention, while those left holding their hats and purses are constantly being told to *Get out of the way!*

Here comes Angelina Jolie. I step off the bottom bleacher. Tatiana's busy with Ryan Gosling and Tracey's stuck with Gwyneth Paltrow, who I could never interview because I'd troll her mercilessly in an attempt to pry a tone-deaf quote out of her that tops her old favorites such as, "I would rather die than let my kid eat Cup-a-Soup" and "I am who I am. I can't pretend to be somebody who makes $25,000 a year." Anyway, Angie's here, and I'm the only one available, so I go for it. Will it be Angie who solves all my problems? Of course it will. This is what it's all led up to—Augusta Noble one-on-one with the queen of celebrities, mom of the year, a superstar who speaks up for the voiceless.

She stops in front of me, says, "Hi!," then immediately glances elsewhere, putting on that enormous smile and waving at her adoring public. She's got chapped lips and is all-around indifferent to our encounter. I feel as if I'm talking to her through a TV, as if I'm imagining the whole thing. She moves and talks slowly and appears frail. Her hair is a brittle blue-black, and layers of makeup cannot hide imperfect skin. If I knew any young girls right now, I'd say to them, *I have seen the truth. The world's great beauties have flaws too, even if you don't see them beneath all the airbrushing and makeup. You will be OK—you ARE OK, just as you are.*

I'm thinking Angie will get a 6.0.

By the end of the fashion parade, my feet hurt, my surgically applied makeup is fading, and I have not had a single revelatory encounter. The instant I see Ryan Gosling's tight butt disappear into the golden theater, I blast through the crowd, out of the security zone, and find the car that whisks me to an outrageously decadent Oscar-viewing party. I make it to the bar, where a hot young guy mixes me one of tonight's specialties: a lemon-raspberry martini with bits of real vanilla bean.

Everything is purple and white and there's a celebrity at every turn. I approach my assigned table and see an imposing, dark-haired actor I recognize from TV and movies; I *love* Mr. Big, aka Chris Noth. I cruise toward the seat next to him, head held high, tummy sucked in, and plop myself down. I situate my drink, my lipstick, my handbag, my phone; then I introduce myself. This guy is one of the few genuinely tall actors, as handsome in person as he is onscreen, and he is nice enough when I introduce myself as a reporter. His face darkens when I mention *CelebLife*.

"What's the problem?" I ask, as if we're old friends. I am genuinely dying to know. He looks surprised at my bluntness. Mrs. Big leans across him and says hello. She's got a healthy glow, excellent manners, and is half his size.

"Your magazine misquoted me," Chris grumbles. "Got me in trouble." He's unapologetically, refreshingly grouchy, but doesn't want to give details. I'm dubious we "misquoted" him, partly because I don't remember the last time we wrote about him.

"That's not like them," I say. "We're usually a very nice magazine. Sorry about that. *I* don't misquote people, so don't worry."

He says something along the lines of, *Grumble mumble grumble*, and picks at his salad, then takes a drink of his something-or-other on the rocks. In the end, I warm him up and he becomes talkative and interesting, and his wife, Tara, is awesome. At one point, Big even brings me a cocktail.

After dinner, the price of a chat with Sharon Stone is a dance. She's got short, spiky platinum-blonde hair, the deep smile lines she's had since before *Basic Instinct,* and a permanent smirk. I conduct an interview while bopping with her to the live band, at which point I learn she is not modest about her work with AIDS.

"I've been at it sooo long, my dear," she coos. "I've been an AIDS worker since you were in diapers."

I hit her with a question from my sheet. "I have to ask how you stay looking so young," I say with long-practiced amazement.

"They've raised $3.8 million for AIDS tonight, baby. Just write that," she orders me, throwing her head back as she gyrates to the music.

I bid her adieu and find a stone-faced Ben Stiller standing in a small group. He strikes me as the guy who's always talking about a *project*, something in *development*, something he's *pitching*. No small talk or schmoozing, even here. When he turns to talk to me for a moment, I find him serious and irritable but not entirely awful, as I expected based on some of the things you read about him in certain online comment sections. Fun facts about Ben: He doesn't like to cook and he doesn't celebrate his birthday.

I set off to look for a bar but pass a Godiva stand first. I pop a dusted cappuccino truffle in my mouth and take a breather. I need to start racking up some interviews *CelebLife* will actually use, but with the awards show just ending over at the Dolby, the scene here remains low wattage. On my way to find actual stars, I see easy prey. Gordon Ramsay is sitting with his wife and some British guy I think I recognize from TV but can't place. No one at *CelebLife* will print an interview with him, but at least it'll look like I tried.

"Hey, Gordon," I grin by way of a greeting, telling him who I am and who I write for. "What can we expect from your upcoming show? More swearing?"

"Cum, bollocks, shit, and piss," the guy sitting next to the TV chef barks bizarrely.

Tana, Gordon's long-suffering wife, glares at me. Gordon ignores me and says something to the weird guy, who I realize I *do* recognize as an aging bit-part actor.

I let it roll off and lean in. "Hi, Tana, I'd love to talk to you, too! For our Oscars issue. What can we expect on this season's show?"

"You've got a *ladder* in your tights," Gordon sneers out of nowhere. "Now, will you fuck off and fix it?"

The bit-part actor snickers like a playground bully, a sort of laugh/snort, and Tana grins like the girlfriend of the head bully who thinks she's cool by association. I feel like I've been sucker-punched. I doubt very much my run-resistant tights have any sort of tear in them, but I can't be sure. "I hate you," I reply in a deferential *ha ha, you got me* sort of tone. "You're a horrible person." I'm back on the school playground, powerless to do anything but laugh along at my own expense.

"It's not very nice to walk around with a ladder in your tights," Gordon snaps back, louder this time, pointing toward my upper thigh area. He means to humiliate and demean me, and it's working. I want to fight back or run, but I'm paralyzed. "I have one? I do? Do I really?" My voice is nervously high-pitched. It's happening so fast there's no time to think about getting away.

"Yes!" Gordon yells. A thick swoop of hair stands up at the front of his head like the comb of a colossal blond rooster.

"Where?" I grab the front of my stretchy dress and pull down, trying to get it closer to my knees so he stops looking up my skirt.

"Up the back! You can't see it, it's right up inside your thigh. I'm being polite, and you tell me, 'I hate you.'" He's talking fast, in a cruel staccato. "Of course you can't see it, because it's right up the side of your bum." Gordon takes a crooked finger and sends it in that general direction, though he stops short of touching my clothing or me.

Don't piss off the celebrities. "I take it back," I say. "I don't hate you." *Ha, ha.*

Gordon decides it's time to tell me about the show, which he does in two monotone lines when all I want to do is retreat. At the end he barks, "Now—go sort your ladder out."

I walk away as fast as I can. This isn't the worst thing that's ever happened to me, so *why am I so freaked out?* I head to the bathroom, sit on the toilet, and, shaking and breathing heavily, I Yammer "Gordon Ramsay" and "misogyny." An encyclopedia of dickheadedness pops up. He's allegedly had affairs and publicly demeaned women. I'm not the first and I surely won't be the last. I collect myself in the stall, freshen up, then find a route out to the garden/smoking section/outdoor bar, hoping to catch up on my notes. The only butt-sized space left is next to a smoking celebrity. Having an ingrained reporter's drive, I can't stop myself, though this guy could be *worse* than my last.

"Hi, Simon," I greet him with a bit of Eeyore in my tone and manner. He pats the space next to him and I perch on the glorified ottoman, one butt cheek threatening to slide off.

"Well hello," Simon Cowell says. "How's it going?"

"Ah," I sigh. "Gordon Ramsay told me I have a ladder in my tights. I don't."

"No," he agrees. "You don't."

I turn on my recorder and fight an odd need to yawn. "Tell me, Simon, what brings you here tonight?"

"This is the only one I had an invitation to. That's why I'm here." He sucks in some nicotine.

"How's everything going? How's that cute family of yours?"

"Great," he says.

"You and the wife doing well?"

He tilts his head to the side and gives me a faux-suspicious look. "Why do you ask? Are you coming on to me? Are you saying you'll have sex with me tonight?"

I try not to laugh. "One-hundred-percent, yes," I hit back. "*Now* what are you going to do?"

"OK, you win," he says, waving his cigarette-holding hand in the air in surrender. "I'm now going to have to have sex with you."

After he responds to a few relevant questions about various musical stars he knows, I walk back toward the party's grand entrance. My file so far is verging on pointless from a *CelebLife* editor's point of view, and from mine. I'm by the door, and bigger stars are now congregating in the entry hall. There are the Beckhams again: I'm so over them. Miley and Liam: *Ugh, I just can't.* I should be focused on coaxing the latter ultra-hot couple to talk to me, but I'm starting to think this entire affair has bad juju, and my calm euphoria of hours ago has waned. There is more trouble coming; as my mom would say, I can feel it in my waters. I watch the young pair for a bit and am amused to see how they interact: Miley is as gulpy and goofy as her public persona, and Liam watches her in a sort of befuddled wonder as if to say, *I don't know why I love you, I just do.*

I move down a wide, dark hallway and bump into Ricky Gervais, yet another fifty-something white male British star who's known to pick on absolutely everyone. But since I'm obsessed with *The Office* (U.K., *not* U.S), I must risk it. He's with his longtime partner, bestselling author Jane Fallon.

Ricky greets my interview request with "Hey, sure. What's up?"

We talk about the luxurious party and how Americans actually do love him despite his piss-taking on our precious stars, and he laughs at every attempt at humor I make. I decide to get his view on the royals. "You know there's another baby coming, right?"

"What?"

"A royal baby. I assume you've already bought a savings bond for the little tyke…"

Ricky bends over and cracks up, giggling with abandon. He laughs a lot at other people's jokes. Though he's known for relentless self-promotion on social media, he doesn't appear to take himself seriously, and it's endearing.

"Oh, yes," he replies. "I've put something aside in case the baby needs it. I popped five million in just yesterday. I can't wait." He's still giggling.

Dan Stevens, the poshly handsome blond actor who bit the dust in *Downton Abbey,* walks up to us. Ricky, who starred with him in *Night at the Museum*, introduces us.

"Meet Dan. He's newly famous. The girls like him. You can see why, can't you?"

"Absolutely."

Finding himself in the *CelebLife* spotlight, Dan reveals an aw-shucks shyness. Soon enough, I figure, he'll be jaded and suspicious of people like me. "Didn't you play Sir

Lancelot in those movies? I mean, you went full knight—talk about a chick magnet, right?"

"My wife, in particular, loves the knight thing," Dan replies, smiling shyly.

I nod to indicate yes, I understand he is married.

"What are your fans like? Do the ladies ever get a bit pushy around you?"

"My wife keeps me in check," he says.

It's kind of sweet the way he keeps mentioning her. Either he thinks I'm lusting after him or he's afraid he'll lust after me and is keeping himself honest (I'm leaning toward Option A). Or maybe he's just a nervous blurter, which I can entirely relate to.

Ricky is laughing again. I turn to Jane and jab my thumb toward her man. "You must laugh all the time living with this guy."

"I do," she deadpans. "I laugh until I'm *sick*." She puts a heavy emphasis on *sick* as if she's literally going to blow chunks.

Ricky doubles over with laughter. When he recovers, he inquires, "So. Are *you* having fun tonight?"

I shrug. "Unfortunately, not all the guests at this party are as gracious as you three."

"What happened?" He sips his drink.

I tell him, but refer to Gordon only as a fading British TV personality.

Ricky listens, then asks, "What do you care what some has-been cunt says to you?"

A quick smile crosses my face. "You know what, Ricky? You're absolutely fucking right."

That's an answer. A solution. It's not *the* solution, but I feel I'm getting close. As I leave Ricky, Jane, and Dan, I try to reset and remember that out of the dozens of stars I've racked up to date, far more have been kind than cruel. There have been more Kevins, Parkers and Rickys than Gordons, Hilarys and J-Los. As I near the end of the road, I'm finally figuring out what's been messing with my head this whole time: It's the *not knowing* that kills me. I can't predict what I'm going to get when I walk up to a star: jokes, abuse, rudeness, kindness, grace, rote answers, gentle mocking, laughter. I have to brace myself *every single time* and simply take what comes; if I can't bear to do that, I might as well get out of this business altogether. Which is definitely a viable option.

I watch Jennifer Lawrence walk by—in yet another dress with a train—and worry she's going to take another tumble. I am only vaguely interested in her at this point and don't bother chasing her. It's time for another forget-you-ever-met-the-has-been-chef drink. I'm heading to the bar when I slam into someone with a thud.

He points at me. "You," he says as if I've done something wrong. "*You*."

57

It's Tristan Catlin, sexy and slick in a coal-black tux. "*You*," he says once more. "The girl who doesn't want me. You never called. What's your deal, girl?" He's slurry, friendly, drunk, high.

"Don't flatter yourself," I respond, tucking a piece of hair behind my ear and running my tongue over my teeth. "I'm sure there are tons of females who don't want you."

"*This* is why I love this girl," he crows to Liv, who's with him again, along with a pretty young woman and a prettier young man I'd bet my paycheck are Ivan Deaver's publicity assistant/babysitters. Tristan pulls me into a hug, his grip stronger than last time.

He takes my hand and leads me into a nook around the corner from the bar that's dark and sparsely populated. He pulls me close until our bodies are touching from knees to chest. He's a little pushy, sure, but he smells great, he's charismatic, and he's a great kisser. And, let's face it, he's *Tristan Catlin*. Buzzed on vanilla-bean cocktails, I let him kiss me. His lips are expert, hard. His tongue is on a mission. But he's not Alexander, and my body knows it.

Tristan pulls back after thirty seconds, and smiles at me like he's won something. He is celebrity perfect. Nose-hair trimmed, a bit of subtle makeup for the cameras, teeth of a color and structure not found in nature. And is that…*eyeliner?*

"Don't look at me like that," I say, wriggling out of his embrace. "It was a kiss. That's all."

"Oh, I don't know," says a voice from a few feet away. "It looked like more than that from where I'm standing."

I know that accent. That *voice.*

I turn and see Alexander in the entrance to the wide hallway, his tailored tux lit up under a purple-hued chandelier. My throat constricts.

Tristan watches with mild curiosity as I hurry over to greet Alexander. "Hey," I say, grinning up at him. "What in the world are you doing here? And why didn't you *tell* me you were coming?"

Alexander does not smile back. "I'll give you this, Augusta Noble," he says. "I thought no one could surprise me anymore. But you—you've surprised me." Alexander nods toward Tristan, who's watching with some interest. "Well. I'll leave you to it."

He turns on his heel and stalks away.

I chase after him, touch his arm. "Wait! *Wait.*"

He stops. "*Hey,*" I say, wanting to touch him more but resisting. I hug myself. "What are you so upset about? I had no idea you were coming."

Alexander is frowning, and his dark mood, while slightly concerning on its surface, has told me something very important: He cares more than I realized—and he's jealous.

"It's a funny thing about surprises," he replies coldly. "It's not actually a *surprise* if you tell the person first."

I stare at the floor and suddenly feel naked. I pat my shoulder; I don't have my handbag. I stop myself from looking over at Tristan, though I'm sure I left it with him.

"You seem to forget what happened the last time I saw you," I remind Alexander. "You were all over a pretty little actress called Belinda. What am I supposed to do? Sit around waiting for a guy who's never in the same place for more than a week? We don't even live on the same continent." Rome seems forever ago now.

I watch his eyes, dark and closed down, but he stays rooted in place as if wants to leave but can't. "I explained that," he replies. "And then you left—you were just gone. You never even said goodbye."

I throw my hands up. "What are we doing here, Alexander? You're constantly traveling, you're changing your plans, you're hanging out with hot blondes, you're texting me on Christmas—but this is the first time I've seen you since Rome. Why *wouldn't* I feel free to make out with Tristan Catlin at an Oscars party?"

His eyes are still dark, but now they're less angry and more hurt. Elton John walks by in a shiny lavender suit with Liz Hurley in tow.

"You're right, Augusta. You're absolutely right. I should've taken the hint. This was a bad idea."

"Wait—what hint?"

"When I suggested you come back to London," he says, "you…well, you ignored it. You treated it like a joke."

Britney Spears is passing by with a massive entourage. I can't have Britney Spears in my face mid-breakup; the image will never leave me.

"Because I thought it *was* a joke," I reply. "How do you see this working, exactly? Your aforementioned travel schedule means I'd probably never see you anyway. I—"

"What about *your* schedule?" he cuts in. "That's why we *can* work—don't you see? I wasn't asking you to come back for me. I was listening to how much you seemed to loathe L.A. and how much happier—how much better you fit in—in London, and I feel the same way. I could *never* live here. I'm thirty-three years old. I've watched my friends spend their adult lives panicking about sorting out the wife, the house, the kids. And you know what? The minute they do, they're looking for a way out. All they want is freedom and adventure. Unlike them, we *have* that, Augusta. We live a rare life. We're good at what we do and we love it." He steps closer to me, points at me, then back at himself. "You and I? We could have both. That's not something you find every day. I learned that the hard way."

I have no ready response for any of this. I never knew he thought of me that way; a part of me believed I was simply another port of call. The truth is, I've been thinking about going back to London for months now, wanting to get back to my serious news roots with the added challenge of international locales and languages, but I never wanted to do it for a guy; I didn't want the impetus, the reason, to be a *man* beckoning me with vague promises of "seeing if it works." The way things stand now, though, I'm basing a decision *not* to go on a man. It's twisted.

"I know you're right," I say more softly now. "About this not being the right place for me. But I don't have a job back in London, or a flat…"

He pauses, seems unimpressed. I feel like I can read his mind: *That never stopped you before.*

"Well," he shrugs, still unsmiling, "I told you I was going to come see you, and I did. It's your turn to make the big gesture. When you figure out your life, you know where to find me." He shoots me one last looks straight into the eyes, then turns on his heel and walks away, disappearing into a crowd of models.

I call after him, "No, I don't! That's the problem." I can't tell if he heard me or not.

I am not at all certain I'll see him again, and the possibility makes me want to throw up. There's another major complication looming between us, too: Alexander has no idea I'm possibly a murderer. There was never the right time to tell him what I went through, and what's hanging over my head. This is all too much to handle on Oscars night, so I keep moving. I turn back toward Tristan, who cannot be trusted to take care of my handbag. He is standing in the same place. And, shit, shit, shit—he's holding…*the book*.

"Wow. I mean—*wow*. Let me ask you something," Tristan snarls as I approach. "Who do you think you are?"

"I'm nobody," I tell him, trying to get my bearings, switch gears, save myself.

"I was going to bring your bag to you, and this fell out. It's been illuminating. You think you can judge us?" He flips loudly, violently through the pages. "Here's a good one—Michael Shannon. Wow. *Woooowww*. The coolest cat in Hollywood and you decide he's 'disheveled' and 'hunched?'" Tristan lets out a sardonic laugh.

I clear my throat. "Well," I say, "he was. If you look closer, you'll see I also said he was 'highly intelligent' and 'better than the rest of them.'" *Or something*.

He flips some more, the crinkling of the aging pages making me wince as he abuses them. I have to get my book back. "Princess Kate. Oh….*the poor girl*. She's got 'a slight underbite'? Um, OK." He meets my eyes. "I guess she's not attractive enough for you? You're right. She's hideous. I mean, wow, Augusta." He pats the book. "This is great journalism. Really."

I cross my arms and stare him down. "*You*, who love to go on about his *craft*, are sticking up for a duchess, of all people? She did nothing but wait around for a man for a third of her life, before he finally caved in and married her when his other prospects balked at a life in that weird family. I mean, the girl nearly dislocated her jaw putting on that fake posh accent. She's a *phony*, Tristan—just like some other people I know."

"Here we go." Tristan widens his eyes, ignores me. "This is interesting. *Christian Bale: Has a big head.* Seriously? Christian's a buddy of mine. I'll be sure to tell him you said so. He can get right down to the hospital and get a head reduction."

"Why not?" I shoot back. "You people get everything else nipped and tucked to feed your vanity. Why not a head-ectomy?"

Tristan's eyes flash as he shakes the notebook at me. "Right. I got hair implants. I got my eyes done and my nose tweaked. I have to look good on camera. You don't know what it's like." His eyes move from my head to my feet and back again. "Who are *you* to judge *me*?"

"Who I am," I tell him, realizing in this moment exactly what has irked me about people like him since I began, "is a *real person* with flaws and a regular-sized nose and yes, a crooked tooth or two, and thighs that rub together and probably always will. You think young girls— and boys—are cutting out their ribs for a smaller waist, getting plastic surgery, starving themselves, because of other kids at school? *No.* It's because of *you*—from the 'reality stars' to the so-called A-list—who hate yourselves so fucking much you cave to a few pervy men who run the industry and decide what's beautiful. A mouth full of novelty teeth, a bubble butt until bubble butts are out again, fake tits, boob reductions, calf implants, lip injections. So I ask you again: Why is the idea of a head-ectomy so outlandish to you?"

Tristan doesn't respond. He's reading again, his eyebrows moving as much as they can with all the Botox. Liv is in view just around the corner, playing on her phone, side-eying us every minute or so. He says, "I particularly love the ratings. Thank god we have *you* to decide where we are on a scale of one to ten." He checks me out. "Maybe I should rate *you* now."

"Go for it," I tell him. "Seriously. Because you know what? You were right about me. I *don't* care about impressing you, or anyone else. I failed for years—I failed every single fucking day to fit in and make everyone like me. It took me a long time, but I finally learned to stop trying. And you know what happened? Nothing changed. I was still the odd one out, but I discovered it's a lot more fun being myself."

I'm hit with an unfamiliar sense of serenity. There it is; I found my fire again. Its return, in the end, has nothing to do with celebrities. Or maybe it does, a little. Perhaps I should be grateful for Tristan and the other stars. Like my old friend Albert Schweitzer said, *We should all be thankful for those people who rekindle the inner spirit.*

I don't think Tristan's heard a word I've been saying, but I've had quite enough of his ranting. It's time to pry the book away from him, whatever it takes.

"I will say there's some deep stuff here," he observes. "Let's see what Peter Dinklage has to say: *I trusted my instincts, in the end, and my career took off. It took me a long time.* OK, Peter rules, bad example. This one looks good: *Hugh Jackman tells me about his close-knit family: 'Augusta, one day this might be over, but we'll all be together. That's what matters.'"* Tristan faux giggles. *"Awwww.* Here's your little note at the end of the quote: *Says my name. Several times. LOVE him.* What are you, in eighth grade?"

My brain begins to short-circuit. I blink; shake my head. "Wait. Go back."

"What?"

"Read that part again. Please."

A memory is rushing by me, too fast to catch. What are the words? How do they string together? I squeeze my eyes shut, reach out to grasp it, but it is gone.

Tristan complies, putting feeling into it. *"'Augusta, one day this might be over, but we'll all be together. That's what matters.'* Good old Hugh."

"The next one," I prod. I'm moving my thoughts around like a jigsaw puzzle. "Was it Jennifer Lopez?"

Tristan happily reads a passage I'd written about J-Lo, adding dramatic flair as if he were in a scene: *"She has blood on her hands—the blood of skinned animals. She wears it with such joy, with a smirk and a strut. So much fur, so much pain inflicted on innocent creatures to make her feel pretty."*

"One more," I order, and he reads another entry—and everything changes.

These observations, my own and the celebrities', are telling a story. Putting it all together, right here, with music blaring and movie stars surrounding me, I know what happened.

I know what happened.

It was *Joe.* Oh, thank God, it was Joe. *Joe* had blood on his hands.

The buried memories were in my book all along. I wrote them myself. The therapist said I wouldn't be able to stop it all from coming back, even if I tried. My mind would find a way to leak what happened. "Please," I say, holding out my hand. "I really have to go. This is my job, Tristan. This is my work and it's due tonight. Give me the book."

Tristan laughs at me. "Now, now. Why would I give this up when I'm having so much fun? It'll make a great party trick at the *after* after party. Do you have an invite to that, by the way?"

"Don't be that guy. Just give it to me."

I stick my hand out, take a step closer. He whips the book away. Liv is poised for action. What can I do? Leo and Tobey are migrating this way and seem to be focused on Tristan. Maybe they all party together, I haven't a clue, but if Leo gets a load of this book it's all over for me.

Before I attempt to take it forcibly, at which point I wouldn't be surprised if Liv put me in a headlock, I try one last strategy.

"Read *your* page," I tell Tristan.

His page, and those surrounding it, contain my early work—not only celebrity observations, but a roadmap of a teenage girl's angsty world and the life-or-death moments she *knows* she'll never get over. He pauses, glances around at the growing number of people at this party dying to talk to him, circling us, ready to pounce.

"Oh. OK," Tristan says lightly. "This should be good. I'm toward the end, right?" He pages through.

"No," I say. "The beginning."

He turns back to the first page. He flips through JFK Jr. and Matthew Perry, sees his name and starts reading. I see a few people edging toward him, but he doesn't acknowledge them and they back off. After a minute, he flips back a few pages to where I wrote about the party I wasn't invited to, and the prom, and my dark thoughts about not wanting to live anymore because I was nobody and would forever be nothing. He reads about how he, Matthew and JFK Jr. paying me attention showed me a world outside the suburbs, and that it mattered not because they were famous, but because the tiniest gestures can dig you out of your rut; the quickest glimpse of sunlight can remind you there's a better world above ground and it's worth burrowing up until you can see the sky.

When he's read enough, Tristan raises his head slowly, his face crumpling, the sneer erased.

"I'm sorry," he says. He hands me the notebook. "I'm sorry for what you went through, and for…for all of this tonight." His eyes are glistening, and I have to force myself to remember he's known for Tristan Tears.

I reach for the book and he lets go. I take a look at the passage I wrote about him so long ago. It's not the most poetic, but it's effective in its almost childlike innocence. *I met Tristan Catlin today. I have a feeling he's going to make it big. He's got great eyes and he's so nice, kind of like a boy in a man's body. Today made me feel like I can go on and be OK. I hope when Tristan gets really, really famous he won't change. Maybe I'll see him again someday and I can thank him for catching me.*

"Thank you." I pat the cover. "You've given me some things to think about—and maybe that's mutual. But I *really* have to go."

"Don't," he says, reaching out for me. "Stay. I—"

"We're good," I assure him.

He watches me curiously. "I get it. Do what you gotta do. But when you're done, call me. I'm not done with you yet."

I smile back at him, wave, and take off. It's a funny thing about celebrities. It never occurred to him that *I* might be done with *him*.

58

I remember.

I recall everything that happened; I think I do, anyway. How does one know what one is *not* remembering? Still, it's enough. I know why I did it, why I had to kill Joe, and that I'm no murderer. I didn't end a man's life recklessly. I did what I had to do.

In the car on the way home from the party, I call my mother. Normal people keep their phones on silent at night, but not Jemima. It's always on *just in case.*

"What? What's wrong? Are you OK?" She's half asleep while also entirely panicked, and now I know where I get my high anxiety from.

"Mom," I say, "I'm better than OK. I remember *everything*—and it's all going to be over very, very soon."

When I get home, I pull off my shoes, bodyshapers, bra, and tights, which do not have a single nick, let alone a "ladder." In a cozy kimono and fluffy socks, I pore over the notebook, reading every sentence I wrote after that terrible day. I've never read it this way, as a whole. What I discover is an unflinching, relentless progression from that first encounter with Colin Farrell to the shock of Bon Jovi, through my trip to Rome, and finally to facing what a plastic lie this industry really is.

I crack open a fresh notebook and write out every thought, fragment, and sentence that sparks a memory. It's all there. Each one adds a piece to the story.

Peter Dinklage: *I trusted my instincts, in the end. It took me a long time.* Jennifer Lawrence: *Sometimes you have to do what you have to do— You can't live in fear of pissing people off.* Roger Federer: *…and the right thing isn't always the easy thing. You do it anyway.* Hugh Jackman. J. Lo. The glint of the blade poking out from Joe's hand, the way he'd palmed it like a magician until he let his guard down. The terror of knowing what I had to do. The agony of not being quick enough to save Caroline, of feeling the fear and doing it anyway—just as I talked about with Robbie Williams. I wrote the ending of my own story before I even knew what it was.

I am not a murderer. It's time to make Barilla and his pals believe it. But first, I have to write up my Oscar reporting. It's not in a journalist's DNA to leave the story unwritten. Even in war, reporters file. I play my recordings and type up my interviews and observations, starting with Angelina on the red carpet. As much as I don't want it to, I relive the Gordon Ramsay encounter. I save the recording but don't include the episode in my story. He doesn't count toward my total. He's not a star, he's a black hole.

When I'm done, I commence a final celebrity count. I should've easily hit, even surpassed, the Number tonight. The place was infested with celebrities. I get to Ricky Gervais when my blood pressure starts to spike, *No, no, no.* The Oscars were meant to be my swan song, the brilliant cap to a brief but intense career as a celebrity journalist. OK, one more…Dan Stevens counts. That's 105. Next: Tristan. But no…*no, no, no.* He was a repeat. Oh, dear Lord. I'm out of celebrities. I ended on Dan Stevens and I'm still *two short.* Two tiny, pretty little celebrities. I could've easily gotten a couple more tonight if I'd had my wits about me. The distraction of Alexander popping back in just as Tristan was shoving his tongue down my throat threw me off catastrophically. My eyes well up from exhaustion and anger; I'm furious at myself. There is no question this matters, even in light of what I'm facing, because for so long it has been the reason for everything. *I have to finish this. Breathe.* I don't know how I will, but I must. Somehow, I manage to quiet my brain and fall asleep.

I wake by nine to check in with the editors. They love my dull red-carpet Angelina reporting and ignore everything else. As I brush my teeth, I decide not only am I never going into the office again, I'm not going to bother telling anyone. I'm just not going to go.

I'm still in boxers and a sweatshirt when someone starts banging on my door. It's not Mom; is it Lincoln again? I leave the chain on and crack open the door. Standing there is a wraith, a memory, a ghost. My Caroline is there in a baggy white T-shirt, faded jeans, and beige Birkenstocks.

"Caroline…" I exhale it like it's air, not a word. "What…*how?*"

I slam the door, remove the chain, and throw it open again.

"Your mom called my mom." She smiles tentatively. "She told me where you lived. Oh, and she got on the first flight out this morning so she's not far behind me."

"But how did *you*—"

"I live in Calabasas now," she says shyly, as if we just met. "With Ginger. Can I…" She gestures inside.

"Of course. Come in." I move into the living room, sinking into the futon, offering Caroline neither a seat nor a glass of water because I'm too frazzled to be a hostess.

She perches next to me and pulls a throw pillow onto her lap, hugging it. She's put on at least ten pounds, most of it muscle judging from her shapely arms and strong shoulders. She's grown her hair out so that it falls to her chin, and has a purple scar running from the corner of her mouth almost to her ear.

"It's amazing, you remembering what happened," she says, clasping her hands together over the pillow. "This can be over now. If you're ready, I want to hear it—I want to hear *everything*. Leave nothing out, and don't you dare worry about upsetting me. I'm done being upset."

I close my eyes for a moment, try to get my bearings. "Caroline. I…" And the tears come, along with a rush of images of her on her porch with her whirly wind toy when we were six, me calling out to her, *Do you want to play?* Of her in that bed, as good as dead, of her in a coma, of me running away.

She gets up and sits right next to me, grabbing my knees with small, scarred hands.

"*You* shouldn't be comforting *me*. I'm fine," I say through sobs. "You're the one—"

"You're fine? Really? Yeah, you seem *totally* fine."

She rises, makes her way to the bathroom, and returns with a cumulus cloud of toilet paper. I blow my nose. "What I wanted to say," I tell her, "is that I'm *sorry*. I am so, so, sorry, Caroline. I let you down, and—"

"Don't you dare," she breaks in. "I *never* blamed you. You saved my life, Augusta. Do you get that? No matter what went down that day, *you saved us*."

We both jump at a loud, sharp banging on the door. "Augusta! Augusta Noble. Open the door. It's your mother."

I slowly lift myself off the sofa. "Hang on," I yell. "I'm coming."

She bangs harder. I make it to the door and throw it open to see Jemima standing with her old rolling suitcase splattered with bumper stickers: *Behind every woman is herself* is bright and new, but *Well behaved women rarely make history* is nearly faded away. My mother has aged since I last saw her. She has bags under her eyes, deeper frown lines, and is wearing no makeup. Her curls are entirely out of control.

"Well?" she says. "Are you going to invite me in, or do I have to stand out in this dry heat all day?"

Caroline and I settle on the futon sofa. My mother, holding a chipped mug of chamomile tea, sits on the bouncy Swedish armchair.

"Tell us," Caroline says to me.

I get comfortable on the scratchy cushion. "I didn't know who to believe," I begin, addressing myself to Caroline. "I knew Lincoln was like family to you, but he was volatile. I knew he'd been hiding things from you, and you'd been hiding things from me."

"I'm sorry, I—"

"No, no, it's OK—it's just, Joe was laying it on thick when I got to your apartment. He told you'd both been battling with Lincoln but that you hadn't wanted to drag me into it. He portrayed himself as your protector, making sure big bad Lincoln couldn't get to you. He said that you two were more serious than ever, and Lincoln was losing it. All the while, I'm looking at that innocent face of his. You know what? Joe would've made a great actor."

Caroline is nodding. "He was a sociopath, Auggie," she says. "He fooled everyone."

"*Mmm hmmm,*" my amateur psychologist mother agrees.

"Still, I knew something was off," I continue. "Nothing he was saying rang true. He mustered up some tears, stroked your head, looked me dead in the eye and told me he'd caught Lincoln attacking you. I was...honestly, I was so confused I didn't know *what* to think."

"So," Caroline says in a hushed voice, "how did you figure it out?"

"First of all, so much time had gone by and there were still no sirens. It seemed so weird that he pushed me *not* to call 911 again. And...he was looking at you lying in the bed and then...he said something."

I shiver at the recollection, pick up my tea, take a small sip. Jemima and Caroline seem to be holding their breath.

"He said, 'Don't worry, my love. It's all going to be over soon, and then we'll be together forever.' Then he paused, still looking at you, and added, '*All* of us.' It made me feel like a million bugs were crawling over my skin. I knew what he meant."

My mother gasps. I continue before she can really lose it. "When he said that, I became hyperaware of every detail, every move he made. He knelt next to you and laid his hands on the edge of the mattress...."

Caroline reaches for her mug, which rattles on the glass tabletop as she lifts it.

"He stroked your hair with one hand. The other was only partly in my view, but I saw something glinting in the light coming through a gap in the blinds. I knew it was a knife—small enough that he could palm it. That's why I hadn't seen it before."

I hear myself talking faster and faster, as if I'll forget again if I don't get it all out. "And then there was the blood on his right hand…it was concentrated on two fingertips. *Why?* I kept thinking, why aren't his palms, *both* hands, covered in it?"

Caroline is focused on me, wide-eyed but calm now, as if she knows the worst has happened and these are just the details.

"I understood in that moment that *he'd* written the letters—the *L-I-N-C*. Not you. By that point, all the conjecturing, the thin-slicing I'd been doing since I entered that room came together: the knife, Joe's words, his ever-changing demeanor, the final look of peace on his face. It was the look of someone who craves total control and finally has it. That's when I knew what I had to do."

I clear my throat, then take a breath. "I asked him if I could go over and hug you. To say goodbye."

Caroline swallows. My mother reaches across and lays a hand on her knee.

"He didn't even hesitate. He knew I was unarmed, so he let his guard down. I stood behind him while he was kneeling over you. I picked up the statue, and then I…"

I stop. I can't say it out loud. The two women are watching my every twitch, prompting me with their eyes to go on.

Yes. I CAN say it. "I hit him on the head as hard as I could. But as soon as I did, I felt a stabbing in my own head, like I was having a stroke or my brain was exploding. It was probably the worst pain I've ever felt. As I stood over him fading out, the cops rushed in. That cellphone call to 911 that Barilla mentioned—Caro, you must have made that call."

I let out a long breath and face them both. "And that," I say, "is everything I remember."

They're both silent for a moment, then my mother says gently, "Augusta, you say you were standing over *Joe* when Emergency Services arrived. Are you sure it was *Joe*?"

My mother and Caroline exchange concerned glances.

"Yes," I say, my voice cracking again. "It's OK...*I'm* OK about it. I hit him because I *knew* he was going to kill all of us. And he was. Caroline, Lincoln, me...we were all dead if I didn't. My next memory after that is waking up in the ambulance."

Caroline closes her eyes for a moment. My mother shifts again on her hard chair.

"Augusta," my mother says, staring into my eyes like she thinks I am, in the end, utterly unwell. "Honey...I'm afraid...well, it seems your memory hasn't entirely come back after all. Lincoln, he—" She starts choking up as she says his name. I suddenly feel sick all over again.

59

Caroline inches closer to me on the sofa and lays a hand on my knee.

"I'm so sorry, Auggie," she says, "but Lincoln…didn't make it. He died in that bathroom. You tried to save him. *You did everything you could.* You untied him, you were giving him CPR when the police broke into the apartment, but it was too late. There was nothing anyone could do."

I am taking it all in, trying to make everything fit, but it's as if I'm working with all the wrong puzzle pieces.

"We thought you probably knew this, deep down, but your therapist and the doctors said not to push you…not to upset you," Jemima says. "I'm so sorry."

"*No*," I cry. "*Please…no.* It can't be…that can't be true. I remember now…I remembered it all because I knew the truth would save Linc!"

I don't recognize my own voice, high and cracking and feral. I'm overwhelmed with a cocktail of emotions. I'd thought I'd gotten used to the panic, fear, guilt…and now this new avalanche of unadulterated grief is unbearable. "I remembered for you, Caro…but for him, too. I can clear his name now." I leap off the sofa. "I have to tell him. *Please.* Tell me how to get in touch with him."

"Sweetie. Augusta." My mother rises too, watches me, reaches out to hug me, but I shrink back. "Lincoln's *dead*, honey. I'm so sorry…"

"No, no, he's not," I cry. "I just saw him—"

Oh. I stop cold. I *didn't* see Lincoln, did I? I had too much Burgundy and I stayed awake working for thirty-six straight hours. I was *wishing* Lincoln were there and I…dreamed him up. I talked it all out with an imaginary Lincoln—a ghost. Or…an angel? *Lincoln wasn't real.*

I begin pacing. "I mean, I thought Lincoln was…I thought he was fine…I don't remember any of what you say. Did I…block it out?"

I stop, turn to face them. Caroline's eyes are downcast. Maybe we both let Lincoln down.

"The doctors said this could happen," my mother says. "There's no way to predict how selective amnesia will play out. It's your mind protecting you, making sure you don't have to face anything you can't handle until you're ready. It all happened the way it's supposed to, I guess." She sighs, puts her head in her hands.

Did it? I'm thinking no, this was not how it was supposed to happen. Lincoln is supposed to be alive. My mind is working furiously to make everything fit, to figure out how I could remember things that didn't happen and forget things that did.

My mother says, "I've already called Detective Barilla. They've moved the meeting to Thursday and the DA's office is prepared to shift gears now that you remember."

The apartment is quiet but for the leaf blowers revving up one floor down. Caroline breaks the thick silence.

"I didn't see this coming," she says. "I thought Joe was my dream guy, and I betrayed Lincoln for him. *I'm* the one who caused this, Augusta. So do us all a favor and quit hogging all the guilt for yourself."

She breaks my heart with those words.

"No one could have seen it coming, Caro," I tell her fiercely, sitting next to her. "It's no one's fault but that dead psychopath Joe Fucking Lannells. Do you understand?"

My mother smiles slowly. Caroline watches me, eyes shining.

Oh. Ohhh. I see what they did there. It's what they do with little children. And boy, did it work on me. They've gotten me to admit that it was Joe's fault. All his. Not mine. And finally, with Caroline's forgiveness, maybe I can start to believe it. We were all lured into a sick trap by one man, and he alone is responsible for the horror that followed.

"See, Auggie?" Caroline asks. "It feels kind of good to put the blame where it belongs, doesn't it? I never wanted you to suffer. Not ever. I'm ready to heal and move past this. Are you with me?"

"I...I think so," I say, and smile at her for the first time in forever. She smiles back like it's all going to be OK.

My mother envelops both of us in her arms and squeezes, and we stay there for a long minute. When we pull away, the air is dense and needs clearing, and Jemima takes care of that. "I'm hungry," she pronounces. "You know what we need? We need the world's best pancakes."

"That would be the Griddle on Sunset," I say. "But trust me, that's not what we want. Those pancakes require a half-hour wait, after which we'll be shoved at a table for two and won't be able to hear one another over the din. No...we want is the world's *worst* pancakes. I know just the place."

Caroline squints up at the café's sign, hands on her hips. "'Flapjacks of Omar?'"

"It opened last year and it's never busy. It's where I go when I need to work in peace."

Omar himself leads us to our terracotta-linoleum-topped table, and I'm happy to see two others are occupied; I want quiet, not for him to go out of business.

"I was wondering, Augusta," my mother says from behind her menu. "What was it that sparked your memory? It all seemed so sudden…" My mother always knows everything. *Always.*

I throw a glance at Caroline, who's browsing the pancake choices. I am loath to discuss anything happy or light or fluffy around her.

Caroline glances up. "Whatever it is, spill. Don't you dare tiptoe around me." She goes back to scanning the many colorful pictures Omar has provided of his various offerings.

The atmosphere is different now, lighter. There comes a time, after you've been burned to the ground, when things have to go back to *all right*. I've been waiting for a natural transition from grief to laughter, from tragedy to good news, but none has come. The time is now.

Omar comes over and we all order pancakes and thick Turkish coffee. When he's gone, I grab the notebook that Jemima gave me so many years ago, pull it out of my bag, and slide it across the table without a word. My mother touches the cover, then looks up at me, and for a moment we are connected by the memory of the day she brought it to my room.

I tell them about the poster people and the goal; that I am still two short, but can't decide whether to finish. And I tell them how it was the notebook that helped me figure everything out—made me *remember*. My mom's flipping through it, shaking her head in wonder, I hope, as opposed to disapproval.

"Anyway…none of this is important right now," I say. "Mom, we can talk about it later. It's silly."

"Of course it's silly," Caroline smiles and shrugs. "I've learned a lot these last months, including the value of silliness. There is no way I'm letting you abandon your goal with *two left*. I know I used to be hard on you about all the celebrity stuff but…I know now that not everything that's trivial is without value. These days, I cling to every scrap of fun I can find, just to get through the day."

Omar stops by and drops three plates in front of us with a grunt.

"So," Caroline finishes as she eyes her stack, "how are you going to bag those last two precious celebrities?" She reaches for a carafe of unnaturally blue syrup from a colorful selection.

"Well…*CelebLife* did offer me an event tomorrow night…" I'd emailed Tatiana this morning to keep my options open, and an hour later she'd sent me a tip sheet for an event tonight.

"You absolutely *have* to do it," my mother insists. She douses her pancakes in a gloopy pool of I Can't Believe it's not Maple Syrup. "Who do you think your last ones will be? Who's on the list? Tell us!"

This is a new one on me. "Your interest surprises me," I say slyly, "considering you both hate celebrities."

"*Hate* is a strong word," Caroline hedges.

"Sure, OK, maybe a little," my mother says. "The cult of celebrity is entirely superficial. But certain *individual* celebrities aren't. Not real, working actors; not people with talent. Speaking of talent, did you know Harry Styles has a third nipple?"

Caroline and I are slack-jawed. "I can't believe you even know who Harry Styles is," I manage through laughter.

I pull up the tip sheet on my phone and scroll through, reading out some names. "Charlie Sheen…Andy Cohen…"

Both get unanimous boos.

"Agreed," I nod. "How about Justin Theroux, Tori Spelling, Kylie Jenner…"

"Nope, nope, and nope," says Caroline.

"Marky Mark, Anna Faris…"

"Brad Pitt!" My mother yells.

I shake my head. "He's shooting in Europe somewhere, so no chance he'll be there."

My mother gives up. "Do they ever get any surprise guests?"

"They do. Absolutely."

Caroline nods and swallows a piece of pancake. "Let's hope for that, then. None of these names are wowing me for your last two."

My mother nods emphatically, too busy chewing to talk.

It occurs to me that, with Caroline as a buffer, now's the time to break the very possible, almost-certain London news—so I do, and my mother is predictably unsupportive.

"But there's no more *CelebLife* in London, I thought," she tries.

"They still assign a ton of stories in Europe; they just do it out of New York now," I explain. "And there are other publications for me to pitch to. I can get back to real news and investigative journalism."

My mother focuses on her pancakes and purses her lips as she saws off a piece. "This thing is like a microwaved Frisbee," she grunts.

"Told you," I say.

"So…your plan is to go back to London with no job and no flat," Caroline says, then takes a minute to finish chewing. She swallows and points her fork at me. "Something's not adding up. What aren't you telling us?"

I glance at my mother, then look back to Caroline. I've been starved for true women allies these past months. The story of Alexander and me comes out in all its messy, dirty, beautiful glory, from polo to the Alps to Belinda the boyfriend-stealing actress, and finally to getting caught with Tristan at the Oscars and how it's now my turn to make the "big gesture" if I want to see him again. I show them pictures—one of us together in Rome and the gorgeous snaps of him from the *GQ* article. Caroline takes the phone and expands the photo of Alexander in the Andes.

"*This* is the guy who's waiting for you in England? Girl, what are you doing here eating crappy pancakes with us? If he wants the 'big gesture,' I say go for it."

She's being rhetorical, of course, but I take her point. She examines me closely. "So what's the problem? Why do I sense Prince Amazing isn't *quite* Prince Perfect?"

"Because," I say, wiping syrup off my hands with a paper napkin, "the hot viscount who thinks he's besotted, but who later realizes he can have a supermodel instead of me, is the person who can hurt me the most. It's scary." I add casually, "And…well, I haven't told him anything about all of this. There was never the right time."

They both nod as if they understand—why I haven't told him, and why I'm now worried about telling him, if it comes to that.

"It's funny," my mother says after a moment, interlocking her fingers on the table, "but have you noticed that you—*both* of you—have been hurt as badly as two people can be, and you're both still standing?"

I stab at a pancake. "You're not even going to bother telling me that if I take a chance and actually trust this guy, I won't get hurt?"

"Nope," Jemima smiles wanly. "Just that if you are, you'll survive it. Look," she adds, more serious now, "you *know* I don't want you to go. I want you to live in Cambridge for the rest of your life and come over for dinner every week. But if you must go, if you *have* to, I want you to spread your wings. I want you to stay brave and be yourself, and take chances—well, not crazy ones. You know…no bungee jumping or anything."

It's what she said to me all those years ago: *Stay brave.*

"You know what none of us will survive? These things. I give up," Caroline says, pushing her plate away.

We laugh, drink our coffee, and signal for the check. Before we go, my mother takes Omar into a corner and whispers her pancake recipe to him while he crosses his arms and glares at her.

Caroline and I part ways by her car, which is still parked in front of my apartment, while my mother roots around for an orange ripe enough to pull off the tree.

Thinking about my recent "visitation"—or whatever it was—from Lincoln, I say, "Caro…did you ever find out if Linc had a job, in the end?"

"Funny you should ask. He did—he had a business, actually." I watch as her eyes tear up. "It turns out he was running a successful bike repair shop and making a *fortune*. His clients *loved* him."

I am too shell-shocked to ask anything else. For now, I'm going with osmosis as an explanation for why I knew this. I must've heard things in the hospital without realizing it.

"Not so long this time, OK?" my friend says.

"Definitely not." I smile at her. "You have to promise to come visit me in London. You can even bring Ginger."

"Only if you visit me in Calabasas first." She grins mischievously, then quickly turns serious, reaches out, and grabs me in the fierce Caroline hug I've missed for so long.

"Different but always together," I choke the words out.

"Best friends forever," she replies, then lets go of me, waves, and gets in her car.

60

#106...?

Miles Teller is walking toward me, buffered by a gang of hyper handlers. He avoids eye contact as he approaches me; his team corrals him, guides him, protects him from my invasive journalist tentacles. Lance, stationed next to me for maybe the last time, dares to shout out a question and receives a death stare from a rep for his trouble. I actually don't care about Miles, so I'll live. But wait—it looks like he *is* going to talk to at least one member of the print press, but only to... *The Times*? *The Wall Street Journal*? No; he stops and does a quick exclusive in lowered tones with *The New York Globe*, a gritty tabloid. I roll my eyes, bite a hangnail, wonder if anyone can see what I'm thinking about all celebrities and reps right now: *You're not saving lives, you self-important twerps. You pretend to be someone else for a living. Get over yourselves!* Don't they know there are meaningful, brilliant, serious, horrendous, life-changing, tragic things—things that *matter*—happening right now around the world? As Caroline said, this is supposed to be silly, fun, light. Miles is walking off the carpet now. He didn't look at me or speak to me, so I decide he can't count toward my total.

Ooh—here comes a good one. I can cleanse my palate with Rosario Dawson. She greets me with a wide, happy smile, and I launch straight into girl talk: *Is she looking forward to the party? What are her amazing skin secrets?* I end up asking her the wackiest thing she ever did while drinking bubbly, because a Champagne company is sponsoring the party tonight.

"It's one of those things where, if you start drinking in the morning, no one looks weird at you because mimosas are totally approved," she says as I nod emphatically. "Champagne is always that not-guilty pleasure. It's totally OK and it's classy." Just like Rosario! *This is going great.*

Then I go and ruin everything. "We're working on a story about celebrities and the loves of their lives," I say brightly. *Who doesn't love love, right?* "I was wondering—"

Her face darkens. "I don't have a current love of my life," she says, effectively ending this line of questioning.

I close my eyes for a moment. To be fair to celebrities, they *do* have to field some insensitive questions. I wouldn't welcome this kind of prying even at a party full of my own friends. I think of how to save myself with Rosario, and decide to go with honesty.

"Neither do I," I tell her, and she nods slightly and smiles. I think she forgives me in the end. As I watch her go, I feel a shot of adrenaline. One more. *One more celebrity.*

A fresh cacophony of yelling blows down the carpet. I lean on the velvet rope and peek past Lance to see what the ruckus is about. A crowd that was congregated around the TV reporters breaks, and I see who's coming down. *No, no, no.* Not tonight—*not now.* I squeeze my eyes shut, then open them and watch him move down the line, putting on his tough-rapper-with-a-heart-of-gold act, touching a male reporter's shoulder, throwing an arm around a female TV journalist's waist.

Surely he won't remember me from Rome. He's probably been to fifty other cities and intimidated a whole new batch of women since then. Then he's suddenly in front of me, because Lance is pretending to be on the phone so he doesn't have to interview McMoney.

The star reeks of cologne and a sickening musk. I can see in his beady brown eyes that he doesn't, in fact, recognize me. Not even a flicker.

"Hey..." McMoney, who is actually Garth Snodgrass from Delaware, drawls, then shoots what he probably thinks is a subtle look at my chest. He steps closer. I'm hemmed in with photographer's equipment behind me and people jammed in on either side. My tummy is pressed into the rope.

This man, with a swoop of brown, greasy bangs falling across his left eye and that same orangey fake tan he had in Rome, stares at me expectantly. I do my job: "You're really breaking out in film. How will you juggle that with your music?"

He begins answering me in a surprisingly articulate and practiced manner. I don't process a word of it. He is touching me. He is doing that thing that too many women—skinny or obese, old or young, pretty or plain—are familiar with: the stealth grope. The one that comes with plausible deniability. I am pushed against the rope by the crowd of journalists I'm stuffed in with. He stands closer to me than he has to. He won't back off and I have no room to move. I would bet money he thinks I like it. That I'm flattered. Turned on. Grateful, even.

His hands are grasping the red velvet rope at crotch level, his fingers flicking firmly against my stomach, then grazing lower. He flicks at me again, hits me below my pubic bone. He does it over and over—it's not the accidental touch of forced proximity. *He* has room to back off, but doesn't. He has a droplet of spittle in the right corner of his mouth as he utters words I can't focus on. *No one* gets to touch me where I don't want him to.

Why didn't I stop it sooner? That's what they would ask me, if I told them. When there is a violation of the body, the brain takes too long to process what's happening. The mind flips over, accepts, wonders, clarifies, justifies, then has to make a decision that could affect the rest of your life. But I have experience now—too much of it. I grip my pen, a hardy one of clear plastic with a fine point, then work it in my hand so the tip is pointing near McMoney's crotch, though I can't see exactly because I have to pretend to be listening to him. People are calling his name; fans, his rep, other reporters. As I run out of questions and give him a robotic *Great, thank you*, he winks; I draw back subtly as I can, pushing into a pissed-off photographer's assistant behind me.

Breathe. Stop being scared. Take back your power; claim it. I have seconds. I exhale and jab him in the nuts. *Breathe.*

"*What?* What the *hell?*" McMoney squawks and shrieks like an angry chicken. He doubles over, grimacing, groaning, and grabbing his crotch. "*What the fuck?* I've been stung!"

I have to cover my mouth because I am instantly crying with suppressed laugher. He appears to think a monster bee attacked him. My eyes well up and bubbles of laughter threaten to erupt. No one ever said McMoney had a high I.Q. At the very least, he seems to realize people are starting to notice his dramatic display, and he stands up slowly and tries to smile. He shoots me a direct look in the eyes, a hard stare that tells me he wants to, but won't dare accuse me of anything. His publicist rushes over and holds him up like he's a child sent home from school with a tummy ache.

I am proud of myself. Even better, I am *OK*.

My heart leaps. Here comes my last and final celebrity. Who will it be? I've been thinking about it since Mr. Number 25, aka Jason Bateman. And look—here comes 107: it's Chrissy Teigen, here to bring me peace. In this moment, I understand why it was so important for me to reach my goal, arbitrary as it seems.

Why *not* Chrissy? Body positive, sensitive, gorgeous, a fellow female navigating a world often hostile to women. I feel lighter. Like I could soar. It's a good way to end. I do a quick Internet search and bring up her quotes on fame. It breaks her heart sometimes; it's claustrophobic, confusing, and a rare privilege. *It's hard to explain because everyone thinks money and fame is pure awesome, so it just sounds whiny,* she wrote. *I get it, trust me…It is just a weird little world that I cannot expect anyone to get.*

She casts an eye on the limping, seething McMoney, then turns back to me. "That wasn't you…?" she asks suspiciously.

I give her the slightest nod. "People can be such assholes," I shrug, launching right into it. "You know that better than anyone, I imagine…you get a ton of trolls on social media. The ones who call you fat when you never have been? What a bunch of losers. I suppose for a top model, those words don't hurt much…" It's more of a statement than a question. A wrong statement, as it turns out.

"Fuck them," Chrissy says, swiveling her head sharply back and forth. "It *does* bother me. It hurts." Her face is scrunched up, and her voice rises an octave.

My goal in life is to stop caring about this stuff, but if Chrissy, *Sports Illustrated* swimsuit goddess and beloved wife, mother, and businesswoman, is still battling the need to be liked and accepted, can I expect more of myself? Does it ever really go away?

"But what about your fans, who think you're the most perfect, beautiful woman out there? That must make it all better?"

"Of course it means the world to me," she says. "But it's an illusion. It's airbrushing." She runs her hands in the air up and down her body. "This is me with an incredible team of makeup artists, hairdressers, and stylists behind me. This isn't what I look like at home."

I take a good look at her. She's not particularly tall or skinny compared to the other models I've met. She's got natural, rosy apple cheeks. "I remember when you Instagrammed your stretch marks," I say. "You were a hero to all of us who hide ours in shame."

"Hey…it's important to remember what's real. You'll drive yourself crazy if you get caught up in all of this."

Everything goes quiet. The flashes cloud my eyes and the people on the carpet blur out. The noise stops. Her words hit me exactly at the right time, in the right place. *Don't get caught up. Let it go.* I blink to come back to the moment.

"Will I see you inside? At the party?" Chrissy asks.

I shake my head. This will be it for me. I'm ready to go. I thank her, and she waves, smiles, and moves on to her next interview.

There is a brief celebrity lull, and the event rep skitters up to me. "Jonah Hill's coming. Do you want him?" I glance down the line.

I shake my head and smile at her. "No, thanks. I'm done."

I drive to the beach to write up my final notes. At Shutters, I order a jalapeno-infused margarita and sit by the window overlooking the beach, and though it's dark now, I imagine the waves and I can see the sand under the hotel's lights. Cindy Crawford is in the corner with her family picking at a shrimp salad, but no one pays them any mind. I open my book and quickly dispose of McMoney, who receives my first and only zero. *Notes: Sexual predator. 0.0.* I stop for a moment to think about what to write next. I'm a professional cynic, and I'm aware some people say the hashtags are PR tactics or money grabs and won't change things, not really, but I'm hoping those people are wrong. If even a few women—and men—*outside* Hollywood find their voices and feel empowered to seek justice, that's a victory in my eyes. I turn back to my book.

#ItHappenedToMe. Thank goodness for the women who came before me—because of their bravery, I can tell people what happened if I want to. I can fight back if I'm up to it. They might believe me. Maybe he's done worse to other women—and maybe I can be one that starts the ball rolling for others to step forward. #ThankYou. #NoMore.

After giving Chrissy a 10.0, I flip to the next page. There's only one blank left in the book before the embossed Albert Schweitzer quote. As I sit alone in a place I might never be again, I write down the last words I'll ever enter here. It is a note to my future self. I log it because it's easy, in a moment of change, to greet the rush of endorphins and vow to be different. This is for later, when the little things creep in and make me crazy, when the glitter settles and I have to face that my real life has been underway all along, while I was making plans for something better. *This is my life*—unsettled, all over the place, full of adventure, and forever imperfect.

I take pen to paper. *The wasting of one moment with worry, envy, or fear is a strike against your future. Let it come, whatever it is; gather your strength and embrace it. Try to hear what's meant for you, tilt your head, cup your ear, listen to the wind, hear the voice that speaks to you. It will work out how it is supposed to. It will be nowhere near as bad as you fear or as perfect as you dream, but it belongs to you and it is beautiful. Hold it tight.*

Epilogue

I finally answer Stanley when I'm in the taxi from Heathrow. *I'd love to work with you. I'm on my way.*

Operative word *with*, not *for*. I plan to stay in business for myself, find new freelance opportunities—Mallory's going to get me a meeting with her editor—get back to investigative reporting, write a book. It's a funny thing about being dispensable at *CelebLife* magazine—it has a double edge. Their lack of loyalty means they don't seem to expect any from me, either. Esdee's emailed a few times asking where I am, and I kept my options open and told her to try me in London. I started to think I wasn't ready to give up *all* free parties with beautiful people, nor was I in a position to turn my nose up at the paychecks. I might keep *them* on a string for a while.

I direct the driver to the flat I've rented in Wimbledon for six months, sight unseen, and ask the driver to wait while I drop my bags. Back in the car, I direct him to Primrose Hill.

I stand on Alexander's stoop and ring the bell. If he invites me in, I'm ready to take the chance—to tell him everything, including that the DA has officially called my actions self defense, and the police are finishing up endless paperwork to close the case. If he doesn't invite me in, I'll turn around and go back to my flat and continue living my life. That's the beauty of wanting, not needing. He'll listen to me or he won't. He'll welcome me back or he won't; and if he doesn't, he never really understood me at all.

Acknowledgments

Self-publishing, it turns out, is nothing of the sort. I was lucky to have a group of wonderful people help me get this book to the marketplace: Thank you to my biggest fan, Chris, who gave valuable feedback and claims to love everything I write; Jed Hammel, who helped fine-tune the manuscript; and Vicki Hammel (aka Mom), Jack Bower and Samantha Bower, chief readers. I couldn't imagine putting this out into the world without an editor who saved me from myself more times than I care to admit, the brilliant Laura Ross. *Thank you,* Laura. Not to mention the genius cover designer Laurie Anne Ernst, who stuck with me through endless changes and revisions and made fun of my font ideas, then came up with a design that perfectly illustrated a very odd sort of book. And finally, thank you to those who helped throughout this two-year journey in various undisclosed ways: Christi & Rob Felt, Liza & Ed Smith, Jason & Angie Hammel, George Emerson, and as always, Aunt Linda.

CPSIA information can be obtained
at www.ICGtesting.com
Printed in the USA
LVHW111529280219
609069LV00002B/474/P